PRAISE FOR **WHERE [THE RAINBOW] ENDS**

"One of the best pieces of gay literature I have ever read . . . The book is about creating a sense of family, and most of all, it is about hope . . . This is one novel that I was sorry to see end."   —*Impact*

"The author writes about love as only someone who has lost it can. Bravo."   —*Poz*

"Currier's smoothly flowing, emotionally charged writing evokes a time now sufficiently far past to elicit a kind of nostalgia. This is strong work on a powerful subject."
—*Booklist*

"Satisfying in a way that the efforts of the lavender literary greats are not."
—*The Weekly News*

"An ambitious work of interest to anyone who wants to take the long view on the crisis. Its breadth and scope give it historical value."   —*Dallas Morning News*

"I have always admired Currier's descriptions of living and loving in dangerous times. Now I have a reason to believe that his words are more than about surviving danger. *Where The Rainbow Ends* is about living beyond the age of AIDS. This is a novel to read and reread as we approach the new millennium."
—DAVID WAGGONER, *A&U*

"Currier's lyrical erotica wakes the heart as well as the flesh—he moves beyond the simple mechanics of sex to explore the emotional and spiritual aspects of two people connecting through love or lust or any other passionate feeling."
—LAWRENCE SCHIMEL, **Editor,** *The Mammoth Book of Gay Erotica*

"Currier conjures up the twin Fantasy Islands of Fire and Manhattan at their zenith with aplomb, and his sex scenes sizzle."   —*Lambda Book Report*

"Currier describes in aching detail the mystery and confusion of the epidemic's early years, when so little was known and so much was feared. Currier tells a very sad story indeed, but one that bears repeating. He reminds us of a time and a place that many would prefer to forget. How deep does the sorrow go? Jameson Currier knows, and doesn't want the rest of us to forget."   —*Harvard Gay and Lesbian Review*

"A nostalgically lush and beautifully written memoir of the "end of the party" and the beginning of AIDS, this lovely, long and involving novel articulates a message about loving life in spite of, and therefore transcending, the sometimes horrible details."
—*White Crane Journal*

"Written in a conversational tone, *Where the Rainbow Ends* often reads like a diary with small, daily musings coupled with thoughts on larger topics. *Where the Rainbow Ends* is full of laughter and celebration, sadness and grief . . . Currier has managed to tell the large story of a time that is also filled with smaller vignettes of people and love and family. When this is all added together, it becomes the story of life and living."
—*Alive*

WHERE THE RAINBOW ENDS

A NOVEL BY

JAMESON CURRIER

THE OVERLOOK PRESS
WOODSTOCK & NEW YORK

First published in paperback in the United States in 2000 by
The Overlook Press, Peter Mayer Publishers, Inc.
Lewis Hollow Road
Woodstock, New York 12498
www.overlookpress.com

Portions of this manuscript have been previously published in:
Synaesthetic, Blithe House Quarterly, Genre, Iris, The Minnesota Review,
Evergreen Chronicles, Backspace, LGNY, Art & Understanding,
GayPlace, The Mammoth Book of Gay Erotica, Best Gay Erotica 1997
and Best American Gay Fiction 3.

Library of Congress Cataloging-in-Publication Data

Currier, Jameson
Where the rainbow ends : Jameson Currier
p.   cm.
I. Title.
PS3553.U668W47   1998   813',54—dc21   98-16591

Manufactured in the United States of America
Book design and type formatting by Bernard Schleifer

1 3 5 7 9 8 6 4 2
ISBN 0-58567-084-7

To
my family of friends,
past and present,
and, especially,
for Debbie

The sun athwart the cloud thought it no sin
To use my land to put his rainbows in.

— RALPH WALDO EMERSON

CAMELOT

In 1978 my friend Denise left her family and moved to New York City to become an actress. She enrolled in drama school and lived that year in a dormitory in Greenwich Village. On Sunday evenings she would shampoo and condition her long, light-brunette hair, put the original cast album of *Camelot* on the stereo and sing along, combing out the wet tangles with a large blue comb and testing herself to see if she remembered all the words of Guenevere's part. Denise had always wanted to be Julie Andrews, or, rather, be the actress that Julie Andrews was, singing and acting all the roles Julie had done on Broadway and then going to Hollywood and making all the movies Julie had made, only doing them all bigger and better, and, of course, achieving more fame, success, stardom, and awards. After reliving Guenevere's trial, her rescue by Lancelot, and her reunion with Arthur on the battlefield, Denise, feeling exonerated, triumphant, bewitching, and clean, would then go to the pay phone in the hall and call her mother in Shelbyville, Kentucky.

"I've been so worried about you," Denise's mother, Mrs. Connelly, would sigh into the phone with an exasperated motherly concern. "I thought you were going to call me yesterday."

"I always call you on Sunday, Mother," Denise would answer, shaking out her hair and rolling her eyes, the lilting Broadway melodies of du-tu-du du-tu-du-tu-du still humming along in her mind. That year she was twenty-two, and what surprised her most was the potency of her mother's disdain about everything in her life and the power it still had to dampen her mood. Denise would lift herself onto the stool that was placed by the pay phone, cross her legs and adjust her bathrobe, settling in for the long, agitating conversation ahead.

"Oh, well, I mean I thought you were going to call me earlier," Mrs.

Connelly would correct herself, Denise recognizing how her mother stressed the last word to apply guilt. "I thought you might have had an accident."

Mrs. Connelly feared everything about New York City, worrying constantly that something fantastically horrific would happen to her daughter, like a chunk of sidewalk garbage would suddenly whirl around like a tornado and butcher Denise into tiny, unequal parts. Every conversation between Denise and her mother could potentially include the topics of crime, rape, starvation, poverty, and unemployment; Mrs. Connelly gleaned the atrocious headlines of the newspapers and the nightly news for assurances that New York City was not the place where her daughter should be. Denise equated life in Manhattan to that of Camelot, continually reassuring her mother that she made plenty of money as a part-time waitress four nights a week at a restaurant on Hudson Street, that she was never at a loss for food because the cook always let her bring home leftovers. And that garbage storms were something she was not afraid of—in fact, they only entertained or irritated her, depending on her mood.

"I'm fine, Mother," Denise would reply. "I had brunch with some friends."

"Brunch?" her mother would ask, as if the word were a foreign phrase she had difficulty pronouncing.

"I went with some girlfriends to Phebe's. It's this restaurant on the Bowery."

"The *Bow-er-y?*" Mrs. Connelly would repeat, drawing out each syllable.

Denise would immediately regret having mentioned the place, knowing her mother was now searching her memory for some unfavorable comment about the neighborhood, knowing the word "bum" was somewhere right around the tip of her mother's tongue. Denise was always trying to remember safe places to talk about with her mother—Macy's, Radio City, the Metropolitan Museum—and she knew that if she kept talking her mother might fail to focus her concern on any one thing. "And then we walked over to the west side, it was a really beautiful day—and watched the boats along the Hudson River." A safe subject, Denise would think: the weather. "The air was so light today. Like spring."

"It sounds, well, lovely, dear," Mrs. Connelly would work her way back into the conversation. "I'm sure you had a wonderful time. You must be meeting so many new people. Anyone special?"

Denise, then, would feel the first stab of tension racing down the knots of her spine like the shock of an electrical current. Since Denise had reached the age of puberty she felt her mother had paid too much attention to Denise's finding that "special friend." And what really irked Denise was that her mother's concern was such an illogical paradox; sifting out clues of reassurance that Denise was *not* having sex, but that she *was* seeing someone and wanting to get married. But the truth was Denise had felt alienated and vulnerable upon arriving in Manhattan. She had not been able to align with any of the other girls in the dormitory; the friends she went to brunch with were a group of girls on the hall who went to the restaurants in the neighborhood en masse. She had been unable to connect with any of the other acting students in her classes. She hadn't thought of many of them as talented; most of the other girls she felt had only bubbles of air between their ears, pretty girls that Denise resented because she knew their looks would get them the kind of parts Denise wanted to perform.

Denise had always been suspicious of her own beauty; she felt she was too short, too thin, too birdlike to really make it as an ingenue. Still, she hoped that one day someone would give her a chance to prove herself, prove her beauty and talent and acting and singing. And so she felt, that first year in New York, that if she kept herself slightly at a distance from other people, perhaps she would be considered special, unique, an enigma waiting to be decoded. The same thing had occurred her first year in college in Louisville. It took time to meet people, Denise knew. It took time to find friends. This was not the time, she felt, to rush things. It was the time she should use for studying.

"No, Mother, I'm not seeing anyone," Denise would answer her mother's question, hoping the subject would change quickly.

"You don't want to be alone forever, you know. You need to find a good, honest man. Are there any decent men in New York?"

Denise felt again another stab of tension; she knew her opinion on men differed from her mother's. Denise was drawn to those men who enjoyed the theater as much as she did, the ones who could quote lines from Tennessee Williams, sing phrases from Cole Porter, mimic the dance steps of Michael Bennett, gossip about the current backstage romances and revenge. These types of men Denise knew would alarm her mother; they were, after all, homosexuals. Denise would gravitate toward them in classes, in the hall, in the cafeteria of the dormitory, eager to hear their opinions and learn their source of laughter. Her attraction, though, was not a sexual one, nor did she consider herself what was then termed a "fag hag." She identified with them because they made her recognize her own difference from other women. What she liked about them was that they were all, well, so open. She had no idea, though, how to begin to describe this to her mother.

"I'm not trying to meet someone," Denise would instead explain. "I don't have time to be involved. I'm working on a career."

"Well, you don't want to come home to an empty house, you know," her mother would reply. "You should find someone while you're still young. What about that boy you dated in college? What was his name?"

"Rick."

"Rick. Do you ever see him?"

"He lives in Florida now, Mother. I haven't spoken to him in about two years."

"I just don't understand why you didn't settle down with him. A mystery to me," Mrs. Connelly would say and Denise would again hear that exasperated sigh. At times Denise was convinced that her misery in life would be not understanding what her mother did not understand. At times like this she felt sure she must have been adopted or dropped by mistake by her true parents— aliens visiting from another planet.

"Your father thought he saw you on TV last week. What was it? A tooth-paste commercial. Was that you? Your father thought it might be you."

"No. I haven't done any commercials yet."

"Well, then, what are you auditioning for?"

"I'm not auditioning yet, Mother. I'm training."

"Training? For what? Your father paid for all that college for you to move to New York so someone could tell you how to walk and smile at the same time? What's there to train? The girl in the commercial just brushed her teeth. You have to take a class to learn how to do that?" Denise would hear her moth-er laugh, that girlish giggle that sent another stab racing down her spine. "What happened, Denise? Don't you miss all those civics classes you took in college? I thought you wanted to be a teacher. Your sister said they were hir-ing some substitute teachers over in Clayton."

"Let her go apply."

"Don't be such a sourpuss, dear. I'm just concerned about you, that's all. I just want you to be happy, you know. Are you careful when you're on the streets?"

"Yes, Mother. I strap a shotgun to my leg before I go out."

"Now, don't be smart with me. Just don't stare at people and they won't pay any attention to you."

"Mother, you're going to make my hair turn gray from all this worrying."

"Well, it's just such an unhappy place. All that violence. Why don't you just come home? I heard they're doing *My Fair Lady* in Lancaster."

Again Denise would feel uncomfortable, her heart would sink at the thought of not being able to do *My Fair Lady*, until she realized this was just another one of her mother's ploys to try and make her homesick, even though Denise had not lived at home for over four years, since she had left Shelbyville for Louisville and college. "I've already done *My Fair Lady* in Lancaster."

"But you weren't the star, were you? Your father just thought it would be wonderful for his daughter to come home from New York and be the star."

"In a community theater?"

"Well, you are coming home, aren't you? Your father's birthday is next month. It's his fifty-fourth."

"Mother, I have classes here. I can't come running home every month. It's too expensive." Now, Denise would detect her own inflection of exasperation. "And don't start up about Thanksgiving. I can't make it down for Thanksgiving this year."

"Well, it won't be the same without you." Her mother's voice, here, affect-ed that thin, tiny, pleading sound.

Again, Denise felt another pang, this time as if a surgeon was about to wheel her mother into an operating room. Why, she wondered, was it so difficult to break away from her mother's grasp? Why was her mother so unwilling to let her daughter live her own life?

"You are going to make it for Christmas?" Mrs. Connelly would then ask. "Your sister, Melanie, is bringing Burt over. She's getting serious with him, you know."

"I'll take the train down."

"The train? Oh, do be careful, Denise."

At this point Denise would feel the loneliness stirring within herself. She would look out at the shuttered doors of the dormitory hall, the long vacant beams of fluorescent light. "I need to go," she would say to her mother. "Someone else wants to use the phone."

Denise would lift herself off the stool, grateful at last that the conversation was coming to an end.

"Dear? Denise?" Mrs. Connelly would ask hurriedly into the phone, a final question before hanging up.

"What?" Denise asked, her irritation rising again.

"Your father wants to know if you have met anybody famous."

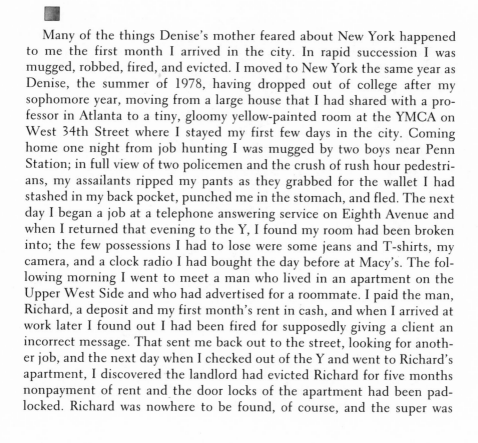

Many of the things Denise's mother feared about New York happened to me the first month I arrived in the city. In rapid succession I was mugged, robbed, fired, and evicted. I moved to New York the same year as Denise, the summer of 1978, having dropped out of college after my sophomore year, moving from a large house that I had shared with a professor in Atlanta to a tiny, gloomy yellow-painted room at the YMCA on West 34th Street where I stayed my first few days in the city. Coming home one night from job hunting I was mugged by two boys near Penn Station; in full view of two policemen and the crush of rush hour pedestrians, my assailants ripped my pants as they grabbed for the wallet I had stashed in my back pocket, punched me in the stomach, and fled. The next day I began a job at a telephone answering service on Eighth Avenue and when I returned that evening to the Y, I found my room had been broken into; the few possessions I had to lose were some jeans and T-shirts, my camera, and a clock radio I had bought the day before at Macy's. The following morning I went to meet a man who lived in an apartment on the Upper West Side and who had advertised for a roommate. I paid the man, Richard, a deposit and my first month's rent in cash, and when I arrived at work later I found out I had been fired for supposedly giving a client an incorrect message. That sent me back out to the street, looking for another job, and the next day when I checked out of the Y and went to Richard's apartment, I discovered the landlord had evicted Richard for five months nonpayment of rent and the door locks of the apartment had been padlocked. Richard was nowhere to be found, of course, and the super was quite unsympathetic. I was so green and naive I should have just had "FOOL" or "SUCKER" tattooed across my forehead.

I suppose you might even say I was raped and pillaged that first month, though what happened happened willingly on my part when an Italian sportswear buyer I had met at a bar on Seventh Avenue took me back to his hotel room and seduced me with champagne and drugs, or, rather, after the booze and the drugs and the backlash of my misfortunes, I willingly plowed my way into him. A few days later I felt an itching, burning sensation in my crotch and which is how, after a few discrete questions at a bar on Christopher Street, I ended up at the clinic for gay men on Grove Street in the West Village.

I was so new to New York City and felt so foreign myself, I was not even certain that anyone knew how to speak English. I was only nineteen years old and not one person I met in Manhattan those first few days could be considered as "friendly" or "civil" to me. So I was amazed when the guy seated next to me in the waiting room of the clinic widened his already large brown eyes, smiled at me and said, "So what are you in for?"

"Bad behavior, I suppose," I answered.

"Ahhh," he nodded his head, and I felt him looking me over and, here, I turned and studied him, too. He was the embodiment of what was referred to as a "clone"—a lean, muscular young man with a thick, clipped black mustache and shiny black hair but whose ears were disproportionately large for his head and tipped out from his face like wings. Even though it was summer, the middle of July, he wore jeans, workboots and a gray T-shirt, the collar of which could not contain the curls of black hair that climbed up from his chest to his neck. "A run of bad luck, eh?" he said.

"Like you wouldn't believe," I laughed, disbelieving it all quietly to myself. "And you?"

"Just making sure everything is back in working order," he said. "And I've got this huge crush on a volunteer here." Here, he took his hand and fluttered it over his heart. "Vince," he said and stretched out his hand to me. "And you're. . . "

"Robbie," I answered. "Robert Taylor," and I took his hand and briefly, politely, shook it. I'm sure I must have seemed anxious to him, darting my eyes around the room and then back to him, trying to figure out if I was in the process of another misfortune.

"Whereabouts you live?" he asked.

I'm sure my puzzlement must have registered on my face. For years I had been told that I was never one who could, well, hide his emotions; my sturdy, too-cute-boy-next-door looks easily crumpled with the onset of confusion. "That's debatable," I answered.

"Oh?" Vince said, as if he had, at last, uncovered a secret.

And what I did next was to begin to explain the whole sorry mess of my saga to him. He disappeared, though, somewhere around the rape and pillage part; his name was called and he was escorted out of the room by a rather handsome man who I took to be a volunteer and who was also wearing jeans, workboots and T-shirt. A few minutes later I was ushered into a tiny cubicle where I dropped my pants and my little itching, burning sensation was diagnosed.

I was given the card of a doctor who could see me that evening and sent on my way. Climbing down the four steep flights of the building I felt as if my miserable luck would never end. I was upset because I still hadn't found a job, upset because I was broke and again living at the Y, upset because I was sick, or, more to the point, inconvenienced, and I thought, as I took each step as if it were to be my last, that maybe I had just made a huge mistake in thinking I could move to Manhattan, and maybe I should just hitchhike my way back to Atlanta where at least everything seemed familiar to me.

When I reached the street, the sunlight was blinding after the darkness of the hall and I stood for a moment wondering what to do next.

"So what's the prognosis?" I heard a voice coming from behind me. I turned and saw Vince leaning against the wall.

"A drip."

"Ahhh, the clap. They give you a referral?"

"Yeah," I held out the card to Vince.

He didn't even bother to look at it. "Come on," he said. "I know a doctor who owes me a favor."

I have often wondered why I invested such blind trust in Vince that day — and why he, too, extended such kindness to me. I think it had something to do with my feeling that, well, things could not get much worse, but something more, too, was at core of it than just willingly accepting the kindness of a stranger. I have often believed that it had something to do with that sexual chemistry that attracts two men to each other in the first place, the way many friendships were first born out of prior sexual encounters.

After escorting me to the doctor, then accompanying me to a pharmacy where he paid for my antibiotics, I expected Vince to just give me his phone number and disappear. My thanks, I expected, would be offered to him weeks later when I was well. I knew there was nothing, really, that I should do with him that day; I did, after all, have my little drip to attend to. What happened next was that he led me out into the street and then he looked up at the sky as if expecting a miracle to happen; it was one of those brilliant late New York summer afternoons, the kind where the air is thin and clear and the sunlight makes everything shine and shimmer and sparkle as if new. "It's too late for the beach," he said, as if I had suggested the possibility. "I bet you've never even been to the Empire State Building."

"No," I answered, shaking my head in response. "But I see it all the time," and turned my head uptown as if I expected it to materialize between the buildings.

"Come on," he said. "I'll take you to the top."

The view was magnificent that day, the visibility stretched, it seemed, for miles. We stood outside on the observation deck, our elbows leaning against the concrete walls, entranced by the strong, warm summer breeze and the twilight painting the sky with deeper and darker hues of blue. The city beneath us, so minute and detailed, seemed to me like one of those miniature enchanted kingdoms where trains run through the mountain slopes, only now on a larger scale there were cars and buses and the microscopic dots of people. So many stories, I thought as I tried to alight my vision, but couldn't. How could I ever find my own—my way to fit in? But then there was a moment, too, when I was seized by the enormity of the city and the luck of having met Vince, finally finding someone who might be a friend, that I felt that I had been truly blessed by something grand, the witness of something special, or, perhaps, as silly as it sounds, embarking at the start of some great new adventure. I was so full of exhilaration that I half expected at any minute to turn and kiss Vince or that, perhaps, he would lyrically spin me around as if we were two actors on a movie set.

Instead I drew in the air, swelled my chest, and hoped to myself that a day and a feeling like that would not end in disappointment. "How long have you lived here?" I asked.

"I was born in Brooklyn," he said. "Somewhere over there. But we moved to New Jersey when I was little. See that building?" I looked to where he pointed, a skyscraper misplaced, it seemed, on the New Jersey skyline. "Near there. When I was in college we were always driving into the city to do something." That, I felt, explained his ease with the city. Vince was twenty-two, three years older than I, and as we watched the sunlight break into pink and violet strips in the west, he told me that he had gone to college in the city and had majored in economics, but was really working on being a writer, a playwright, actually. He was taking some courses and working on some scripts in some workshops, though at the moment, he was unproduced, unpublished, and unknown. For money he worked part time at a bank three days a week, sorting through checks, though he also mentioned that his grandfather had left him some money, which explained to me, too, his ease in other matters. He talked some more about his writing, saying he wanted to some day write something witty and significant, but what he was still searching for were the themes and subjects he needed to explore. "I can't just write about sex, you know, although I think sometimes I might be an authority on it," he said, followed by a quick belly laugh at himself, which led him to explain that he had been in love exactly four times, but preferred for the most part to maintain his independence, or, rather, to play the field.

We stayed until the sun had disappeared completely; the stars, so vivid and precise at that height, began to appear in the sky as if a tube of glitter had been tossed in the air. On the way back down to the street Vince suggested we return to the Village for something to eat and I agreed to go with him. Later, after dinner, I expected him to want to be rid of me at any moment, but we set out walking again, and he lead me to the entrance of a café on Bleecker Street.

"I'm on the top floor," he said, motioning to the door beside the café.

He must have sensed my hesitation. I was not only nervous but confused. What exactly did he want from me?

"You can sleep on the floor if you want," he said. "I've got some extra pillows and a blanket." He pushed his key into the lock and opened the door. "It's got to be better than the Y."

"Why are you being so nice to me?" I asked. I watched his face, lit by the street lamp, move through his confusion. It was clear he was not used to being asked questions so bluntly.

"You're a cute guy," he said, trying to dismiss the intensity that I felt move into my own expression.

"Cute? That's it?"

"Yeah, and you've just had some bad luck. You just need one good thing to change it." It was here that he shrugged his shoulders in exasperation. "Look, I've met a lot of guys," he said. "I can tell when someone's honest, you know?" And this was where he locked his stare into mine and I felt, in that second, the certainty of his trust.

"Everybody needs a friend. Maybe some day you'll do a favor for me." He pushed the door open and stepped inside. And I turned and followed him up the stairs.

"I collect favors," Vince said as he unlocked the door of his apartment. "Someday I'm gonna be a rich and happy man just from favors." As he flipped on the light it was clear to me that he collected other things too; his apartment, a studio, was crammed with piles of magazines, manuscripts, books, and newspapers.

"I keep thinking I'm gonna move out of here," he said, as if he had detected my shock. "So I really haven't invested in a lot of furniture." The furnishings were, well, almost spartan: a table, a chair, a typewriter, and a single bed.

"Problem is, this place is real cheap." He flipped on a stereo that rested on the floor and the piercing voice of Gloria Gaynor filled the room. In a matter of seconds I found myself seated on the floor next to a pile of books on top of which was the script of *Philoctetes*.

It was such an odd moment witnessing this mixture of disco and Sophocles, but Vince seemed not to notice, or, perhaps, think it commonplace. But he did lower the volume to allow us a conversation.

"Want a beer?" he asked, but before I said that I probably shouldn't, he realized it too. "Sorry," he said. "Soda?"

I shook my head no; I was, at that moment, satisfied. Vince opened a beer, took a few swigs from the bottle, then opened a closet and withdrew a blanket. "If you put this on the floor it won't seem so hard." Then he tossed me a pillow and as I caught it I noticed a glass bowl behind a stack of magazines. I lifted it up to examine—it was a large fishbowl, the kind normally used for goldfish. But into this one Vince had stuffed business cards and scraps of paper where names like "Mike Lavaca" and "Todd Luther" were written alongside their phone numbers. It was clear, too, that Vince collected people; they would, after all, be necessary for collecting all those future favors.

"One day I'm gonna paint this place," Vince said, sitting down beside me on the floor. "I want to get a bigger bed and put it against that wall, and get a real nice print or something and hang above it. I want to turn this wall into bookcases," he waved his hand in the air. "But look," he said, and, here, he got up off the floor and walked over to the place where the two walls intersected. "They don't meet at a ninety-degree angle. I'll probably have to get them custom built."

"That's not hard to do," I said. "I could build them for you."

"You know how to build a bookcase?" he asked, with almost a laugh.

"Bookcases are easy. You know someone who has a saw?"

"A *saw?*"

"An electric saw would be best."

"An *e-lec-tric* saw?" he asked, somewhat flabbergasted.

"To cut the wood. You probably already have a hammer."

"A hammer?" He looked at me, disbelieving. "What kind of guy do you think I am?"

"Well, you must know someone. Collect a favor," I said, with a sort of wry smile.

"Where did you learn how to do this?" he asked, his hands resting mockingly on his hips.

"God," I answered rather soberly. "God taught me."

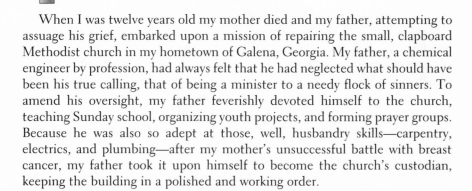

When I was twelve years old my mother died and my father, attempting to assuage his grief, embarked upon a mission of repairing the small, clapboard Methodist church in my hometown of Galena, Georgia. My father, a chemical engineer by profession, had always felt that he had neglected what should have been his true calling, that of being a minister to a needy flock of sinners. To amend his oversight, my father feverishly devoted himself to the church, teaching Sunday school, organizing youth projects, and forming prayer groups. Because he was also so adept at those, well, husbandry skills—carpentry, electrics, and plumbing—after my mother's unsuccessful battle with breast cancer, my father took it upon himself to become the church's custodian, keeping the building in a polished and working order.

I had always resisted my father's religion, as minister's children are often wont to do, and as the years went by I felt my father hid a lot of his flaws behind his religious mask: his narrow-mindedness, his bigotry, his fear of change, and yes, even his alcoholism. But the winter that my mother passed away, I followed my father to the church, hoping myself to find some sort of alleviation and wisdom from my own loss. It was then, during those cold, wet days that my father set about repairing the pews, or, rather, rebuilding them one by one. He had set up a small workshop in the basement of the building, having brought over his lathe and vise and electric tools and sawhorses from his workroom at our home. My father and I, dressed in layers of shirts and pants, would puff out our cheeks and blow hot air into our palms, then set about drawing the outline with a pencil onto the wood we would later cut and sand. My father must have hoped that the experience of us building together would bond us, rebuild our relationship too, but what happened was that it distanced me even further from my father, his blustering mannerisms and paradigms about the godliness of carpentry were such a bitter paradox to me when I measured it against the sour stench of his whiskey breath. What happened as I turned away from my father was that I turned into the work, sawing and sanding like a demon in the temple of God, my pride and joy attained from each new notch of craftsmanship I achieved.

It only took me two days to build and stain Vince's bookcase for him; Vince had remembered that Alex, a friend of his from New Jersey, ran a construction business out of a loft on 17th Street and had all the tools that I needed and had agreed to let me use them because he owed Vince a favor as well; a few months earlier Vince had helped him get a large group of theater tickets for some relatives who had come into town for a vacation. Vince was so impressed by my work that he began to recommend me as a sort of handyman to his other friends, including pushing Alex to use me as a freelance carpenter whenever possible. A few days later I found an apartment on West 19th Street in Chelsea, a small studio walk-up on the fourth floor above a Chinese restaurant.

I always expected Vince to drift away from me, but what happened was we began going to the gym together; Vince loaned me money for a membership at the YMCA in Chelsea till I could pay him back, his stipulation was that I would be his work-out partner, a favor for a favor as it were. Vince preferred the larger but more seedy gym at the Y over the tiny high-tech health clubs that were springing up in the Village and Chelsea; he took his workouts seriously, moving quickly from one set of exercises to another till his body and clothing were coated in sweat. "No pain, no gain," was his philosophy, but during breaks he would love to talk about philosophy, pondering Kant's definition of rational understanding or Neitzche's rejection of Christianity at the same time he was ogling a guy's buttocks on the other side of the weight room. I confess, even now, that I have only a little grasp of what he was talking about—philosophy was never my strongest subject—but I was awed, certainly, by the absurdity of the situation: the reps to achieve the peak of, say, a bicep, juxtaposed against the idolatry of, perhaps, the guy with big arms in the navy blue tank top matched against the primal existence of man or, a favorite of Vince's, the ontology of existentialism.

The sexual tension that had initiated our friendship was always there between Vince and myself, but instead of being a source of frustration it now became an accepted fact; at times, it even introduced a healthy competition between us—we were, by then, too close of friends to want to jeopardize our friendship by having sex with each other, so instead we would often point out men we would like to, well, meet, or, perhaps, we sensed would like to meet us. Vince loved to cruise, especially on the street, and, walking beside him along Seventh Avenue on our way back to the Village after a workout, he would suddenly stop talking as a handsome man approached us; then, just as the stranger was out of earshot, he would whisper, "Did you get a look at that one?" and, if I hadn't noticed, he would always add, "Well, he gave you a look over."

Being with Vince turned the city into an erotic adventure: eyes met, glances were exchanged, smiles bequeathed like presents. It happened everywhere: the subways, grocery stores, theaters, and banks; cruising was the recognition that bound gay men to one another. Vince loved to scan his eyes over a crowd of men at a party; his gaze exploring and lingering, almost tauntingly. Vince collected invitations to parties as easily as he did business cards; he never worried about what sort of opening line he should say to a guy who caught his attention—he had no trouble drawing men in with an alluring smile and a nod. Sex was an easy and uncomplicated accomplishment for Vince, and, though his religion was the same as mine was—the worship of the male body—he was not after the same thing that I was—finding a lover. In fact, it was my quest that often set us apart.

I went with Vince to those parties and bars and restaurants and beaches full of expectations, thinking and, well, believing that I just might stumble onto the man with whom I was destined to fall in love. I was such a young, incurable romantic that everything had such a heightened sense of possibility for me. On the nights Vince and I would go dancing at the Flamingo, a gay disco not far from the curbs of Soho, moments after we had entered the club together, Vince would disappear in the direction of a cluster of friends or a guy who, perhaps, he felt he had to meet. I would nod him away and go and stand on the perimeter of the dance floor, watching the crowd of swirling, sweating bodies spin and twist into the pinspots of flashing lights, the bass line of a song passing through my skin like a thunderous heartbeat.

I was no stranger to clubs—those dark, music-filled places were where, years before in Atlanta, I had discovered there were other gay men, learned, too, that there was nothing really wrong with myself. In high school, tormented by the confusion of my homosexuality, I would borrow my father's car and drive to the discos in Atlanta, and stand and watch men dancing with other men. Those clubs and those men, to a naive suburban teenager like myself, was like being granted free admission to a glittering, urban amusement park; each step and each man contained the possibility of a new adventure. The first man I ever had sex with had first asked me to dance. The first man I fell in love with I had first met at a disco.

And on those nights at the Flamingo in New York, I would scan the crowd the same way I had done a few years before, pausing to study the way a particular man danced, the way he moved his hips and feet, shifted his shoulders, or tilted back his head into a spotlight, wanting at first to be like that man, wanting to grow up looking like that, moving like that, then wondering what sex would be like with him, then wondering, too, what life could be like with him, wanting him, then, as a lover.

At some point Vince would return and tweak my nipples or clutch my crotch or breathe a heavy "errr" into my ear and pull me out to the dance floor. We would dance until we were sweaty and wet, removing our T-shirts and dangling them through the back beltloops of our jeans, our fists shoving in tempo to the music like synchronistic pistons. A rag soaked with ethyl chloride would be passed before my nose, and I would crunch up the muscles of my face before the bleachlike scent expanded into my brain. By then, Vince had usually disappeared and I would be dancing with someone else, watching this other man shift and tilt before me, then suddenly sweep his eyes across my face to find my own. And then I would find myself waiting in a line to piss, some tiny pill pressed into my hand or, on occasion, right into my mouth, and I would be back out on the dance floor again, perhaps, now with another man, caught up in the magic of the moment: the swirling lights, the heaving drum beat of the music, surrounded by dancing men who played tambourines and whistles and cymbals and fans like a band of traveling gypsies.

I would dance until the Flamingo closed, into the early morning hours, and back on the street, squinting at the light and with some guy's arms tucked around my waist, I would feel, as the cool, oily air of the city swept over me and chilled the sweat at the base of my back, my father's disapproval hanging over me. My religion—my worship of men—was what had caused a rift between me and my father and his religion, as wide and impossible to bridge as that of the Grand Canyon. I was also, in those early days of mine in Manhattan, enthralled with the decadence of it all, of urban gay life. I would be so tanked up after a night of dancing I would have to stop in the archway of a building and pee, or, waiting with a guy at a crosswalk we would instinctively slip into a kiss in full view of the morning traffic, without any sort of thought that this might be illegal or immoral to someone else, moving, certainly, without any fear. At the heart of all this was my hope that all this dancing and drugs and booze and sex were only the beginning of something else; what really was so shameful about wanting to fall in love with another man? But even though I still had a boy's raw and naive consciousness, I nonetheless had the cravings and needs of a young man on the prowl. And as much as I saw myself as an optimistic romantic, there was still so much delicious joy and satisfaction in being bad every now and then.

That was the same year that Denise was paired with a young man in her acting class named Jeff, a tall, well-built guy with a strawberry-blond crewcut and a regal looking face, long and rectangular, with narrow blue eyes and a squared off chin as broad as his forehead. At first glance Jeff appeared to be haughty and aloof, but the truth was, Denise was soon to learn, he possessed the burly and playful personality of a four-month old lion cub. Their first assignment in front of the class was to perform the rape scene from A *Streetcar Named Desire* and Denise and Jeff seemed to be a perfect cast to play Blanche and Stanley: Denise, petite and frail-looking; Jeff, large, virile and athletic. But there was also something a little, well, too-too about the both of them—Denise, too young, too bright, too Miss Junior Majorette-looking to be regarded as someone so decaying and mentally delicate, and Jeff, too handsome, too wholesome, too, well, All-American-Bible-toting-football hero, to be believable brutalizing such a pretty young woman. It was Denise's lighthearted suggestion one afternoon while they were rehearsing in the basement of her dormitory that maybe they should change roles, maybe she should be Stanley and Jeff should be Blanche; wouldn't this, after all, be a true test of their talent? This struck Jeff as a wild and outrageous possibility; already at the ripe old cynical age of twenty-three he had grown to dislike the constant effort to fight being stereotyped into bland, heroic roles, tired of being considered nothing more than just another vacuous chisel-jawed matinee-idol-mannequin. Denise would often remind Jeff, however, that it was these same drop-dead looks that had helped get him into this school with a scholarship.

Jeff and Denise's resulting reenactment of Blanche and Stanley's pas de deuce became something of a scandal to the class, several students objected to Jeff's frank, effeminate portrayal but others were even more horrified by Denise's precise, streetwise Stanley. But it was a liberating exercise for both Denise and Jeff, its ramifications lasting well beyond the confines of the classroom. This was the moment that Denise broke out of her shell, found both her self-confidence and creative spark, and Jeff, so confused before as to how much of his sexuality to portray not only on stage but also off, opened his closet door partially and showed his fellow actors that he could, well, wear a dress and not at all be ashamed of it. Not that he stated, specifically, anything about who he really was, of course, but the instructor was so taken by Jeff's new candor that after class he pulled Jeff aside and asked him for a date.

Not that Jeff ever had a problem with suitors or dates before; just walking down the street Jeff could cause quite a stir. Jeff kept his "interests" private, however, as was the wont of most handsome would-be actors trying to find a break, his needs satisfied by late night excursions to bathhouses and members-only clubs. He had been worried, in that midwestern Christian sort of way, that his proclivities would somehow taint him, criminalize him before the public, though now, with his new friendship with Denise, Jeff felt comfortable enough to tell her about his joy of being privately gay. He would come to her dormitory room in the early morning hours, having just been with someone, a man named Stan or Bill or Peter or Jerry, and sit on the floor at her bedside and describe his newfound passion to her, the adoration of other men, and Denise, so intrigued and polite, would curl herself up in her blanket as if she were settling down to read a novel, and listen to Jeff describe the men he had found, reveling in the way he would compare the firmness of one man's ass to that of a basketball, or describe the striated muscles of another man's shoulders.

It was during these early morning confessions, hunched over the cups of instant coffee that Denise would make for them, that Denise would realize she had at last found her first New York friend. Denise loved being bitchy and queeny with Jeff, as she had secretly witnessed the gay boys in her class do amongst themselves, and she would ask Jeff questions, in her campy, tiny, affected voice, "Dahrling, are you only interested in size?" or "But dear, didn't all those tattoos scare you?" Her concern for Jeff's safety was genuinely honest; as large and intimidating as Jeff could appear to be, he also possessed a cautious streak, as though he were a titanic waiter balancing a miniature tray of crystal champagne glasses. Denise, however, preferred to get a comic rise out of Jeff, something to stir a waggish retort from him. "But he must have had terrible breath," Denise would wonder out loud about one of Jeff's more, well, oral connections, for instance. Jeff, playing along with the game, would respond with a coy, "But how would I know? He wasn't anywhere near my mouth." But what gratified Denise most about her new friend was, when he had expended his revelations, his puppylike candor of sexual joy, he would look up at her on her bed, pull her into his cool-blue stare and say, in the boyish tone that Denise had so come to love, "But what about you? What have *you* been up to?"

What Denise did, after finding Jeff, was to let the joy of him, the ecstasy of his doting, easy-going friendship, push her out into the city. Now she went out buoyantly with the girls on her hall to find new restaurants, with fellow actors to ride the Circle Line around Manhattan or tour the United Nations or for a shopping jaunt at Bloomingdale's, happy, at last, to have a purpose and to be able to retell, hours or days later when seeing Jeff again, all the things she had done, share with him the details of her happiness. And it was here, too, she began to affect her own opinions, though often mimicking the gay spirit of the day. She would look at Jeff and smile and say something with mock exasperation, "Oh, dahrling, you should have seen the windows at Macy's yesterday. Those poor designers must certainly be on drugs. They have misplaced a statue of Cupid amongst the Easter lilies." Jeff, in turn, would continue the bitchy banter. "But dearest," he would implore to Denise, "They aren't designers. They only maintain their employment for those literal fifteen seconds of fame they are granted." Denise, here, would show her mock confusion. "The parade, dear," Jeff would explain to her. "Just to be able to say to their coterie how they were captured in all their beauty on television at Thanksgiving pulling a giant Goofy balloon down Broadway." He would laugh, then sigh, then lure Denise in again with a tilt of his head. "Did I tell you about the beauty I met at Macy's?" he would ask, and then he would be off again, detailing the glory of the male physique.

Their friendship spilled over on one another in many ways. Denise brought Jeff to the parties she was invited to and Jeff, in turn, introduced Denise to guys he met, guys whom he would describe in beautiful and explicit details and who would, eventually, make their way into Denise's acquaintance and offer her discounts on things like clothing, jewelry, shoes, and haircuts. It was sometime near the end of the spring term that year that Jeff, through one of these tricks, heard of a large apartment in the West Village that was cheap and vacant. Denise had no qualms about living with Jeff, jumped, in fact, at the opportunity to move out of the dormitory and into a real apartment, even if it was a fifth-floor walk-up located near the end of Bethune Street.

Jeff often referred to that first apartment they shared as "the tenement," though Denise preferred to describe it as "a railroad flat with character." The apartment was a series of four large rooms and a bathroom, designed so that one had to pass through one room to enter the next. The "character" of the space was acquired from the overpainted walls, the broken window sills, the stingy water pressure available in the bathroom, a wall of electrical outlets that refused to work, and the floors that slanted so much they seemed to belong inside one of those lopsided carnival fun houses. They decorated their home as many New Yorkers often furnished their first apartments, assembling a collection of boxes and crates that became coffee tables and bookshelves, a couch or a chair found from garbage piled up on the street at night, waiting to be picked up by the city sanitation department. Jeff moved into the last room of the apartment, the one where the door could be closed for privacy. It was decided between them that Jeff should have the private room because, well, he hoped to entertain a lot. Denise took one of the small middle rooms as her bedroom, accepting a sofa bed bequeathed from one of Jeff's friends, and stringing up curtains for her own privacy, though she rarely found the need to close them.

Jeff and Denise never even locked the bathroom door; whatever personal restraints they harbored had evaporated after the first few days they lived together. Jeff loved to roam around the apartment draped in a towel, singing at the top of his lungs, *"The truth is I ne-ver left you."* The truth, of course, was what thoroughly alarmed Denise's mother. On top of all of Mrs. Connelly's fears of New York now loomed the fact that Denise was unmarried and living with a man. Denise explained to her mother that there was nothing wrong with living with Jeff; she slept on the sofa bed entirely by herself and Jeff had his own room and that, well, Jeff was gay, so what was the problem? That, of course, was the problem; and only another in the string of things that convinced Denise's mother that her daughter's life was deteriorating into decadence.

Jeff, on the other hand, was amused by Mrs. Connelly's provincial concern. Jeff would often tease Denise after her phone conversations with her mother, asking her if she had told her mother about the Hispanic guy he had tricked with the night before, or about the young man he had met in the porno cinema near Union Square. Jeff told none of this to his own mother, of course. Jeff had moved to Manhattan from Ohio and he explained Denise to his parents as "someone special;" they, in turn, accepted Denise as Jeff's asset.

Denise, in fact, never worried about the guys Jeff brought into the apartment, not even the ones late at night who would bump into the edge of the sofa bed on their way to Jeff's bedroom. Denise was actually intrigued by it all; but at the time she was more concerned about her career than about sex. And she wasn't really jealous of all the men Jeff was able to attract, though she once told me that she was envious of all the attention Jeff was getting. Denise always looked upon Jeff's "guests," as she liked to call them, as new faces to meet in the morning—those who stayed till morning, and most did. Denise would invite Jeff and his friend of the moment to join her for breakfast, sitting down opposite them at the café table that crowded the tiny first room of their apartment. She confided to these strangers, on those mornings, her fear that really, deep down, she knew she looked too thin and birdlike to be considered a serious actress. She knew, too, she was much too short to ever make it as a fashion model. Her greatest claim to fame to date, she would explain with her light-hearted sarcasm, besides her debut as Stanley, was the time in Louisville she had worked as a shampoo model at a department store; she knew her best feature was her Pre-Raphaelite hair: thick and long and wavy brown. Jeff and his guest would nuzzle one another and Denise would hunch over her coffee mug and draw them into her stare and say her time would come, years from now; she felt she would make a great elderly character actress. All she had to do was to train and hope.

It was into all this hope that Vince appeared one morning at that little kitchen table, having met Jeff the night before at the Flamingo. Denise has often described that first morning with the two of them as being something akin to breakfast with two kids in hyperdrive—Jeff pumped up from his night of dancing and sex and Vince chattering away from the side-effects of too much booze and drugs. Denise knew instinctively to fix decaf that morning, staying away from caffeine or any other sort of stimulant that might only heighten the animated state Vince and Jeff had reached; they could not remain still, could not contain their infatuation for one another, could not keep their hands off each other's bodies, their tongues out of each other's mouths, except, of course, when they had something to say.

Vince, suspicious at first of a woman's presence, tested Denise's composure by talking about the various pecs and nipples and biceps and yes, cocks, on view at the Flamingo the night before, comparing them to Jeff's own beauty and checking Denise's expression for any perceptible sign of disapproval. Denise, of course, was enthralled by Vince's monologues on male beauty, and Vince, satisfied, drew her into the conversation. But she then drew Vince into another conversation, one of hers, about her concern over the current state of the Broadway musical, and about the presence of Sondheim and Strouse and Hamlisch and was it all just becoming, really, just one big messy nonsensical revue. Jeff, still elevated by his evening of stimulants, started singing whatever phrase crossed through his euphoric mind, and Vince was only too satisfied and eager to offer his own opinion on theatrical matters. Then, once Vince realized he had been accepted, had been taken into both of their confidences like an old friend, he took one look at that tiny, cramped kitchen and proclaimed, in his best imitative Bette Davis voice, "*What a fuck-ing dump!*"

He got up from the kitchen table and began walking through the apartment, running his fingers along the cracks in the plaster walls, inspecting the missing light fixtures, the warped door frames, the floorboards creaking beneath his steps, Denise rambling on and on in defense of the charm and the bohemian quality of their lifestyle. Vince began to see the apartment as he felt it should be seen, saying, "You should paint this wall a real light color and the woodwork in a darker color, maybe something in peach or dust tones," and, "A couch would look nice here—a large floral design or a thick tweed look." When he reached Denise's room, the floor tilted so much that Denise, where she stood, appeared as tall as Jeff. Vince shook his head and asked, "Are you sure this is not a structural hazard?"

"No, I don't think so," Denise said, though she knew nothing of what Vince was talking about, but then neither did Vince. Vince reached out and touched the curtains Denise used to define her room but which were never drawn, and here, turned to Denise and with a nod of sincere concern, said, "You really need more privacy than this." He lifted his chin toward Jeff, capturing, too, at that moment his understanding, and said emphatically, "You should build a wall or something," and then gestured his hand toward the ceiling with a wave, "Maybe something dramatic—like Japanese screens."

Denise backed away, captured by her imagination of Vince's suggestion; she had, up until that point, not taken anything Vince had said with any sort of seriousness.

"But it would be so expensive," she said, fighting back her disappointment.

Here, Vince reached over and grasped Denise's hand, bequeathed her a warm, knowing smile as if he had a secret he would share, and this was the moment that they would both recall, years later, as the beginning of their friendship. "I have a friend who can build it for you," Vince said. "He'll do it for you very cheaply." Then he turned to Jeff, caught his eyes and, here, smiled even wider as if to assure his promise. "He owes me some favors," he said, and, then, reached out his free hand and placed it on Jeff's bicep, bonding the three of them together as a minister would before prayer. "You'd really like him," he added, arching an eyebrow at Jeff. "Short. Dark hair. And very cute."

By that time I owed Vince many favors, one of which was for introducing me to Alex, a short, stocky man in his forties who kept his monk's ring of gray hair closely cropped against his broad face. Alex ran a nonunion construction management company out of a loft near Union Square, a tall dusty pipe-lined space lit from the spill of sunlight around the neighboring buildings of the Flatiron district. Alex was responsible for hiring freelance construction crews and workers for sites around the city. His loft was often full of potential employees, usually a mix of immigrant latinos or blacks or expatriate southerners: large, bulky, beer-bellied men dressed in jeans, tool belts, T-shirts and workboots and who hunched over coffee cups or stood and jiggled the coins in their pants pockets, their feet nervously pawing the floor while waiting for the chance to light up another cigarette.

Alex's loft was a hothouse of testosterone and tension, some guy was usually complaining about last night's Knicks or Jets game or about a girl-friend or wife nagging about something or another. Alex sat in an unpainted office at the rear of the loft, wearing out a ragged spiral notebook that contained a list of names and phone numbers, his shirts sleeves rolled up to the elbows, his bulky and hairy forearms dandered with sawdust. Alex hated more than anything having to be tied down waiting for phone calls to come in, but knew it was the necessity of his business; he was, after all, the link between his clients and workers. Often, he would rub his fingers through his hair or chew on the cap of a ball point pen till the phone rang. In the morning he kept his conversation contained to short, staccatolike phrases, waiting to hear from a guy who could sub for another worker, wanting to get off as quickly as possible so he could move on to the next call, his index finger loudly punching the plastic buttons of his phone with a "chink," "chink," "chink" as he moved from one line to another.

More than anything Alex would have preferred to sit and bullshit with the other men in the loft who congregated outside his office door, but even when the opportunity presented itself he was treated with the reverence of someone more like a coach than like one of the guys. Not that that bothered him, though; Alex was always a man of his own agenda. He was one of those men whose aura is highly sexual around both men and women, which perhaps was another contributing factor to his employees' unbelievably boyish manner in his presence. Alex had a wife and two kids who lived in New Jersey, two boys in their early teens and whose photographs of growing little league baseball and junior varsity football triumphs lined the metal shelving of his office as if it were a trophy room. But Alex saw himself as something more than a married man; he had married late and separated early, and he had worked hard not only to support the family he had left behind but to settle back again into his own independence, though he would often move mountains to rearrange his schedule to spend more time with his sons. He had lived for the last four years in an apartment on 72nd Street that had a view of the East River, and he had moved into the sort of lifestyle that a decade before would have been labeled "swinger." Alex seldom required a full night's sleep; instead, for Alex nights meant going out to a club for a drink and bringing home whomever interested him. At the time I met him he had a particular fondness for dark-eyed beauties—Italian women and Puerto Rican boys, settling for whichever he believed would offer him, well, the least amount of emotional complications.

Not that Alex was ever the type of man to discuss these complications with anyone; he kept the temperament of his changing sexuality hidden from his workers. I found all this out from Vince, of course, who had known Alex since Vince was a boy and they had lived in the same apartment building in South Orange. Alex, in his twenties then and studying evenings at Rutgers, had recently begun weight lifting, and Vince, because he had no friends his own age in the building, would hang out in the basement where Alex and his best friend Len had set up some gym equipment. Vince once told me those afternoons watching Alex and Len work out was his first erotic experience, and he mentioned that Alex had even once modeled for a prominent physique photographer. Alex, however, had never taken bodybuilding all that seriously—he always felt his height had hindered him from achieving any sort of perfection in the sport.

It was one of those hot, hazy August days that Vince tracked me down through Alex and explained over the phone that he needed a favor done for some new friends. Why Vince felt so compelled to help Denise and Jeff I have never been certain, but I have always felt that it was more than just because of his tête-à-tête with Jeff, since both of them had already moved on to other sexual partners. I believe it was because Denise and Jeff, like Vince, were struggling artists, actors on the verge of their craft, and Vince, himself a struggling writer, felt that if he befriended them now, passed some favors along to them, that perhaps, years later, he might collect on them, as he did so immediately and frequently from me that summer.

It was still brutally humid the day I showed up at that tenement apartment on Bethune Street to measure Denise's room. Vince was conveniently absent, having accepted an invitation to go out to Fire Island for the weekend, though he had left behind a sketch of how he felt the wall of Japanese screens should look. Vince, as a friend, I could never fault, but Vince as designer I never much appreciated. Jeff, too, was missing that day, having ended up in New Jersey with a man he had met the night before at Uncle Charlie's. Denise was uncomfortable with me from the moment I arrived; she was worried about being alone in the apartment with me, a sweaty brooding stranger clunking around her apartment in workboots, worried about the expense of it all, thinking Vince had perhaps duped her into something she could not really afford. After measuring the room, modifying Vince's sketch into a practical solution, and figuring out the hardware I would need, I gave Denise an estimate for what the materials would cost, mentioning that the labor would be free, according to Vince's instructions.

"That's all?" she asked, flabbergasted at the price.

"You're a friend of Vince's," I answered, a little too mechanically.

She looked at me, then said, "You're not at all what I imagined."

I was taken back by the statement, "What exactly were you expecting?" I asked.

"I don't know. You look so young. But you also seem so, you know, so practical."

"Practical?"

"It's just that I know so many guys who are, well, you know—high strung."

I laughed. I knew exactly what she meant. "I think I know the same guys," I said.

She looked at me and, here, I met her stare as she asked, "Who do you want to be?"

"Be?" Now she had me confused.

"Everybody always wants to be someone else. You know like a designer or an actor or a writer. What do you want to be?"

"It would be fun to be an actor, I guess," I said, not having given it any serious thought. "But I don't have to be that. I don't really have that sort of talent. I suppose if I had a wish—what would I be? I suppose I'd want to be in love with someone."

"A romantic," she said, somewhat surprised.

"Hardly," I lied, shocked at revealing too much of myself too quickly to a stranger.

"Let me see your hand," she said, and reached her hand out for mine.

"Do you read palms?" I asked, and lifted a hand out towards her. She took my hand, rubbing her fingers over the calluses at the base of the joints. "No," she answered. "These are not the hands of a romantic."

Jeff rematerialized the day after I had carried all of the lumber and tools and hardware and materials I would need to install Denise's screens up the five winding and poorly ventilated flights of their building by myself. By the time Jeff emerged from his bedroom that morning, the old, shredded T-shirt that I wore was already drenched in sweat, a tape measure on my belt loop pulling a flimsy pair of cutoff jeans below my waist. Jeff wore only the small towel that he twisted around his waist to prove he had some modesty around strangers, and it was clear both to him and to Denise when he approached the beams I had laid out on the floor that he provided me with a source of both interest and agitation. Even then Jeff's physique was both startling and seductive—the definition of his muscles appeared to be chiseled into the unblemished ivory of his skin, as if Rodin's Thinker had discarded his dark, pensive mood and changed into a sexier position. Denise, who had decided it was her mission to monitor my work as though at any moment she was about to be overcharged, wanted nothing more than for Jeff to disappear, for he was not only a distraction for me, but obviously somewhat curious about me himself.

"He's not interested in you," Denise said to Jeff while I attempted to flush a beam against their misalligned wall. "He wants love not sex," which was, of course, not what I wanted from Jeff at the precise moment.

"Really?" Jeff asked her. "And how do you know this?"

I began hammering, hoping the sound would drive them both from the room. I could feel the T-shirt clinging against my back and swore, at that moment, I could smell the stench of myself. When I stopped, they were both still there.

"Rob, this is Jeff," Denise said. I looked up and nodded and pretended to be measuring the beam again.

"Where did you learn how to do this?" Jeff asked. This talent, it seemed, was of interest to everyone.

"My father," I answered this time, hoping to keep the subject closed.

"My father's a shit," Jeff said.

"So's mine," I answered, almost as a mumble. From my peripheral vision I could sense him fidgeting with the towel around his waist and I avoided the urge to turn and study him.

"Want something to drink?" he asked.

I looked up and, here, caught his eyes, my turn to lock into his friendship. "Sure," I said.

"Denise, dear," Jeff said, in his most mock chauvinistic tone but with a queeny stance with his hands on his hips, "Don't you want to make some lemonade. Or *some-thing?*"

I did not have sex with Jeff that day, nor did I at all that summer. What happened after Denise disappeared to make *some-thing* was that Jeff began to talk about his father, who was a continual source of frustration for him. Jeff had spoken to his father on the phone the day before, and in conversation his father had asked Jeff, who had only last month received his acting degree, "But when are you going to get a *real* job?" Jeff had fallen into a trap of working odd jobs to earn extra money in order to keep auditioning for acting parts—selling ties at Barney's, spraying cologne at Macy's, stuffing envelopes at a public relations office—all which, if they didn't pay that well, could at least offer the promise of someone inviting him out for something to eat.

"Why is it parents don't want their children to be different from them?" he asked me, not really expecting, I believe, any sort of answer.

"Genetics, I suppose," I replied, not wanting to seem uncaring. I felt it was a little too early in the morning to begin such a heavy conversation, but I was also somewhat relieved to take a break, and I sat on the window sill hoping the breeze that hit my back would dry the sweat that still dampened my T-shirt.

"My dad is a real hypocrite," he said. "He's a high school football coach. One of those big fat slobs who drinks too much and never exercises, but treats everyone like he's this military sergeant." The tone of his voice, the gesturing of his hands, reminded me of all those late-night, after-sex, confessionals of so many of the men I had met. I sat there for a moment wondering if I had missed something, if Jeff and I had already had sex and we were now reaching another level of intimacy, but it was obvious that Jeff needed someone to talk to, someone who could provide him with a little more understanding than Denise could, someone who, well, was another gay man.

"If you had a choice to be straight or gay, what would you pick?" he asked me.

"Is this multiple choice or free association?" I asked, trying to keep the mood light.

"No, come on," he said. "Are you happy being gay?"

"I could think of some things that might make me happier, you know, like more money and a lover. But I'm not unhappy. Certainly not because I'm gay. I don't think it was a choice I ever made. I believe I was born gay. But I made a choice not to be straight."

He nodded his head in reply and I noticed his face moving through a thought. "When I was fifteen my father caught me messing around with another guy on the team," he said, seating himself on the floor, draping the towel so that it continued to provide some respectability to his arrangement. I have never understood why it is so easy for people to open themselves up to me, but by then, that summer, I had accepted the fact that I must sometimes simply be a good listener. "He took me to see a psychiatrist," Jeff continued,

"And I told the doctor that I thought I was gay. This doctor thought that it could be cured so he suggested that I check into a hospital for some tests. Since everyone thought there was something wrong with me, I went into the hospital—only this hospital the doctor was talking about was one of those fucking mental hospitals. And my parents went along with all this. The first day I was there I was strapped into a chair at my wrists and ankles and a nurse came in and told me that everything was going to be all right. They fastened electrodes to my fingertips and a flashed slides of nude men and women on the wall in front of me. When the male pictures appeared I was electrocuted. It was so fucking painful.

"This stupid shit continued for about a week, then one day it just stopped, but I was still kept in the hospital for observation. A week later I mentioned to a doctor that I had had a dream in which there were mostly men. Not even an erotic dream. Just a fucking simple dream. They started the electric shock therapy again but this time it was even worse. They gave me thorazine and strapped me down to a table, and I was hooked up with an IV and pumped with something that made me drowsy. Electrodes were placed at my temples and they put a rubber plate into my mouth. They had my head confined so I couldn't look around the room, so I had to just stare at those fucking little holes in the ceiling tiles. The shocks were so painful I tried to spit the bit out of my mouth. And then I lost everything. I just went out of it. I couldn't remember my name. They kept me strapped to my bed, didn't change me for days. Just let me lie in my own shit.

"Finally, my parents decided I had had enough and had me released. This was in 1970. For a long time I pretended nothing happened. I just went back to school, studied, and went back to the football team. Then I left home for college and never looked back. I got a track scholarship to Ohio State and paid the rest with a student work program. My father didn't pay a dime for my education. I can't even speak to him now without shaking. He was a fucking asshole to do that to me. I was fifteen fucking years old. That's probably why I'm such a slut now—still looking for proof that there's nothing wrong with me. Either that or I just like sex."

I felt the enormity of Jeff's story hovering in the humidity of the room and I struggled with the awkwardness of it needing a reply. I lifted the corner of my T-shirt and twisted it up to my face, wiping away the lines of sweat. "You shouldn't judge yourself by your father's morality," I said.

He looked at me as if he remembered, suddenly, that there was another person in the room, someone who was not merely an extension of himself.

"We're brought up to believe that sex is dirty," I said. "Something bad and unnatural. So instead of accepting it as something instinctive and pleasurable, we attach such emotional baggage to it that it becomes confused with love." I felt, then, the emotional history of my own words. "Sex is not always an act of love," I added, trying to reassure him and myself, even though I was seldom able to separate the two.

Jeff looked away from me, giving my words great thought. "I bet your father is a minister," he said, at last, with a laugh of recognition.

"No," I answered. "But he's real close to God."

My first lover was a man much older than myself, older, even, than my father was at that time. Will was a college professor—had been my Russian Lit instructor—but I had first met him when some friends of mine introduced us at a disco not far from campus. Will was, the year that I fell in love with him, fifty-five years old. I was barely eighteen, a college sophomore. Will was a tall, thin, elegant-looking man and before a classroom he was somewhat magnetic, expounding on the gifts of Chekhov, Tolstoy, and Mayakovsky; he appealed, at first, to the bookish, academic student within me. The year after I first met him at the gay disco, I enrolled in his class, but when he invited me over to his house one evening, it was clear his intention was more than his offer to show me the photographs of Meyerhold's productions that had instigated the invitation. I, of course, had sensed that this would be the case; and I was only too willing to accept him as my guide, needed him, in fact, to be my guide.

And what a guide he became. He changed the way I cut my hair, the clothes I wore, the courses I took, the books I read, the way I thought and spoke, and, especially, the way I looked upon sex. Our sexual sessions were long and explicit; he would talk to me as he made love to me, describing how he was touching my nipples, what my skin felt like, the way my ass would taste before his lips. And he was full of questions, too, wanting to know what I felt as he rubbed two fingers across the head of my cock, what I was thinking as he kneaded the muscles of my shoulders, if I was scared as he would slip first one finger into my rectum and then another. He did this all with a tenderness he would not admit to, to do so would be to break one of his private vows, that of never imbuing the sexual act with a sense of love. Will was always cautious of maintaining his distance from me; he would never refer to me as his lover, never, either, admit that he was in love. In fact, he would often invite other men—mostly students, but once, even another professor—to join us in bed. This was done not only for the pleasure it afforded us, but also, purposely at times for my sake, to make sure to keep me grounded, to keep us at a distance from one another, to make sure I was not falling in love with him, or, at least, not falling so hard that when the time came for us to conclude our affair, I would end up feeling hurt or misused, which, of course, I nonetheless did.

"Imagine what your father must think about all this," Will would say when we were in bed together, before he would slip his mouth over my cock. My body would tense, of course; I had told Will all about my father. "Now imagine yourself as a bird in that tree," he would lift his head away from me and say, looking out at the window. "First flying into this room, looking at us on the bed, and then soaring back out into the world."

I did just has he suggested, and this was how I began to distance myself from the shame my father had instilled in me, this visualization that I was free of feeling and restriction, liberated as it were. And I discovered, too, the joy, the physical pleasures of sexuality, and it was how, too, months later when my affair with Will ended, that I was able to keep from feeling so abandoned and disheartened. This is what I told Jeff that morning after he had spoken of his father, how it was important for us to now look beyond the way our parents saw us. Denise had joined us again by then, the glasses of iced tea she had made dripping with condensation even before she reached the room.

"Sex, sex, sex," she said, at once lightening the mood of the room. "You boys don't ever seem interested in love."

"On the contrary," I answered. "Some day I'd love to be in love."

Denise's wall of moving Japanese screens was finished within a few days; Vince returned from Fire Island and those hot, humid summer afternoons slipped fitfully into fall. Vince had finished a draft of a play he had written, a episodic farce involving twenty-seven characters in search of a hotel in the Bloomsbury section of London, and once a week for a whole month he would have readings, either at a midtown rehearsal studio or a friend's loft in Chelsea. The people who helped Vince with those readings were nothing like the parts they were asked to read. Jeff and Denise and I were each given roles: Denise played a Russian secretary trying to defect, Jeff, a Dutch librarian with a stutter, and I was an English butler addicted to morphine. The play itself, Vince even admitted to me, was not very good, though he often mentioned when he pulled me aside on those evenings that this play was written solely to keep him visible to his other theater friends. Vince assembled and orchestrated each of those readings as if it were a party; bouquets of fresh flowers were strategically placed under spotlights, a waiter with hors d'oeuvres circulated through the crowd, and golden oldies from the Sixties played softly on a tape deck so that people would impulsively start singing or dancing as the songs changed throughout the evening. Vince would not even attempt to contain the cast in one area, but preferred to let the dialogue ripple through the crowd of rooms, spilling around the pockets of laughter; the result gave one the feeling of having stumbled into a spontaneous avant-garde event.

Afterwards, Denise, Jeff, and I would tumble out into the chilly night air and walk to a nearby café, order cappuccino or espresso and pastries, and set our dreams in motion, or, rather, set about talking about our dreams. Denise was always the first to bring up the subject of what she hoped to accomplish in her life; most of the time it was a litany of the roles she felt she would be right to play, a wish list she could readily recite from memory and augment on a moment's whim. Jeff's dreams were often more immediate; sometimes it could involve our waiter or perhaps another customer within his line of vision; other times, he, too, talked endlessly of acting. I was silently drawn into the romantic notion of everything: the vaulted, shadowy ceiling of the café, the dark carved oak furniture, the stubby candle burning at the center of our table. But what I felt so gratifying about those evenings was my own willingness to become absorbed in other people's lives.

"I could get you into one of my acting classes if you want," Denise said to me one night.

"I don't think I really have any desire to be an actor," I answered, waving my hand in front of the flame of the candle.

"You did the English accent real good," Jeff said.

"You could be really good, I bet," Denise added, as though she and Jeff had rehearsed a scene in order to convince me of converting to their profession. "You have that look."

"What look?"

"My new drama coach would go nuts for you," Jeff said. "He'd let you in his class in a minute."

"Vince even mentioned that he thought you would be good," Denise said.

"Is this a setup for one of his favors?" I asked, with a laugh.

"No," Denise said, with the slight gasp of acknowledgment.

"Not at all," Jeff frowned.

"We just wanted to be able to help you with something, that's all," Denise said, her hand reaching for the base of the candle and tilting it a bit so that the hot wax dripped onto the table.

"I've just never imagined myself as an actor," I said. "I guess I would prefer to do something more solid."

"Solid?" Denise asked. Now, I noticed, she had become confused.

"Stable," I explained. "Or maybe go back to finish school someday."

"*School?*" Jeff replied, horrified. "How much fun could that be?"

"Fun?" I asked. It was my turn to be confused.

"But what would you really like to do?" he leaned across the table toward me. "What would you really like to wake up in the morning and just have to do?"

"Do?" I asked, tilting my eyes up in wonder at the darkness of the ceiling, knowing where he was trying to lead me with the tone of his voice, but trying, instead, to find some sort of other answer for him. "Do," I repeated. "I'd love to build something some day."

"*Build some-thing?*" they both answered in unison. I knew by the concurrent tone of their voices that I had completely mystified these two thespians.

"Like a house, you know."

"Like an architect?" Denise asked.

"Sort of. But build it with my own hands. Something I can be proud of. Or, you know, renovate something. Like a brownstone or something."

"Our apartment needs painting," Jeff said, perhaps a little too flatly.

"Now you're trying to take advantage of my good nature."

"Well," Denise said, as if trying to sum up the conversation. "We'll just have to find you something to build."

Then in early November, walking across Washington Square one morning, Denise slipped on a patch of ice, the first of the season, fell, and broke her leg. Jeff met her at the hospital, took her home, helped her up the stairs and into their apartment. A doctor had prescribed Darvocet for Denise's pain, but Jeff brought her instead one of the joints he hid in his small, carved wooden jewelry box, the ones he saved for special occasions. Denise was propped up on pillows in her bed and had pulled back the screens so the entire room was once again open and exposed. He sat beside her on the edge of the bed, well, next to her Raggedy Ann doll, really, lit the joint and drew a long toke and then passed it to Denise. They sat this way, smoking and laughing, until Denise felt better, or, at least until they both became stoned and hungry. Jeff disappeared into the kitchen and brought back crackers and orange marmalade, the only thing he could decide that he wanted to eat at that moment. They smoked some more and Jeff said he wanted to inaugurate the cast that extended from above Denise's knee down to her toes. Jeff took one of the pencils that Denise kept in a cup on the window sill and drew the comic face of a woodpecker on the cast. Denise was so impressed she asked Jeff to show her how he drew it.

"Don't you remember all those ads in the magazines that said, 'If you can draw this picture you can be an artist?'" Jeff said.

"Right," Denise answered, squinting her eyes with her memory.

"I could never draw it. So I traced it."

"You *traced* it?" Denise asked, here, assuming the mock surprise of someone stoned.

"Over and over," Jeff laughed. "It's the only thing I know how to draw."

Jeff found a sheet of paper in a notebook in his room and presented it to Denise as if it were a gift. "Just trace it," he said, proudly.

Instead, Denise sketched it. This, now, rather impressed Jeff. "Let me draw you," she laughed, and then sketched Jeff. Soon Denise began sketching everything in her room, then hobbling into the kitchen and sketching everything there, then even sketching Jeff again, this time draped with only a towel around his waist.

Because Denise was essentially homebound, trapped like Rapunzel in their fifth floor walk-up, Jeff bought and brought Denise all the things she needed: diet soda, Chinese take-out, colored pencils, nail polish, sketch pads, and shampoo. Denise was surprised she actually liked drawing so much, liked making all these tiny, precise little sketches. Once, when I visited her and brought her some vegetables and fruits from the corner market, she told me her sketches filled up her mind, filled up her days, too, and more importantly, gave her a sense of accomplishment. In less than a week Denise had filled up seven sketchbooks. Vince, looking through one of Denise's sketch books one night, said, "These are really good, Denise, you should show these to someone. I think I might know an art teacher." Which is exactly how I found myself

helping Denise into a cab the following week, taking her to see an art instructor on 12th Street.

When Denise told her mother that Sunday on the phone, that she was
changing her career from acting to art, Mrs. Connelly, who had not yet recovered from the shock of her daughter's accident, was now thoroughly convinced
her daughter's life was in desperate need of salvation.

"It's not like I'm giving up acting," Denise tried to explain to her mother.
"If Woody Allen offered me a part, then I would be an actress again. But this
is a real talent I have. Everyone says so. And I don't have to sit around and wait
for someone to give me a part or tell me I'm a great actress. I can generate my
own work."

"I'm not exactly sure how your father will feel about all this," Mrs. Connelly
said, not even attempting to hide the exasperation in her voice.

"I hope he will at least be happy for me," Denise said. "And Mother,"
Denise added, here, with a slight trepidation in her voice. "I won't be visiting
for the holidays."

"At all?" Mrs. Connelly gasped.

According to Denise's mother a family was needed for certain things, such
as Thanksgiving, Christmas, arriving at airports, hospitals, birthdays, funerals,
and Disneyland. That was not the first year that Denise had missed returning
to Shelbyville for at least one of the holidays, but Denise pointed out to her
mother that her brother would not be home for Thanksgiving, her sister would
not be there for Christmas, and that her mother was trying to inflict all the
sibling guilt on her. That, of course, upset her mother even more, and her
mother said, finally, "Your father will be very disappointed that you're not at
home this year," as if to give Denise a final stab in the heart before hanging up
the phone.

This, of course, amused Jeff even more. That Christmas was the first of
many that I spent with Jeff and Denise. Denise's mission, that year, was to
connect all of her friends who were adrift during the holidays, those who were
single or unattached, too far from home, preferred, well, the "bachelor"
lifestyle, or like myself, were alienated from their families. That Christmas Jeff
was involved with a guy named Hank, a short, beefy mime who wore a crooked
toupee. Vince was dating several men at once; the ones I remember were
named Stephen and Frank—both of whom were there that day. Denise had
just met a director, Peter, whom she was convinced would do Vince's play, and
thus would, in effect, repay Vince for all the favors she felt she owed him by
then.

There were seventeen of us at that apartment that afternoon, an oddly
warm, muggy day—the rooms had the feel of some sort of bizarre East Village
art gallery. Jeff had opened the windows and let the damp breeze float through
the rooms, ruffling the tinsel and the edges of Denise's sketches that were
taped everywhere throughout the apartment. The food was a ramshackle
what-could-be-afforded buffet, plates scattered on counter tops, bookshelves,

and a coffee table, nothing festive, really—cold cuts, appetizers, chips and dip, small squares of pizza. I had left Vince and Denise and Peter, who were talking in the kitchen about how a play about two gay prisoners during World War II was being staged on Broadway, and I wandered through the other rooms of the apartment, not really wanting to settle into any conversation. I was feeling fidgety; I have never felt comfortable during the holidays, never felt relaxed at parties either, really. For many years I have been described as a man of few words; I've never been good at small talk and chitchat, and especially wasn't good at it in my youth. Most people would probably find me boring or think me snobbish and I had come to prefer to just sit on the edge of a couch or a chair and just listen to everything everyone else had to say.

That afternoon I sat on the edge of Denise's bed, near a night table where a bowl of cashews had been placed next to the phone, and tried to relax and not look too conspicuous and at the same time listen to Jeff describe an audition he had had to the guy who stood next to me, a slender boyish-looking blond named Nathan, a friend of Hank's whom I had not yet formally met. I had been eyeing Nathan since he had arrived with Hank, wondering what his story was, why was he with Hank if Hank was with Jeff, then mentally undressing him, thinking what it would be like to spend an evening in bed with him, using my imagination of him to fight back some of my own holiday loneliness.

And then the phone rang. Nathan instinctively leaned over and answered it, saying, "Santa's House of Passion." Denise's mother, who was calling, spoke in a startled voice I could hear even from where I was seated. "*Who* are *you?*" she asked.

"And *who* are *you?*" Nathan asked in reply, his voice deep and breathy. Denise's mother, now completely flustered by hearing an unrecognized voice, worried that her daughter might be in the hands of some mad holiday deviate, answered in a harsh, frightened voice, "I want to speak to—*the mother.*" Nathan lifted the receiver away from his ear and yelled, "Is there a *mother* in the house?"

That, of course, set everyone to laughing and joking, and when Denise retrieved the phone from Nathan, Nathan ended up sitting next to me on the bed. "And *who* are *you?* he asked me in the same manner Denise's mother had spoken.

Surprised, I momentarily forgot my own name. "Not a mother," I answered, a little too quickly, a bit stunned at being drawn in as his accomplice.

His eyes widened. "Good," he replied. "That's not what I had in mind."

Denise once said that Nathan and I reminded her of two choir boys lost in a candy store, an image, Nathan replied to Denise, that must have been ground into her mind because of some sort of bizarre maternal Christian self-persecution complex. But it was true that Nathan and I looked younger than we were: I with my dark, somber looks and working class clothes and Nathan with his straight, choppy blond hair and oversized shirts. And it was also true, I will readily admit to anyone, that I first fell in love with the way Nathan looked: the symmetrical squareness of his face, the thin, toylike slope of his nose, the light green center of his eyes—the outer ovals of which were edged the color of shamrocks. Though we were the same height, he did not share my big-boned stockiness; he possessed, instead, the lanky physique of a runner— a combination we found suited us well together in bed.

Bonded by the loneliness of the holiday, we had left Denise's Christmas party together and walked up Bleecker Street to Broadway and over to Nathan's apartment in the East Village; that odd, muggy December afternoon in 1979 had blown into a clear and chilly winter night, but the moonlight now drifting in through the window beside his bed still betrayed the enchantment of a summer night.

Stretched out on his bed before me, Nathan became a willing supplicant to my desires, and it was at moments like that that I have often wished my hands were not so calloused and chapped from physical work. As my touch tested the firmness of his flesh, the taut pull of his skin, I realized I wanted more of him and I pressed my lips against the base of his neck, then ran my tongue slowly down the knots of his spine. I gripped my hands at the contours of his waist, lifted his ass up slightly and pressed my face into the spread of his cheeks. I could feel him squirm as my tongue explored him, the molecular fabric of his skin heating as the stubble of my day-old beard teasingly rubbed against him. He stayed that way, sighing in large gasps of air, till he broke free and reached for a bottle of lubricant he withdrew from the drawer of a nightstand beside the bed. He pushed me back down on the bed but I bent forward slightly to watch as he lathered my cock with the oil and then straddled my body, his knees digging into the mattress at my waist. He opened himself first with one finger, then another, then lifted himself, now teasingly over my cock, till my body begged for the feel of him, then slowly, assuredly, guided my cock inside himself. He leaned back into his arms and I felt the desire of him flush into my lungs, my body tense and then relax into a light sweat. The smell of the eucalyptus from the oil he had used floated in the air above me and Nathan appeared to enter some sort of state of unconsciousness, till he began gently swaying as if moved by an inner rhythm and I settled back against the bed and rocked my cock into him, as if my body, too, had locked into the same song.

We stayed that way for what seemed like forever, for I surely did not want him to stop—I felt powerful, desirable, and possessed, but my mind battled with that confusing state of ecstasy my body was enjoying, searching for an explanation for all this heightened pleasure. It was thoughts of my father that loitered about me, or, rather, the religious condemnation my father had so explicitly articulated with the grimaced spit of, "It's a sin." How could something this pleasurable be so condemned? Was sex a sin simply because it was a basic, instinctual, animalistic act? Or was it that sex between two men—raised for centuries to be such restrained and impassive creatures—was what was so taboo? Or was it that Nathan and I had so clearly communicated our desire for one another in our own subliminal, pious manner? Was that what scared so many people, the forming, as it were, of our own denomination, conceived from our own emotions as homosexuals, our own gay ethics and codes for living?

"Relax," Nathan said, as if he were indeed as much inside my head as I was inside him. He shifted his weight and we rolled over so that I was on top of him and I settled his legs against my shoulders and pressed deeper into him. This was the reason why I had fought so hard against myself, the reason why I became gay, the desire of being with another man. Nathan looked only at my eyes but I was caught up in all of him, the grainy feel of the hair on his legs, the unwrinkled freshness of his complexion, the lean, athletic muscles at his shoulders. I grasped his cock, thick and stubby, and stroked it slowly with a determined grip, feeling the hard, fleshy vein which circled down to the head. When I caught Nathan's gaze once again I felt that I was no longer pushing into him but he, now, was willingly pulling me deeper and deeper into himself. I shivered and felt myself come but I was still hard when I withdrew from him, still hard when he reached up and brought my cock together against his, rubbing the palms of his hands against them as though starting a fire. He came the moment I took his cock in my hand again, squirming as I moved my fist up and down, the warm, pearly-white liquid spilling over my fingers. I rubbed my finger across the slit of his cock, still slippery with come, letting my touch burn into his body till he couldn't stand it any more, and he took my hand and pulled it away.

Nathan quickly fell asleep, a blissful, childlike sleep, and I lay there for a while, my body wrapped around his, feeling him breathing and the blood pulsing beneath his skin, a pillow tucked underneath my head so that I could see beyond him, out through the window beside the bed onto a courtyard surrounded by the dark, blocky shapes of the tenement buildings. This view wasn't much—rooftops and sooty bricks, a string of Christmas lights twisted around a fire escape one floor above—and the window of Nathan's apartment was enclosed by black iron window gates. But what caught my attention was a small, clear ornament hanging from a string that was tied to one of the beams of the grating, a tiny, teardrop crystal, really, drawing in the deep purplish colors of the night like that of a black prism.

Aside from the bedroom, Nathan's apartment had only one other tiny room, a combination kitchen and living room that he kept in a fanatically precise order: a spice rack organized in the descending height of bottles, an alphabetized record collection, sweaters neatly folded on the top shelf of his closet. But his apartment had the feel, too, of an adult being let lose in a kindergarten playroom; his furniture was painted in bold, primary colors, bright scatter rugs covered the varnished wood floor, even the steam radiator was painted red and white to resemble a candy cane. Near the window the bright blue painted top of a drafting table was tilted upward, a pad of drawings held down by a bold yellow plastic ruler. Stacks of what appeared to be magazines on a bookshelf turned out instead to be comic books; the walls were covered with framed animation cells from cartoons: Betty Boop, the Road Runner, the fairy godmother from *Cinderella*. As I got out of bed and began to search for where I had left my jeans, the thought occurred to me that Nathan and I would never hit it off; I was, of course, his squallish evil twin, my apartment was littered with tools and nails and scraps of wood, everything draped in a layer of sawdust. But this thought was also the initiation of a reflex, really, a sort of self-preserving defense mechanism—for as much as I wanted to be regarded as someone special, my greater concern was that if I didn't stay the night at someone's apartment then I wouldn't attach myself emotionally, and not attaching myself emotionally, I wouldn't have to face the fear of being rejected in the morning, or, even worse, just being considered as last night's trick. Unlike Jeff and Vince, I hated the morning awkwardness, hated putting myself in the vulnerable position of: "Will he see me again or will he just kick me out?"

"You're not going?" Nathan asked, his voice a syrupy, sleepy whisper. He had rolled to the edge of the bed and was watching me dress.

"It's late," I said. "I thought I could just let myself out."

"Don't go. It's Christmas."

I gave a nervous laugh. "Yesterday was Christmas. It's already the day after

Christmas."

"You don't have to work, do you?"

"No," I answered. It was true—I was not scheduled to start another assignment for Alex until January.

"Then we can stay in bed as long as you want."

The thought of a night beside Nathan, waking up against him, a day of just enjoying him, pulled me back toward the bed. I undressed and slipped into the bed again, first feeling the crispness of the sheets, then the warmth of Nathan's skin as he drew himself nearer. Nathan had revealed a joyous sexuality the moment he had discarded his clothes that night, as if he were delicious candy that had been wrapped in bright, shiny paper, and his body slipped easily against my own.

"Christmas can be tough if you're not a kid," he said, and as he pulled himself through a beam of moonlight I caught a glimpse of his face moving through a thought. "Or if you don't have a kid," he added, and then leaned toward me and we met in a slow, thoughtful kiss. There was, too, simply with his kiss, a comfort with him that hadn't been present with any man I had known before him, and I was now too delightfully awake to fall back to sleep easily, though I could feel the darkness and Nathan once again settling around me.

"I bet our kids would be beautiful," he said.

"What?"

"If we were able to have kids. They'd be beautiful. With your bone structure."

"My *bone structure?*" I laughed with a heave of my chest and I felt Nathan move, could see him smile from the corner of my eye.

"Sure," he said and ran a finger along my cheekbone to the slope of my jaw.

"They'd probably be nervous and hyper and a psychotic mess."

"Ohhh?" he asked, drawing the word out as if it were the end of a song. "Would that be from your side or mine?"

Feeling both cautious and coy I kissed his brow, the part of him that was nearest to my lips, and whispered, "We'll let the jury decide."

He turned away from me, toward the window, but I followed him and drew my arms around his waist. "Don't you want to have children?" he asked.

"I never gave it much thought. I have a hard enough time supporting myself."

"I bet you would be a good father. You seem like the good father type."

"Good father type?"

"Sure. You probably should have been a doctor or a dentist. You have that kind of demeanor."

Now I laughed again and rolled away from him and, here, he turned and followed my body and encircled me.

"Do you like children?" he asked. I felt his voice reverberating to my bones.

"I suppose. I haven't exactly been exposed to them a lot since I moved to

Manhattan."

"They're all around. You just don't notice them. I wasn't a very successful child—I suppose that's why I'm still stuck in the fantasy of it. My father was killed in Korea. My mother died in a car accident before I was even three years old."

As I imagined the early years of his life, I felt the walls of Nathan's bedroom expanding, blowing apart, really, and leaving only the two of us wrapped together against the infinity of space.

"She just, like, couldn't take the grief of it," Nathan said. "After he died. I can barely remember anything about them. My mother had a wave in her hair, here," he said and ran his fingers close to his left eye. "Very Veronica Lake. She had no money. Her family had no money. I'm sure this sounds sexist, but she was probably some white trash whore who got pregnant by accident and the guy had to marry her. At least that's what I hope, you know, so I don't have to miss her. My foster parents are really wonderful though, but I also feel, well, distant from them. I always knew they were never my real parents."

It has always amazed me how effortlessly Nathan's life became exposed to me, layers and layers of himself unfolding as easily as the way the wind would scatter his blond helmet of hair to reveal the subtly darker colors closest to his scalp. As a boy Nathan had been drawn to the imagination of comic books, at first intrigued by the bright colors and bold actions, he could later detail specific adventures of an assortment of characters from Little Lulu and Archie to the Green Hornet and Spiderman. But the comics also afforded Nathan a view of places like Gotham City and Metropolis, glimpses of what he dreamed he might one day discover for himself. This infatuation produced in him a yearning to travel and discover the world, but thus far, this ambition had led him only away from his foster parents' home in upstate Connecticut to the East Village of Manhattan. Nathan was also full of the big dreams of a young man—always wanting to do something like rock climbing in the Alps, windsurfing in the Caribbean, or traveling on a barge through the Amazon. But he was not without a practical side. His ambition was to be an artist, an illustrator of children's books, but he knew he really did not have that sort of creative talent, that he was more imaginative in his design than in the execution of the art, and when I met him he was working as a draftsman for an architect on Park Avenue, learning at night school how to draw architectural renderings, a precision he felt he was more suited for and which, in its own odd pseudo-psychological way, made sense to me when he explained it—an orphan meticulously imagining the fantasy of the future.

"I always used to think that being gay eliminated the possibility of having children," Nathan said later that night, "but there are ways to have kids. I go once a month and donate sperm."

"You donate sperm?" I said, unable to disguise the shock in my voice. Nathan always reveled in my surprise; years later we would both use it as a test for our love and concern for one another.

"Sure. There's a place in the Empire State Building. I get a big kick out of it. You go in a room and jerk off into a cup—give it to a nurse, and then, boom, they pay you. It's fun walking down the street and thinking, well, you know, that baby could be mine."

"How long have you been doing this?"

"A couple of years. Since I moved to the city. But I don't ever hear if it was a success, you know—that someone got pregnant. The patients have no contact with the donors. But I'd love to have a kid of my own some day. I love kids—playing with kids—but I'm not sure I would be a good father."

"It would be hard raising a kid with gay parents," I said, wondering how in the world our imaginary lives had already become so complex.

"The child would not have a problem," Nathan added. "Kids can be remarkably accepting. It's the parents who need help. I don't know if I could take the responsibility of someone who was that dependent on me. I'm really too much of a flake to be good father material."

"A flake?" I laughed. "So all these women lining up for the gorgeous blond stud sperm are really in for a surprise."

"Funny, isn't it? Sort of like nature's little joke." With that he kissed me and drew me back into the moonlight.

That was the Christmas that it occurred to me that my life could encompass something I never felt possible of gay life, becoming a parent and creating a family—believing that a way of living, really, could exist beyond the diversions of the bars and parties and discos and baths. Desire came to me that night imagining Nathan and myself as two boys who could grow old together, a pair of lovers visited on a future Christmas by their grandchildren. There we were in a room with a huge sofa and a fireplace and tree covered with tinsel, bright-colored wrapping paper covering the thick carpet, kids squealing at the sight of games and toys and bikes. Simple but luxurious thoughts, actually, that kept lifting me out of sleep throughout the night.

I was already awake when Nathan opened his eyes the next morning; I held him from behind, as I had held him throughout the night, matching my breathing against his. Instead of studying the view I was watching the morning light break through the crystal in his window into a small rainbow that fell along the sheets of the bed and slipped over his body and ended at my arm. Nathan lifted himself out of my embrace and moved to the edge of the bed, and, once he had shaken the sleep from himself, looked back at me and noticed the rainbow, now mostly violet and blue, painting a part of my chest. He reached with his fingers and touched the crystal, sending the spectrum of colors spinning madly around the bedroom.

"From the planet Krypton," he said.

"*Krypton?*"

"When Clark Kent was sent to earth, shards of his exploding planet became embedded in his space ship."

I lifted my eyes to meet his, then watched the pendulum of colors spin back and forth, back and forth. "This must seem so silly to you," he said.

"Silly?"

"All this stuff," he said and waved his hand at his brightly decorated room.

I had no answer for him; instead I gave him only a smile. I was, at that point, already stupidly infatuated with him; I wasn't interested in being judgmental. What he only wanted, after all, really, was just to be noticed and thought interesting, as most of us do. I pulled my foot from beneath the sheet and poked my big toe against the ribs of his chest to make him laugh. He grinned and jumped at me, tickling me with his fingers, our bodies falling into a wrestling embrace.

We never made it far from the bed that day, our bodies were drawn to each other again and again without permission. Our temptation for one another was something akin to what an addict must feel reaching for a hit of cocaine. I wanted nothing more than to revel in the solitude of Nathan; his apartment was one of those overheated New York apartments, the kind where it is much easier to wear nothing at all than to pretend to be modest by draping yourself in a robe or a baggy T-shirt. We laughed and giggled and embraced one another in every possible permutation in every possible space of that apartment. In fact, we were, well, so boyishly open with one another: confiding our deepest fantasies, holding hands in front of the TV set, staying in bed until noon, leaving only to bring back plates and boxes of snack food.

Vince once remarked that Nathan reminded him of a wild pony. It was true Nathan had a wild streak; he had a roving eye and an unsatisfied appetite for sex. His biggest flaw, however, were his beautifully white teeth: the top row was slightly overlapped and gave him a bit of an overbite which he compensated for at times by jutting out his lower jaw. His bottom teeth were a crooked mess and he often smiled without showing any teeth at all. This gave the impression, to those who did not know him well, that Nathan was something of a snob instead of a young man with a disdain for patience. I found all these imperfections quite endearing, especially as I discovered them again and again, and I began to consider Nathan as, well, sort of like a good looking man impersonating a very attractive one.

When I brought Nathan with me to the gym one day during that holiday week before New Year's, I could tell Vince was jealous of this new-found romance of mine. In his not-too-subtle way, Vince heaved and spat through his workout, tossing weights around with a cavemanlike aggression. Nathan was bored and uneasy and he kept whispering to me, "What a jerk," every time Vince slammed the dumbbells back on the rack with a vicious clank. At one point Vince pulled me aside and asked, "So what does he mean to you?"

"Everything," I answered, for I was, at that point, a young man glowing with joy, not interested in being disturbed by the uncertainty of others.

"Just be careful you don't get hurt," Vince said. "He looks like a self-absorbed, selfish bastard who would drop you in a minute for someone he thought was better than you."

"Oh?" I answered, a little put out. "Your kind of guy, huh?"

"Yeah," Vince grunted, his eyes brightening with recognition. "A real asshole."

Nathan's friend Hank, the toupee-wearing mime, made a similar impression on me the night I accompanied Nathan to a dance class that he took once a week at a grimy loft overlooking Times Square. I never imagined Nathan to be such a wonderful dancer, but watching him warm up it became apparent to me how he had achieved the lean, threadlike muscles of his body. Hank taught the class, beginner's jazz, and I, of course, had had no sort of experience with brisés and arabesques and pirouettes. Hank was not much taller than I was, and our builds were similar, but my body had not been trained to move in the ways that his did. Normally Hank would have dismissed me entirely when he discovered my joints were not as flexible as his, but he was pissed off at me because I was a friend of Jeff's, who had dumped him to start dating another guy—a chorus boy in *Grease* who looked a lot like Hank except that his hair was real. Toward the end of the class, Hank pulled me in front of everyone and asked me to demonstrate the combination of steps he had just taught. I giddily stumbled through them and when I had finished Hank said, in a very sarcastic tone, "Ladies and gentlemen, please take note. This is what we mean when we say a person has two left feet."

It was Denise, however, who unleashed and captured Nathan's charm and sincerity. Nathan was always polite and gracious, especially with women, and he adored Denise, flattering her endlessly about her talent as an artist. In many ways, I always believed that Nathan saw in Denise the serious artist that he, himself, wanted to become. It was Nathan who gladly led Denise out to children's bookstores, gossiped with her about the art of animation, rummaged with her through bins of old comic books in the East Village. And it was Nathan who first suggested to Denise the idea of drawing an urban comic strip, a sort of fairy fairy tale—gay Manhattan seen from the perspective of a naive sort of *Alice in Wonderland* heroine. We spent hours laughing together imagining the possibilities—Alice asking for tea at a tea dance, Cinderella discovering a drag queen wearing her same gown, Dorothy Gale and Toto stumbling into the S&M shadows of the Mine Shaft and discovering the Munchkins, muttering the oft-quoted line, "I don't think we're in Kansas anymore."

As winter settled in, Nathan and I fell into a pattern of seeing each other on Wednesdays and Saturdays. That suited me just fine, because we spoke every day on the phone, and all day long, from my first bright moment of morning consciousness to the last black second at night, I was aware of Nathan's power over me. I even began to fantasize about our living together and raising a child. Walking from my apartment across town to Alex's loft, I began to notice children, Nathan's children—babies in strollers, backpacks, and papooses—one child had his green eyes, another his nose or chin or his tight-lipped smile. Children were suddenly everywhere in the city to me—from the advertisements on the sides of buses to the thrift shop clothing bins near Canal Street. It was a ridiculous fantasy, of course; I knew Nathan and I would never have a child together, something even Nathan might have considered silly, but I was caught up in the implausible but romantic notion of it all: Nathan and I changing a diaper together, zipping up a tiny figure into a down-filled jump suit, soothing tears with the promise of ice cream.

Still, with all this dreaming, I was unprepared for what I saw in Nathan's eyes every time we would get together—a passion and intensity I felt so truthful it was impossible to doubt. Days would pass where we wouldn't see each other, but meeting up again, we would tumble into bed, our clothes scattered across the floor like forgotten toys, our fingerprints stained into each other's skin like tattoos. Sometimes I believe what connected us so urgently to one another was our shared, though unspoken, dread of loneliness. As Valentine's Day approached I began to imagine Nathan and myself as one of those immortal couples, forever in love: Hepburn and Tracy, Stein and Toklas, Pears and Britten. By the time the day arrived I had planned to bestow on Nathan an elaborate spectacle of my affection, everything from a gourmet candlelight dinner, purchased take-out, of course, but complimented with champagne, cards, flowers, and chocolates.

That was also the same day I received a letter from Elaine Crowder, my father's neighbor in Galena, explaining in it that she had tracked me down through my former college. Her letter said that my father had remarried a younger woman who had a three-month old daughter. They had met when the woman, Shelly—a girl, really—had been refused admission to return to Galena High School after giving birth to her baby out of wedlock. It had been my father's mission not only to convert the sinner to the ways of the Lord, but also to shame the school board into forgiving Shelly and allowing her to return to school. In the process, my father fell in love with the girl and that in itself had caused another scandal within the community. The letter and the news took me by surprise—my father had long ago stopped all communication with me when he realized redemption was not to be a part of my plan—but it's impact, that my father had now replaced my mother and myself with another family—was deadened by the importance I had given Nathan in my life. Nathan had made me feel important and invincible, and, most of all, loved, and I would have loved to have rubbed the existence of Nathan in my father's face, as proof that what two men can feel for one another is nothing unnatural, and I slipped the letter into the bag I was bringing to Nathan's apartment to read to him later, as further testament of my admiration for him. When, after the dinner and champagne and chocolates, Nathan and I lay in bed together, I unfolded the letter and propped it up on my stomach to read out loud. It was then that I noticed the tiny black flecks within the hair near my navel. Thinking they were chocolate crumbs or soot, I brushed at them with my hand but they did not disappear. Seconds later, when I realized what they were, I jumped out of bed.

"*Jesus Christ!*" I yelled. "*How did I get fucking crabs?*"

"Oh *shit!*" Nathan said in a tone of voice that revealed every possible indiscretion.

"Are you seeing someone else?" I asked somewhat hysterically.

"No. Not really. Not one person."

"*What?*" I began to get dressed as quickly as possible, rushing around the room, grabbing my socks and jeans and shirt.

"I went to the baths the other night," he said. "That's all." He watched me for a moment and then said sternly, "Where are you going?" as though trying to assert some control over the hysterics.

"Somewhere else, obviously," I answered.

"You can't just leave like this," he said and tugged at my shirt. "We need to talk about this."

I yanked the shirt out of his hands. "We should have talked about this a long time ago."

"You never said anything about not seeing other people. We never talked about dating each other exclusively."

"I didn't think I had to," I answered, flabbergasted. "I thought you knew how I felt."

"But I can't give you that—that total devotion," he said, his eyes looking away from mine, down to the floor. "You'll break my heart. Don't you understand? I can't fall in love with you."

His words stunned me. "So then this would have ended anyway sooner or later?" I asked, grabbing my coat and opening the front door.

"Don't do this now, Robbie."

"Save the sympathy for strangers," I said and ran down the stairs and into the street. It was almost midnight and a misty chill clung to the night. At St. Mark's Place I was surprised to find the street crowded, faces changed almost instantly from white to Asian to latino to black, every other person a pusher chanting in front of my face, "Smoke? Smoke?" The spikey hair, love beads, black leather jackets, and studded clothing all caught me by surprise; in fact, the whole time-warp-psychedelic-feel unnerved me, and I began to jog through the traffic. I ran for blocks, not really certain of my destination, past the tenements, diners, and bodegas that smelled like cat piss, past the brownstones, fruit stands, and shuttered storefronts with illegible graffiti written across the boards by thick-tipped black pens, the sandy particles of the sidewalk at my feet, ridiculously sparkling under the street lights. And then I was astonished to find myself in front of Vince's building pressing his door buzzer over and over till he answered.

"Crabs," I said, out of breath, when Vince opened his door moments later.

"In the bathroom," he yelled and briskly pointed for me to come inside. "If

I catch one of those fucking pests, you're dead."

I stripped and put my clothing into a plastic garbage bag as Vince ordered, then smeared a pungent oily lotion that he gave me over every imaginable body part. Vince shouted through the closed bathroom door, "Don't forget your underarms! And even behind your knees! And don't forget the crack of your ass, too!" I was grateful for Vince's no-nonsense approach to my problem though I was now shivering, waiting the required ten minutes before I could shower the lotion away.

"I told you he was a good for nothing," Vince yelled through the door, even though I had, at that point, explained nothing to him. "You're better off without him."

None of this made me feel any better. I was twenty years old by then and felt I had already been through dozens of lovers, and no one seemed capable of, well, wanting a real relationship. Even though the steady, hot spray of water quelled my body's tension, my mind was still in shock, still disbelieving Nathan's admission.

By the time I came out of the shower, Vince was seated on the floor sorting through the cards he had dumped out of his fishbowl.

"Here," he said, handing me a stack of business cards. "Go find yourself a date."

It was Denise who made the first contact with me on Nathan's behalf, explaining when she phoned me the next day how upset Nathan was—wouldn't I call him, at least try to be friends? By then I had moved into a state of depression I had only imagined divorcees must feel, but I refused to call Nathan and only reluctantly agreed to meet Denise and Jeff later for dinner.

It was Jeff who tried to set my emotions in order when we met at a café in Chelsea: Wasn't I passing the same sort of moral judgment on Nathan that my father had on me? Wasn't I sentencing Nathan, after all, by the righteous terms initiated by heterosexuals? How could I define promiscuity—sex, really—a physical act—with such prudish condemnation? Didn't we—as gay men—so set apart from accepted social structure, have to create and reinvent relationships that would, after all, work for us?

I knew Jeff was right—or, rather, knew that Nathan and I had not even attempted to define the parameters of our relationship—if, indeed, it was a relationship at that point. How could I judge him as dishonest when we had never established a basis for fidelity? And did fidelity, really, exclude the possibility of having sex with other partners? Or wasn't I, as Jeff accused me, attaching too much emotion to the behavior of sex and defining love, like all straight men, as an act of possession? I was aware that I was reacting with the same emotional ideology as a straight man: I was jealous, wildly so—the thought of Nathan sleeping with someone else was driving me crazy. But in my opinion, Denise and Jeff, as sincere as their concern was, were trying to cover a gunshot wound with a Band-Aid.

"Are you jealous or just envious?" Vince asked me a few days later, when he met me for a drink at the Ninth Circle, a bar in the West Village. Vince was cruising the crowd and I was nursing a bottle of warm beer, mashing the clumps of sawdust on the floor with the heel of my boot. Vince said the best therapy for a broken heart was to date and have as much sex as possible till I was either ravishingly in love with someone else or thoroughly disgusted by the whole notion of sex or love. And indeed, if there was anyone to blame beyond myself or Nathan for propelling me on the search for Mr. Right, a quest I found as futile as the search for the Holy Grail, it would have to be Vince. Vince took me back to the bars and the baths and out dancing, pointing out the dark, brooding look one man gave me, the military physique of another, the Greco-Roman slope of someone else's profile, all the while feeding me business card after business card as another possibility, leading me, really, through the labyrinth of gay life in search of a relationship or a boyfriend or even just a date. I could never remember what all those codes and clues meant. Did keys on the left side mean passive or aggressive? Did a yellow handkerchief stuck into the right back pocket mean the wearer was into fist-fucking, water sports, scat, or merely had a sunny and cheery disposition? And what if the wearer was a tourist from the West Coast and I didn't know it? Didn't that confuse matters even more? All I wanted, after all, was pure, unabashed, unadulterated love. Denise, flabbergasted by my search asked, "Why don't you just get yourself a dog?"

But I didn't want a dog. Neither did I want to begin a relationship with myself. I had to find and meet Mr. Right. I scouted the personal ads in the *Village Voice* and the *Native*, roamed up and down Christopher Street, loitered by the bulletin board at the Oscar Wilde Bookstore, convinced, really, that a partner, a true significant other, existed for me somewhere in this city— I simply had to find him. Jeff said I should redefine my expectations to expect disappointment—finding Mr. Right means a lot more than being at the right place at the right time with the right attitude. "Even if you do find him," he said, "What makes you think you're going to be *his* Mr. Right? Isn't that what happened with Nathan? What if that just happens again?"

Vince, who never concealed his indulgence with so many men from me, thought I was too particular. I replied that I only expected the same qualities in a boyfriend that I enjoyed in my friends. Then what was wrong with the Italian banker? he demanded. Or the stockbroker he had introduced me to? Or the blond jogger? (Too short, too much hair, too, well, on the move.) Jeff thought I placed too much emphasis on looks. (This coming, of course, from an extremely handsome man, I answered.) Jeff then turned huffy and said I was being shallow and insincere. Even Denise sided against me one night when we all went together to a cinema in midtown. "Don't you think, Robbie, you're trying too hard? Are you sure you're just not trying to make Nathan jealous?" That, of course, made me go furiously wild.

At some point Vince even registered me for a dating service, run by an over-weight woman on the Upper East Side. And so I began a series of dates that were, for the most part, brief and unfortunate. One date barely spoke English, another was too spaced out on drugs to even try to attempt a conversation, another never showed up. The worst was the young boy who paid for his dinner in quarters, and then had to borrow money from me when he found that he didn't have enough to pay his portion of the bill. But I did have sex with any who were willing, and most of them were. And I developed an appetite for sex that I imagined was even more ravenous than Nathan's, but about as emotionally satisfying to me as, well, as Chinese take-out was physically filling.

What I wanted, however, was something that went beyond the sex. What I wanted was an end to the frustration. What was missing in every man I met was Nathan, though I found a part of him in every one I dated—the way one guy held me in bed, the palm of his hand pressed against the small of my back, the way another man coughed to clear his throat. Another date held his coffee cup with his hand tilted over the rim of the cup just as Nathan had done on the mornings I awoke in his apartment. I even discovered Nathan within myself—the childish glee I felt one night after keeping a brightly colored cock-tail swizzle stick, something he would have done. Nathan had set a standard, both good and bad, that I couldn't ignore. Sometimes I would wonder what he was doing, who he was dating, what he was eating, what he was watching on TV. This, of course, would drive me into a frenzy and I would have to find something to do to distract myself: work out, read, or draft the design of a project for work—a new bookcase or night stand or desk. And then, just when I thought I had erased him completely from of my mind, I'd notice a piece of him again in a child on the street. Nathan was everywhere, everywhere except where I wanted him to be. With me.

I avoided every possible confrontation with Nathan himself, however, refusing to talk to him on the phone when he called or feigning illness when Denise invited me to join Nathan and her for dinner. Nathan had developed his own friendship with Denise; they continued going together to museums and galleries and bookstores without me. Even Jeff had begun liking Nathan; he and Hank had repaired their aborted affair into a casual friendship and I had heard through Vince that they had gone with Nathan to see the Broadway revival of *West Side Story*.

Gossip is endemic even in the best of friendships—and every time I heard that Nathan had done something with Denise or Jeff, I would call them and make arrangements of our own to meet for a movie, a play or, perhaps, just go out for dinner. I had become very protective of my friendship with Jeff and Denise; I was worried that one or both of them would announce, at any moment, that they liked Nathan more than they liked me, found him more interesting, better looking, smarter, or funnier. I, of course, clung to every clue or euphemistic mention of Nathan that could provide me with information on his current state of affairs without asking directly. What I wanted to hear, without a doubt, was that he was miserable without me, but I knew, realistically, that one day I would hear that Nathan was dating someone else or had met someone and fallen in love. I was prepared for that, but it came as a surprise to me one Saturday morning when I went with Vince to a sale at Bloomingdale's and Vince mentioned in passing that Nathan had helped Denise get a freelance job with an artist who ran a greeting card company that specialized in novelty postcards. I knew I should have been happy for Denise but instead I took the news as if I had been deceived, stabbed in the back, betrayed by an ex-lover and a close friend.

Denise soon became aware of my anger, of course; gossip flows in many directions, after all, and when we met for dinner, a few days later, we were both keyed up for a subtle war. Denise immediately began talking about all the ideas she had had for her postcards, speculating on the merchandising possibilities—from matchbooks to T-shirts to coffee mugs to, yes, well, comic books. I talked about all the sex I had had, positively, of course, expressing the awe and admiration for the various body types of men I had recently encountered, even discussing in detail some new fucking positions I had tried. We were both drinking heavily that night, and by the time dinner was through our bitterness was about ready to explode. We politely split the check and I walked Denise to the corner of Sixth Avenue and Bleecker Street, knowing for certain we had reached the end of our friendship, that I would never see her again, never really want to see her again. We said our goodbyes graciously, paradoxically vowing to call one another the next day and, as I was beginning to cross the street, from the corner of my eye—my peripheral vision—I noticed some movement by a building. I turned and looked back and noticed a man, a boy, really, emerge from the shadow of an alley and head toward Denise. It was clear to me that he was after her purse and I turned back and rushed in Denise's direction to warn her.

What happened happened so quickly Denise was not even capable of screaming. The boy noticed me but continued toward Denise. I lunged for Denise's purse, trying to grab it before the boy did. The boy, confused, turned to me and smashed his fist into my face. Denise clutched her purse to her chest. I fell to the ground and the boy rushed away. The boy had been wearing a heavy, gold ring, and though I was still conscious, my face was covered with blood; the ring had cut me just above my eye.

Denise flagged down a cab that dropped us off at the emergency room at St. Vincent's Hospital; she had removed her panties in the cab and used them as a compress to stop the flow of the blood from my cut. Later that night, when a doctor finally saw me, he said my options were either stitching the cut together, which would mean losing a portion of my eyebrow, or allowing the wound to heal normally with a small scar that would bisect the eyebrow and that would eventually, someday, disappear. I opted for the scar and, on the cab ride back to my apartment, I tried to deflect my discomfort and fragility and Denise's anxieties by joking that I could now tell people that Denise and I had gotten into a fight and she had won. Denise was not at all amused by that; she had decided that the boy had wanted more from her than just her purse, and my gentlemanly act of scaring away her robber had also prevented her possible rape. She stayed at my apartment that night, feeling both custodial and vulnerable, cleaning my kitchen over and over, as though she were obligated to repay a favor.

The next few days I suffered through the misery of a black eye. A small pocket of pus had begun to form near the cut, and the skin had taken on a variety of colors, from the deep violet of the impact of the punch to the sickly yellow tint at the edges of the wounded skin. To be honest, I began to relish my malady actually, walking to the bank or the grocery store and willingly encouraging the startled looks and sympathetic nods from as many stalwart and self-absorbed New Yorkers who would cross my path. Suddenly, I felt worthy and worthwhile again. Vince decided it was the butchest I had ever looked, and when I met him at the gym that week, he said, in his most lisping, affected voice, "Mary, you should get yourself to the baths—they'd be all over you in a minute. Those girls just love that rough and tough look."

I privately assigned this to just another sequence of misfortunes Nathan continued to inflict unknowingly upon me. If I hadn't been so curious about him, I wouldn't have pressured Denise into dinner. I know Denise told Nathan about the incident; how could she have not? But now I began to believe in the source of my own anonymous courage, that I had really saved Denise, that I was, perhaps, too good for Nathan. But something also frightened me internally. A young boy—a child—had sent me reeling unexpectedly to the street. I was the victim of an unanticipated assault. As a result I began to consider taking a course in karate or judo or self-defense, but instead I began to push myself harder and harder at the gym. I wanted to get harder and tougher and bigger and stronger, to widen my lats and thicken my delts, shape my pecs and enlarge my biceps, to be unapproachable, really—to make it impossible to be victimized.

I went to the gym every day now, bulking up with weight-gain and vitamin supplements. I spent hours and hours lifting and straining and pulling at weights and dumbbells, strapped into machines or lying on benches, flushing myself with water from fountains and plastic bottles. Some days I would be so sore from exercise I would canter down the street back to my apartment, my legs weak from lifting too many heavy weights. I began to feel aches and sores in every part of my body, from the swollen pads of the arches of my feet to the ligaments and tendons stretching toward my elbows and knees. One day in late May I began to feel a pressure in my groin, a tenderness and a stabbing pang, really, on the right side of my lower abdomen, a sensation that left me once again feeling susceptible and insecure. I rationalized this as being caused by an intense workout and the sudden humidity of the day. But the next morning I felt nauseous and the pain was much worse, so bad, in fact, that I could not even bear the touch of underwear against my skin. By the afternoon a small lump had swelled at my groin.

Vince met me that evening at the emergency room at St. Vincent's. By midnight my pubic hair was shaved and I was prepped for spinal anesthesia. I had a hernia that had to be operated on immediately.

This, too, I blamed on Nathan.

If I were able to look back on my life and draw up a list of idyllic days, one of those days, I know, would be the day I came home from the hospital following my operation. I had felt so ashamed of my predicament that I refused to allow Vince to tell anyone that I was in the hospital, particularly Denise and Jeff, but the morning Vince brought me back home to my apartment, they were both there waiting for me.

The three of them had not made any special preparations for my return home; there were no "Get Well" or "Welcome Home" banners, no crepe paper streamers, no plates of hors d'oeuvres or champagne or strippers jumping out of cakes. What it was was a beautiful early summer day, the sunlight bursting through the courtyard window. We spent the day doing nothing, really—playing Uno or Gin Rummy or Go Fish, watching TV and eating potato chips, picking out our favorite songs on the stereo. My record collection was mostly pop and cast albums since I bought, most often, the music I had often heard at friends' apartments. Vince made us listen to the complete scores of *Porgy and Bess* and *Candide*, then Jeff played the first side of *A Chorus Line*. By the time Denise put on *Camelot*, our conversations centered completely on the theater.

"What Pinter misses is the consequence of betrayals, the revenge or compromises or apologies," Vince explained to Jeff. "The backward structure is a hindrance." Denise had moved to the window where she was dancing in place to "The Lusty Month of May." Jeff was seated at the foot of my bed laying the deck of cards into seven rows to show Vince a trick he had learned as a boy.

"Betrayal is not an act but a mental process," Vince said, tapping Jeff on the wrist to make certain he had his attention. "There is a thought attached there that the action shouldn't be done. Betrayal is a thought. The action is infidelity or adultery."

"If that's the case then fidelity doesn't exist as a thought," Jeff answered, surprising me that he had so completely tapped into Vince's logic. "No one is mindfully, consistently, faithful. There's always temptation."

Denise had moved into a beam of light, and I watched her profile shift and change, that Pre-Raphaelite outline of hers, and realized it was a face I loved, the hollows and glints of her nose and lips, the sunlight disappearing into the ringlets of her hair.

"Pick one," Jeff said. "But don't tell me which one it is, just tell me what row it's in."

"This one," Vince said. Jeff scooped up the cards, then laid them down in seven rows again. I was compelled now to look more closely at Jeff, to regard him as if he were a painting or a sculpture in a museum, to try to see the whole and its parts at the same time, to attempt to regard him objectively as though he was a work of art, the shape of his forehead, the bone beneath his eyes, the slope of his jaw, but I realized, here, too, that I could not detach my feelings; this was a face I had also come to love.

"Which row now?" he asked Vince.

"This one," Vince said and pointed to the middle row. "Temptation is merely one of the levels of betrayal. Temptation is a thought."

Jeff scooped up the cards and again laid them down in seven rows. "But some sort of allegiance must occur before the act occurs. Which one now?" Jeff asked.

"This one," Vince pointed. It was here that I noticed Vince's hands, the thick stubby fingers, the flat squarely trimmed fingernails, the dark hair that sprouted at the lower joints and curled around the wrists. These were hands, I thought, that even detached I would know anywhere; hands that had offered me a wealth of favors and comforts. Vince looked up at me, aware, instinctively, that I was too concentrated in thought. "Oh, dreary, dreary *Camelot*. Where everyone is so unhappy," he said. "Denise, can't we put on something more up? Something like *West Side Story*?"

"He dies in *West Side Story*," she answered succinctly. "There's no strength there. Love prevails in *Camelot*."

Jeff shuffled the cards again and flipped one over. "That's your card, isn't it."

"Amazing," Vince said, smiling and shaking his head in disbelief. "Then put Sondheim on. We all like him."

I was just about to say that I found his music too fast, too loud, too, well, pretentious, when the thought occurred to me that perhaps my life was destined to be just one that was full of good friends—faces and figures and personalities and arms and hands to which I must attach the depth one ordinarily does to lovers. Perhaps I was to be a man whose life was to be elusive of long-term lovers; were my relationships, then, to be defined through friendships? And was that so horrible a life? Wasn't their presence, like now, at least medicinal? Wasn't I happier now in this moment than all the days I had spent moaning over the absence of Nathan?

By the end of the day I was even standing up and helping with cleaning, putting things back in order. As Denise was leaving I turned and gave her a smile and mentioned that when she spoke to Nathan again, would she mind asking him to give me a call; I was ready to talk to him.

"Nathan?" she said, in a surprised voice. "I thought you knew he moved." Here, she threw a startled glance across the room to Vince.

"What?" I snapped at her, anxiety rushing to my face. My fear of all fears; Nathan had met someone else and was in love and they were already living together. How had this happened? Why had I let this happen? I looked at Denise, tried to meet her eyes, but she pitched them to the ground. I turned and looked at both Vince and Jeff, but they, too, looked away from me, remaining silent, sheepish, and uneasy.

"What's going on?" I asked.

"Nathan moved to Europe," Jeff said.

"*Europe?*" At once I felt dizzy, angry, and cheated.

"Two weeks ago," Vince said. "It wasn't the right time to tell you."

"I don't understand." I sat at the table to steady myself.

"He answered an ad in the *Times*," Denise said. "It's all a little unclear to me. It happened so quickly. Some sort of Greek prince was looking for an assistant."

"A Greek prince?"

"He's some sort of builder or architect," Vince said.

"An architect?"

"You know Nathan always wanted to travel," Denise tried to explain in a deliberate, matter-of-fact tone, as if she knew him better than I did. "And this guy was willing to bring him into the business on the ground level to train him to take over some day."

"They're not sleeping together," Denise added, before I could even ask.

"But he doesn't know anything about business. He doesn't care about business. That's not Nathan. Nathan can't even balance his check book," I said.

"I think he just wanted a change of scenery," Jeff answered.

"He wants to move through life on a grander scale," Vince said, waving his hand in the air, as much to dismiss the subject of Nathan as to indicate his own bewilderment over the matter.

"Is this permanent? Did he give up his apartment?"

"He put all his stuff in storage," Denise said. "Near his parents' house."

"Did he leave an address?"

"Yes," Denise answered. "I'll call you with it when I get home."

"Don't bother," I said. "I don't want it." That, I had decided, was finally the end of Nathan, and all at once I felt both powerful and powerless.

I have often felt as if I stood slightly outside the world, watching from the sidelines of life, detached, remote, and reserved. I have also felt that way about being gay, my connection to gay life rarely extended beyond the desire to have sex with another man. Most gay men would find my statement foolish, what else is there besides sex that connects us? But the gay world is broken down into smaller, more precise subcultures, lives unified by such token signatures as leather jackets, Broadway playbills, pierced nipples and rare opera recordings. All I know is I have always been uncertain of my place in gay life; I liked or wanted to try all of those things, still, none of those things had the ability to capture my passion. At times that made me feel as if I were not a very good gay man; by that I mean it never felt natural for me to gossip and camp it up as my peers did on something like the art of musical comedy, never felt interested, really, in matching my humor against the wit of my friends on subjects such as closeted Hollywood homosexuals, antique memorabilia or what's faux pas to serve at brunch, never felt capable, either, with most of the men I met and bedded, of moving beyond the connection granted simply through the sexual act associated with this identity. But I've never stopped believing in what I wanted from gay life; to be in love with a worthy man—a man who could help me discover my joy and humor and lifestyle, a man with whom I could, essentially, share my life—and to really, in all actuality, find a normality in such a relationship.

I used to believe my estrangement from other gay men was because of my youth, and, optimistically, what lay ahead for me was akin to a boulevard of stores: I merely needed to discover where I liked to shop. Instead, I found myself sampling merchandise, never really buying anything; my gay relationships handled the way a car is leased for the weekend, simply signed for, used, and then returned, or, perhaps, more in keeping with the sexual slang of the day, I was merely another ship passing by in the night. My first lover, Will, opened a desire within me to fall in love, settle down, create a comfortable, homey life, but that, unfortunately, was not what he wanted of me. Relationships are, of course, two way streets—but Will did instill in me the recognition that the possibilities and discoveries of life are wide and multi-colored. It was Will who pushed me out into the world, suggesting that what I needed was to continue growing and learning—not just academically—and not to look back at the past in a nostalgic way, but to look forward to life as an adventure, to face each challenge optimistically. It was Will who suggested that since I was having so much trouble in deciding who I was in college that perhaps I should just leave it behind, unfinished, and move to New York or San Francisco to be better able to find myself, cities where uncloseted lifestyles were permissible, places where crashing up against reality would also continue my education.

When I moved to New York City I hoped I would find a larger, more comfortable niche for myself within the urban gay landscape; instead, I found only a handful of close friends. In many ways I am happier for that; one thing I learned early on was that I am much more at ease with one friend than with many. Still, I hoped to find something to pull me further in, not only into the gay world, but also deeper, more passionately, inside myself. Dating Nathan, if only for those brief six weeks, had reawakened, or, rather, disturbed into consciousness, that longing I had felt in the early days of falling in love with Will, that desire to build a relationship on certain grounded principles: trust, commitment, and, well, yes, love. The absence of those things, not only from Nathan, but also from the gay life that I was bashing and bumping around in, made me once again feel alienated. I could be easily sucked into the glamour and pleasures of gay life by the handsome and varied assortment of faces and cocks that the city offered up to me, and in many instances, I could achieve a certain plateau of satisfaction and pleasure and, yes, humor, in and with all those men. But I also looked on all that activity as a means of hopefully reaching another level of contentment, a stepping stone as it were, to a sort of relationship with another gay man, akin, really, to a heterosexual marriage—two men bonded by a passion and fidelity and trust for one another.

My mission also felt edged at times by desperation. I was approaching, then, the ripe old age of twenty-one, and though now, so preciously aware of how young I was then, I was also so consciously aware of time running out on me. I had always felt my life should have reached an order with adulthood. As a boy I remember lying on my bed or on the lawn or on the slick hot cement of the driveway and daydreaming about the fact that by the time I was on my own I would have an enormous house with too many rooms and lots of expensive furniture and so many cars I would have to think about which one I would want to drive that day, like a millionaire in the movies who stands before a closet and tells a butler what suit he should withdraw. I imagined, then, that life would be, well, worth living, and could be done so, in a thoughtless manner. But at twenty, I had not yet reached any sort of success, financially, emotionally, or even spiritually, and I felt like a boy distracted in a toy store. I was, to be honest, caught up in the great amusement park of gay Manhattan— wandering through the adventures of the Rambles of Central Park, the piers of the Hudson, or the movie houses of Times Square without too much fear; sampling the alternatives of showtunes at Marie's Crisis and the disco beat of Studio 54, investigating the heavy action at the Mine Shaft or simply retreating to an evening alone with Jack Wrangler pornography. It wasn't always necessary for me to feel connected, really; to be single and available for tricks in the park or a toilet or at his place or yours was all part of the escapade of being young in a big city. It wasn't even necessary to contemplate a connection with other gay men; what bound us, simply, was the great island of Manhattan, living in the fast lane at the cusp of the new decade.

But in the days following my release from the hospital after my hernia operation, my depression grew worse; the Demerol the doctor had prescribed for my pain kept making my mind reflective but my body too woozy to knock it away with any sort of physical activity, the best kind of therapy I knew how to pursue at that point in my life. I couldn't work out at the gym, couldn't refinish the set of chairs I was working on, couldn't even, really, clean the bathroom or sit in the laundromat on Seventh Avenue. Vince knew that I was sinking, knew instinctively without me even mentioning it to him, and it was he who decided an outing was in order for us, that perhaps we should get out of the city for a few days. I, of course, hesitated about taking such a trip. But Vince was insistent: the summer season on Fire Island had just begun. I wanted, though, to avoid being caught up in the great social and sexual swirl of the Pines, particularly to steer clear of having to feel the need to participate in this hedonistic revelry, or, at least, have to repair the damages from it. But Vince had wrangled an invitation from Michael, one of the guys from the Flamingo he had met and had a short and passionate affair with and who had a half-share in a house on the bay side of the Pines, a quieter retreat, I was assured, than those in the heart of the beach. What I didn't know, or, rather, what I had to relearn that summer, was that Fire Island was still Fire Island no matter where you landed or what house you stayed in.

Fire Island, particularly the Pines, was not exactly the most restful and relaxing place Vince could chose for me. One of the beachfront resort communities along the narrow sandbar off the coast of Long Island, the Pines is a place you either love to worship or love to loathe. Alex once described it as one of the most breathtaking places on earth, a reflection not only on its natural scenery of dunes, anchored against the wind and the Atlantic Ocean by the roots of pine trees and long grass, but also on the scantily clad gay men imported from the mainland by ferry. Beauty, therefore, is the essence of the Pines, the swimsuit the great social equalizer. Many gay men find the superficial atmosphere of the Pines frustrating or intimidating, pretentious and phony—the magnified glory of the male physique, the insistent ritual: tea dance, nap, dinner, drugs near midnight, dancing till dawn, crash, breakfast, beach—and then starting it all over again. Only the year before, when I had come out to repair the planking of a deck for a house on Ocean Avenue, Gus, a summer resident of the Island for over twenty years and the house's owner, had waved his hand out to the sea and decried the absurdity of it all. "A swimming pool—only breaths away from the ocean? How can one be more ostentatious? All this attitude could easily be washed right back into the sea." He explained this to me only moments before downing his afternoon cocktail; then he disappeared inside to pick out an outfit to wear to tea dance.

That summer, though, the summer of my hernia operation, the summer of 1980, life in the Pines had no reason to change. Pairs of men still waited to see who stepped off the ferry, whispering asides about the arrivals, kisses of greetings exchanged as freely as heated looks. The clones were well-muscled that year, theme parties were grand, porno stars could be spotted holding hands with celebrities; life in the Pines was anything but simple. Michael's house, though, was nestled into a bank of woods like a mountainside cabin, isolated, it seemed, from the carnival promenade of the Pines. I found great solace just from the moldy mildew smell of the walls, but this did not please Vince at all, and from the moment of our arrival Vince kept pulling me away from the interior of the house, first outside to the deck, then to the beach, then to the boardwalk and the activity of the marina. Conscious of my limp, cognizant of the pain from my operation every time I took a step, everything seemed unsteady beneath my feet that weekend: the planks of the walkway, the floor of the house, the decking of the harbor. I was relieved when Vince and Michael plopped me on a beach blanket the next morning, shoved an umbrella in the sand and then disappeared into the Meat Rack, that cruisy area of scrubby brushes that separates the Pines from its sister village, Cherry Grove.

Why they disappeared I could not figure out; everyone, it seemed to me, was out at the beach that day, parading between me and the quiescent, shimmering pond of the Atlantic. Sitting on the beach alone too long can become narcotic—the intensity of the sun, the brightness of the sand, the glimmer of the water, the blue mindlessness of the sky, empty except for a boxy kite or a banner dragged behind a seaplane—can all contribute to a lazy, blisslike lethargy. Filled with insecurities about myself—everything from the fact that my hair had not been trimmed in weeks to that uncomfortably rough feeling of my pubic hair growing back and scratching against the fabric of my swimsuit—I thought, then, the best thing I could do would be to just obsess on things of the moment that I could enjoy, so I sat for a long time and counted the number of boys I spotted wearing thongs, the faddish swimwear popular that year. Vince had left me with an irregular stack of reading, *The Journal of Human Sexuality, The World According to Garp, GQ* and *Mandate* magazines, and a new paperback by Felice Picano, but I wasn't in the mood for reading, or, rather, I wasn't inclined toward concentration. For an instant, I thought about trying to go see Gus or walking to one of the other houses I had worked on last year in the Grove, but Wes, another friend I knew from the gym, came over and we talked about various vapid things, one man's biceps, the music played last night at the Pavilion, the ridiculous price of drinks, till he tired me and he left and I took a nap beneath the umbrella.

Awakened by a gust of wind that suddenly blew the umbrella over, I groggily stood up and felt again in that instance the weakness of my legs against the instability of the sand.

"Need some help, mate?" a voice called out.

The accent caught me off guard, but before I could answer a lanky redhead with an indecently narrow waist was helping me shove the umbrella back in the sand.

"Name's Pat," he said.

I nodded and brushed my palms together to rid myself of the sand, recognizing his accent as Australian. "Robbie," I answered in that silly, precise intonation Americans always affect in the presence of foreigners.

"Spring this beat last summer, did ya?" he asked, following me back to the blanket without even as much as an invitation.

"I worked at a few houses here," I said. "Repairs and stuff."

"Thought I spotted you before," he said. "Did Gus's house, did ya?"

I nodded, quietly inspecting him. He had the lean hungry body of a drifter but the face and personality of a golden retriever, a combination I found, at that moment, rather too delicious to snub, even in my weakened condition.

"I should really go see him sometime this weekend," I said.

"Not out this week. He's in the city," Pat said. "Bad cold. Lousy to be sick on such a beaut of a day." He looked first at the sky, squinting, then back at me. "Want to take a break?" he asked. "My house is just over that dune." This one's a fast mover, I had thought, not even any small talk about the books and magazines I wasn't reading. I smiled and pitched my eyes to the blanket, consciously aware that someone was hitting on me after an absence of what seemed to be, well, like years.

"Get a drink or something?" he asked, tilting his head down to search out my eyes.

"I have a little problem walking," I said, and began to explain my hernia and my recuperation, and then, suddenly, into the whole misery of breaking up with Nathan four months ago over having discovered, well, he had given me crabs.

Pat's face moved into a smile at the end of my story. "I've got plenty for your troubles," he said. "Come on, I'll help you walk."

On the way back to his house he told me he was originally from New Zealand, not Australia, and had been coming to the Fire Island every year since the late Sixties; his uncle, a painter, had owned a small clapboard house in Cherry Grove. The house we walked to in the Pines, however, was a two story creation of weathered cedar and glass, perched high on stilts above a dune. Pat explained, in his benign offhanded manner, that his uncle, now dead, had left a sizable inheritance to his favorite nephew. After briefly meeting Pat's housemates, a giggly quartet who danced unabashedly around the high tech living room to the soundtrack of *Fame*, we made our way into the kitchen where I watched Pat mix vodka and orange juice together into glasses in decidedly unequal portions.

"Cheers," he said and we lifted our drinks into a toast, but before I could take a sip he took my hand and said, "Come on back here, mate," leading me through the house, up a flight of stairs and into a bedroom that overlooked the ocean. "These are from Timothy Leary," he said, and held up a vial of pills.

"*Timothy Leary?*" I answered, somewhat disbelieving.

"Well, some actress, really. She said she got them from Timothy Leary." He opened the vial, broke a tablet in half and placed a section on my tongue. "You're gonna feel great," he said. I held the pill on the center of my tongue, worrying about what I had gotten myself into. "It's easy, mate," he said, noting my concern. "The boys downstairs love 'em." As much as I wanted to be part of the great adventure of gay life and experiment with all of its temptations, I was still full of hesitations and guilt, instilled, I firmly believe, from my father telling me for years and years and years that everything was a sin. I sat on the edge of the bed, lifted my drink to my mouth, and washed down the tablet, the alcohol burning a path to my empty stomach. Pat joined me on the bed, rubbed his hand along my thigh till my eyes met his and then he leaned over and kissed me, pressing me fully back into the mattress. He held me for a long time in his arms, his lips and tongue leisurely exploring the territories of my eyes and chin and nose and neck. He slowly worked a hand down my stomach to the hem of my swimsuit, then cupped the fabric that held my straining cock and balls, and then slipped the swimsuit down my legs. He hovered over me a moment, uncertain; I knew he was taking in the angry red scar left behind by the surgeon's knife on my groin. Then Pat took his hands and gently cupped my balls and cock, kneading them together like dough but also in rhythm to the music the giggly boys continued to play downstairs and which filtered through the thin walls of the house. Pat, looking up again to my face and matching my eyes, asked in a whisper, "Does this hurt?"

"No," I answered. "Only if there's pressure against the skin."

He leaned down and took my cock in his mouth, his hair gently floating up and down against my stomach. Things began to decompose and detach at that point. I remember studying the tan, leathery creases of the skin near Pat's eyes, the way he worked his own cock into an erection, the slight pain I felt as he pressed it into me, the slow precise revolutions of his hips. And then things began to lose their corporeality, a warm vibration journeying from my bowels to my lungs turned into a weightless heartbeat echoing from Pat through me; the sheets of the bed became a bottomless space like Alice's rabbit hole, Pat and I fucking in somersaults like tumbleweeds. The music grew first louder, then muffled, the basslike kettle drums in an orchestra, and I became convinced that Irene Cara and Donna Summer must be sisters or cousins or maybe even the same woman, the treble of their voices so high and similar.

Then the music fell apart, too, notes sustaining themselves like chimes, turning into pictures in my mind like *Fantasia*, first into things like long, shiny threads of film, then rolling together like the wheels of a bike before fading back into the solid shape of a stationary pinwheel. Other things seemed to fall apart as well: the freckles on Pat's back multiplied to look like a sequin jacket, cottony clouds of the sky marched into the room like an army of Casper the Ghosts, the watch on the bureau angrily sat up and chastised me like a preacher from a pulpit. Logic seemed to find other shapes, too. The pain I had felt earlier from my operation washed away from my skin like a stain from bleach, fear was only a piece of clothing discarded on the floor. My detachment from gay life now seemed as silly as a beach ball—here I was, after all, with a man from another country going down on me, fucking me—weren't we speaking the same language, no matter how different the accents?

My orgasm came like an explosion of carbonation, pent up inside a bottle, shaken and then released. I remember we showered together afterwards, my fingertips searching out the cool, slick feel of the bathroom tiles. And I remember helping Pat prepare dinner, giddily chopping green peppers and mushrooms into a large glass serving bowl, sipping another drink, one of his housemates slipping me a Tuinal to dull the edge, another opening his closet and letting me try on his clothes, a joint passed around while the roast was cooking, more drinks during dinner, and afterwards another pill before heading out to go dancing at the club in the harbor.

The next morning I woke up on a slick, varnished wood floor of a bedroom, the thick arm of a latino man with a circular tattoo of a braided rope around his bicep next to me. I recognized no clothes on the floor or the chair that I could distinguish as my own, not even my swimsuit, so I slipped on a white T-shirt and a pair of yellow shorts that I had noticed on the chair. I walked out of the bedroom, my groin aching with every step, and into the room of a house I had never seen before. Confused, I began looking around the kitchen, a pressure growing behind my eyes as if someone were blowing up a balloon inside my skull so that it almost obliterated the pain of my limp.

When I found the kitchen there was a tall guy with a thick mustache and wiry brown hair I had never seen before, spinning things in a blender.

"You're Bill, aren't you?" he asked when I entered the room.

"Robbie."

"Ahhh, Robbie," he repeated, as if it mattered.

"Where's Pat?"

"Pat?"

"Tall. Red hair. From New Zealand."

Nothing I said seemed to register with this guy. He shrugged his shoulders. "Don't know him," the guy said. He stopped the blender and lifted the lid off and pressed his nose to the rim. "You out here all week?" he asked.

"Till Sunday night."

"Sunday?" he asked, bequeathing the word a bewildered expression on his face. "You mean you were supposed to leave Sunday."

"What?"

"It's Tuesday," he said smugly, as if delivering the correct answer on a game show.

I looked out the window trying to sort out this information, as if the sky itself could convince me that time had not passed without my notice. My head was pounding and my vision stumbled around disorientedly, focusing on the pots of geraniums and petunias by the door, a child's red wagon, flip flops lined up on the deck like empty shoes at a Japanese restaurant. How did I lose two days? Not one. *Two.* How could this have happened? Had I lost all sense of self-control? All sense of self-worth? Did this happen because I was a man who was depressed or because I was a man who was a homosexual, or simply because I was an aging boy going for a ride on the brightly painted merry-go-round? Is this what it must always feel to be gay? I remember thinking at that moment. How could I ever let myself do this?

"Can I borrow the phone?" I asked the guy with all the politeness I could still muster.

"On the wall," he answered and pointed.

I called Vince at his apartment in Manhattan, hoping I would not reach him, that he wouldn't be home, that I had, instead, awakened within my own nightmare. "Vince?" I asked when I recognized the voice on the other end.

"Robbie?" Vince answered. It was true, two days of my life were missing. "I've been calling you since yesterday. Michael and I brought your stuff back here when you didn't show up at the house or even call."

I couldn't say anything and I felt, then, like I was adrift in a lifeboat waiting to be found. There was a long pause of silence on the line. "Are you okay?" Vince asked finally, the line now crackling brilliantly with static. "Where are you?"

"I'm here," I answered. "I'm lost again."

I stayed away from the Island the rest of that summer, throwing myself mercilessly back into work, telling Alex that I wanted the worst jobs that he could find because I didn't want to have to come home and have the energy to do anything else, didn't want to have to think about anything else, didn't want, really, to have to believe my life could be better or even different. All I wanted to do, I explained to him, was to just function: work, eat, and sleep. That was it. No distraction. No deviation.

Alex tried to convince me otherwise, mumbling through some sort of unrehearsed speech about how the desire and finding of amusement was one of the great dividends of life; his chief concern, however, was that I would not be so overworked that I could be injured on the job, that my depression, really, would not distract me from the work that I was doing. But I moved with an internal combustion made up of both fury and frustration; if New York was such a great epicenter of gay life, why were the guys I was meeting so shitty? So unavailable? Why couldn't I meet a decent guy? Why was I so unhappy? Was something wrong with me? Was I the only guy who wanted to fall in love?

I did not give up on gay life that summer, of course, did not give up on men and sex, did not relinquish, either, the bars or baths or discos. Sex and men were still my own narcotic: one evening with a lawyer who lived in Brooklyn with a collection of Streisand albums could easily encourage another night at the baths on 15th Street, which in turn could lead to a trip to Uncle Charlie's and another night with a stockbroker who lived on the Upper East Side. I could, with each of them, slip out of my own skin and into their lives, into, as well, my imagined life with them. It seemed I had trained myself to fall in love instantaneously, to be available for it if it was to be returned; each minute, quirky habit of a man could provoke a tenderness within me, the way, for instance, one guy sucked air through his teeth as he talked, or rubbed his hands together furiously when excited, as if wanting to warm them before a fire.

Each time, though, with each man, I thought I would walk away having learned some lesson about either life or about myself, that Mr. A was not right because he was too cynical in conversation or too self-absorbed in bed, or Mr. B's hygiene was too unruly or unkempt, or Mr. C smoked too much or drank too much, or seemed, for instance, to just float in space, his brain removed as if from an overuse of marijuana. But instead of learning things, each time I had my heart taken away from me, such was my good but unfortunate nature, I guess, removed like a coat borrowed from a closet, stretched out of shape and then returned, misshapen and smelly and tattered around the hems. I suffered, too, through another case of crabs that summer, shaving all the hair on my chest, stomach and groin this time to get rid of the eggs, then got a case of urethritis from a rather aggressive session with a man at the Ansonia baths, then hammered a nail through my thumb while I was replacing the planking of a platform bed. But I handled those scars and misfortunes, then, with the aplomb of a veteran, with the knowledge that with each test, each mishap, I would end up being if not a better or wiser person, then at least a tougher one. Some nights I would walk alone on the empty streets and believe it was my destiny to wander through life alone, that I would forever be searching for a Mr. Right who was never right, always flawed, my quest as improbable as discovering Atlantis. For a while I shunned seeing Vince and Jeff and Denise, sometimes I felt weary and drained in their company, a depression and loneliness rising from the pit of my stomach and remaining stuck in my chest till I had to excuse myself and flee, going back out again to find something I was uncertain of, making another trip to the bar or to a club or cruising along

Christopher Street, waiting to be picked up by someone, *anyone*. But no matter how much I craved the sex, craved the physicality of another man, I also knew it was impossible for me to emotionally detach myself. Perhaps that was one of the reasons why it seemed to me that I moved through the darkened streets of Manhattan like an island myself, a tragic, though sometimes optimistic, romantic.

That was the same summer that Denise began to yearn herself for romance, though at first she felt as if everyone was deserting her; everyone, she decided, was making plans that excluded her. Jeff spent most of his weekends out at Fire Island, usually as the guest of someone he had met in the steam room of his gym; during the week he was busy floating between auditions, acting and dance classes, and whatever lucky guy could hold his attention for more than a few minutes. Vince was busy writing and arranging readings of a new play he had written, a farce in which all the roles were for gay men and which meant that there was nothing for Denise even to consider wanting to audition or campaign for. Alex continued to keep me busy, and he found an assignment for a friend of a friend of his who owned an old farmhouse in Duchess County and wanted the kitchen remodeled. My days were spent building custom-designed cabinets and counters for him, but I refused to stay over at the house to complete the work; instead, I commuted ridiculously long hours back and forth each day on the Hudson rail line, at my own expense, but grateful to be slumped down in the seat between the other commuters and absorbed in a book.

"I don't know why I put up with all this," Denise said to me late one evening when she had managed to reach me, yanking me out of a nap I had retreated into on my couch. She had discovered Jeff had gotten complimentary tickets to a preview of *42nd Street*, the latest Broadway extravaganza to hit town and a show that she had been mentioning over and over to him that she wanted to see and to which Jeff had taken some guy named Ramon whom he had known less than seventy-two hours when he had gotten the tickets from a connection of a friend who worked at Actors' Equity. She was particularly incensed because only a week before she had taken Jeff to see the Richard Burton revival of *Camelot* at Lincoln Center. Didn't he at least owe it to her to invite her? she mentioned to me. "Couldn't I at least have been offered the courtesy of declining so he could take his trick?" she protested.

"There are not many joys to maidenhood," she complained some more to me over the phone, trying to remain in some sort of detached yet cheerful mood. "If I wasn't so busy chasing my friends to get together I'd think about dating." But the truth was that Denise had not really dated anyone seriously since she had moved to New York. It wasn't that she wasn't interested in meeting someone, it was that she found the company of her friends—most of whom were gay men—more interesting than the straight men she had met. But Denise was also feeling the pressures of an art career that was growing in ways she had not expected and it kept her busy and confused; she had grown unhappy at the greeting card company where she found herself concentrating more and more on graphics and layouts and had quit the job to spend more time drawing and painting, subsiding once again on a series of odd jobs to meet her bills.

The owner of a gallery just north of Houston Street had seen some of Denise's sketches and was encouraging her to find a studio where she could work on larger and more detailed paintings. The suggestion had sounded like a good idea to her but it had also left her with mixed feelings. There was, unfortunately, the expense of it all. There was no way she could afford it without trying to hunt down some wealthy patron, a pretty much improbable task, she felt, with all the other artists in Manhattan searching for the same thing, and she refused to call her parents for a loan, because her mother would only remind her that she was single, poor, miserable, and alone. One night on the phone with me she bitterly mimicked what her mother's response might have been: "Denise, dear," she parodied her mother's heavy southern drawl, "Maybe what you need is a husband, not a career."

It was true that Denise worried her drawing was isolating her too much; she often wondered how the hours could disappear so easily from her day as she hunched over a bright white sketch pad, drawing lines back and forth into shapes and ideas. Evenings, especially, could escape quickly from her; often at midnight she would lift her head into the overhead spot light that illuminated the kitchen table where she worked and realize she had spent yet another day there trapped, womblike, within the ideas of her head. And so on the nice, warmer days that summer, before the oppressive humidity or afternoon heat could make the sidewalks boil unpleasantly, she began to walk to Washington Square and sketch a folk singer or a jogger or a couple that walked their German Shepherd or anyone who could gain her attention. Often, she hoped all this drawing would start up a conversation with someone, and there was invariably a drug dealer who always approached her wanting to communicate something, but she seldom found anyone interesting enough to maintain a conversation with for more than an afternoon. All she wanted, really, was someone who could talk enough about himself without boring her. Usually, however, she fell into sketching as the conversation dulled.

Denise had also been sending to several magazines around town the series of cartoon strips she had been working on about a naive Dorothy exploring urban gay life, but none of them had shown any interest, until she decided, impulsively, to send a note and a few photocopied samples to a weekly art newspaper that was published in Soho. The editor, a man named Perry Doherty, called her almost immediately after opening her envelope and said he wanted to use them, but had to run the strips through an editorial meeting later in the week and would get back to her. When Perry called back, he said he could only publish them conditionally; there was a catch: Could Denise do a few more panels so that they could be more inclusive, or, rather, to put it more correct politically, could they not be so exclusively about gay men? Perry, who had a deep, authoritative voice like an English actor, asked her, "Couldn't you do some about lesbians as well?"

Lesbians? Denise thought. What did she know about lesbians? Thespians, yes, but *lesbians?* She knew of gay male life, of course, vicariously through Jeff and Vince and myself. And she knew a few lesbian women—Rhonda, an actress from her scene study classes, Caryn, one of her art instructors and her lover Holly, and Joanne, a young punkish-looking girl Vince worked with part-time at the bank. But what did she know about being a lesbian? What did she know about a lesbian that she could draw?

She asked Jeff first, as she always did about anything, and he suggested she go see Gwen, the Asian-American cosmetics sales girl at Macy's. "Remember when we worked there?" Jeff said. "She knew all the scoop."

"She's a lesbian?" Denise asked, shocked by her own recollection of Gwen. Gwen was barely five feet tall and painted her face with makeup as if she were about to go on stage and perform Kabuki. Denise and Jeff had gotten to know her the Christmas season Denise had passed out cologne samples to shoppers.

"Don't you remember?" Jeff replied. "She was hitting on one of Santa's Elves."

"Of course," Denise answered, nodding her head. "The girl that looked like Audrey Hepburn."

■

Denise has often reminded me that that was the summer she really set about discovering who she really was, though I have often reminded her that who she became really evolved from a series of events over many years.

"I was literally yanked into being a dyke," Gwen had said to Denise that day she had found her way to Macy's ground floor. Gwen was rubbing a pale beige rose-smelling foundation onto Denise's skin. Denise was convinced the color was too light for her skin but when she looked at her reflection in the mirror on the cosmetics counter she could only see the frown lines which were creasing in her forehead. Gwen moved in over her shoulder, looked at Denise's image in the mirror, and said, "Finding out my sexuality was a real jolt to me." She thought Gwen was speaking much too frankly and loudly for the ground floor of Macy's, but Denise knew, remembered, really, while Gwen was dabbing at Denise's cheek, that that was just Gwen's style—she reveled in being as shocking and jolting as possible.

"I was fifteen and my mother's brother, my Uncle Alan, moved over from Korea and I had to share my bed with my cousin Evie. She was a year younger than I was and could barely speak a word of English. The first night she slept with me, she just reached into me and that was it. I never looked back. And I hadn't even done it with a boy yet, but she had done it with everything she could get her hands on. But the crazy thing was I didn't expect to feel this way. I mean, I had David Cassidy posters on my wall and Evie wasn't even American like I was. But Evie was so pretty. We were lovers for about a year before her family moved to Seattle. She's married now to a guy who is a chiropractor who I'm sure contorts her into all sorts of strange positions." Gwen laughed as she said this, a silly sounding noise that was like a dog sneezing, and then dabbed a light blush at Denise's left cheek. "You ever thought about darkening your eyebrows?"

"Darkening them?"

"I like that look," Gwen said. "I can't stand it when they look too fake and painted-looking." Denise looked at Gwen's eyebrows and noticed that they were so dark they looked phony.

"Evie grew out of it," Gwen said, raising an eyebrow pencil toward Denise's face. "I, on the other hand, can't keep a girl interested enough for a second date." Gwen laughed again and then leaned her wrist against Denise's cheek as she darkened her eyebrow, then began to work on Denise's eyes.

"That looks really good on you, you know," Gwen said, drawing back and looking at Denise's reflection again in the mirror. Denise studied herself, thinking Gwen had made her look too whorish—she had outlined her eyes so that they were as masked as a raccoon's. "So you want me to fix you up?" Gwen asked her.

Denise didn't answer at first, thinking that she meant did Denise want to buy the cosmetics Gwen had used on her face. "*Fix me up?*" Denise replied, deliberately and a bit too loudly when she realized exactly what Gwen was implying.

"I could take you upstairs and introduce you to Norma," Gwen said, drawing back and regarding Denise's face, then taking her thumb, wetting it in her mouth and rubbing it into Denise's cheek as if to correct a mistake. "No, maybe not. You're more Bea's type. I could introduce you to Bea."

"No, no," Denise answered quickly. "That's all right. You don't need to do that."

"But Jeff said you wanted to meet someone."

"Only for a project I'm working on."

"A project?" Gwen said, her hands suddenly against her hips. Her face turned downward, in traditional tragic Kabuki fashion. "What kind of project?"

"A drawing," Denise answered.

"*You need to draw a dyke?*" Gwen said so loudly that Denise felt the stares of the other women shopping around them as they turned and pointed toward the two of them.

"Well, yes, sort of," Denise said shyly, trying as much as possible to blend into the cosmetics and not draw attention to herself.

It was then that Gwen spread her lips wide into a large, fake, theatrical smile. "Here's a pretty face to draw," she said, framing her face with the palms of her hands.

It was then that Denise realized that the first thing she had to do was to find her way out of Macy's as politely and quickly as possible.

Denise phoned Rhonda next, but the moment she had done so, she realized she had made another mistake. Rhonda spent the entire conversation talking about every audition she had been to in the last month, so much so that it made Denise a bit regretful for having given up actively pursing an acting career. When she hung up the phone she realized she had not even asked Rhonda any questions regarding her idea for a comic strip, so instead of calling her back, she placed a phone call to Caryn, her former art instructor. Denise had always found Caryn somewhat intimidating—she was a tall, broad-shouldered woman with tri-colored hair, which she wore in a long brown, gray, and blond braid twisted into a bun at the top of her head and who had a penchant for plaid or patterned scarves and shawls that she could tie in knots or pin to the blouse of the black outfits she usually wore. Denise had always found in Caryn an admirable intelligence and rationale, a woman able to focus on the reason why she was so interested in teaching a painting or demonstrating a technique. Caryn had had careers as a gallery owner and as an artist, had been friendly with Pollack and Krasner on Long Island, could get Andy Warhol to take her phone call, and had married a man and raised three children in Connecticut before even embarking on the first of her varied careers. When Caryn answered the phone, Denise explained in a rather unflattering stutter that she could not break, the idea of her project and the stumbling point she had reached. Caryn, such a perceptive and polite woman, had also known the need for artists to have mentors and never dismissed the concerns of her students—which was how she had come to be involved with her lover Holly. Before Denise could even finish explaining all the details of her idea, Caryn had invited her over for drinks the following night.

"It's an admirable idea," Caryn said when she handed Denise a glass of diet soda. "But you must be careful about presenting stereotypes. We're certainly as diversified as the men are, though I've always felt we've been much more invisible than they have." It was then that Holly, Caryn's younger lover, moved into the room with a plate of crackers and sliced cheese, which she placed on the coffee table. Denise took a seat in a chair opposite the couch where Caryn and Holly had placed themselves so closely together.

"The best thing about it is that it gives that visibility to an audience that might not be aware of it," Holly said.

"Oh, I'm sure the downtown art crowd is well aware of lesbianism," Caryn said. "How well they're aware of feminism is another, completely different, matter."

"I don't think I'm out to teach or convince anyone about anything, really," Denise said. "More to present just a slice of life, or at least comment on it."

"With a sense of humor," Holly added, as if she were part of the concept.

"And a naive point of view," Denise said and watched Caryn lean forward and drink from a cup of decaf espresso she had placed on the table—she had given up alcohol some years back—and when she leaned back into the couch, Holly draped her arm around Caryn. It was such a beautiful moment—a younger woman possessing a much older one—that Denise immediately wondered if she would be able to use it later—something to summon up again and to draw.

"Have you ever slept with a woman?" Holly asked Denise.

The question embarrassed Denise, and she buried her eyes into the glass she held in her hand and said, "No. Never."

"A virgin," Caryn leaned forward and quietly clapped her hands together like some kind of character out of a civilized British novel.

"Hardly," Denise laughed and rolled her eyes.

"Then we must find you someone," Caryn said and turned to Holly as if to draw from her the names of some willing dates.

"No, no," Denise answered quickly. "I'm not looking to meet someone."

"But how can you draw it," Caryn replied, "if it's not part of your vocabulary?

"But that's why I'm here," Denise said, again looking down at her glass of soda. "That's what I need to know from you."

When Denise got home that evening she realized that Caryn and Holly had not provided her enough inspiration to draw, or, perhaps, had provided too narrow of an angle for the point of view she hoped to depict; Caryn, after all, had said that they were only two of many several different kinds of dykes. "I think I grew into being a lesbian," Caryn had explained. "Holly, on the other hand, never even made a choice. She just was." Denise decided she needed to know more and when Vince called for Jeff that evening and Denise answered the phone, she began to question Vince about his coworker Joanne while explaining, at the same time, that Jeff had not yet returned from Fire Island.

"Do you think she could take me out to a bar?" she asked Vince.

"I could take you out to a bar," Vince replied. "I'm not afraid of those women," he said, and then with a pause and a laugh of air, added, "Too much."

"All I need is a few minutes," Denise said. "I guess I could go on my own— I'm not afraid of those women either. Too much."

"I'll get her to go with you," Vince said. " I think she must owe me over a thousand favors by now."

The Duchess was as dark and smoky as any bar for gay men that Denise had ever walked into with Jeff, any bar she had ever walked into period, for that matter. Immediately inside the door, Denise found the smoke irritating her throat, and she began coughing in short, high-pitched spasms, embarrassingly so, so that she was immediately noticed by everyone in the bar. Joanne, who had never really liked Denise, was mortified by this unexpected behavior and immediately escaped to the bar and ordered a beer. Only after Denise stopped coughing did Joanne return and offer Denise a swig of her beer, and then, impulsively, as if to make up for abandoning her, decided to just give the whole bottle to Denise. Beer was not a drink Denise really liked, but she sipped at it until her throat was successfully coated and she felt a light buzz. Denise had not eaten, and soon began to worry that she was growing too dizzy to remain totally comfortable in her new surroundings.

Denise's coughing spasms had also attracted a small crowd within her peripheral vision, and Joanne spotted a woman that she knew—a thin, boyish-looking girl in her early twenties with thick black-frame eyeglasses, a slicked back businessman's haircut with a cowlick right at the crown of her head, and dressed in blue jeans and a white Fruit of the Loom T-shirt. Joanne introduced the woman to Denise as Nina, and they made brittle little remarks about the smoke and the beer Denise was drinking. Denise found herself studying Nina too intently though, and she would turn her gaze away from her and out at the other women at the bar, realizing in a matter of moments that she was at a lesbian bar, of course, and would then return her attention back to Nina in a more sheepish manner. Nina was slightly taller than Denise and there was a boniness to the shape of her face so that the dim overhead light highlighted two prominent cheekbones and a pointed slopping nose. Denise found her gaze repeatedly distracted and disturbed, however, by the small, pointed nipples that poked out against Nina's T-shirt. It's not as if Denise were prudish or anything, she had certainly gone braless at every opportunity she could find; for her it was a way to express, well, a certain kind of feminine freedom, though even braless she often realized that she would often augment her outfit with a vest or second blouse on top of the first one, hoping for more of a funky look than, well, a liberated one.

And then across the room Joanne spotted two friends she knew from the Gay Women's Alternative, and before Denise knew it she was suddenly alone with Nina and her pointy nipples talking about, of all things, cars.

"I got it from an ex-lover," Nina said, pulling a pack of cigarettes and a lighter from the hip pocket of her jeans. "We were living together in Brooklyn Heights and she worked out on Long Island. She kept the cat." Denise watched Nina effortlessly slip the lighter and the cigarette pack back into her jeans, wondering how the cigarette that Nina held just at the left side of her lip could not look crushed after all that time in her pocket; Nina's jeans were so tight that she looked as if she had sewn herself inside of them. "It's a red Skylark," Nina said proudly, blowing smoke up into the ceiling. "But I keep it out at another old girl-friend's house in Queens."

Nina talked and smoked, waving her hands to emphasize a point, rocking her hips back and forth subconsciously to the rhythm of the songs that filtered out of an old jukebox in the corner; at times she tilted her head back and let out a huge belly laugh, though Denise never said anything remotely funny, or so she thought. Denise thought it might be because Nina wanted Denise to admire her long, pale cariboulike neck—certainly Nina's best feature next to her prominently displayed nipples. Denise didn't understand anything about what Nina wanted from her. Was this an attempt at seduction? A pick-up? A pause between an evening's conversation before a scavenge for another partner?

Nina excused herself and disappeared to the bar and Denise found herself instantly relieved to be alone. Nina returned a few minutes later, however, with a tumbler of a heavy liqueur which she wafted beneath Denise's nose with a wry smile. She dipped a finger in the glass and then rubbed it onto Denise's wrist as though it were a perfume. She then lifted Denise's palm to her lips and began to lick her skin. Denise felt herself flush in a way she had never experienced before, and she horridly glanced around to see if anyone was watching the scenario, but the bar was crowded now—women were huddled into groups, talking, shifting themselves back and forth as if ready at any moment to break out into some heavy disco dancing.

"I'm not who you think I am," Denise said, drawing her hand back to herself.

"I'm sure you're much better than you give yourself credit," Nina responded. "It's nothing to be scared of."

Denise felt herself blush again. Was it that obvious that she was not a lesbian? Or, if not, had she envisioned herself as one incorrectly? Had she dressed inappropriately? She looked down at her docksiders and tried to imagine how she must look in her faded jeans and the white Oxford button down shirt she had inherited from one of Jeff's ex-boyfriends. She thought, well, she had dressed rather dykey.

"I won't make you do anything you don't want to do," Nina said. "But I think you should know you'd be missing a really good time if you don't seize this opportunity."

"I wasn't expecting this," Denise said, crossing her arms across her breasts as if to protect herself, or at least protect her emotions. She had failed to mention, of course, that she was at the bar for a specific reason—a kind of sociological research, after all.

"This is a bar," Nina laughed. "What else would you expect? Just to get drunk?"

"I don't really drink," Denise said.

"Then what do you do for fun?"

Denise, insulted, turned and looked quickly around the room for Joanne, but couldn't spot her, so she walked toward the exit, her mind now as far away from drawing as it could possibly get. But as her hand fell to her side, Nina reached down and grabbed it to catch Denise's attention again.

"I'm sorry," Nina said, pulling Denise back toward her. "I didn't mean to hit on you like that."

And this was where Denise scooped her hair behind her neck, not really ready to leave, willing, though, to accept some sort of apology.

"Can I call you?" Nina asked. "You're the prettiest girl that's ever walked into this bar."

Denise, now flattered and apologized to in less than a minute, suddenly found a spark of happiness within herself for the first time in months.

"Okay," she answered. "I'm listed in the book. Connelly on Bethune Street." And this was where Denise extended her hand as if to seal the exchange with a businesslike handshake. But Nina reached out and only took hold of Denise's fingertips, drawing them toward her lips with a bow of her back.

And this was when and how, Denise remarked later, that their courtship really began.

Nina had called the day after their encounter at the Duchess, and their first date began a few hours later at a coffee shop on Bleecker Street. Before Denise had even finished eating the grilled cheese sandwich she had ordered, Nina had asked her, "When was the last time someone made love to you?"

It wasn't that the subject of sex was so foreign to Denise; God knows she had discussed it enough with Jeff and Vince and Nathan and even myself—it was the fact that within the last few years she often felt she experienced sex vicariously through other people, particularly her friends, especially her gay friends. She looked at Nina that afternoon with what she realized later must have been a rather horrified stare—she wasn't at all used to talking about sex with another woman. Denise, unable to reply, unable even to focus on her sandwich, did not have to worry about her uneasiness for long. It was here that Nina reached out for Denise's hand—right there in a public restaurant—and said, "I could make you never forget me."

Denise was not used to being wooed with such immediacy or with such force, not used to being wooed at all, really, but found a moment of clarity amongst all the headiness she felt from the flattery, and asked, "So you plan to bed me and just disappear, is that it?"

Nina, surprised by Denise's straightforwardness, pulled her neck back and thought for a moment. "Not at all," she answered. "I plan to spend a lot of time with you."

Jeff was out on the Island that day and by the time Denise and Nina had walked in and out of all of the handbag and shoe stores on Bleecker Street, Denise felt her resistance fading and her infatuation escalating. And there was, of course, as she explained to herself over and over again, her need to know more about all of this lesbian stuff in order to draw about it accurately. And so, by the end of the afternoon, Denise had rationalized and reasoned everything in her mind so that when they reached Bethune Street once again, she invited Nina up to see her apartment.

Denise had not even made it through a glass of Tab before Nina was kissing her on the mouth and working at the buttons on her blouse while they were still standing in the kitchen by the refrigerator. Denise tried not to feel rushed or pressured into the suddenness of sex—focusing individually on each sensation—the bitter taste of nicotine on Nina's breathe, the smell of Nina's hair, the feel of Nina's skin as she wrapped her hand around her waist and slipped it up her T-shirt and against the flesh of her back—but it was impossible; Nina's presence was so enveloping it was as if all the lights had been shut off and Denise was forced to wander through her apartment without sight. And so each moment seemed, then, as if it were a test for Denise, as if she were waiting for something to repulse her so she would pull back, something she would feel but could not identify, but Nina's hands and lips were making her body ache for even more attention.

"Is this too fast?" Nina pulled back momentarily and asked, not really expecting an answer from Denise, instead slipping her hand through the opening of Denise's blouse and fondling the fabric of her bra. Before Denise could even breathe in response she found her bra on the floor and Nina sucking at her nipple. Denise ran her fingers through Nina's short hair, amazed that it felt like rubbing fur. Nina slipped out of her T-shirt and Denise stroked her hands against her breasts, amazed, now, that the touch of another woman could make her feel, so, well, feminine—and not at all repulsed. Nina slipped her hand beneath the skirt Denise wore that day, and worked her hand under the panties, stroking at Denise's pubic hair till she slipped a finger inside her and began to massage her.

And then Nina began rocking Denise with the cup of her hand, back and forth, back and forth; Denise held onto Nina at her neck and hipbones, as if strapped precariously onto a carnival ride that somersaulted against gravity. Denise came almost immediately, however, shuddering right there standing up in the kitchen. She felt so odd for having reached an orgasm so quickly and with a woman—a combination of guilt and inexperience—as if she were too easy but had also failed a test. Nina, however, was not yet ready to back off at all. Instead, she leaned into Denise's ear and whispered gruffly, "Now show me to the bedroom."

Denise has often mentioned to me that it was Gwen's remark about being jolted into her sexuality that haunted her thoughts the most those first few weeks she saw Nina. Denise had never believed then that she was a lesbian herself—something in her mind refused to acknowledge it. Instead, she convinced herself she was interested in the person, not the lifestyle, believing, really, that their affair would only be a one-time fling and that what she would experience, she could use to draw and sketch ideas for her cartoons.

Denise had always believed that she was an unconditional romantic, so the very notion that sex—and such frequent amounts of it—could so potently knock her off her feet and change her life came to her like an aggravation. It changed the way she woke up in the morning, the way she moved through the day, the way she organized her day, really, so that it fell around Nina's unexpected schedule. She didn't like that she could lose pockets of time or bequeath such power over herself to someone else—but she didn't try to amend it, either, or, at least, refuse to let it happen.

Denise had always believed that what had attracted her to Manhattan in the first place was the potential romance the city maintained, a quality that her home town in Kentucky had been unable to possess during her school years. Growing up, Manhattan conjured up for her a sea of elegant and sophisticated images—listening to Bobby Short at the Cafe Carlyle, ice skating in front of Rockefeller Plaza, two figures embraced in a silhouette in front of the Brooklyn Bridge. But after living in the city for just a few weeks, Denise had found that the city's charm and romance lay in its unpredictability, the way you could turn a corner and instantly change neighborhoods, from the noodle shops of Chinatown to the pastry stores of Little Italy, for instance, or the way you'd sense the air was becoming thinner and cooler but not realize it was fall till one day an amber sunset washed over the facade of an apartment building.

In many ways Denise and I were alike in this regard, this quixotic romantic image we carried around with us throughout our lives in Manhattan. There was, for us, a vibrancy to New York that was generated through the glances of everyone you passed on the street or stood next to on the subway or nearly missed coming out of a bank or a grocery store. There was a fervent sparkle within the lights of storefronts and restaurants spilling out onto the sidewalks at night, a passionate beam to the headlights of taxis and traffic, an ardent sound produced by the street musicians singing or playing out of tune violins, even a nostalgic smell to sandalwood incense drifting down the block from the line of peddlers hawking old paperbacks.

But Denise was also aware that a solitude could haunt you in the city, too—that too many choices, too many options, too many people, too many things to do could easily burn you out. Denise had never been able to develop a close friendship with another woman—a straight woman—they had all seemed too vacant, silly or competitive. Had it all started when her mother had criticized all of the friends she had brought home from school, or was it, perhaps, that she noticed too much of her mother in other women? Nosy, overbearing, and manipulative traits she had been afraid of developing herself? Or had she simply disconnected from herself—from her own femininity by submerging herself, instead, amongst gay men? Before she had met Nina, Denise had seldom dated any man more than a few times, had not been able to emotionally connect with anyone other than the gay men who had become her friends. She had also reached a point where she was frustrated from looking for someone to meet, as tired as she had become of hustling and trying to make a career— first from the demeaning process of theater auditions, then from the equally demeaning process of trying to shop around her drawings—the art of business,

she had found out, dictated the art of an artist and was as equally disappointing as, well, dating was. "There's too much phony baloney going on," she had
remarked to me one day on the phone when I asked her if she had gone to the
opening of a gallery I had seen written up in the *Village Voice*. "Eccentricity is
now being confused with ingenuity."

Denise once explained to me that Nina had awakened things within her that
she had long since repressed while learning to live and survive in Manhattan.
Living in the city beyond it's initial giddiness period, Denise explained, had
toughened her up; a cynicism had crept into her behavior—anything or anyone
that could spark a feeling of happiness within her could easily be deconstructed
and reduced to a set of emotional mechanics, and, well, examined for potential
problems. And so as much as she looked forward to the sex with Nina, there were
things Denise found that she did not like about Nina: foremost, there was the
smoking and the drinking; secondly, there was the fact that late at night, when
Nina was over at Denise's apartment, Nina could not stop eating, roaming
through the kitchen cabinets devouring potato chips and chocolate chip cookies as if she were a roach. But then there was the aggressiveness and the hyper-
activity, too; Nina seldom seemed relaxed—she was always on the prowl, her
eyes constantly wandering through a room, taking everything in before they
would eventually meet up with Denise's. And then there were the ex-lovers.
Denise had no idea how many ex-girlfriends Nina had had, but walking through
the West Village with her was a constant test of patience—someone usually
had something to say to Nina, even if it was just a hiss across the aisle of the
grocery store. Nina would smile, a crooked, smug sort of smile, and say something like, "Oh, we dated for a while but it didn't work out. Too jealous for me."
Too jealous? Denise would think to herself. If she was anything like she was
around Denise, when did Nina have time to woo other women?

And it seemed to Denise that Nina was spending most of her time over at
Denise's apartment—in less than a week she had two changes of clothes, a
toothbrush, and a vibrator in residence, much to the dismay of Jeff, who had-
n't hit it off with Nina from the moment they met as she was coming out of
the bathroom one morning with a cigarette hanging from her bottom lip. But
all these ex's and problems proved to be an unexpected boon for Denise—they
provided her with the comic perspective she had searched for for her cartoon
strip—Denise's hook was to have Dorothy's lesbian guide through Oz always
quoting advice from an ex-girlfriend, an image Perry, her editor, enthusiasti-
cally embraced and which quickly found its way into print. No matter how
unflattering this prototype of Nina could be, Nina was nonetheless flattered,
delighted that she was to be the stimulus for Denise's art.

What kept Denise connected to Nina had nothing to do with her finding her
muse; nor was it due to the companionship nor to the growing friendship that
occurred between the two women. What attracted Denise more and more to Nina
was, blatantly, the quality of the sex they had together. Denise's skin glowed, now,
as if it had been scrubbed with a loofah brush and then moisturized with an

expensive cream; as she walked or worked at her drafting table she felt a tenderness at her nipples, as if they were just waiting to be caressed by Nina's lips or fingers. Still, Denise wasn't really convinced that she was a lesbian. Her feeling was that she had been romanced into the practice by Nina's aggression, though each time she tried to rationalize it in this way she couldn't shake a mental image she had retained of Gwen's tragic and comic theatrical poses until one day she recalled Amanda Shinn instead. Amanda had been the girl she had liked in first grade and they had kissed one afternoon in the coat closet. But hadn't Amanda initiated that too? Hadn't it been her idea and not Denise's? Maybe there was something to Denise that, well, attracted other women to her. But had Amanda seen something in Denise that Denise had still not recognized on her own?

It wasn't that she was a virgin; she had slept with Johnny Barton in eighth grade and had been steady with Kevin Adair throughout high school. And in college she had learned from experience the emotional distance between lust and love. She knew, for instance, that she felt all swoony around Eric Golder, but didn't have a thing to talk to him about and couldn't trust him the minute he was out of her sight, and she knew she wanted, instead, for example, to spend Valentine's Day with someone more like Rick Fulton, someone who was bright and interesting and could at least bring her a thoughtful gift. Denise had discovered—with boys, at least—that if you didn't have anything to say to him outside of bed that there was little that would happen in the realm of love. Nina, however, had willingly shared details about herself out of bed, even though Denise felt that they had too few subjects in common to talk about. Instead, their affair became an education for Denise; Nina took Denise to a women's poetry reading on the Upper West Side, a potluck dinner at a performance artist's loft off the Bowery; they played racket ball at one of Nina's ex's health club near Wall Street, ate at a vegetarian restaurant that Denise had walked by almost every day but had never tried, went back to the Duchess and spent the evening dancing and necking in public.

And then Nina began to talk about their future together, about how they could go to Vermont in the fall or take a trip to Seattle, or drive down to New Hope in two weeks to go to a dinner party. Denise found herself thinking so much about what they could do together that whenever Nina wasn't around she felt a perceptible loneliness, as if she were incomplete or no longer existed on her own. She would run through conversations in her mind, trying to figure out where Nina was, what she was doing, if she was doing something with someone else, wondering too much about the "ex" Nina had said she was seeing that afternoon, for instance. Denise never confronted Nina with any of her suspicions; an ex-girlfriend was an "ex" after all, certainly not a threat to their relationship. And when Nina returned they would talk more and more about their plans together for tomorrow or the weekend or for a trip at the end of the month. And Denise found herself falling in love, or, rather, falling in love with the idea of falling in love, even though she reminded herself continually that what she felt for Nina was simply pure, old-fashioned lust.

5

It was Vince who called and said that Jeff was moving out on Denise, or as
he said it, to get away from that horrendous new girlfriend of hers. Nina's presence had spilled over into every inch of the apartment, much to the annoyance
of Jeff. It wasn't that Jeff wasn't a tolerant person, he was, and God knows, he
certainly owed Denise his fortitude and patience; after all, hadn't she waded
through innumerable evenings of witnessing Jeff's tricks pass by her bedroom
in the deep of the night?

But Nina was impossible, even Vince admitted to that—she was so possessive of Denise that Jeff could not even have a conversation alone with Denise
without Nina hanging around the corner and eavesdropping or trying to get
Denise to join her somewhere else in the apartment. Nina was so afraid of Jeff
turning Denise against her that she tried everything she could to turn Denise
against Jeff. Wasn't Jeff forgetting to buy paper towels? she nagged Denise.
Wasn't he supposed to vacuum every other week? Wasn't he forgetting to
flush and put the toilet lid down? Nina stomped around the apartment in her
heavy hiking boots whenever Jeff was around, as if to assert her presence
through the creation of noise. Jeff said to me, when we ran into each other on
the street one day, that it wasn't the noise and aggressiveness Nina generated
so much that rattled him so, it was her goddamn cigarette butts all over the
place. There were butts on the carpet, on the kitchen counter, floating in the
toilet. *Everywhere*. And whenever he wasn't home, Nina would go into Jeff's
bedroom and lie on his bed and watch TV, making sure the ashes dropped on
his sheets and pillows. "I've been concentrating on fiber all year," Jeff wailed
in a rather overly dramatic queeny manner, trying to inject some humor into
his plight. "Now I'm gonna die of secondhand smoke."

Jeff, however, would neither confront Nina on this nor complain about it to Denise, his reason being that the apartment was his home as well, and he didn't want to hate having to be there, or, at least, dread going back to it, though lately Nina had taken to playing the stereo late at night so loudly that Jeff could neither fall asleep, read, nor watch TV with any sort of concentration.

"What can I say?" he remarked to Vince the afternoon they passed one another on Seventh Avenue and Vince noticed Jeff was looking tired and unhappy. "I'm a 200 pound wimp with eighteen inch arms." Then Jeff began to explain that he was now renting rooms at Man's Country, the Ansonia, or the St. Mark's baths almost every night just to get some sleep.

"If I wasn't getting so much sex out of it," Jeff said with a wry smile, "I'd really be pissed," though what Jeff was feeling, he told Vince, was betrayed by Denise. "We were really good friends before this," he said, "and now it's as if I only exist to be in the way."

Vince had offered Jeff the possibility of moving into his apartment for a while, on a temporary basis, but Jeff had quickly nixed the idea, knowing how small Vince's apartment was and how possessive of his space Vince could sometimes be, more possessive, it seemed, than Nina was of Denise. "We'd either end up lovers or hating one another," Jeff had said to me a few days later when he told me of Vince's plan. So instead Vince had called his friend Wes at his house on Fire Island and suggested that Jeff could be the perfect coordinator for Wes's annual Labor Day party. Jeff, after all, was always short of cash that year, and being paid to live in the Pines for two and a half weeks to answer the phone for RSVPs was an action that required little forethought or planning from anyone.

I never made it to Wes's party that summer; I was, at that time, still so exasperated with gay life that I moved through days loathing myself because of my single, unattached fate, still aware of the mess with my hernia and my disastrous attempt at a relationship with Nathan. And it wasn't until September that I saw Jeff again; it was sometime after Labor Day and though summer was not officially over, Jeff was back in town, back not living at his apartment, back moving between a night at the baths or a night at a trick's. It was then, running into him outside the cinema on Greenwich Avenue, that I said to Jeff that if he needed to he could crash on my couch overnight. The offer was genuine though we both knew that Jeff's physique was much bigger than the tiny love seat sofa I kept by the window in my apartment. I followed my offer, though, with a promise of making Jeff a set of keys so that he could come and go as he needed until he found another place to live.

When Jeff appeared at my apartment the next afternoon with his shaving kit and a gym bag full of clothes, he mentioned he had gotten an invitation to the opening of a new disco in the East Village, a private club, he said, that a friend of a friend had put him on the invitation list for and was I interested in going to the opening night next week with him? His treat, he informed me, for letting him stay with me. As tired and disenchanted as I was about gay life, I never refused the opportunity to go dancing when it was suggested. Dancing, I was often convinced, was one of the few things that kept me gay.

By the time Jeff and I reached the club that night it was close to midnight; a line of thickly built men wearing tightly fitting bomber jackets stretched out of the entrance onto Second Avenue around Third Avenue and then back down Sixth Street. A sense of anticipation clung to the air like a chilly condensation and Jeff and I passed several guys we knew and we stopped to chat or air kiss one another, a few waving, like church fans, invitations that bore a drawing of a nude St. Sebastian pierced by laser beams, before we took our place at the back of the line. A guy Jeff used to work out with at the Body Center was not far from us in the line, and he turned around periodically and spilled facts about the place: a dome, five million dollars worth of renovation, on the site of the old Filmore East where Janis Joplin had once performed. Before we even made it into the Saint that night there was an exclusive members-only type feel to it on the street, eyes glistening as much from excitement as from pre-disco prescription stimulants, high-pitched giggles punctuating the sounds of the passing city traffic.

I'm not sure if it was the bright sheen of the gold and black marble floors when we entered the Saint that night that first transported me into another frame of mind, as if time itself did not exist, or if it was the heavy sound of music that wafted through the locker room where we left our jackets, or if it was the fact that everywhere the eye roamed a handsome man could be seen smiling, talking, sipping a drink, and shifting his weight back and forth to the heavy bass beat of the music. Perhaps it might have been the fact that Jeff took my hand, as if I were a VIP or certainly the most important person in the room, and led me purposely through the lobby toward a set of twin spiral staircases, nodding at everyone he passed as if he had arrived with the evening's prize. Had we never reached the dance floor at all that night, the trip across the lobby would still have been something close to Nirvana—such it was, the sheer beauty of everything and everyone.

But the music, spilling out into the lobby, kept tugging us upstairs, and when we entered the disco, I felt as if I had stepped off a spaceship that had just landed on the moon. Above us a white planetarium type of dome was recessed into the ceiling and framed the room; in the center of the polished blond wood dance floor a circular light tree constructed on a hydraulic lift raised and lowered banks of lights that twirled and spun as if it were dancing itself, the porous skin of the dome above magically darkening into a blanket of stars.

Jeff and I hit the dance floor right away, our excitement rising like helium balloons. I had fallen into a territory of resplendent happiness long before we had reached that palace of high tech decadence, however. I had fallen in love with Jeff by then, or, rather, replaced my obsession over Nathan with the obsession of wanting Jeff to be my boyfriend. As I watched Jeff dance in front of me I was aware that the full intensity of my affection was turned onto him, my eyes mesmerized by the way he moved his hips and shoulders, my psyche undressing him inch by inch, then penetrating his skin till I found the core of him, the way his heart and mind pumped and ticked so that I could reside deeper into his body, engulfed somewhere between his chest and arms.

In the days just before that opening night party at the Saint, Jeff had opted to make the best use of my apartment. Often, upon coming home from work or the gym, I would find him stretched out on my bed watching TV, reading, or napping. We would eat dinner together, usually something I had picked up—Chinese take-out, pizza, sandwiches—and afterward we would settle back again onto the bed, talking or watching a movie till one of us fell asleep. It was senseless to ask Jeff to sleep on the couch, he would have been too cramped even trying to sit on it; but I had also expected the nature of our friendship to provide a stronger restraint against the forces of sex, even though I was so perceptively aware of our subtle and undisclosed carnal attraction to one another.

In retrospect, I realize how young I was when all of this happened, how easily I could be seduced by anyone, how much I, too, was in love with the idea of being in love. What happened happened naturally, without any forethought or premeditated intent from either of us. It began the second night Jeff stayed over—a casual brush of one leg hitting another sometime deep into the night and then a shifting of a body to find a closer warmth beneath the sheet. Jeff slept in his underwear and it was hard not to be drawn to him, his body emanated a brawny heat simply because of its muscley bulk. And the deeper recess into the mattress his heavier physique created than mine made me feel as if I was always trying to prevent myself from pitching into him. The first night he stayed over I remember I had to hold myself in check—my sexual energy repressed as I kept myself from literally tumbling into him. The second night, however, I was tired, worn down from trying to avoid him, and in the middle of the night I turned my back to him so that my body mirrored his fetal position. As I did so, Jeff stretched his legs out and turned onto his stomach, his hand coming to rest against my hip. His head was turned toward me and his breath, feverish and moist, hit my neck, and as I rolled over to settle into another position, Jeff's hand followed my body and he closed around me like a spoon.

I knew I was hard before I was consciously awake; I felt Jeff's fingers flutter up against my ribs and I lifted my arms to allow his forearms to slip tighter against my waist. I held myself in his embrace, feeling my body tense when his lips then brushed against my back. I rolled over again and settled my face into the crook of his neck, at the same time breathing in the musky smell of his skin.

Jeff's arms moved down and cupped my buttocks and I felt his cock jump and flatten against my stomach. We played that way for hours that night, rolling, shifting into one another, brushing, groping, kneading our fingers against bones and muscles, till our mouths found each other and we drew together into long, deep-tongued kisses.

During the following day, while working, I found myself thinking about Jeff, worrying if he could distinguish me from his other tricks, afraid of even wanting to confront him with any of my emotions, worried, too, that it would break the magical spell that had enveloped us. Night after night that week our bodies discovered one another beneath the warmth of the sheets, moving consciously together at the outset, then, from the desire for sex with each other. I hadn't imbued so much feeling into sex since I had been with Nathan and I was constantly trying to ground myself, worrying in my mind that I was placing too much emotion into how I felt about Jeff. He was, after all, one of my closest friends. By the time of the weekend of the opening night party at the Saint, ten days later, I could not keep my emotions separate from the sex that was happening between us. I had come to believe, because of what we were doing with each other, that Jeff had no intention or desire of settling elsewhere.

There was a tribal feeling to the Saint that first night. Dancing is never just dancing for gay men; Perhaps even more than sexuality, it's a communal celebration of who we are. It was easy to spot the little cliques of men dancing, unpunctured adoration usually swallowing up the handsomest of the group. The music that night slid effortlessly from track to track, the dancers as much athletic as erotic. Around us a few guys were dancing only in shorts; on the risers just beneath the slope of the dome I could pick out men shaking tambourines, sticks, or cymbals as they danced. Across the room I noticed a guy spinning with two fans and I easily recognized the silhouette as Michael's, and I realized I hadn't spoken to him in several months. He made me immediately wonder about Vince and I felt momentarily guilty about not having phoned to tell him we were going dancing tonight. I had purposely been avoiding Vince, uncertain how he would regard my growing infatuation with Jeff. What would I tell him? How would I explain it? How could I make it sound logical? *Oh, by the way, Vince, Jeff and I are groping each other in the middle of the night and I'm falling in love with him because of it.*

In a way Jeff and I had nothing to do with one another as we danced together that night, there was no physical contact between us, after all—I kept one eye on him thickly bouncing as I tilted my head heavenward to study the lights. But I could feel a restlessness growing within me, though, and I didn't feel right about lusting for another man in front of him, nor did I even want to consider the possibility. And I also sensed a restlessness within Jeff; he continued to cruise and study one dancer after another as we moved about the floor. We danced for close to two and a half hours without a break, the music and the mood were that infectious. We parted back downstairs in the lobby; Jeff headed for the restroom and I went to wait for him against a wall. I hadn't expected that he would be gone long; he had clutched my hand coming off the dance floor with the same design as when we had entered. I leaned against the wall and rubbed my fingers through my hair, collecting the sweat with my fist and then shaking it to the ground. As I looked up the staircase I thought I noticed a blond figure that seemed familiar to me, but just as I was trying to figure it all out, a hand clamped on my shoulder and I felt a stubble of beard brush against my cheek.

"Dearest, you look as magnificent as always," Sal said. Beside him was his lover David. Sal was the darker and better built of the two, but David was the startling beauty—creamy white skin, bushy black hair and ice blue eyes framed by lashes so thick and dark they looked as if they had been painted on him. That night, David's eyes were wildly dilated, and I knew he was tripping on something because he giggled and pressed his hand against my chest, slipping his index finger against the indention of my clavicle. Sal was delighted by the physicality of it all and he stood lolling his tongue around his mouth as David slowly inched his hand around my neck.

"You must need me for something real bad," I said, teasingly, leaning down and running my tongue along David's forearm. Last year I had built some window seats for them in their nearby Village loft, and I knew from my boss, Alex, that they were thinking about framing off space to make a private bedroom.

"We don't need you," Sal smiled. "We want you. We've been trying to get you to party with us for years."

I smiled and cocked my head back into a spot light, as if to tease them further. Sal and David had as much of a reputation for fooling around with other lovers as they did for fooling around together with a third party; their sexual appetite was as insatiable as their innuendoes. But I had no desire to become part of a threesome, and I never understood, either, how they could handle the jealousies of their infidelities with each other.

"Such a pretty boy," David said, moving his hand to cup my chin.

"Still searching for Mr. Wonderful?" Sal added, his eyes darting away from mine and out into the lobby. "He'll only break your heart sooner or later. Better just to have a good time. Look what happened to Alex."

"Alex?" I asked, suddenly alarmed by the remark, realizing that Alex had been out of the office for almost a week.

"His latest," David slurred. "Now over."

"He was smitten with this wild young thing named Lance. Lance, of all names," Sal chuckled. "Dirty blond, thin as a rail, tattoo of a hammer on his inner thigh."

"Jail bait," David said.

"Not even a driver's license," Sal added. "But divine, just delicious."

"Amoebas," David explained. "The boy possessed parasites of such fury that Alex could not even sit down."

"He had a doctor make a house call," Sal joined in with a squeal. "And the doctor absconded with the boy."

"He wails," David said, rolling his eyes. "That girl just feels betrayed."

I felt instantly deflated. Even Alex, with all his money, had problems holding on to someone. Even money doesn't prevent heartbreak, I thought, nor does the objective of promiscuous sex. Then I felt the music tugging harder at me and I wanted to dance again, wanted to find Jeff, wanted to get away from Sal and David, wanted to escape all this mental confusion. I kissed them both goodbye, this time graciously on the lips, wondering if Jeff hadn't seen me and had gone upstairs.

Jeff wasn't inside on the dance floor, and when I went back to the stairs and looked down at the crowd in the lobby, I spotted him by the water fountain. I was instantly hot with jealousy, frozen into place as I watched him tweak a short, big-chested guy's nipple then lean down and slip his tongue into the man's mouth.

"I see Jeff's found his true love," I heard someone say behind my shoulder. I turned around, relieved to see it was Vince standing a stair above me, watching me watching Jeff. "At least for tonight."

He stepped down and kissed me on the neck and I slipped my arm around his leg, tilting my face up to him.

"You've been avoiding me," Vince said.

"Not really," I answered. "Just busy."

"But not careful," he added. "You're the simplest guy I've ever known, Robbie. You just need a good fuck to forget him."

I felt myself blush, embarrassed and culpable that I had not confided in Vince. "How do you know?" I asked.

"Denise."

"*Denise?*"

"They had a fight because he stopped paying her rent," Vince said. "And Nina doesn't give her a dime. She needed a sympathetic ear. And she knew where Jeff was staying."

"I thought you would be angry with me," I said.

"Because he's not staying with me?"

"Well?" I asked, waiting for him to answer his own question.

"I've been sleeping with Jeff for years," Vince said. "I *still* sleep with him," he added, emphasizing the current tense. "That doesn't mean I need him to live with me."

I unraveled myself from Vince's embrace and I began walking back down the stairs, determined to leave, not wanting to be caught up in all this, well, complexity, suddenly trying to sort out just how many men Jeff wanted to sleep with.

"Robbie," Vince yelled behind me, trying to catch up with me. He caught me in the lobby, taking my hand as Jeff had done earlier. "You don't have to go."

"Why not?"

"You're being too hard on yourself. You need to loosen up. You need to learn to have some fun."

"*Fun?*" I spat back at him a little too bitterly. "This is not about fun."

"Things are not always black and white," he said, and it was here he shoved his hand into his pocket and withdrew a small yellow capsule. "Take this," he said, in a tone that almost made it an order.

"Why?" I asked, looking at the pill in the palm of his outstretched hand.

"You're gonna need it," he said, and slipped it through the corner of my mouth.

I backed away from him but held the pill in the center of my tongue. "What do you mean?" I asked.

"Did you swallow?"

"No."

"Well swallow."

"Why?"

"Trust me."

I swallowed the pill, feeling it become caught momentarily in my chest before it eased its way down my throat to my stomach.

"Okay?"

"Okay."

"I've got some bad news," Vince said, running his hand then against my chest.

"I saw the guy Jeff was with," I answered.

"Worse, girl," Vince replied with a snap of his fingers. "Nathan's back in town."

I regretted the drugs and the drinking the next morning—a headache split across my forehead and resided somewhere behind my left eye before I even woke up. I regretted, too, dancing too hard—an ache in my calves made me wonder if I was becoming rheumatic. But how could I regret the fact that I had ended up at Vince's apartment, in Vince's bed with Vince? Hadn't I wondered for years why we had never ended up like this?

What I regretted, then, was that I was unable to remember any of it. I remember a cab, kissing Vince in the back seat, telling him I loved Jeff but that I loved him more, had always loved him more even if he was right about Nathan being wrong for me. And I remember Vince kissing me back, digging his hands into the back of my jeans to cup my ass, squeezing the cheeks with his fists as if he were wanted to tear them apart and look inside. But I remember nothing about climbing the stairs up to his apartment, nothing, either, about what might have followed. I might have thought that perhaps nothing sexual had happened at all between us, if I hadn't seen my clothes in various positions about the room, as if they had been taken off hurriedly or tossed giddily about. From where I lay in the bed that morning I could see a sock sitting on the bookshelf I had built for Vince. How in the hell had it made it up there? But it was the jar of Vaseline on Vince's nightstand that gave everything away.

I reached down and felt my asshole, coming back up with a greasy swipe.

Vince was still sleeping when I stepped out of the shower and I was glad not to have to confront him, not to have to unravel my feelings and place them up against his, or, perhaps, notice his lack of them. I didn't know how to handle the situation of sleeping with your best friend—is it something you want to escalate further? Or is it something you just dismiss? Protocol for this behavior varies from person to person, different in circumstance as it is to any relationship. But I knew several guys who had slept with someone first and who were not interested in developing any further relationship together and ended up becoming best friends. I knew nothing about the process happening in reverse.

By leaving Vince sleeping alone that morning I indicated to him how I wanted him to handle things—that perhaps things should remain status quo, or, rather, status quo before the sex occurred between us. I didn't hear from Vince until the following day; I attributed that to the fact that he was perhaps sleeping off even more booze and drugs than I had done. His reason for calling me was not to discuss what had happened between us and how we both felt about it—instead, he phoned to let me know that Jeff was staying with him for a few days.

I suppose, then, I could have felt hurt, upset that Vince had dismissed the event between us as coolly as I had. I suppose, too, that I could have been upset that Jeff now seemed to be avoiding me. The two of them probably had a lot to talk about, I thought, feeling oddly relieved but nonetheless wounded at the turn of things. But by the time the weekend's stimulants and exhaustion had worn off, I found myself even more confused. Nathan was once again at the front of my mind.

In the days that followed I looked for signs of Nathan wherever I went. I expected to see him turning the corner on 14th Street, waited to find him in the aisle of the grocery store, thought he would emerge from the shadows of Uncle Charlie's. I invented different scenarios on how I would greet him should our paths eventually cross: blasé in one encounter, not remembering his name in another, kissing him with outstretched arms if he should happen to catch me by surprise. The fact is I had already seen Nathan. Vince had pointed him out to me on the dance floor at the Saint that opening night; the familiar blond figure that I had seen disappearing into the dim echoes of the balcony had indeed turned out to be Nathan. While Vince and I danced together I had positioned myself so that I could watch him dance without him noticing I was even present. Nathan was there, that evening, with his friend Hank, and I studied their movements carefully as they danced in front of one another, trying to discern if they were sleeping together, wondering, as well, if Hank would spot Jeff. Occasionally, Nathan would pull a vial of poppers from his jeans and inhale first in one nostril, then in another, then offer the vial to Hank, who would wave it away and watch Nathan replace it in his pocket. Later, I noticed Nathan dancing by himself on one of the risers, barechested, his T-shirt bouncing between his legs like an eager puppy's tail, and it was then that I decided that he and Hank were not there as boyfriends. I still had no desire to approach Nathan, neither to reveal myself as being functional and happy nor with the hope to become wrapped up in his life again. I was content, really, at that moment to dance beneath him and watch him from afar.

And he danced magnificently that night, too—unrestrained, without a partner, he would tilt his shoulders up and down, like the inner workings of a watch, lifting one leg up slightly, his sole carefully parallel to the floor while his other pumped in rhythm to the music. And then he would squat for a second, his energy residing in his thighs, till he exploded into a spin and started the process over again.

Vince goaded me to go over and say something to Nathan, but I wanted, then, nothing of the sort. I soon grew annoyed with the idea of Vince watching me watch Nathan, and I left Vince to dance by himself for a while, and when I returned I noticed that Nathan was gone from the risers. That was when I went back downstairs for another beer, and when I returned later, not finding Nathan on the dance floor again, went and searched for Jeff. Not finding him either, I had another beer till Vince found me in the lobby and offered me a joint.

It was then, as we passed the joint between us in an out of the way corner, that Vince filled me in on Nathan's most recent escapade, facts that he had found out through Denise and that he had kept concealed from me for almost a month. Had I not then been so eager to know more about Nathan I could have been furious with Vince for being so secretive from me. It seemed that Nathan's Greek prince, the builder and architect who had hired Nathan to help with his family's business, had turned out to be a fraud.

Even drunk and drugged up that night I remember the facts finding their way to my consciousness. The story went that Nathan had flown to Geneva, purchasing his own airline ticket. The price of the ticket had been promised to be refunded—and as per the prince's instructions, Nathan went to the hotel where he was to meet the prince in his family's suite. When Nathan got to the hotel, there was no such record of a prince, a reservation, or even a family suite. Not even the local Swiss authorities could help with Nathan's dilemma. Nathan had never been given a phone number to reach the prince, not even initially in Manhattan. Everything had occurred through the mail or through phone calls that the prince had placed to Nathan, because, as it was reported back to me, "the prince was always traveling."

What kind of scam could be going on, I had wondered, if the prince never profited from Nathan's mishap? But Vince also revealed the motive for that. As Denise had related it, it was a case of misplaced trust; Nathan and the prince had been, it seems, well, sort of "fooling around" with each other, a contradiction, I pointed out, to one of her earlier bulletins on Nathan's where-abouts. Denise believed, as she told Vince, that the prince probably found, well, you know, "something better."

By the end of the week I had convinced myself that I had to see Nathan again. I called Vince and Jeff, both of whom I had been purposely avoiding, and suggested, in my most rehearsed but casual manner, that we all get together on Saturday night. "Let's go back to the Saint," I said. Both of them were more than eager to agree.

And neither of them had the slightest perception of my motive.

By that return visit to the Saint, word had gotten out around town about the club; the next Saturday it was twice as packed as the week before. Nathan was nowhere to be seen, and Vince went crazy upon seeing so many guys head-ed for the balcony looking for a quick sexual release. "He's such a pig," Jeff said, irritated that Vince had so swiftly deserted us to explore the balcony him-self. Jeff, in the interim week, had renewed his infatuation with Vince since they had started sharing living quarters, an unexpected turnaround since Jeff had never vocally indicated to me his desire of wanting to be so emotionally grounded to someone. But the truth was there was always another layer to Vince and Jeff's relationship—a fact neither of them wanted to admit or act upon in that delightfully sybaritic period of their lives. "All he thinks about is sex," Jeff had added that second visit to the Saint, working himself up into such a bad mood, that he began ranting about the DJ. "Disco is dead," he announced at the top of his lungs, an ironic statement, I thought, from some-one who worshipped musical comedy, an art form that had not progressed since the 1940s. "How can we let this define our lives?" he screamed at me on the dance floor, just at the point the crowd became so compressed that it was impossible to dance except by simply shifting your shoulders. "We have to leave," he said to me, looking as if he had witnessed a pedestrian sideswiped by a taxi and he had to report the injustice of it to someone.

"Not yet," I said, fighting with my own bad mood. I was angry at myself for thinking that I could draw Nathan back into my life by simply running into him at a disco of all places, angry, too, that I would even consider wanting to chase someone who clearly no longer wanted to be with me. I was angry at Jeff because I still felt attracted to him. And I was angry at Vince for not even acknowledging our night together, even though I, in turn, refused to acknowl-edge it to him.

Jeff and I soon left the dance floor and on the way to the lobby we ran into Sal and David who were making their way inside. Sal took an immediate dis-like to Jeff for being one of those beautiful, aloof muscle boys, but David, on the other hand, was immediately intrigued by the possibility of an orgy and offered to counter our bad moods with a quaalude. Sal didn't stick around to see Jeff grow wobbly from David's little blue wonder pill, however, nor did David once he spotted a Catalina porn star he wanted to meet. Jeff passed out in the taxi back to my apartment. When he came to we were groping once again beneath the sheets of my bed.

For some of us—some of us gay men—sex is not the primary modus operandi of our daily life. Yes, our sexuality defines us—men wanting to have sex with other men—but like heterosexuals, there is a wide spectrum to gay sexuality and ethics—some of us want a monogamous relationship, others settle for a sort of "mock" monogamy, some gay relationships are blatantly "open"—each partner fooling around with other partners but coming back emotionally to one another. Some gay men have no desire at all for a permanent or long-term partner—hot, anonymous sex is like a drug for them and all they want.

Sex has an incredible power, of that there is no doubt. It is a vivid, human desire—an intoxicant—and that was why, perhaps, I could not resist Jeff or Vince when the opportunities finally fell into place. My first lover, Will, once said that the human skin needs to be touched, and that was why, when he was ready to begin sex with me, he would start by rubbing the palms of hands beneath my shirt or jeans, searching out the cool patches of my skin to warm against his own. A blind date once told me, however, that we, as gay men, place too much emphasis on sex. A guy I once met at a bar in Atlanta, a psychiatrist, said that the admission of one's own homosexuality was, in itself, an emphasis on one's sexual need.

And so as troubled as I was by the turn of events, there was a certain headiness to it all; I was, after all, a young man barely in his twenties, flattered not only at the thought of sleeping with my two closest friends, but with two men I found both handsome and sexy. I also wanted desperately to be loved by someone, so much so that I had no self-control when it came to sex because that was the path I thought would take me there. But there was also a nervousness encased within this delight that I was experiencing sexually, as if a dark demon seed would be uncovered like the pit of a cherry, indigestible amongst all the sweetness of the fruit. I considered myself to be the source of that potential dissatisfaction, for at the root of my feelings was the desire for something that I also felt was unattainable for myself from either Vince or Jeff. What I wanted was a relationship, something that I felt that they—neither Jeff nor Vince—expected or wanted of me other than one of friendship. But I was also conscious that if I vocally raised this concern with either of them— my wanting "something more"—that I also risked the possibility of losing that friendship.

It was Nina who oddly escalated my affairs, veered the course of events into a direction I hadn't anticipated. She had threatened to throw Jeff's things out onto Bethune Street if they were not moved out of the apartment by the end of the month. Denise, unable to assert herself on Jeff's behalf, caught in a bind between Jeff not paying rent and Nina not having any money and always borrowing from her, sided, with no uncertainty, with the person she was sleeping with, the one she was trying to make into her significant other. Although Denise had confided to Vince that Nina was beginning to drive her crazy—the smoking, the sloppiness, the constant drinking and belching—trouble in paradise as Vince later relayed to me—she decided that if by Jeff being out of the apartment Nina would be happier, then she would have to help make it happen.

Jeff, himself, could have openly showed his feelings of betrayal at this point. But as it happened he was more than willing to oblige and remove his belongings from the apartment, but not before he gave Denise a piece of his mind. Wasn't she aware that Nina was an alcoholic? he asked her. Couldn't she tell that Nina was controlling and manipulative? Had Nina ever repaid even a penny that she had borrowed? "Just wait for the day she really screws you over," Jeff said to Denise at the end of a rather bitter and heated exchange. "It looks like she's already screwed a lot of people. It's only a matter of time before she gets to you, too."

Jeff arranged to store some of his stuff at Vince's apartment, some at mine, the rest he put into a storage locker on 43rd Street near the Hudson River. I had always believed that Jeff was a man who possessed more clothing than furniture, but over the years of living in that tenement on Bethune Street he had amassed quite a collection of record albums, scripts, and magazines, none of which he was willing to part with simply because of Nina. The Saturday Vince and I helped Jeff disperse his belongings throughout sites around Manhattan was a long, tedious and tension-filled one. By dusk we had ended up back at my apartment, cranky and shoving down slices of pizza and drinking beer. Jeff lit a joint he had discovered in one of his drawers and passed it around the room, hoping it would take the edge off the situation. I was lightheaded almost instantly from smoking and I stared around my apartment, alighting on things—a wooden candle holder I had made, a green coffee mug I had bought in Savannah, a black plastic ashtray I had stolen from Jimmy Day's on West 4th Street—trying to find their significance and sentiment in my life. Jeff could not let go of his complaints about Nina, and he was working himself into a more animated state when Vince ordered him to lie on his back on the floor and relax by taking deep breaths. Vince then straddled himself across Jeff's waist and began massaging Jeff's shoulders.

Jeff's shirt soon came off and it was clear to me that Vince's intent was more than a massage. Not wanting to witness the seduction, I lifted myself off the couch and went in the bedroom. Jeff caught me by the ankle as I passed by his neck and I heard myself emit a nervous chuckle, realizing, at that moment, that I was exhausted, drunk, and stoned. The next thing I knew I was on the floor, kneeling as Jeff unbuttoned my jeans, withdrew my cock and began to suck on it. I, of course, offered him no resistance. How is it that that dictum goes? A hard cock knows no conscience?

We ended up in the bedroom that night, smoking another joint, embellishing the sex with a variety of creams and lotions. Somehow I seemed to have been the one who had collected all the residue and afterward I left the two of them in my bed and went to shower. When I returned they had both fallen asleep, Jeff's pale, overmuscled body curled up within itself and using Vince's darker, hairier chest as a pillow.

I dried my hair, slipped on a sweater and jeans and went upstairs to my roof and sat on the railing. Below, on the sidewalks, I could see the tops of heads moving toward Seventh Avenue. Across the street I noticed two guys walking closely together, as if huddled for warmth, but I recognized that it was a different sort of warmth that made them huddle so closely.

While we had been moving Jeff's belongings we had found some of Nina's cigarettes and a lighter in one of Jeff's drawers, and I had shoved them quickly into my jacket before Jeff had a chance to discover them among his things and go into another tirade. Sitting on the roof I found them again, still in my jacket, and I took the package out, shook out one of the cigarettes and lit it. I hadn't smoked a regular cigarette since I left Atlanta, over three years before, and the first puff of nicotine racing into my bloodstream made me instantly dizzy. I held out the feeling though, savored the heaviness in my eyes, wondering how I could extricate myself politely from this burgeoning ménage à trois, without any of the friendships being irreparably damaged. How had I let this happen? Was I that needy? That horny? Was my libido so out of control that I did not let my mind steer it correctly? Would it mean avoiding Vince and Jeff to make my point clear that I didn't want this continue? I began to move into a more nervous, frenzied state. I didn't want to lose them, but I didn't want things to continue on this course. Could they both drop me? Would I have to move to another city?

Keep looking, a voice inside me urged. Get out of this and find someone else. Perhaps, I thought then, if I could convince them that I was falling in love with someone else, wouldn't I be able to graciously bow out of this mess? That logic seemed to me, at that moment, such a clear course of action.

But the first step was the hardest one, of course, one I had been trying to make, after all, for years and years—meet someone. I decided, that night, I would start all over again, and I began by heading downstairs at that very instant and out into the street, walking downtown toward Greenwich Village. But where to go—a bar, the baths, back to the Saint? Wasn't the emphasis of those places primarily sexual? Wasn't it the intent of most of those patrons to get laid? Wasn't my intent—a relationship—hopefully to encompass more than that?

The weather that night held a breezy autumn warmth, and I walked for a long time, closing my eyes against the onslaught of the wind. As it was, my search was fruitless again that night; I ended up in a room at one of the baths in Chelsea avoiding anyone who looked my way, just so I could avoid going back to see Vince and Jeff together in my bed in my apartment.

As it turned out, Jeff and Vince had their own plans. Jeff, now officially homeless, had asked Vince the next morning, realizing the intent of my determined absence, if he wanted to look for a larger apartment to share together. Vince, confiding his own jealousies about Jeff's unending sexual contacts, also revealed his concealed feelings for Jeff, saying he couldn't live with a promiscuous roommate who was also the object of his sexual attention and emotional affection. Jeff, never realizing the depth of Vince's emotions for him, agreed to a compromise: a trial relationship—a "don't ask, don't tell" scenario that at the same time revealed his own jealousies and intimate feelings for Vince. And so a plan was constructed: Jeff would move in with Vince at his current apartment, and if things were still comfortable at the end of the month, they would begin looking for a larger apartment.

In essence, they had shut me out of their relationship before I had had my own chance to decline the invitation.

October folded into November, Jeff and Vince began looking for an apartment, my obsession to see Nathan faded and I continued to prowl the city searching for some sort of avenue into a relationship. Why it meant so much to me, I cannot forthrightly explain, except, perhaps, that it was an instinct to mate and nest and had become, once again, my most important mission. I'm surprised my zeal continued unabated, especially as I began to hear the troubles Denise was having with her own relationship. Mr. and Mrs. Connelly, Denise's parents, had decided to drive up from Kentucky and spend Thanksgiving with Denise in the city. Mrs. Connelly, of course, complained at the very outset of the trip—the long ride in the car, too much holiday traffic, all those tolls they had to pay on the way up—the idea, she let it be firmly known to Denise, had been her husband's not her own. She clutched her purse everywhere she walked in the city, refused to go down into the subways and frowned at the homeless people who slept on the sidewalk grates. She complained bitterly about the five flights up to Denise's apartment, which she was convinced was sucking out all her optimism and strength. It did not prevent her, however, from reorganizing Denise's kitchen cabinets or nagging Denise that the greasy oven racks were destined to be harbingers of bacteria. Throughout the week she kept sighing and dropping her shoulders, "Denise?" she would ask with the disappointed tone of a mother, "How can you live like this?"

Upon her arrival, Mrs. Connelly did possess some satisfaction in the fact that Denise was no longer living with "that man," Jeff, but she was appalled to find that Denise could put up with such squalor from Nina. What appalled her most, though, was Nina's chain-smoking; and Nina purposely overdid her cigarette intake in the hope of driving Mrs. Connelly out of the apartment and

back to her midtown hotel. The two women, without a doubt, were never destined to get along, but what angered Nina the most was that Denise refused
to inform her mother of the exact nature of their relationship. Denise had
boxed up the sketchbooks she had used to draw portraits of Nina and had hidden her lesbian cartoons in drawers that her mother wouldn't disturb.
"Roommates," is how she described her relationship with Nina to
her mother, which infuriated Nina so much that she purposely left her vibrator out on display on the top of the toilet.

"This woman has too much control over your life, Denise," Mrs. Connelly
said shortly after their arrival, her eyebrows arched into a frown. "You were
never this messy before."

"Yes I was, Mother," Denise replied. "You just kept picking up after me."

"Well, can't you find another roommate, then? This one seems, you know,
so mean."

"I like Nina," Denise said, catching herself not to add too much emotion to
her words, in order to keep her feelings secret from her mother.

"You never listen to your mother," Mrs. Connelly said, ending her sentence
with an exasperated breath of air.

"I listen, Mother," Denise answered. "But you're not always right."

"Trust me, darling, a mother knows. Something's different. I can tell something's not making you happy," and it was here that she reached out and
placed her hand fondly against her daughter's cheek. "Your father thinks
you're acting too mannish."

Denise wanted to scream at her mother that it was her visit that was making her a wreck. But it was also Nina's silent combative attitude that was
driving her crazy. What infuriated Nina the most, that long holiday weekend,
was that she had been excluded from Thanksgiving dinner. Mrs. Connelly was
so aghast by the squalor of the apartment—Denise's easels propped up in corners, her artwork still taped to the walls, Nina's panties draped over the shower rod—that she had promptly announced when she arrived that no one would
be cooking or eating in this apartment. They were taking Denise out for a
Thanksgiving dinner. And Mrs. Connelly had made it clear that Nina was not
invited. Denise knew she should have stood up for Nina, insisted that she
come along, but she also recognized a nagging truth caught in her throat that
she didn't want to have to deal with both her mother and Nina at the same
time. Her resistance had finally been worn down. Or was it that she first recognized then that she needed something from Nina to sustain her beyond the
sex?—the only fact, she felt, that was keeping them together.

Nina had retaliated by going to the Duchess that night, getting drunk and
bringing back to the apartment one of her ex-girlfriends. When Denise
returned from her holiday dinner and had dropped her parents off at their
hotel, rattled by having to spend over two hours listening to her mother grill
the waiter about the cleanliness of the kitchen, and discovered Nina in bed
with another woman, she had picked up the phone and dialed my number.

She knew that I could offer her some immediate help since Vince and Jeff were spending the evening at Vince's parents' house in New Jersey.

Denise arrived at my apartment that night all teary eyed and flustered. Her biggest worry, though, was not that Nina had deceived her but how to find a way to get her out of that apartment—permanently. One thing she had learned from her parents' visit, she told me, was that she could no longer live with Nina's temperament. "I've learned to deal with the fact that I'm a lesbian," she said. "What I can't deal with is the fact that I've gotten myself into such an unhealthy relationship."

"Change the locks," I suggested, "and throw her stuff out on the street."

Denise, however, was afraid that Nina would try to drag the super into the quarrel. "Maybe Jeff could move back in," Denise wondered.

"Jeff?" I replied, startled by her suggestion. Jeff and Vince had just moved into an apartment on Greenwich Street and they had already asked me to build a wall of bookcases and slender table that they could use in the kitchen. "But that's not being fair to Vince."

"Not forever," she said. "Just till he drives her out. She hates him. On second thought, maybe they could both move in and force her out."

As it happened a plan did not need to be hatched. Denise's parents went back to Kentucky, Vince and Jeff returned from New Jersey, and Nina, recognizing that she had lost Denise's affection, promptly returned to her ex-lover in Queens.

And so Denise hibernated into her solitude, concentrating more and more on her drawings and cartoons, Jeff and Vince went shopping for a king sized bed, and the holidays settled into the city, the first snow that year falling shortly after Thanksgiving. I seemed to walk more and more across the city, up and downtown, east and west, running errands for Alex, taking last minute jobs of building Christmas tree stands and roping garlands around staircases; I even built a platform for a miniature train set for a guy who lived on York Avenue.

As a child, Christmas was always a lonely time for me; I never had a brother or sister to work up the excitement of the holidays and after my mother died, my father and I exchanged gifts the way construction workers trade sandwiches. Every year I always believed that I would stumble across a way to handle the holiday depression, but each year it got harder and harder, engulfed in a tidal wave of advertising, decorations, and sentiment from everyone from Charles Dickens to Monteverdi.

I've always wanted to have a lover during the holidays, but the opportunity was never there, or, if it was, something always seemed to go awry—at least a lover would burn off the depression of not having a family to go to or not wanting to be with the family I did have—at least that's how I imagined it to be.

Will, when I lived with him, always disappeared back to his family in Florida during the holidays, and Nathan had never lasted long enough to make it to another set of holidays. And so that year, the Christmas of 1980, walking around town and peering into the store windows and lit apartments, I felt my own solitude and misery bunched up again in my shoulders, conscious of having had both the good and bad fortune of meeting Nathan just the year before. My depression, however, nagged me deeper and deeper into my coat, despite the fact that there was so little cold in the weather, and I often felt myself snapping my head out into the air like a turtle suddenly awakened, in hopes that I could try and reinvigorate myself.

The city seemed to me like a vast empty playground without any toys or children, and at night I would walk to a bar on Christopher Street, study the one or two guys who looked as miserable as I did, drink enough to feel a buzz and then leave and find my way home. I never met anyone at the bar those evenings; never even had a conversation—that was not my intent—my intention was solely to get drunk. At home, I would climb back into my bed between the chilly empty sheets and sleep just enough to make it to work the next morning, hung over and still depressed, my mind so thick and clouded I had hoped it would prevent me from being able to think about anything.

Work continued to be a string of odd jobs; Alex apologized every morning I showed up, hungover or not, for the lack of work or the mundane tasks he assigned to me. Finally, Christmas slipped behind us and Denise called and asked if I would go to a New Year's Eve party with her. "Mourning's over," she said, referring to her own plight over Nina. "I'm ready to have some fun again."

I accepted because I was lonely too, tired of drinking alone, tired of getting drunk, tired of waking up in the morning and wondering if I had become the horrible monster my father, miles away, had imagined I had become. The party was at a loft on Spring Street, and on the ride up to the eighth floor apartment in the freight elevator next to Denise I noticed the scent of jasmine and roses, so deliciously out of season, and I turned to her to say something but caught myself noticing the way the curls of her hair were hitting the collar of her coat instead.

Inside, the loft was crowded, too many people, too many dressed in black, and I was suddenly not in a mood to talk to anyone and I headed for the bar at the back of the room. There must have been close to two-hundred people crammed into the space; the apartment was owned by an agent who had taken an interest in some of Denise's drawings. Before Denise parted from me she had pointed him out—a large, graying, overweight man with a ponytail and dark tinted eyeglasses, surrounded by an arrangement of freshly scrubbed All-American young men in tight-fitting black shirts or turtlenecks.

After a few sips from a glass of wine, I was already feeling tired and ready to leave, but I noticed an outdoor terrace encircling the loft and a door next to a shelf of poinsettias. I followed two guys outside who must have had the same idea that I had had—that some fresh air would feel good, but I left them alone and walked to the darker corner of the terrace. Before me was a slender man wearing jeans and a purple silk shirt which fluttered nervously in the cold breeze, leaning over and looking at the street eight stories below.

"Happy New Year," I said, noticing I didn't even startle him, though I had approached silently and cautiously, not wanting to disturb his space, but on recognizing him, I knew I had to say something or I would regret not having seized the opportunity.

He didn't look at me, however, didn't acknowledge my voice, his eyes continued to pitch toward the street, and I could tell there was some kind of drug or drink pumping through his blood, working some sort of introspective sorcery on him. There were a few drops of moisture at the cleft above his upper lip, a strand of his blond hair bobbed in front of a vacant set of eyes. He seemed lost in thought, or either lost in drugs, as if he were hallucinating, and I placed my hand against the base of his back as if it might steady him. "Nathan, are you okay? Aren't you cold?"

He turned and gave me the dimmest sort of recognition, as if we had been schoolchildren together and he was trying to recognize the kid's face within the adult.

"I don't *feel* anymore," he said and closed his eyes, as if looking back through his memory to find a thought. "Something was in the punch," he added and here bequeathed me a wry smile. "I put something in the punch. *My* punch." He wobbled away from me, his arms outstretched like a cross, the wind slapping his shirt against his body like a flag. He walked a bit unsteadily, one foot in front of another, as if treading a tightrope, then stopped abruptly and turned to me, his face pouting like a child's. "You never gave me a chance," he said. "That hurt."

I was stunned to hear him say this; he was, after all, the one who had hurt me, or at least that was the way I believed it to have happened, or the way I had reinvented it after all these months. He walked back to the railing again and leaned out as far as he could into the night. I was suddenly frightened that he would topple over accidentally and I reached out and caught him by his belt, feeling him defiantly pitch his weight over the rail, leaving his fate in my grasp.

And then, that night, I felt him shift his weight out a little further into space. "Take me out of here," he said, throwing his voice more into the wind than to me. "Take me away from all this. *Please.*"

It was Nathan who aggressively pursued me to date again; the evening I arrived at his new apartment he had candles and incense burning through the rooms. He had fixed only a salad and spaghetti for us to eat, and we spent most of the evening sitting around the table weaving comfortably through subjects—movies, books, Broadway musicals, our families, and our pasts.

"I didn't expect you to be so patient," he said when we had cleared the table and I was in the kitchen washing the wine glasses as he loaded leftovers into the refrigerator.

"When you've been burned you learn to keep away from the flame," I answered, not knowing for sure what he was referring to, but knowing my answer could respond to any of several subtexts, whether it was that I had not been sexually aggressive with him throughout the evening, for example, or that I had agreed to see him that evening in the first place.

"I think it helps that we had something going before," he said, "even if it didn't work out exactly as we hoped it would."

I gave him a weary smile and started to leave the kitchen thinking he only intended us to be friends, but this was where he caught my hand and slipped it around his waist. He pulled his body up to me and his eyes searched out mine until they connected. "I mean that in a good way," he added and pecked at me with a kiss. He drew his head back for a moment, as if he was embarrassed by his sudden outpouring of intimacy. But this was where I took my free hand and grasped him at the back of his neck and pulled his mouth back toward mine, parting his lips with my tongue and breathing a rush of air into his body with a passion that even surprised me.

What I had learned in the time since Nathan had first appeared and disappeared was that it was impossible to know completely another person's life, that no matter how much history or knowledge or insight you have of someone, there is always a side that you will never know exists. Nathan never detailed the stories of his own dates during our absence from one another, never explained or admitted to the existence of his prince, but I sensed that something else, something beyond me, had hurt him, for there was, those first few times of seeing Nathan again, an aura of sadness that clung to him, as if a lotion had been rubbed into his skin to numb his feelings. My intent with Nathan, as we began to spend more time together, was far from just sexual— I wanted to be sure I still liked him—and we went shopping together or walked through the city, just hanging out informally with one another, as friends are wont to do, stepping casually into a store that we had no intent of ever buying anything in, just to have another experience to share together. In a way it made us both laugh with each other again, shopping for items we would never want to own—who could ever wear a chain link skirt, for instance, or could you eat off of a $1000 butter plate?

It was a way, too, to bring our dreams closer together; Nathan always pointed out things he liked—sheets, lamps, rugs. "My next apartment," he would always say, and point out an object and where he would place it. I was always caught up in the dream, of course, wondering, for instance, what it would be like to sleep in a bed with a headboard made of thick wooden slats, feeling Nathan's body curled up against mine every night, his breathing against my neck.

But Nathan was full of questions for me as well—he was the one who adamantly wanted to maintain some sort of relationship on a daily basis, refused, too, to let the dynamic of our relationship consist merely of friendship. Every evening that we hadn't arranged to see one another he would call and ask about where I had worked that day, what was I building, what was the client's reaction, what did the office or apartment or loft look like, what did I think about all of it. In this way he came to find pieces of me I had never shown to anyone before: a distaste for expensive china (useless, I felt), poor circulation in my toes (why I always wore socks to bed), a childhood fear of heights (the reason why I had reached out to keep him from falling, that evening, even though he said he always maintained his balance—which wasn't true). But he also would draw me purposely into a kiss when I least expected it, coming out of the bathroom, for instance, or press his hand against my crotch or my ass while we were watching TV, or while walking through the city, take his hand and slyly cup my elbow, as if I were an elderly man who had lost his balance.

In fact, those first few weeks Nathan and I were together again, I worried about his balance a lot. When I suggested one evening that we go dancing at the Saint he turned angry and vehement. "That would be the easiest place to lose you," he grumbled, dismissing the suggestion. Another time, he said his concentration was no good when I wasn't around, which is why he wanted to do some drawing while I was over one evening at his apartment—he thought about me too much while I was away from him, as if he were fearful of losing me again, and before I arrived he called and suggested that I make sure I had some reading material to keep myself entertained while he worked. Once, in a diner on Eighth Street, he asked me if I still found him attractive—it had been a couple of days since we'd had sex. "Of course I do," I answered, alarmed by the question, worried that perhaps I had not proved enough my infatuation to Nathan. "I'll take you into the restroom right now and fuck your brains out, if that's what you want. That's how attractive I find you. But if I did that, Nathan, I know I would lose you too quickly. It would burn out like that," I said and snapped my fingers. "I want you to stay around."

That was, in fact, exactly what he wanted to hear and I suppose an impartial bystander could accuse me of nurturing an unhealthy relationship with Nathan. The truth is that I fed off Nathan as much as he did off me. There was something chemically—emotionally and physically—that I got from Nathan that I never felt with anyone else, not even Vince or Jeff.

When does a boyfriend become a lover? Is there a progression in feelings? A sequence of events that determines when the definition changes? Does it follow a pattern like heterosexual rites into manhood: first fist fight, first erection, first shave, first girlfriend? Perhaps something on the order of first kiss, first date, first night over at his place?

When do you stop agonizing over whether he will call you or is it too soon to call him? When does he begin to sit inside your brain and you wonder what he is doing when he is not with you? When can you repattern his day in your mind into one of a faithful or, at least, trusting lover?—trusting, in the sense, that he will want to return to you. All I know is what I felt for Nathan the first time I met him. What I felt the first time we had sex together. I know what I felt when I broke up with him the first time, too, when I realized he was seeing other men. I know how difficult it was to move through the days without his presence beside me or comfortable within my thoughts, how miserable it was to understand the conflict between my own jealousies and obsessions. And I know how much I wanted a relationship with him to work. And I know, truthfully, that I loved Nathan as much as a friend and a companion as I desired him sexually. Love was a match that had suddenly flamed in my chest, windless and unwavering, with no concept of burning out over time, as if it had been placed, protected and enclosed, by a glass dome and set up high on some kind of imaginary altar. Why, then, was I so worried that my happiness, finally unearthed and polished, the thing I had yearned for so desperately since my journey to Manhattan, was once again making me feel too vulnerable?

"Every question in the universe does not have an answer," Will said to me one night while he was cooking dinner, though for every fault or flaw I ever confronted him with, he tried to generate an explanation. What I liked about

Will—no, what I loved about Will—had a lot to do with the quantity of time we spent together, or, rather, the passage of time that we had together—the longer I spent with Will the more deeply I fell in love with him, despite the fact that the reverse was true for him. For one thing, there was the warmth and security I felt from sleeping with Will every night; six weeks after we started dating each other, I moved out of my dorm and into the house he owned behind the campus library. For the next five months I spent every night with him, even when I realized he had begun seeing someone else in the afternoons.

At first there were the intensely passionate nights—often, we could not even make it through dinner before we tumbled into bed or, perhaps, began consuming one another on the rug or the kitchen floor, a pot or a plate crashing onto the tiles, heightening the brutish physicality of it all as we wrestled our bodies from one position to another. At night, exhausted from lying awake and just holding him in my arms, I would run my fingers lightly through the thick gray hair at his temples, or outline the profile of his nose and the cleft of his chin with the tip of a finger, listening to the rain tap against the black window panes or the wind lift and swing the rose bushes that grew outside and would brush up against the bedroom wall nearest the bed, and then, finally, I would fall into a light, conscious sleep, only to be aroused by him again nudging me into sex or asking me questions about what I wanted to become of my life with him. Lust, I learned, in that young, impressionable era of mine, soon faded into feelings, feelings much deeper than I had ever imagined possible from myself, and I found I could not bear to be out of Will's presence. I showered with him, fixed breakfast with him, memorized the clothes he wore so that when I left the house with him when he went to his office, my mind could follow him throughout his day—sit with him during his appointments with graduate students, know where he was going for lunch, what he would lecture about to his classes, what he said to someone he was leaning over to and speaking with in the hall. I wanted to be entirely with him, wanted to know how he felt, how he reacted to everything in his world.

That desire turned into possessiveness, and that possessiveness turned into an ugly jealousy. But before that happened, before I reached that nasty point, I found a comfortable place with Will and how I came to need his body. There was something to the familiarity of his skin, night after night, that continued to arouse me, the way the hair grew sparsely around his navel and traveled up his stomach in a thin line and then unfurled like an eagle's spread at his chest, covering two small brown nipples that I could suck and twist on in my mouth like the head of a pin. Some men find rapture through the variety or newness or anonymity of sexual partners—strangers who quicken the pulse—but what I loved about Will was the way I came to know how he felt in my hands, the nubby texture of his back and the padded flesh at his shoulders that he had once built up with muscles, but most of all I loved how Will explained to me what he wanted, desired, and needed from me physically, in essence, what felt good to him. Communication was always Will's most admirable asset, even as we were breaking up, a fact that he would announce over and over, even as he would draw me more forcibly and desirably into sex.

I knew how he liked me to sweep my fingers through the hair of his chest, the tips of my fingers running along his shoulders, how he liked me to angle my body through the tweezers of his legs and go down on him, my hands buried beneath his ass, squeezing them forcibly as if kneading dough. I knew he liked me to graze my fingertips along the length of his body, that he enjoyed my massage of his feet as much as my licking the underside of his balls like a cat.

But what came to happen, though, was that he began to keep his body away from me, or, rather, he began to remove his mind from the physical act as mine buried itself profoundly within his skin. In bed, sex together came to be me having sex with him, me pleasing him almost selflessly, as if he were an inanimate object whose lust I would have to shake almost violently awake to arouse. It worked, of course; this was the way that Will had designed it to be, that I would have to knock him into his passion. But the passion was soon hardly ever reciprocal, however, and it came to feel as if it were a test for me to see how much it would take before I could make him feel for me. I would find myself hovering over him, straining with an erection, sucking him, rimming him, fucking him, pushing and pushing for him to feel me till my orgasm came like tears of animosity.

It was only when the photographs and magazines began appearing regularly in bed that my feelings really began to be hurt, not that I had shunned such visual aids before—they had been hot, diverting scenarios at times, especially when Will would create one that included me in it—a police officer or an army sergeant, for instance, interrogating me on some minor misdemeanor, making the good boy beg before the bad one—but now he began to use them to exclude me—as I would lean over and begin to blow him, for instance, he would enter into the fantasy of being with a beefy centerfold model, completely shutting my presence out of his head.

How do you keep a man's attention? I wondered. By being distant? By pushing too much? Was there too much sex with Will, or, rather, too much emphasis on sex to make things work? Did he desire not to be with me when we were outside the bedroom? Questions came to me in a frenzy and I began to miss my classes, began to feel like I was going to jump out of my skin. I would sit in the library, trying to read, staring, fidgeting, thinking of nothing but why Will was purposely hurting me. And then one evening he brought a young man home named Stephen—tall, lanky, thick brown hair and a beautiful boyish face marred only by acne scars at his cheeks. When the three of us ended up in bed later I knew it was time for me to leave, that things could not be with Will as I wanted them to be in my life. I promised myself I would never let another man hurt me like that. Two months later, at the end of the term, I was on a train to New York City, vowing I would never let another man have that much power over my life—a vow I would find over and over again too difficult to keep.

"Of course I feel guilty about it," Vince said to me one afternoon at the gym while we were waiting for a rather sweaty and hirsute, overweight man to finish with the chest machine. "I'm doing exactly what I asked him not to do." Vince leaned over and shook his head so that the beads of sweat that had collected at the ends of the longer black bangs of his hair that curved against his forehead plummeted like rain drops into the flat gray pad of the floor carpeting. But he still could not hide his grin from me. "Three months into a relationship and I'm already fooling around big time. Have I no shame?"

Vince had met his current infatuation, a waiter at Clyde's, one morning when he and Jeff had stumbled into the restaurant after dancing all night at the Saint. I knew exactly the man Vince was describing before he said his name—Matt. In my opinion, he was as close to a physical clone of Vince as anyone could find in the city: dark, short cropped hair, bushy mustache and a hairy, pumped up body framed by a flannel shirt and jeans.

"He's really sweet," Vince said, as if Jeff were not, and I frowned and it was my turn to shake my head in disgust, gathering my sweat up into the arm of my T-shirt. I was, at that point, already thinking about looking for an apartment to share with Nathan. And Vince had hinted it would be good for me—good for us. I only wanted for him and Jeff what he had indicated he had wanted for me.

Vince always felt that Jeff was too independent to be successful in a relationship; he didn't need Vince, drifting through life in his own little world, narrowly focused on the person and the moment he was in—and for an actor Vince felt Jeff was also pretty stingy with his emotions, at least whenever he was off the stage. Vince felt he could never expect any sort of spontaneous gift from Jeff—a rose or a box of cookies, or even a kiss on the cheek upon walking through the door. Everything always felt so planned and scheduled and timed.

Jeff once explained to me that it was because he was never an outwardly affectionate person. It had a lot to do with the competitive nature he developed as a boy—always trying to be the best—the best outfielder, the best hitter, the best receiver, the best scorer. In fact, during conversations, he always found himself trying to tell a better story than the previous anecdote someone had just related, for instance, another trait which irritated Vince to distraction.

"I'm not giving Jeff up," Vince said, a dark wave of realization coming across his brow. "Why is it the more sex I get from him the more I want it from other people?" The sweaty guy jumped off the machine and Vince frowned at him as he passed us by, then Vince stepped up to the blue painted steel machine, brusquely wiping the sweat off the back cushion with the white hand towel he had carried slung across his shoulder. He seated himself into the machine, and I moved to stand beside him. He looked up at me, trying to make me knock away my now very conspicuous frown. "I'm addicted to him," Vince said, adjusting the weight bar. "And I'm addicted to sex. What can I say?

There's nothing wrong with me. This is the Eighties. Relationships are different. Why should I change my life because I'm falling in love?"

But the truth was Vince and Jeff were friends first, foremost against the fact that they were experimentally living together as lovers. They genuinely thrived on talking to one another, thrived, really, on annoying one another, too, of having a safety net, for example, when they had no desire to go to see a movie alone. Vince said it worked for him because he had never had a close friend when he was growing up, that he was too bookish and razzed for being an academic nerd. Jeff felt it was, in part, because his family had failed him. His father was too distant and his mother too self-absorbed in her own miseries. In many ways Jeff felt that Vince fulfilled one of his most intimate fantasies. "Friends," he said to me one night while we were walking across town to the opening of a new dance performance piece in the East Village, "are the family you make for yourself."

His concept had struck me, then, as such a powerful logic for a gay man to recognize and hold passionately as his belief. I had always placed a strong value on my friendships. I found my first friend at the bus stop when I started first grade. Craig lived about a mile from my house and once my mother accepted the fact that I could walk to Craig's house after school without her help, I began to spend afternoons there with him, climbing up into the dusty attic of the old Victorian house Craig's grandparents had owned and passed along to his parents, lying on a cot and blowing dust off of old magazines and books, watching Craig give me a tour of his life, as if he already possessed the contents of a museum.

Craig was two years older than I was and I had embodied him with a sense of wisdom I desired myself to possess. He loved to tell stories, loved to draw out the objects he stored in the Dutch Master's cigar box he had acquired from his grandfather, loved to embellish these very stories with fantastic details. A raven's feather, for instance, had come from the witch's pet who lived where the Little Pigeon Creek began, a string of beads he had stolen from an Indian near Cherokee Falls, the wire-rim eyeglasses had been his great-great-grandfather's in Switzerland, the lenses handmade by a superhero who compressed together Egyptian sand, the seeds were from the orange tree from his grandmother's—his mother's mother—back yard in Florida and could grow into magical fruit.

Galena was growing from a small, sleepy south Georgia town into a suburban retreat from Atlanta, and often after school, Craig and I would walk through the woods and over the ridge to where a new subdivision was being built. Craig loved to pick up large chunks of dried red clay and send them smashing to bits at his feet. Even more, he loved to catwalk along the basement foundation of a new house that was being built, his arms outstretched as if he were a circus gymnast. My father had forbidden me to play near the construction trailers and empty new houses, so every time Craig and I ended up there I felt as if I had become the disobedient and disrespectful son.

It's hard for me, even now, to explain the manipulative hold my father had on me, even at that early age. I was raised in a religion of shame and fear and guilt; life was black and white to my father, good and evil, redemption and temptation, and I came at an early age to think like that as well, that life was a series of cause and effect circumstances, so when, in second grade, I fell off the foundation of a wall and broke my arm, my father called Craig the most evil influence that could happen in my life. Craig had begun sneaking cigarettes from his mother's purse, and I, too, had the keen sense that I was doing something wrong whenever I was in his company. So when my father prayed for me to repent my evil ways, I really tried to do so, but I also struggled with losing a friend for reasons I did not understand. For weeks after I had broken my arm, I dreamed at night I was falling off ledges and cliffs, over and over, a bad boy being plunged into hell. I only wanted to feel better, stop the dreams—the only advice my father offered me to make them stop was, of course, for me to change my ways.

And so Craig passed on to another group of friends, or, rather, he began to hang out with an older crowd, sixth graders, and after a period of moping about the house, I settled into becoming a more dutiful son. Still, life in those years was not to be without other villains; my father could resurrect a temptation at the drop of a hat. Whenever unfortunate events happened, for example, my father was happy to invoke the wrathful judgment of God. So it was no joke to me that when in first grade, for instance, my teacher began drilling us to curl beneath our desks and clasp our hands together at the back of our necks in order to live through the bombs the communists were sure to launch at us. I would arrive at home shaking, scared, worried the world was soon to end. My father also magnified that fear; the communists to him were surely the devil undisguised, and so it was little surprise to me when a few months later, President Kennedy was shot and my father, sobbing, blamed it all on the Russians.

I remember this now because it is an important part of my past, a piece of my history as it were, a footnote for how my mind works today—how when I hear of something, some event, I immediately try to connect it with some plausible past behavior. It was why, when Will began to look for other lovers, I felt there must be something wrong with me, or something, perhaps, that I had done wrong. And it was why, when Vince said to me that afternoon he was fooling around on Jeff, I felt an ominous sensation that something unfortunate was to happen. God, history, and my father were intertwined into my past and present inexplicably; years and years of this way of thinking had unfortunately bequeathed me my own set of dysfunctional insecurities.

And then in May of 1981 Vince's father died unexpectedly; while working at his desk at a freight shipping company in Newark he suffered an aneurysm in his brain and was dead before the ambulance arrived. The wake began the first hot, humid day we had had that year, a forecast of another sweltering summer, and Nathan and I took the train out to Hoboken with Jeff, the three of us silently reading a newspaper or a book, trying to make the best of our expedition out of the city.

Jeff was dressed in a pin-striped businessman's suit that day, and though he was strikingly handsome he was miserably uncomfortable, his muscles straining the seams of the fabric every time he moved. The section of the train where we had found seats was not air-conditioned and though the trip entailed only a few minutes journey out of Manhattan, I could feel my shirt sticking to the back of the seat before we had left the station. By the time we got off the train in New Jersey the collar of Jeff's white shirt was transparent from his sweat. Nathan, however, had the ability to never look overheated; preppily attired in khakis, a white shirt and a blue and red tie, he had even managed to read the newspaper without his fingers being stained gray from the ink. When we were outside the station Jeff pulled a sheet of paper from his coat pocket where he had written down the instructions when Vince had called. He studied his notes for a moment as I shifted uneasily beside him from foot to foot, dizzy from both the heat and hunger. Jeff handed me the sheet and sighed loudly and then pulled a joint from another coat pocket. He lit it and took a deep drag while Nathan and I watched him. "That way," he said, looking to his left and he passed the joint to Nathan, who took a small, polite toke and then passed the joint along to me. We walked single file then for a while, passing the joint back and forth to one another.

Vince had been raised as a Catholic and the wake was at a tiny storefront funeral home. Upstairs, in a darkly paneled room, short, portly men with black hair, black eyes, and black suits were clustered near the vent where an air-conditioner hummed a poor attempt at a breeze into the room. Jeff made his way over to Vince and his mother, who sat in a row of chairs near the open casket, her white gloved hands folded across a purse she held in place on her lap. She looked stoic but stunned by the loss of her husband of thirty-seven years, her gray hair pinned in a bun at the back of her neck, a single strand of pearls lost in the folds of her black dress that began at her collar and continued below her knees. Vince was dressed in a black suit and he had lost that elegant evening Manhattan edge of his that day, or, at least, left it behind in the city. He looked older and more tired than I had ever seen him before—not a young man at all, more like an executive returning home from a stressful day on the job, a slump about his shoulders and his brow lined with creases. It made me so consciously aware, once again, of how we never see or understand the complete picture of someone else, no matter how well we think we know them.

Vince's mother leaned her head up to Jeff when he approached her, nodded and accepted his kiss on the cheek when he bent down toward her, their faces momentarily frozen together like a photograph. Nathan and I awkwardly shook Vince's hand, as if we were teammates about to begin a game of baseball, and he introduced us to his mother and two cousins who were standing nearby. It was then that Vince's older sister Julia appeared, a thin, nervous looking girlish version of Vince. Instinctively she relieved him of the familial duties of attending to his mother, and he walked with us over to his father's casket.

It was clear where Vince had gotten his good looks, his father appeared to be a patrician, elderly version of him, and as the four of us stood before the casket, I felt the fuzziness in my head from the pot I had smoked escaping into sobriety. "He never knew about me," Vince laughed nervously. "I told my mother, but not him. And I know she didn't tell him. I think he suspected it, though. I could never seem to make him proud that I was his son. When I was seven he took me to see my first Broadway show. *Camelot* at the Majestic. He had no idea what he had done to me. I bought the cast album; I memorized the lyrics; I made him take me to see the show again. I didn't disappoint him till he realized that I didn't want to be a hunter. He and my uncle used to take me deer hunting in Pennsylvania, but they never got how much I hated it. I used to stamp on branches purposely and cough a lot, just so they couldn't get a buck. My thirteenth birthday he gave me a .300 Savage rifle with a scope. I wanted to see *Hair*. He didn't understand why I was just as disappointed as he was."

Vince walked back and took his place beside his mother. Jeff looked at us for a moment as if we were two scrawny boys asked to play on a big boys team, then went and stood beside Vince. Vince seemed momentarily shaken by Jeff's presence at his side, but no one seemed to give it any notice, and Vince relaxed for the first time since we had arrived, introducing Jeff to the steady stream of visitors as "my roommate Jeff."

"I never thought they would want to be together," Nathan said as we sat in folding chairs at the back of the room. From where we sat it seemed to me that Vince and Jeff could even be mistaken for brothers; though they looked so dissimilar, their body language betrayed an unspoken bonding and intimacy with one another, as if they had known each other for generations. For a moment, it seemed to me as if Vince ached to be embraced by Jeff, the way he leaned into Jeff's profile as if he were out to detect his scent.

"They're both so independent," I responded, placing my left hand so that it rested against Nathan's leg. This was one of those moments that a gay man wishes he could show a public intimacy with his lover, but instead must find ways to adapt in order not to shock or disturb people who might not understand. Across the room, I watched Jeff steady himself by placing a hand on Vince's shoulder as he leaned to shake the hand of a shorter man who had approached them, as if he knew, intuitively, that Vince wanted to be touched by him.

"Maybe that's why they work so well together," Nathan said. "They haven't given in to one another."

"But they feed off each other," I said, sensing at that moment a connection more spiritual than sexual. "Vince wasn't himself until Jeff got here."

"They're hardly role models," Nathan said, as if ready to start a fight.

I turned and gave him a surprised look. "Vince has been seeing another guy named Matt. From the gym," he said. "Jeff told me. Jeff knows all about him."

"And he puts up with it?" I asked, fighting not to show my alarm that Jeff knew everything Vince had been up to.

"It's obvious that they get something from one another besides just sex."

"Who?"

"Vince and Jeff." Nathan squirmed uneasily in his seat. "None of us are saints," he added and then squirmed again. "Even straight men can have gay sex," he laughed nervously. "Especially Italians," he added with a whisper. "I mean, look at Vince's mother, then look at his father. I'm sure he must have had a mistress or something else on the side."

"Not all of us have your sex drive," I responded, with a more bitter edge to my voice. "Or your lack of faith in relationships."

"Sex isn't the only thing in a relationship," Nathan added, a bit too hurriedly. "And I'm not saying that his parents didn't love each other. It's the same with Denise's parents. Her mother fooled around on her father."

"Her mother fooled around?"

"Mrs. Connelly has had a dancing partner for years. They take classes together. They go out square dancing. They go to the State Fair every year."

"What makes you think they're fooling around?"

"They buy each other gifts. She wears a ring he gave her. You figure it out."

"Did Denise tell you this?"

"Not exactly in those words."

"How do you know all this then?" I asked, raising my voice above a whisper.

"People talk. I listen."

It was then, at that moment, that I stopped talking, ready to shut Nathan out of my world, wondering how much of our own lives had floated out into conversations he had had with other people. Nathan sensed me closing him off; there was, after all, some sort of dynamic, some sort of spiritual connection between us as well.

"All we can expect of someone is that they will be there when we need them," he said. "Good and bad. Like now." And it was here that Nathan took hold of my hand, slipped his fingers through mine and placed our hands together on my thigh. I was embarrassed by his outward expression of affection, worried how the response might culminate around us, but Nathan refused to give in to my discomfort. "I'm serious about us living together," he said.

I nodded my head, still worried about our hands. "I don't want there to be any secrets between us," he added. I nodded again, sending my gaze out into the room. "I think you should know I slept with Jeff before we met."

My stare jolted back to our hands still clasped on the top of my leg. Had I not slept with Jeff myself I would have been disturbingly jealous. But I also couldn't yank my hand away from Nathan, it was rooted in place; Nathan was grasping my hand even tighter now. "Nathan," I announced his name in a forceful whisper. "Do me a favor. Some things I don't want to know. I'm not interested in hearing about your affairs."

He tilted his head toward his lap, as if boyishly ashamed he even mentioned the subject. "I just want you to know you have my heart," he said.

There is a way of walking in Manhattan that breathes a sense of suddenness into life, how the unexpected can happen at any turn of any corner—a prostitute in hot pants and a halter top throwing up in a garbage can, film crews of men with paunchy stomachs and oversized workboots redirecting traffic because of a movie shoot, klieg lights unnaturally lighting a normally darkened street. Part of the joy I found from tumbling into and around this kind of world was due to my feeling that I was always at the edge of things, watching, as it were, as if from a balcony or ledge. Nathan, however, made me feel as if I were part of the world. Living in Manhattan one spends a great deal of time navigating the streets, one feels a certain investment in current history, too— everything seems to be reported in the terms of the latest trend or event—a new fashion designer, a new exhibition at the Met, a new opening night on Broadway, a new band discovered on the Lower East Side. But as the new decade unfolded there was also a consciousness of how it might be defined, a sense of novelty surrounding everything that was introduced, from Reagan's ascendancy to the Presidency to cable TV to hand-held Donkey Kong computer games.

Walking through Manhattan it is possible to define yourself through others' looks, your good mood reflected, for instance, by a stranger's too long stare or lifted eyebrow, your looks or sexiness evaluated by a glance over your shoulder to see if a cruise is perhaps returned. As Nathan and I began to date one another more seriously, I found my strides through the city full of joyous expectation; I found the better I felt about myself and him the more attention I received on the street. I loved walking around corners at a too fast pace, some tune bouncing through my head, loved strolling through a store aware only of my peripheral vision, loved walking to meet Nathan at the deli, looking for him in a bookstore, or finding him waiting for me in the queue for a new movie. Nathan was still drafting for an uptown architectural firm, still wanting to shift into the rendering department. Wherever we walked in the city Nathan carried a small notebook that he kept in his coat pocket and we would often stop so that he could sketch the facade of a building, the moldings around a window, or the frame of a doorway. Sometimes I would lean against the side of a building and watch him as he stood across the street from a lobby, trying to capture the angle for the perspective of his drawing.

Not long after Vince's father's funeral, Nathan had escalated his desire for us to find our own apartment to share. And so I agreed, without any sort of hesitation, to search for an apartment that we could share together. And so that Friday morning in 1981 before the Fourth of July, a day Alex had given me off, I had packed a light lunch in my backpack and walked from the West Village up Ninth Avenue to meet Nathan by Tavern on the Green in Central Park, to look at apartments on the Upper West Side of the city.

So I was stunned while sitting on the bench waiting for Nathan to show up by an article I read on the back page of the first section of *The New York Times*: "Rare Cancer Seen in 41 Homosexuals." I studied the facts it detailed over and over: Kaposi's sarcoma, gay cancer, men in San Francisco and New York City. I remember feeling, in those moments, as if the world had slipped from under my feet, as if some sort of earthquake had happened, some seismic shift had occurred but that I had managed to keep my balance. Nevertheless, it rattled my soul as much as any other unexpected historic event.

It wasn't that I expected, then, the worst that was yet to come; it was the belief, contained somewhere within the article, that homosexuality could be somehow biologically predisposed. My attraction to Nathan, then, could be explained in chemical terms, the way I always believed it to have happened, and it was not something I chose or a behavior I had mimicked or learned. It was proof to me that being gay was not an indulgence in lustful behavior, not a sin, but that something far greater, biologically, was at work within myself. But what rattled me even further was the thought that there could be a gay cancer. A cancer that was gay? How did disease fit into this pattern of behavior?

It's amazing to me now that I remember so much from that day and that moment, the way the sunlight hit the leaves of the trees above me when I looked up, as though to ask God a question. I remember the jeans I wore, shredded into white threads at the knees, the red T-shirt emblazoned with the *New York* magazine logo that was a size too small for me and pinched me beneath my underarms, the fact that I had not yet shaved that morning and I ran my fingers vigorously against my upper lip and chin, listening to the sandy sound of my hand against the stubble of my beard.

Nathan had not seen the article, and when he arrived he sat and read it after I pushed the newspaper at him.

"I don't understand what it means," he said when he had finished and I took the paper out of his hands. "What would make a cancer gay?" His eyes met mine and then suddenly followed a pigeon that lifted off the ground and into the sky.

"What makes you and me gay?" I asked him back. He stood and brushed the soot from the back of his pants, looked at me as though he had found a book in a library that he had once read and loved. I shrugged my shoulders and followed him through the park, my legs feeling rubbery, as if I were treading on the thin foam of a mattress.

"I just am," he answered, twisting a leaf off a tree and rubbing it in his hand. "It's just what I feel. Why are my eyes green? Why is my hair still blond? I don't have answers for those questions."

"But you inherited those," I said. "They're part of your roots. It's your genetic map. Maybe there's a gay chromosome or something."

"But what makes you realize you have it?" he asked, not entirely convinced. "There has to be something psychological there as well."

"So is a gay cancer psychological?" I asked. "Is it caused by what you think or believe?" At the back of my mind was my father's belief that disease was caused by sin or a lack of faith in God. When I was six years old and had my tonsils out my father had said I had not prayed enough. And when my mother got cancer, he blamed himself for her illness; my father had once been tempted by another woman, he had confessed to me one night while we were driving to see my mother in the hospital, though he neglected to state if that desire had been consummated.

"Being gay doesn't make you sick," Nathan said with an annoyed tone, and began walking at a faster pace so that I trailed a few feet behind him. Then he stopped and turned, looking me straight in the eye again, this time his expression uneasy and more compressed. "Why do you always worry so much?"

Feeling a defensive response flash up my spine, I narrowed my eyes and said, "I don't worry. I wonder about things. There's a big difference. We can drop the subject."

That was the end of that conversation that day though I walked for a while with an anger simmering within my body, stepping spasmodically now on top of what seemed like the huge chunklike foam squares of the ground, trying to sort out my relationship with Nathan and trying to evaporate the fear that was brewing within me that I could become sick because I was gay. We looked at several apartments that afternoon, none to Nathan's liking, then went and saw a movie near Lincoln Center. By dinner time, fortunately, I had forgotten why I had become so upset.

But in the days that followed the conversation kept materializing over and over, repeated with the urgency of the best kind of gossip. Denise believed that everyone was potentially gay, every person possessed a feminine and masculine side, though it was expressed differently around each person with whom we came into contact. But the *Times* was wrong, she said to me over lunch one day. What about lesbians? If a cancer could be homosexual, then why weren't women getting it, too? How could the *Times* be wrong? Jeff laughed when I told him what Denise had said. Don't they consider themselves the "newspaper of record." Denise later pointed out to us that the reporters didn't actually do the medical research themselves, they only wrote the story, so of course there could be room for mistakes. Vince, still upset over his father's death and his mother's mourning, told me he thought I was becoming too existential again. "Things just are," he snapped at me the afternoon when I called and woke him up from a nap. "Some things just happen."

I had always wanted Alex to become more of a friend than an employer, but the truth was, he wasn't interested in that kind of relationship with me. My sexual orientation was no secret to the other workers who found jobs through him—many times I had gone out on assignments that required a crew of three or four men and I had soon learned which guys were comfortable with me and which ones weren't. For that fact I think that Alex was always on his guard with me, conscious of not showing me any special attention, or, rather, more conscious of not swinging open his own closet door, or, worse, worrying if I was going to rattle the doorknob a bit too loudly. Still, I talked openly with Alex about my growing relationship with Nathan, but I only learned of his involvement with other guys through my conversations with Vince. Alex's bisexuality had evaporated the more he found himself involved with young men—even the skittish, just-off-the-bus-soon-to-be-hustlers he was so strongly attracted to. Vince was always telling me about who Alex was dating or whom he had encountered at the baths and at times it was difficult for me not to enter Alex's office with a smirk on my face, knowing, for instance, that the reason why he was so sleepy looking was because he had been at the Anvil the night before.

"I'm not aging well," Alex yelled and slammed the phone down one day when I had wandered into his office. "Why is it that every queen wants a trompe l'oeil on her wall?"

I was seated across the desk from him, and I watched him take both hands and pound them against his skull. "Too many people read *Architectural Digest*," I said, hoping to make Alex laugh, but watching him, instead, restlessly click the buttons of his phone. Alex, I knew from Vince, was not in good spirits. He had been battling an ongoing stomach problem and had dropped close to ten pounds, losing, as he did with the weight, his healthy demeanor. A gastrointestinal specialist had recommended exploratory surgery, which Alex was adamant about not even considering. On top of that the guy Alex had been seeing had dumped him for a college student from Germany, and Alex's experiments with a hair-growing tonic had yielded only minimal results, a bit of gray fuzz and a few scaly red patches on the top of his head—blotchy, puffy patches which looked like they were painful if touched. I had even heard Alex was considering a hair transplant, willing to try to surgically move some of the hair that ringed his skull up to the top of his brow to make himself look younger and healthier. It was odd, I thought, to hear things secondhand about someone I worked so closely with, relied on, really, as the source of my income, counted on, as well, for the way I could live my life. I wanted to ask him what was so upsetting to him, what was wrong, but I feared too much about breaking that superficial relationship that worked so well between us.

"Everybody wants to believe they have a bigger apartment," I said, having just finished the day before tearing down Denise's wall of Japanese screens that I had built for her years before to give her sagging tenement apartment an airier and brighter feel.

"Robbie," Alex said, scratching at the bald plate of his forehead, "if I sketched some shelves for you, could you build them in my apartment?"

"Your apartment?" I answered, a bit too flabbergasted by his suggestion.

"I want to make the room warmer."

"Warmer?"

"Homier," he added.

"Homier?"

"I'm gonna move some more of my stuff out of Jersey," he said.

"Sure," I said, somewhat surprised by this new assignment. Homier, after all, meant the accumulation and acceptance of one's history, and Alex, I knew, seldom regarded his life in New Jersey, except, well, when he felt it could connect him to someone—emotionally, financially or, even, sexually.

"Sure," I said. "When should I start?"

"No rush," he replied. "And I want this to look really solid."

"Solid?" I answered.

"Like it was built into the apartment," he said. "I don't want anyone to ever be able to tear it down without a lot of help."

I was never to build those shelves for Alex. Something or another was always postponing it—Alex had the flu and was out sick or he had just met a new boyfriend or his son was visiting for a few days. For a while I kept trying to reschedule the time to devote to Alex's project, then finally gave up on it when I realized that if he wanted it bad enough, he would reschedule the time with me.

And then in August Jeff signed with an agent and almost immediately landed a role in a television commercial that was shooting for two days in a suburb of Philadelphia; the story board cast Jeff as a husband and father protecting his family with a well thought out insurance plan. Filming took place at a house and a pool as photogenic as the cast; Jeff spent the first day jumping in and out of the pool in boxer shorts and lying on a deck chair lifting the baby who was cast as his child up into the air above his head.

It was clear from the outset that the actress who was cast as the wife and Jeff possessed little chemistry together—she wouldn't allow Jeff to kiss her and wouldn't stand close to him for more than a few seconds at a time. By the end of the day, it was apparent that something was greatly amiss—the real mother of the baby wouldn't let Jeff hold the child, and the director was busily rewriting the next day's scenes. It was the first time Jeff ever felt discriminated against because he was gay, a victim, he said, of apparent homophobia. How they knew, Jeff did not explicitly explain to me, though he hinted it might have had something to do with the way he had flirted with the union grip on the shoot during one of the breaks.

Jeff sucked in a lot of his own pride that day; he kept telling himself he needed the work, needed the exposure, needed the money, too, so that he could buy the rug that Vince had seen at Bloomingdale's and wanted to get for their bedroom. The next day, sitting around waiting for the director to work him into a scene, Jeff found his mood sinking even lower—he missed the camaraderie of his friends at the gym, missed the beach towel gossip of the Pines, missed the witty dinner talk and bitchy phone conversations, missed Vince's casual affection as they worked through their chores in the apartment. But it was also his part in this shameless display of heterosexuality that really began to bother him, and as he sat there in the shade of a table umbrella he found his thoughts wandering more and more to his own family, and how his hatred of his father kept making him gloomier and gloomier.

It wasn't so much the history of the electroshock therapy his father had demanded be done to cure Jeff's homosexuality that so bothered Jeff, it was the memory of his father's buddy-buddy behavior throughout his life. When Jeff was a boy, his father had touched him and patted him, tweaked his ass when he hit the ball to the outfield or intercepted a pass, so that when, as a young man, Jeff began to mimic his father's behavior with other young men his same age, his father immediately regarded it as offensive and perverted. It produced in Jeff, then, an isolation and withdrawal, a distance from others that he would not let anyone penetrate, and waiting there that afternoon for the director's instructions, he felt himself closing up again. He went inside the house and asked the production assistant if he could use the phone. He dialed Vince at the apartment in Manhattan and when Vince answered the phone, Jeff said, succinctly, "I think it's getting too serious, Vince. I need you to stop seeing Matt. And I think you should know I love you."

We had seen five apartments that Saturday afternoon at the end of the summer. By the time we had reached Chelsea my feet were so sore from the new boots I was breaking in that all I wanted to do was to give up and go back to my apartment and take a nap. Nathan had insisted we see this last one, however—he had gotten an early edition of the real estate section of the *Times* from a friend of a friend he had hounded—and he felt certain that this apartment, on the cusp of the Village at 13th Street between Sixth and Seventh Avenues, would be taken if we waited another day. Nathan's mission to find the perfect apartment for us to share was honestly wearing me down; he was a lot more specific than I would ever have been on my own—the kitchen of one apartment we had seen was too small, the bedroom floor tilted in another, the one on Eighth Avenue was too noisy from the street traffic. It wasn't as if we had such an expendable income to be so picky. We didn't. Trying to find a decent, affordable apartment in Manhattan was a full-time job in and of itself; everyone, it seemed, was in the market for a better, cheaper, and larger apartment.

Nathan had convinced the broker from the pay phone on the corner to meet us at the address and that if we liked the apartment we would be willing to up his commission. When Nathan explained to me where the apartment was I remembered that I had always liked that block of the Village, a few years before I had briefly dated a waiter who worked at Reno Sweeney's and the image that I had often retained was not of the guy, but of waiting on the dark, leafy sidewalk for him to get off work. That block always seemed to me more remote, more removed, rather, from the rest of the city, perhaps because the street seemed to narrow because of cars parked on both sides or that the brick town houses seemed closer to the sidewalk or the arched growth of the trees on the block gave it all an enclosed effect, as if to magically transport you into the image of what living in the Village should be, actually—quaint, inexpensive, and bohemian. The apartment building was nestled in between a row of brownstones hidden behind sheets of ivy growing skyward toward the roofs; the apartment was a fifth-floor walk-up through an airless, circular shaft of black-painted concrete stairs.

But I saw the joy hit Nathan's eyes the moment the man unlocked the door and let us into the apartment. The apartment stretched from two windows overlooking 13th Street to a bedroom overlooking a quiet courtyard behind the building. The building was taller than all of those immediately surrounding it, so the view was of the fading sunlight glimmering over the rooftops of Greenwich Village. The apartment itself was in a miserable shape, however— the kitchen floor tiles were cracked and curling at the edges, wallpaper hung in thick tatters in the bedroom, and it looked like it had been a decade since the woodwork and detailing in the apartment was last painted or cleaned— black smudges from fingerprints stained the areas around the light switches and soot covered the window sills. But what made the apartment so captivating were the architectural details: Arched doorways separated the rooms, the ten-foot high walls and ceilings were framed together with a thick molding, in the kitchen heavily painted wooden cabinets had beveled glass insets, a louvered door opened onto the fire escape as if it were a terrace. It was so different than the tiny, modern square boxes we had spent the day inspecting. In the bedroom there was even a fireplace, though one of the previous occupants had painted over the marble mantelpiece. Someone had obviously spent years running this place down—but there was something, too, that immediately announced that this was a home, not just an apartment to come to at the end of a day to go to sleep.

"The cabinets need to be fixed," Nathan said to me when we had found our way into the kitchen for the fourth or fifth time; he pointed out a cracked glass inset, testing me, really, I knew, to see if I liked the apartment as much as he did.

"That's not hard to do," I said. "I know someone who can cut the glass for me." I took a few steps toward the window, but then squatted down and balanced my hand on the floor. I lifted one of the cracked red kitchen tiles, studying the health of the wood underneath it. Above my head I noticed a smooth patch of spackling on the wall that had been painted, where, years ago, someone must have put a fist or a bullet through the wall.

"I could help sand the floor," he said. "Or if you think new tiles would be better."

"I take it you like it here?" I replied, with every ounce of coyness I could muster.

He didn't answer me, but when I looked up at him he was smiling, the same mischievous, boyish grin that had made me fall in love with him so easily. Had we been alone I would have kissed him, taken his clothes off piece by piece and made love to him right there, he was so seductive at that moment. As it was I could only give him a smile and place my hand on his shoulder and pull him into a hug, because the broker, a rather portly man who wore a little too many gold chains around his neck to convincingly make me believe he was straight and who had been sitting on the fire escape catching his breath, was now approaching us as if he knew his commission was a distinct possibility. When he reached us he shook out a packet of cigarettes and offered us each a cigarette. Nathan and I both shook our heads no, and the man slipped the pack back into the front pocket of his pants. "Did you know," he said in a raspy, Long Island accent, "I once met Truman Capote at a party across the street."

Months later, close to Christmas, Nathan and I were still painting the apartment; for a while we bickered on how peachy a shade of beige to paint the trim in the bedroom, but I knew, really, it was an apartment I would never be finished repairing, which oddly was one of the many charms I found in our new home—the desire to keep making it a better place in which to live.

What Nathan liked about living together, he said to me one night when we were still unpacking boxes, was the ability to see the impact of his life on someone else and vice versa—the way, for instance, we had assigned a corner of the bedroom to my sloppiness. Nathan, always a bit too neat for comfort, had designated a few hooks on the wall and a chair as the place where I could toss my dirty clothes and coats. But he learned, really, that I could not be entirely changed or contained, he was forever moving magazines or books I had opened and read and then been distracted away from. Nathan never considered this cleaning up after me; instead he always considered it cleaning up our apartment. Nathan always liked to feel busy doing something, whether it was ironing his button-down shirts or sitting quietly at work on a drawing.

Nathan had moved all of his furniture and artwork into our new apartment and the effect of his bright, cubist furniture reminded me too much of a college dorm, but the animation cells and cartoon backgrounds he had collected and framed over the years and which I had spent evenings studying when we first met, began to have a sentimental hold over me. The moment we unwrapped them from the box I offered to hang them on the walls. Nathan's drafting table and stool we set up in the kitchen, next to the door that led to the fire escape. Though the room only caught the afternoon sunlight it was the warmest room in the apartment; the furnace six floors below never seemed to produce enough heat through the bedroom radiator.

I think, though, the most personal touch he added were the crystal prisms he hung with thread or string looped through bored holes or taped to the side, suspended from the oddest places—the window grill, a doorknob, the back of a chair—in hopes of catching the changing light through the apartment and sending more colors about the room. The longer we lived together the more obsessed Nathan seemed to be about finding more crystals to hang about the apartment; at one point there must have been twenty hanging at various heights in the bedroom alone. Not all were crystals, many were pieces of cut glass, but he could find them in the unlikeliest of places—a paint store, a head shop, an airport souvenir stand. Not all were purchased, however; one he had salvaged from the chandelier of a soon-to-be-demolished Broadway theater, another constructed from an automobile headlight, a few were pieces from a disassembled set of chimes. Nathan actually enjoyed telling stories of how he had acquired the prisms, or, sometimes, enjoyed being coy and mysterious about their origins—how he obtained the crystal he stole from a wall sconce at the Ritz Carlton, for instance, he refused to embellish with details.

In many ways when Nathan and I started living together, we shut out a lot of the rest of the world, as couples falling in love are often wont to do; we certainly cut out a lot of gay lifestyle accoutrements. Gone were the disco days and cruising Christopher Street. Gone, too, was the desire of wanting to go to every new nightclub that had just opened. I had no need for that then; work and love and friendships sustained me. I had a family of friends to support and entertain me: Vince, Jeff, Denise. I had a steady job and a healthy income: Alex had always kept me working. And I was in love. Not for the first time, but this time in a stronger, more assured manner. I remember riding the subway one rush hour and being packed into the downtown train thinking I am doing this because this will take me home faster and taking me home faster takes me quicker to Nathan. Some people could view this sort of behavior as restrained or restrictive, but those people don't understand the unbridled freedom that can accompany the decision to love someone.

And so I found a joy and a purpose and a place for my life. Walking home from the subway or the grocery store, I would breathe in deeply when I reached our block, hoping to catch the smell of garlic and burning olive oil that wafted out of the basement restaurants so that it could give the happiness I felt a concrete sense of smell or taste. As dusk entered the street, I would look up into lights popping on in the windows, through scalloped curtains I could catch pieces of hanging portraits, bookcases, or gilt bronzed chandeliers. All these things—the glances into other apartments, the quiet hush of the street, a softness to the block that didn't exist in other places of the city, so quiet, at times, I could hear the sound of my sneakers against the sidewalk—were only things that I knew in the end would bring me home to Nathan.

Why was Nathan so special to me, I often wondered on my walk, or, rather, how had he become so special to me? Perhaps it had started from that electrical attraction between us, that chemical first impression that drew us so sexually to one another, but it had, over time, metamorphosed into a deeper and more passionate possession. Nathan made me feel lucky to have met him, lucky to love him, lucky to have someone to laugh with and care for other than myself. And so Nathan came to define my world—I will eagerly admit—and in the evenings and afternoons and mornings and whatever time I had with him I would drink up his presence. The books I read were because I was with him, the television shows I saw were because I was with him, the walks I took were because of him, the jobs and subways and everything came to me because I was in love with Nathan. I felt blessed, really, smiled upon by some divine spirit in order to love this man.

I'm not saying that my type of love or our type of relationship is the right kind of relationship for anyone or everyone, certainly not for every gay man, but I am saying that it worked for me, or, rather, it worked for us. I came home happy, and at night watched Nathan move naked and unselfconsciously through the routine of brushing his beautifully white but crooked teeth, scrubbing his face too hard till pink patches formed, brushing his hair away from his forehead to make himself look older, pulling back the covers of the bed and slipping in next to me, holding me too tightly in his arms as he slept, as if I were the one who would so easily float away. Nothing, I felt, could disturb this happiness. I had even rationalized that if Nathan, at some distant point in time, should take other lovers, casual or even more serious, I would not deny him that as long as he came home to me every night and I could still feel this way together with him.

And then one night the phone rang deep in the night and I heard myself groan out loud, "Oh God," before I even answered the call. It was moments before I realized it was Vince calling, saying he was sorry to wake me up, but he needed to talk to someone. Immediately I sensed that he must have had a serious fight with Jeff. "What's wrong?" I asked, shaking the thickness from my head.

"I didn't even know," he said.

"What?" I asked, the alarm in his voice awakening me.

"Robbie, you won't believe this," he said.

"What?"

"It's Alex. *Alex is dead.*"

KRYPTON

7

This was the order in which they died: Alex, Sal, Wes, Michael, David, and Hank. One by one my family of friends began to disappear. Sal had invested hope in macrobiotic food; David had gone the spiritualist route: imaging, crystals and meditation. Wes had been on a new drug protocol at NYU Medical Center; his side effects were a rash across his chest and diarrhea, but he went blind from a sudden and unattended herpes infection. In his last days David had gone home to South Carolina; I never even knew Sal was sick till I read it in the newspaper. But the inescapable fact was that they had all died. And they had each, somehow, been a part of my life.

The city was full of supposition; everyone (except the mainstream press, it seems) was talking about AIDS. One theory had that it was caused by rags soaked with amyl nitrate passed around in discos, another believed it sprang from the government's secret genocide plan to exterminate the black race, others believed it was from a tainted polio vaccine run amuck. Jeff had read in a supermarket tabloid that it was a dormant curse unleashed from opening Tutankhamen's tomb, another magazine had labeled it "Saint's disease," after the disco that had opened on the Lower East Side. One guy told Vince it was spread through pigs in Africa; another guy at the gym quipped he was certain it started from the falafel they sold at the Ninth Avenue Street Festival. Jerry Fallwell and Pat Buchanan, those self-appointed messengers of God, proclaimed it a heavenly retribution against homosexuals. Everything came under scrutiny, from mosquitoes to semen to gay waiters.

It was not long before we knew the symptoms by heart: fevers and night sweats, swollen lymph glands, weight loss, diarrhea, thrush, blurred vision, skin rashes, unexplained bruises and bleeding. Nathan and I examined our bodies for any kind of evidence; we stared at ourselves in mirrors a little longer, half expecting a boil to emerge from underneath the skin and erupt as in a grade B horror movie. I studied the color and size of a mole near my pelvis, scrutinized the wart I had had since a boy at the knuckle of my thumb, examined the back of my tongue daily, monitored, even, the visibility of the scar that still lightly bisected my eyebrow. I memorized, too, the pattern of freckles on Nathan's back, memorized the visibility of the veins of his arms and legs, silently memorized, too, the size of his wrists, chest, waist and thighs. Often in bed Nathan would begin massaging my shoulders but his lean, bony fingers would feel out the tender flesh beneath my armpits, neck and groin. We could never figure out exactly where those lymph glands were, but we combed each other's bodies for signs, finally deciding, one evening, that we would just know when they were swollen. Still, there were plenty of things to keep us worried. Nathan had a knack of clearing mucus from his throat which would always escalate into a cough, the pale skin about his neck and chest flushing briefly from the sudden, forceful rush of blood through his body. One week I went to see Dr. Jacobsen because I was convinced my skin seemed spotted with tiny measle-like blisters, only to be embarrassed into the realization that it was a mild case of psoriasis aggravated by tension.

Fear also shook Vince and Jeff out of their domestic bliss periodically. Vince's worries came to him in lists: lists of people he had slept with, lists of people already dead, lists of people sick, lists of people he was worried about, lists of people he had lost track of. He would often spend hours on the phone trying to locate someone he hadn't spoken to in months, someone, he remembered, for instance, as having been incredible sex. He once called an actor as far away as Alaska just to make sure he was still alive. Jeff accepted each illness and death with the more assured force of denial, carefully sequestering himself from the similarities of the dead. "Didn't he do cocaine?" he would ask, or, "I heard he picked up the boys from Port Authority." But he was only doing something that we were all trying to do—remove himself, inch by inch, if necessary, from the pressing uncertainty of risk and the possibility that he might be next.

There was, really, no way to escape the news, even if it was only reaching us through coded phrases in the media or an underground network of gossip. Nothing much was known but everyone was grappling for information, and then the phone would jarringly ring with the news that so-and-so was sick or in the hospital or was dead. Nathan and Vince and Jeff and I went to the hospitals and wore gowns and masks over our faces, warning signs plastered on the door and above the beds. We scanned the obituaries for clues—single, no survivors, died of liver cancer or bone cancer, lymphoma, pneumonia, or, simply, after a long illness. We attended funerals and memorials dressed in black, standing around enormous vases of flowers we didn't know the names of, eulogizing men we referred to affectionately as always great with the tambourine at 12 West or as wildly campy in that off-off-Broadway punk version of A

Christmas Carol. Medical terminology became a necessary vocabulary to learn to speak; as necessary as checking in with everyone close to us, trying to maintain our sanity, trying the hell to understand, terrified whom the next one was going to be. I remember that there were nights I would be unable to sleep, tossing back and forth, breaking out into a sweat, trying not to disturb Nathan who was himself tossing, worrying who would be the first of us to lose in this crazy game of roulette.

Denise phoned us every day to tell us what she had heard or read: a baby who was ill, a Haitian with symptoms, an Air Force man threatened with discharge because he was sick. Denise felt it was important not to be frightened to talk about anything, not even our fear of speaking the word AIDS, a word we had quickly learned to hate and fear as much as the disease itself. Denise was relentless in her pursuit of what was happening; she continued to grill us: What had we heard, who was in treatment, who had died? She was always, too, making us all join her for dinner, individually or as a group, politely probing for tiny details, wanting to know, as we all did, what was causing this craziness, eager to discuss the possibility of everything from poppers to pork to promiscuity. And then she would change the subject, suddenly lighten it with a joke or a self-effacing remark, or draw a cartoon on a napkin with a pen she would always ask if she could borrow.

In many ways Nathan and I regarded Denise during those years as a sort of combination older sister and surrogate mother—someone in whom we could confide and share our anxieties. Denise would sit opposite us, as she had done years ago when Jeff was her roommate and she had entertained his morning guests, and lure us in with her concern. Denise had come to believe that the solution to everything now was to look for the small joys of life. This was how she had repaired herself after Nina had left her. "Let's eat something extravagant with lots of calories," Denise would say when she felt things were becoming, well, too serious and glum. "Something to make us happy."

"You mean, something gay?" Nathan would add with a mock hint of surprise.

Denise would reciprocate with her own startled look, as though she were a mother shattered by the revelation of her beloved child, then find something girlish to do to deflect her worries about these uncontrollable events, like unfastening the barrette that held back a string of lazy brown curls from her face and clasp them together into a pony tail at the nape of her neck, along with a heap of others that had wandered into variant directions.

Denise's mother was alarmed by everything that was happening. What little appeared on the news about AIDS was enough to convince her that her daughter's life was in jeopardy. Denise's mother believed Denise would become ill simply by association. "Are you careful?" Mrs. Connelly would ask whenever Denise would call her.

"Careful?" Denise would answer in her annoyed-with-her-mother tone, frowning and curling up tighter on the sofa or the bed or wherever she had been lying when the phone had rung.

"You shouldn't let them use your silverware. Or the phone. They don't use the phone at your apartment do they?"

"Mother, they're not sick."

"Germs, dear. You can never be too careful."

"They're my friends."

"That's no reason for you to put yourself in jeopardy," Mrs. Connelly would say sharply. "I would just get out of there if I were you."

"What? Just run away?"

"No, no. Move. Go somewhere where you don't have to worry as much."

"But you would worry no matter where I lived."

"I am your mother, you know. It comes with the territory."

"So why should I move? At least you've got a reason to worry since I'm living here."

And then Mrs. Connelly would let out an unforgiving sigh. "There must be some place safer."

"Safer?" Denise answered. "People are dying everywhere, Mother. I could be hit by a bus anywhere. I don't believe anywhere is safe."

As more friends became sick and others died, Nathan and I tried desperately to escape our anxiety, fleeing the city, just as Mrs. Connelly had suggested; Manhattan, it seemed, had become the epicenter of the epidemic. Nathan and I tried desperately to reach places that we felt were untouched by AIDS—an inn on the Jersey shore or a cabin in the Catskills, any place, where for just a few days we would at least not have to think about it, waking up guilt free in some foreign bed to the smells of coffee and frying bacon, our bodies curved around each other like spoons, our morning beards bristly and coarse as sandpaper. Nathan now preferred to stay secluded from gay life; in the evenings we remained home, escaping into a mystery novel or a movie or a documentary on some exotic subject, such as the penguins in Iceland or the evolution of the Great Barrier Reef. At times I worried that Nathan was withdrawing from me as well, but we had always prided ourselves on being independent from one another as much as possible. Besides, the weekends we always managed to spend together, though usually we visited his parents in Connecticut instead of accepting an invitation from friends to stay in Fire Island or the Hamptons. The architectural firm where Nathan worked had continued to grow, and more and more he found himself pulled away from his drafting table to become involved in administrative work. At times I believe he relished the opportunity to be overworked, to sit at his desk worrying over a sketch of a column or a column of numbers instead of worrying about our lives. Nathan and I were well aware of our fear and denial; Nathan once remarked it was like a story he had once read as a boy in a Superman comic book—everyone attempting to flee the exploding planet of Krypton.

Jeff and Vince had their own strategies of denial; Jeff would often take the phone off the hook in the evening, when bad news always seemed to arrive, saying to Vince he just wanted two uninterrupted hours to watch a movie or to read. Vince had abandoned his quest for writing a "realistic" play; now he had become intrigued with the notion of writing a fantasy, studying fairy tales and theories of parallel worlds, surprisingly seeking Nathan's opinion and advice on the specifics of the genre. Still, Denise kept us all grounded in reality, suddenly retelling a story of a friend who went to the doctor because of the suspected spots on his tongue, only to be told to stop eating so much bread and carbohydrates.

Time passed and we read and watched, daily, the horror and progress and confusion of an epidemic: the announcement of the discovery of HIV, the start-up of blood tests, the shocks of Rock Hudson being flown back from Paris on a chartered 747, Ryan White barred from attending school in Kokomo, Indiana, and the unexpected infection of the population of poverty stricken Belle Glade, Florida. And then at the beginning of the spring of 1986 Nathan and I took a trip to England, spending a few days in London and renting a car and driving through Wales and then up to Scotland. It was, for us, another pastoral retreat, but here, in Great Britain, Nathan became possessed with an incredible passion for adventure, veering our car off on a side road in search of ruins of a castle, peering through the rubble and rocks and stones as if he expected to find remnants of the Round Table, stepping through the dark doorways of taverns to try the local, bitter ales, making love to me at night atop chilly sheets on a squeaky, down mattress. Just before we left, I caught a cold, which the plane trip across the Atlantic only magnified and made more uncomfortable. Back at work the next week at the construction company I had joined after Alex's death, I couldn't shake it, caught now between sweating, the city's rising humidity, and the chill of air-conditioners being cranked into service. One afternoon I felt feverish, short of breath, and a strange pain in my chest, as if I had pulled a muscle at the gym, and I made an appointment to see Dr. Jacobsen only to find myself a few hours later admitted into the hospital with pneumonia.

Dr. Jacobsen had not said I had AIDS, but he did not rule out the possibility either; I was, after all, in that high-risk category, which is why, I am convinced, I was sent hastily to the emergency room at St. Vincent's Hospital. I was, to be exact, a healthy gay man in suddenly declining health, which is why, too, from different corners of the city, Nathan was scrambling to reach Denise and Vince and Jeff before he came to the hospital.

In those first few hours, left alone and lying on a trolley in one of the subterranean halls of the hospital waiting to be examined, I felt as if I had crossed a line from which there would be no retreating, my life was changing and I was powerless to do anything about it. "It's just a cold," I kept saying over and over, convincing myself that this wasn't the end, this wasn't AIDS, and all that was really necessary for me to feel better was to see Nathan again, get some rest and I would be back on my feet.

In the emergency room a group of interns immediately ruled out PCP, Pneumocystic Carinii, the AIDS pneumonia, but my chest X-ray showed pleural effusia on my lungs, and my blood gases revealed a reduced oxygen flow to my lungs. One doctor suspected it was either a pulmonary embolism or pneumonia of a bacterial or viral type, perhaps TB. TB, I thought when he told me his suspicion. *Tuberculosis?* Hadn't science cured that? I could tell by the look on the doctor's face that he hadn't a clue what was happening to me.

This was the first time I had ever realized how weakened and physically vulnerable I could become, how hard it is to ask for help, how important it is to get precise medical explanations from doctors and nurses, questioning them to repeat themselves over and over, to express themselves in laymen's terms, how necessary it is to be surrounded by friends and compassionate people, lessons I would recall too often over the next few years. Hours later I was hooked up to an IV in a room on the fifth floor, my temperature spiking between 103 and 104, Nathan and Denise at the foot of the bed, Vince and Jeff sitting vigil beside the window. I found myself looking up at all of them, certain of the fear in my eyes, expecting at any minute a doctor to walk in the room and pronounce AIDS and find myself abandoned. Nathan and I had heard stories about lovers leaving one another, families shunning their kin, nurses refusing to offer care. And then I tried to calm myself; the thought came to me that perhaps I was just the one in our circle who was always to be sick or in trouble.

"It's just a cold," I kept saying over and over with what strength I could find to speak. The hospital gown pressed against my chest as if it were a heavy blanket, my side ached, my eyelids were swollen and fleshy, but I was too scared to sleep. Vince came over and held my hand, rubbing his thumb slowly back and forth against the center of my palm. Nathan paced back and forth in the room, his patience abandoned, demanding to know from anyone who would catch his eye where the doctor was, what was in the IV, wasn't there something someone could give me to ease my pain?

That night, the infection in my body, still undiagnosed, made its presence known through a river of sweat. My temperature soared again and when I awoke my hospital gown and the sheets of the bed were soaked. Nathan was floors below in the cafeteria when a nurse, a large black woman named Dora, came in and changed my sheets. She helped me out of bed and into a chair, lightly humming as she went about her business.

"You know, I was in here just last year," she said and looked over at me, catching my gaze. "That's right. Second floor. I know it's no fun, everybody poking at you or twisting them hands." She flattened the sheets, tucked in the corners and helped me back into bed again. "You too healthy to be here," she said, again catching my eyes, but all I could think about was how unhealthy I must look—my hair matted to my skull, the puffy eyes, the stubble of beard, the silly, hospital gown, already tangled around my legs. "You be home soon," she said, and it was here I detected a hint of an accent. Jamaican? I thought. Caribbean? How far had she come to get to this room? And then before she left I heard her say, "You okay. You have a lot of work ahead for you."

The next day I was moved to a trolley and pushed through corridors from test to test. The pain in my chest was still present, and at one point while being moved into an awkward position by a technician for an X-ray, the pain became so unbearable I simply blacked out. One specialist decided it was necessary to identify the fluid trapped in my lungs, and back in my room a resident, a dark-skinned Indian man, inserted a three-foot long needle into my back to get an extract of the fluid. Jeff and Denise were in the room at the time of the procedure and I could sense their horror, but the resident, an avid theatergoer, kept asking Jeff about his favorite musicals, then singing snippets of lyrics from *La Cage Aux Folles*. "You may be dancing with a girl who needs a shave," he laughed softly in rhythm in my ear. I knew he was only trying to ease the tension, but I felt myself buckling from the immense pain of the needle, anger gnawing at me: *Why is this happening to me, I only have a cold.*

The tap was unsuccessful, the singing resident could not locate the precise site of the fluid in my lungs. I was again placed on the trolley, and wheeled to another floor for an ultrasound, so that a picture of the lung could reveal where the fluid resided. For some reason the ultrasound never happened, and I was wheeled back to my room for another lung tap. By then Nathan had reappeared in the room, having finished shading a drawing for a client he had been working on in the cafeteria, and he held my hand as the resident again inserted the needle into my back, singing "La da da da, I'm young and in love." Apparently there was so little fluid in my lungs that the resident was having difficulty locating it, and if you poke around too much there is a possibility of making the lung collapse. Nathan, terrified by the sight of the needle, began squeezing my hand so hard that I had to pull away from him to relax his grip.

The lung tap was again unsuccessful, but by the end of the day it was ruled out that I had a pulmonary embolism. Vince was in the room when my doctor reappeared later that night, and I was startled that they greeted each other with little pecks on the cheek until I remembered I had first gone to Dr. Jacobsen on Vince's recommendation. Dr. Jacobsen turned to me, asked me how I was doing, and checked my charts. Then he oddly shrugged his shoulders and said, "Sometimes people just get sick, Robbie. You don't have PCP. Your bloodwork was fine. I don't have any evidence that it's ARC or AIDS. We'll just keep you on the antibiotics. You should be home in about two days. You're a very strong man."

When he left the room Vince began to cry, in large heaving gasps, and I knew instinctively the source of his tears was as complex as any medical diagnosis. Here I was, a twenty-six year-old gay man with a benign, unspecified form of pneumonia, why was I so lucky?

"So you thought you were gonna die?" Nathan said flippantly three days later while walking back to our apartment from the hospital, though I detected, still, the fine whisper of nervousness in his voice. It was an early May morning, a strange, vacant time in the city, the streets already heavy with humidity and the stench of urine, trash motionless at the curbs and sidewalks. Nathan had meant to be upbeat but I also understood the underlying restlessness of his question; that things were beginning to change for us, would find us and bring us down no matter where we were. In a week I went back to work and we settled into a summer of escape, spending Memorial Day weekend at a campground in upstate Pennsylvania, Nathan and I trying like Lucy and Ethel to pitch a borrowed tent in the black of midnight. But each day as my health returned, instead of feeling liberated, instead of being seized by that carpe diem sensibility so many people have after a horrifying experience, I grew only more confused and depressed. There had to be a reason why I was so lucky, why I had escaped. What was it I was supposed to do? Was there something I should have known?

And then in August Vince had a play produced in a small theater in Los Angeles, a fantasy in which a man, suddenly struck ill with a fatal disease, is given the opportunity, through a wish, to trade places with a healthy man so that he and his wife can have a child before he dies. Vince had insisted to the producers, in a fit of nepotism, that Jeff be given a leading part. No one really seemed to object to it though; Vince, after all, had written the role of the husband with Jeff in mind, and Jeff seemed naturally suited for the part, both physically and emotionally. So Jeff and Vince disappeared to California for rehearsals, calling us with each new discovery: the block-long Sports Connection gym in West Hollywood, the boys at Malibu, a noted celebrity with a new hair weave spotted eating pizza at Spago on Sunset. Denise, Nathan, and I flew out to attend the play's premiere at a tiny 99-seat studio theater in West Hollywood, deciding to make a party out of our own trip, renting a suite at the Chateau Marmont for the weekend.

The play was a success; the audience accepted Vince's fable as a comment on the times. At the opening night party at a restaurant on Santa Monica Boulevard, Vince went on and on about how much inspiration Nathan had been with the concept and the play, how Nathan's imagination had helped Vince really open up his own feelings. From a table near the window, Denise and I watched them like proud parents as they circulated through the room, stopping to talk to someone, Vince reaching for Nathan's hand, Nathan planting a kiss near Vince's ear. Jeff arrived late, but he was greeted with applause as he entered the restaurant, and he later found our table and begged Denise to come with him for a minute and meet this agent who was sitting near the bar, wanting to see if she thought the man's praise was sincere or if he was just another Hollywood phoney-baloney. It was then, as she crossed the room, that Denise first noticed Linda, the sister of one of the producers of Vince's play. Linda had the tall, willowy look of a hippie, dressed in a peasant blouse and a long, baggy skirt, her dark blond hair braided in the back. She wore a paisley print headband, large hoop earrings, and several strings of bead necklaces, the effect of which summoned up the image of a sort of ethereal earth goddess. In her arms Linda held her seven-month-old baby named Amy, whose fingers opened and closed about Linda's neck like an electric toy. When Linda found a seat in the corner, slipped her left breast out of her blouse and began to nurse her daughter, Denise's face froze into a smile as though she were posing for a photograph, that amiable but distant grin held just before a flash.

Denise had no desire to meet Linda at that moment. She was only an object of affection, someone, perhaps, Denise could file away in her memory—an image she could summon up later to use for a drawing. What struck Denise was Linda's collected composure, the temperate way, for instance, she attended to the baby's needs, at once both sensual and mothering. They met, however, later in the buffet line when Linda seemed to be losing that very composure, trying to balance a plate of slippery food and a wiggling Amy at the same time. Denise offered to help, taking Linda's plate of food and filling it with the items Linda requested. They sat together in a corner by a fountain, at a table with a candle whose wavery shadows made Linda's long, dark eyelashes look like those of a fashion model of the late Sixties.

Denise soon discovered Linda was recently divorced, because, as Linda explained, shrugging her shoulders and sighing, her husband did not understand her needs for individuality and identity. "Zack tried to define me,"Linda said. "But we're still friendly." And Denise, smitten in that moment, detected a hint of Linda's southern accent.

Uncertain how to regard Linda, how to even comprehend her own infatuation, Denise asked Linda if she had grown up in the South. "Tennessee," Linda answered. "But I couldn't wait to get out of there. People were just so stubborn." Denise laughed and explained her own southern roots, her exasperating mother in Kentucky, the small-town mentality she had tried to escape. Linda turned and studied Denise, but the intensity of her stare was deflected as Amy reached for a strand of Denise's hair. "Change keeps us interesting," Linda said, throwing a flirting smile to Denise, then holding Amy up in the air and shaking her lightly to make her gurgle. "I love people who have been somewhere before."

Nathan and I flew back to Manhattan the following day; Denise had planned to remain behind for a week because of appointments she had made with some gallery owners about her work. She had recently joined a more prominent and serious artistic circle after a gallery in New York had exhibited one of her paintings, and she was trying to find a patron to mount a full-scale exhibition of her more recent works. After we left, she rented a car, even though she always harbored tremendous fears about driving, and moved out of the hotel and onto a sofa bed at the apartment Vince and Jeff were subletting a block off Sunset Boulevard near West Hollywood. Denise's plan was to recapture some of those lost moments she had had so many years ago with Jeff, those late night revelations, the admissions of secrets and desires over early morning coffee. She never willingly neglected Jeff; instead, she found him too busy with the sudden success of the play and he slept well into the early part of the afternoon, and after all, she told me later on the phone, Jeff was perturbed at her for not liking the agent he had introduced her to on opening night. So instead of waiting for Jeff to come around, she met Linda for lunch the following day, then again the next evening to see a movie.

What developed between Denise and Linda was nothing like she had experienced with Nina, but a bond Denise often compared to the girlfriends she had had back in Kentucky—the giggly, silly ones prone to both confessions and critiques. When Denise called Nathan at the end of the week, she mentioned she was now staying at Linda's and that she had extended her trip a few more days to do some sketches. When she called the following week she asked me how my health was, as if I had been prominently on her mind. I told her I was fine, annoyed, even, that people were so concerned that I might still be sick; then she asked if I would put up a card for her on the bulletin board at the Actors' Equity office in midtown, a notice offering her New York apartment for sublet. She reappeared in Manhattan a week later, staying only long enough to pack and interview potential subtenants.

Denise's mother found all of this alarming, of course, worrying out loud that California had too much sun, smog, traffic, and was just asking for earthquakes. Denise reminded her mother that it was her suggestion that she leave New York, though her mother could not even find any consolation in the fact that Denise would be rooming with another southern expatriate; Denise, at that point, had explained nothing about her relationship with Linda, did not even mention the baby, Amy. Instead, Denise kept her descriptions confined to the air-conditioned apartment and the well-lit street it was located on in West Hollywood. Nothing, however, appeased her mother. And she was worried, as we all silently were, that Denise was simply being impulsive again.

Jeff and Vince seemed to find a comfort in California that they had not had in many years: Jeff going to one audition after another; Vince trying his hand at writing sitcoms. Vince would call often, asking me if I were becoming as thick around the waist as he was, which was, in his own subtle way, his method of checking up on my health. He and Jeff loved the West Coast life: the warmer weather, the studio pitch meetings, the parties in the Hills. But Vince said he also missed the energy of the city, missed the surly East Village restaurants, missed the way the wet Central Park ground smelled in the fall, missed, too, the cruisy way of walking through city streets. And Jeff, Vince complained, had become so addicted to the gym that he was becoming so broad-shouldered with muscles that he tilted forward when he walked. As much as we bulked up our bodies and fortified our hopes, we could not escape, even in California, the age of anxiety, the fear of cholesterol or the diminishing number of T-cells, or merely the fading of youth exhibited by extra pounds around the waist.

Vince had said to me one night on the phone that life in California was just as difficult as Manhattan. Perhaps even more. They had not escaped. "Everyone's frightened of it here too," he said. "But no one talks about it openly. It's all hush-hush, everything on the sly. I heard about an actor who travels to

San Diego to get his prescriptions filled because he's afraid of never working again if somebody finds out about him."

But I did feel rocked by Vince's absence in Manhattan. I missed calling him up in the afternoon to see if he wanted to go for a walk, missed his bowlegged, out-turned stride, missed the way he would stop and pull me in a store and point something out to me that I would have never noticed on my own, such as a candle made from the fallen limbs of a birch tree or the first edition of *Daughter of the Revolution*. Even Nathan admitted that he missed Vince's opinions. And I felt, then, with Jeff and Denise gone too, that Nathan and I had been abandoned, left to navigate a mine-strewn landscape. But I also knew they needed a change, needed a chance to get away, escape, really, as we all sometimes do, needed to grow on their own. But I was also afraid that perhaps they were outgrowing us. I know that that was a very selfish thought, but with so many people disappearing so untimely from our lives, it was hard to accept someone willingly moving away.

And then December settled into Manhattan; the trees were empty of leaves and replaced by tiny white holiday lights the afternoon I met Nathan at the south corner of Gramercy Park. Even though I was running late, he was still waiting for me, sitting on the stoop of a brownstone, his hands slipped into the side slits of one of those two-toned football jackets that were so fashionable that year. Nathan had not wanted to go inside by himself and when we walked inside the Players Club a porter took our coats and waved us up into a small auditorium on the second floor. The service had not yet started and there were clusters of well-dressed men scattered about the dark, wood-paneled room, rowdily talking and laughing in an overly animated, cartoonish sort of way. On the other side of a row of metal chairs, Gene, a friend of Vince's, brightly waved to me, then looked at his watch and shrugged his shoulders. No one, it seemed, wanted the memorial service to start; to do so, of course, would be to admit that Michael was dead.

Vince had called from Los Angeles and given me all the gossip; Michael had wanted the service to be held at the Harvard Club but some of the big university boys had balked, it seems, at the idea of, well, so many of our kind assembled together in such an esteemed place. Another friend had tried for the Yacht Club, but they, too, had declined once they learned, well, that it was a service, for a uh-em, you know, well, one of them. Then an old boyfriend of Michael's whose current lover's cousin belonged to the Players Club had agreed to contact the Club on their behalf. Vince had rationalized the choice, because, well, Michael had really loved the theater, and hadn't his life been infused with drama, after all? I was compelled to remind Vince that perhaps the reason The Players had agreed to the service was because the theater was, well, so full of so many of us.

Vince had been adamant that I go to the service because he couldn't afford to fly back to Manhattan. It was important, he said, to remember the details, to know what had happened to Michael, to remember how witty and arrogant and gorgeous he had been, to repeat the stories of what a good friend he was, what a horror his illness had become. "These are the things we have to do now," Vince said to me, not trying to be pretentious, but trying to move me through guilt yet allowing his own fear to surge through the phone lines like a jolt of electricity. Vince and Michael's affair years before had been short but quite passionate, the details revealed to me at the time like the unveiling of a report card with all "A's."

Nathan had tried to find an excuse not to attend the service, saying he was running behind on a drawing that was due, but I knew that these memorials made him feel uptight and worried, didn't they do that to all of us? He didn't even really know Michael, he said to me when I tried to argue him into going. What about that time we all went to the circus? I sternly reminded him. Hadn't he sat there and sketched Michael that day? Hadn't they wandered together that afternoon through the subterranean tunnels of Madison Square Garden, looking for the room where they kept the elephants? "If you can't go for Michael or for Vince," I said as a last resort, "then at least you should go because of me. I want you there."

The last time I had seen Michael was shortly before Vince left for California; Vince and I had gone together to see Michael in Lenox Hill Hospital. Michael lay on a bed with an oxygen mask on his face, his thin, brown eyes wide and astonished as though ready to scream, *When will this be over?* Two years before Michael began to have low grade fevers in the late afternoons, which a specialist—a specialist—recommended controlling with aspirin. Then he developed thrush, which was easily controlled with Nizoral, then came a case of anal herpes. His cellulitis cleared up when a dermatologist prescribed tetracycline, which left him, however, with severe stomach problems. By the time he was switched to Dapsone, his internist discovered lesions in his mouth, which were quickly biopsied and identified as Kaposi's sarcoma. Ozone gas injections, vitamins and Ribavirin flown in from Mexico all failed him. Even the DNCP that he applied directly to the lesions on his arms and legs failed to make them disappear. One doctor had said perhaps this had something to do with a racial characteristic. He was completely baffled, he said to one of Michael's friends—he had never seen KS in an Asian before. But Michael was only half Japanese; his father was American and Jewish, which had bequeathed Michael with an exotic, feral-like quality. Michael always considered himself an expatriate of Japan, but lived in New York the way most gay men do anywhere in the world, settling somewhere far from their families, aligning themselves with others who think and act and believe as they do. The customs of his native country were too conservative, Michael had once told me; his parents had disinherited him because he was gay, long before he died at the age of thirty-three.

Before I ever met Michael, I had seen him dancing at the Flamingo. Short and lean—his skin was like cellophane against his muscles—he was always dressed in black and dancing with fans—two, four, one night he had as many as eight. Michael had specifically requested that his service not be religious in any way; he was adamant, in fact, as I had been told, about Jesus not even being mentioned, or so a friend had repeated it to a friend who had repeated it to Vince who had repeated it to me. Something about there being too many names for one supreme being or something like that, but when I heard the request, it made me remember how he used to dance with his fans. When he twirled around they would catch the light, making it appear as if they were his wings and he was not really a part of this planet, but rather some beautiful, ethereal god sent down to entertain the mortals.

Instead of a sermon, Francis, Michael's best friend, read a passage by Evelyn Waugh—in his later years Michael had become something of a devoted Anglophile. Then someone sang a Burt Bacharach song, then an Asian woman got up and spoke about how Michael had helped her not only learn English, but also to navigate the webs and mazes of Manhattan. Someone spoke about how good and trusting Michael was at his job, how he really didn't care about climbing the corporate ladder of international banking; instead, he preferred to be an ear for office complaints, his office door always open, ready to listen to the next person with a problem. Then randomly, one by one, people began to stand and tell little stories about Michael, all mostly funny, about the time he had streaked through Cambridge in the snow or how rude he could be or what it was like the summer he had been a waiter or how they had discovered one another in the balcony of the Saint. I laughed until I developed a headache, so glad to be relieved momentarily of the tension of grief. How is it that funerals can make you feel so alive and yet so helpless? After each story I felt a prick of depression; I wished I had known Michael better, and I felt that maybe I hadn't been a good enough friend. But then he had always been Vince's friend, not mine, I tried to justify silently to myself, though I knew that that wasn't entirely the truth.

No one mentioned, of course, the way Michael had taken to spitting at the hospital staff when they entered his room, or when he was sent home, how he would crumple up wads of tissue or paper towels and toss them at the television or the stereo. No one told of the effort it was to get him to the bathroom in time because of the IV he was hooked up to, or of the fiery diarrhea that he was plagued with in his final days, though I knew these details were commonly known by those at the service. Vince, too, had passed these details along to me.

Nathan kept squirming in his seat, clearing his throat and rubbing the palms of his hands up and down the sides of his cheeks. I knew he was growing more and more uncomfortable each time a new person started in with another story. Finally, he leaned over to me and hoarsely whispered, "I can't do this, Robbie. I'll meet you back home."

I felt a gasp of air enter my throat in protest, but Nathan had not waited for my response. He slipped out of his chair and walked down the aisle and out of the room. I felt a hot flush of anger and embarrassment, wondering if I would have to explain his actions to someone later. The service went on for more than an hour. Afterward, everyone reassembled into little clusters and a handsome waiter in black tie—a would-be actor no doubt, with wide ears and a face blue with day-old stubble and who momentarily reminded me of Vince—circulated with glasses of wine balanced on a silver platter. I made small talk with Gene, said hello to an overweight actress whom I knew was a friend of Vince's, then wandered around the rooms of the Club, studying the garishly framed portraits and paintings that lined the walls along the stairs to the top floor.

On my way downstairs a slender man with a red crewcut stopped and smiled at me. "I think we met years ago," he said, lifting his wine glass toward me, his voice deep and buried within an accent.

He was wearing a fitted black suit which cast a silvery sheen at the wrinkles, a bleached white shirt and a dark skinny tie. There was something, however, familiar about the way he tilted his head into the light of the chandelier, the way the creases at the corners of his eyes looked as if they were about to squint into a wink.

"I'm not used to seeing you in clothes," I answered, realizing a face and body from my past had crossed my path again, though I struggled to remember the man's name.

He blushed a bit, then pulled his mouth back into a grin. "It's good to see you still 'round."

The accent came to me now as faintly British, till I remembered he had come from New Zealand, but I still couldn't recall his name. "Likewise," I answered. "It's always comforting to see a familiar face."

"You get to the Island at all this year?"

"No," I answered. "I keep a slower pace now."

"Ahhh," he nodded. "Pity about Michael."

I nodded, thrown back momentarily to an image of Vince's flushed face the day Michael dumped him. Michael had outgrown Vince before Vince had had the chance to want to move on, himself, to another conquest.

"That sort of heavy stuff is really tricky."

"Stuff?" I asked.

"Chains, ropes, fists," he said. "Michael was gloriously kinky, you know. Or at least his reputation was."

"Whatever it was," I said. "He didn't deserve this."

He pulled back a bit because of my attitude, then looked down the stairs at the crowd below us, my eyes following his, watching the Asian woman who had spoken weave through the crowd. "Still, don't know many like him who've been sick," he said.

"What?"

"This ever hits Asia there'll be bloody trouble," he clarified.

"Of course," I answered, suddenly startled at the concept, realizing, however, that it was probably already there, that in years, months, maybe minutes, ten-year time bombs could start going off at any second. I reached for the banister with my free arm to steady myself and took a step away from him, as if to leave, but he caught my elbow.

"You seeing anyone, mate?" he asked.

I turned and nodded. "Nathan was here, but he seems to have disappeared."

"Ahhh, lot of that happening lately." He reached inside his jacket, withdrew his wallet and handed me his card. I looked at it briefly, smiled and said "Pat," then slipped the card into my pants pocket. "Call if you get bored," he grinned. "Or need a change."

I nodded and began to head down the stairs. "Careful going down," I heard his laugh behind me in what I felt had shifted into an oddly sinister tone.

It was raining when I left the building, not really raining, but a cold, gray drizzle, dampening and darkening the sidewalk and creating an uncomfortable heaviness to the coat I wore. I stopped under an awning on Park Avenue South, wondering if I should take a cab or just walk home. I felt so confused in that moment, a bit hungry but not knowing what to eat, missing Vince, flustered at running into Pat and trying to forget him, then becoming annoyed at Nathan for abandoning me. How could I yell at him though? Hadn't I freaked out too many times on my own? Maybe Michael had been lucky—he had escaped before things could get worse, before things escalated in Asia and Africa and Australia or right here on Park Avenue South. Looking uptown at the patchwork of windows that were lit in the office buildings that jutted into the air like stacked boxes in a warehouse, I wondered how was it possible for man to create and build such elaborate structures of steel and wire and glass, but not be able to rid the human body of a ravenous microscopic virus. Was there any way to escape this? I thought. Hadn't Vince told me things were just as bad in Los Angeles? Then the chain came back to me—all in an instant: Michael to Vince to Jeff to me to Nathan. We're all going to die, I thought, there is no escape. An Asian boy shot by me on a bike, startling me as he came around the corner on his way to deliver dinner to someone.

And then I was out in the rain again, running back across my history to Nathan.

That year, 1986, Nathan and I spent Thanksgiving with his foster parents in upstate Connecticut, Mrs. Solloway doting on us as though we were under-fed boys. Mrs. Solloway was a no-nonsense, practical sort of woman; she accepted me now as a part of her son's life—as if Nathan and I had been legal-ly wed. When Nathan was a boy, Mrs. Solloway had angered him with her unyielding opinions of what was right and wrong, what was good and bad; Nathan had not been allowed to go out of the house by himself until he was almost seven, not allowed to go out on a date with a girl till he was a sopho-more in high school. Nathan often accounted these things as helping him to find his own adventurous and romantic nature. Mrs. Solloway once remarked that Nathan was such a serious child; even when she would suggest a trip to the park he would prefer instead to retreat to his room with a book. To her credit, however, was Mrs. Solloway's ability to adapt to the changing facts; she knew enough, for instance, to once ask Nathan if our sexual habits were safe. In fact, she had easily accepted Nathan's sexuality when he announced his preference to her while he was home from college one weekend.

"Who in their right mind would willingly give up loving a child because of this?" she asked me the afternoon I had first met her when she came into Manhattan, not knowing that that was precisely what my father had done. Nathan's father was a bit more stubborn on the matter of Nathan's homosex-uality, a bit stubborn, too, at recognizing my place in Nathan's life. While Nathan was in college, his father had originally suggested that Nathan see a therapist to correct his sexual attraction to men; Mr. Solloway had not been present, either, at the luncheon in Manhattan when I first met Nathan's mother. I did not meet his father until almost a year later; he was cold and distant, fumbling for words. It wasn't until many months after that, when Nathan had me rewire their dining room and install a ceiling fan, that Mr. Solloway began to acknowledge my presence, though Nathan often joked that my accomplishment hadn't helped his image one bit.

That Thanksgiving the ceiling fan whirred and stirred the aromas of Mrs. Solloway's cooking from the kitchen into the dining room long before the table was set, the swinging door between the two rooms propped open in an effort to keep the kitchen cooler. As an adult Nathan had never been able to remain in his parents' house for more than a few hours, fearful of not being let go, or, perhaps, of not wanting to leave; children sometimes only want their parents to protect them from the dangers and complexities of the rest of the world. After dinner, after Nathan helped his mother clean the kitchen and I replaced a light switch for Mr. Solloway, Nathan announced that it was time for us to leave. I saw a flicker of disappointment pass through Mrs. Solloway's smile. What parent, after all, wants to see a child leave home?

"No presents for Christmas," Nathan said on the train ride back to Manhattan, our laps covered with bags of leftover food.

"What?" I asked, shaken from a dreamlike trance from overeating. "What do you mean?"

"We're not going to do presents."

"Who?" I asked.

"You and me."

"Why?"

"Because. I'm giving you a surprise," he said, bequeathing his secret with a devilish smile.

"If you're giving me a surprise then I have to give you something."

I turned and watched him think about it for a few seconds.

"Fine," he said. "Eighty bucks."

"*Eighty bucks*? For what?"

"For my present."

"You just said no presents."

"If you want to give me something I want—I want you to give me what I'm giving you. It costs eighty bucks."

"But how do I know I'm going to like it?" I asked.

"Because I know you."

Nathan insisted that my present to him remain a surprise for me; the only clue he would provide was that it involved a plane trip. When I mentioned that most plane trips cost more than eighty dollars, Nathan informed me that I was paying for the event, not the air fare. Nathan had had a good year at his firm; he had more new assignments than he could handle, and his boss, Brian, promised him a large end-of-the-year bonus. My plane fare, Nathan informed me, was to be a perk of his success.

"I don't understand why you had to pack so much," Nathan had said that morning, early Christmas Eve, when the cab dropped us off at LaGuardia airport. "We're just gone for two days."

"But I don't know where we're going," I had answered, a bit too testily. I was aggravated that I had not known what to take and I had stuffed an extra sweatshirt and a pair of dress pants into my suitcase at the last moment.

"It's a surprise," Nathan said, adopting that same slightly irritated-with-you tone. "It wouldn't be a surprise if I told you where I was taking you."

I'd spent years trying to second guess Nathan without much success, his spontaneity was one of the reasons why I fell so deeply in love with him. If he had asked me to guess where we were going, I would have supposed it to be one of the more romantic spots in the world—Paris, Venice, Vienna—for that's where I had always wanted to go. But for two days how far could we fly from Manhattan and still have time to do something wonderful? I felt our destination must at least be within our own time zone. We made it to the departure gate before I discovered that he was taking me to Miami.

"*Miami?*" I said out loud, now, perhaps with a tinge of too-much disappointment. "Why Miami?"

"It's a surprise," Nathan said again, irritated that my excitement did not match his.

On the flight south I had imagined we would be staying at the Hilton or one of the renovated grand Art Deco hotels of South Beach. I had imagined a terrace overlooking the beach, imagined, too, a seven-course Christmas dinner—that was worth eighty bucks, right? Moonlight, dancing, trendy shops. Nathan surprised me again at the Miami airport when we approached a car rental counter.

Key West? I had then thought. Maybe he's driving us to Key West? Or Fort Lauderdale? I hated all this supposition, really. I would have preferred to just know where the hell we were going.

We ended up at a motel south of Miami, somewhere beyond one of those meaningless exits off of Highway 1. There was no beach, no pool, just a flashing neon sign and a bar. Our room had stains in the tub, stains on the wall, stains, too, on the carpet and bedspreads. I pointed none of this out to Nathan, however; this was, after all, his gift to me. Nathan, of course, gave me no explanation for any of this; I could even sense him crowing silently with glee as I tried to figure it all out. For a while I became lost in the novelty of it all—a fantasy that we were robbers on the lam, fugitives from justice, or simply two lovers escaping the fears of their generation. We had dinner at a table just beneath the flashing neon sign, a surprisingly good one in which everything seemed to be deep fried in the same hot oil.

There was a thickness to the air that night, and we drew closed the heavy, plastic-lined curtains and cuddled up together on one of the single beds, watching the flickering light of the television till sleep overcame us. This was all I really wanted, I thought sometime before I drifted off into sleep—to be with Nathan, to spend another Christmas with him.

"I have a present for you," Nathan said, nuzzling his cheek against my face the next morning, then pressing his lips against mine till I opened them to receive his kiss. I squirmed a bit to wake myself and he rolled on top of me and pinned my wrists against the mattress with his hands. I smiled up at him, tensed my body to shake off the rest of the sleep. "You said no presents," I said, my voice a hoary morning whisper, taking in, now, the stains of the hotel room, our clothes discarded on the floor from the night before. "You'll need this," he said, and jumped off the bed, opened his suitcase and returned with a small box wrapped in slick gold foil paper.

I shook the small box in front of my face, wondering if it was a confirmation of this outlaw-renegade motif I had imagined, something like a pistol, a Bowie knife or maybe, even, a hand-grenade. The box was too light to be any of those things, and I thought as I unpeeled the gold wrapping paper that it was probably a stash of condoms. I was surprised when I opened it up and discovered a shiny, red bikini swimsuit. "I need *this*?" I asked with a laugh. It was nothing I would have considered purchasing myself.

Nathan bit off the tag, flipped the sheet off me, and began to slip it over my legs. "Stand up," he said, after he had pulled it on with my squirming help. For a moment I believed this was all some sort of kinky experiment Nathan was up to. Against the dark hair of my stomach and my pale complexion, the bright red fabric of the suit made me look like, well, a tourist. I knew it was too skimpy for me, the fit was too snug, and when I looked at myself in the mirror above the desk, I could see it accented my ass a little too much.

"It looks fab-u-lous," Nathan said. I gave him a frown and placed my hands on my hips. "And you have to wear it the rest of the day."

"*The rest of the day?*"

"You'll need it later. Our appointment is at one o'clock."

"*Appointment?*"

Nathan gave me one of his smirks and for a moment I had wondered what our appointment could be. A fortune teller? Then why the bikini? Then the thought occurred to me that perhaps there was some spa down the road, some spectacular oasis of which I was not aware. Or maybe we were headed into an orgy. Could this be one of Nathan's attempts at opening up our relationship? We had passed through that point long ago and Nathan, I knew, was now smarter and more caring than that. But he did love mystifying me, though, and I knew that he might be getting more pleasure out of baffling me than in what might reasonably lie ahead for us.

At a few minutes before one o'clock we turned down a gravely road about five miles from the motel. We parked next to another car that leaned up a hill toward a fence made from planks of wood and chicken wire. At that point I was convinced that Nathan had indeed turned us into some sort of criminals, and we walked up the hill toward a small stucco building that looked to be an electrical shed.

A young boy, maybe eight or nine, met us at the side of the shed. "This way, this way," he said quickly and waved his hand from beneath a towel that he had wrapped around himself. The boy was dressed in short swimming trunks, which were wet, clinging to his legs and sending streams of water ribboning down his white legs; a small orange life preserver was strapped around his chest like a jacket. I watched him shiver in the warm air and adjust his towel over the humps of the jacket, then followed his darting, sparrowlike steps around the building.

We headed down another hill, below us was the ocean and its wide panoramic sweep, a string of popcorn white clouds bisecting the sky. At the bottom of the hill was a rectangular lagoon filled with black, motionless water, squared off from the sea by what appeared to be a wall of sand bags. Another boy, this one a thin, tanned teenager sporting the beginnings of a mustache and the ragged patch of a goatee, met us on our way down the hill. He was dressed only in cut off jeans and a twisted leather chain that rested just above his collar bones, his wavy, surfer-blond hair slicked back away from his face. He yelled up to us that his mom and dad were away for the day, in Fort Lauderdale, doing a "Christmas thing" with his grandmother, and he was in charge and his name was Tad.

Nathan, who always seemed so boyish to me, became at that moment a grown-up man. When the boy approached us, Nathan reached out and firmly shook his hand. We were led to a picnic table that stood beside the lagoon and introduced to a family, the Lamberts, who had traveled to Florida from Wisconsin: Wayne; his wife, Sherry; his oldest son, Marshall—the boy we had met by the shed; his daughter, Jennifer; and his youngest son, Cliff, a small, bald boy about six years old with bulbous brown eyes who wore an even smaller version of the orange life preserver than his brother did. They stood before us, smiling and bowing; Wayne's top-heavy physique was inverted, pear-like, and resembled his wife's figure—the children, however, were surprisingly lean and wiry. Tad asked us if we needed to change, the Lambert family was already in their swimsuits. Nathan shook his head, and indicated we were wearing our swimsuits beneath our jeans. Here Nathan gave me a glare as he unbuckled his belt, warning me not to start any trouble. I ignored him and lifted my T-shirt off first, and then, unhappily, removed my jeans, revealing to the small crowd my skimpy red bikini.

No one seemed to take notice of it though; that was the same moment that

Tad let out a piercing whistle, a sound which at first startled and embarrassed me, until I looked out at the lagoon and saw two silver dolphins rise and flip in the air. This, then, was to be Nathan's and my Christmas present to one another—swimming with the dolphins in a large black lagoon just outside of Miami.

Tad had Nathan and myself don rubber masks, snorkels, and flippers; the Lamberts, we discovered, were already pros at handling all this equipment; they had been swimming in the lagoon since early morning. As the dolphins reappeared at the surface of the water we were introduced to them: Mickey and Judy—each, we discovered from the Lambert children, had its own peculiar personality.

"Mickey is the fastest," Marshall said to Nathan, and I realized the children had abandoned their parents and were gathered around us. Mickey was also the larger of the two dolphins and kept flicking water at Marshall with the point of his nose. "Judy likes girls best," Jennifer said, sucking on one of the beige straps of her life preserver. I watched Nathan lift his eyebrows at the announcement, then turn to me and give me a wicked grin. Nathan had had difficulty containing his smile since we had arrived, and he kept checking my reaction periodically to make sure I was experiencing his same sense of delight. "I helped feed them," Cliff, the youngest, said to me, clutching my knee. The thought occurred to me, here, that maybe Nathan had chosen this event for us not to swim with dolphins, but to swim with children, and for a moment I had wondered how Nathan could have known the Lamberts without my knowledge of it. But before I even had a chance to figure anything out, Tad had interrupted my thoughts by demonstrating how we were to grasp the dolphin's dorsal fin to be taken for a ride.

We followed the Lambert children down a ladder into the water and waded over to a chain link fence where the dolphins were to pick us up for our rides.

"Are you scared?" Cliff asked me when we were in the water and I realized the boy was holding onto my neck instead of the fence. The water was surprisingly warm, but I felt a thin shiver where the wet skin of my chest met the cooler air. My heart was hammering both from excitement and anticipation.

"Does it show?" I said to the boy, trying to give him a laugh.

"Let them find you," Tad said, and I realized he was almost behind us, sitting on the ledge of sand bags.

Nathan and Marshall edged out into the lagoon; Marshall easily clutched Mickey's fin when it surfaced and went skimming through the water to the other side of the lagoon. Nathan floundered a moment by himself, till I realized that the smaller dolphin, Judy, was circling him. Then suddenly Nathan had grabbed hold of a fin and went traveling across the lagoon.

"Mickey's the smartest," Cliff said, and it was here that Mickey reappeared at Cliff's side and Cliff let go of my neck and grabbed onto the fin. Jennifer had waded out to meet Judy and the four of them were off to the other side of lagoon.

"Mickey'll take you out," I heard Tad say behind me, and I let go of the fence and waited for the dolphin to appear and arch its fin to the surface of the water.

How can you explain something that feels like flying through water? When I grabbed Mickey's fin and went riding through the lagoon, I was neither swimming nor floating; it was, really, more like, well, flying. When Mickey dropped me off and I surfaced, I saw Nathan pop up on the other side with Judy. He lifted his mask off his face, to show me his smile, and I waved to him. This was when Mickey appeared at his side and he grasped hold of the fin; Mickey brought him over to where I was treading water. Before Mickey disappeared beneath the water, I thought that I had caught his eye, an eye that seemed perhaps too human; perhaps knew, too, that Nathan and I belonged together.

"Smart dolphin," Nathan said; he was, at that moment, radiantly smiling. He looked out at the three Lambert kids clutching the chain link fence. "Happy?" he asked me.

"Always hope to be," I answered.

Sherry and Wayne were now making their way down the ladder and, as quickly as Sherry had eased into the water, Judy was taking her for a ride.

There is something about being in the water with other people, everyone near nude in their swimsuits, that can create a bonding and an intimacy between people. Perhaps it is the way the body breathes, the way one person helps another float, the way the eyes become enlarged, sensual, and reflective from the nearness of such a large quantity of liquid. The dolphins carried us back and forth across the lagoon that afternoon. Mickey, Nathan and I decided between ourselves, must be a gay dolphin; he loved to tap Nathan on the chest and spit a misty burst of air from the blowhole at the top of his head at me, a habit, we later learned from Tad, that Mickey did to keep the attention of someone he liked.

"They can read your bodies," Sherry mentioned to me later when we were together at the chain link fence, our fingers touching one another as they curled around the wire. She looked out at her son, Cliff, waiting in the middle of the lagoon for Mickey to surface. "This has helped him more than any sort of radiation," she said. "There's no price you can pay for that."

By the end of the first hour Nathan and I were carrying Cliff and Marshall on our shoulders, fighting and falling into the lagoon, the dolphins chattering at us, as though they were trying to scold us humorously. We stayed longer than the hour we had paid for, however; Tad rolled a joint and started smoking, and when he saw that it did not disturb any of us, he relaxed and let us just play. I sat out with him a while, passing another joint between us, watching the two boys chase Nathan around the lagoon, below them Sherry and Wayne waiting with Jennifer for the dolphins.

That was the day I noticed that Nathan's body was no longer a boy's: the texture of his skin was thicker, there were slight hollows beneath his eyes now, his hair had thinned—he now kept it cut short and businesslike. There is a point when a boy becomes a man, though, that is neither through some physiological change nor through some tribal rite of passage. It has, I believe, something to do with the acceptance of responsibility—for yourself, for others, for the world in which you live. In the time that I had known Nathan I had watched him mature from his young, restless, disco years into a responsible businessman. That day he seemed to become the sort of father that I had never imagined possible of him; I knew he was drawn to children, drawn, too, to childish things, but that day, that Christmas of 1986, was the first time I ever noticed the way he regarded things so carefully before acting—for instance, looking closely before leaping into the lagoon, making sure he was not diving into a child or a dolphin. I watched him help Jennifer adjust the strap of her mask and realized that Nathan, well, would make a good father.

Later, when Nathan and I were back together in the lagoon, Judy dropped Cliff off beside us. "I saw a rainbow," Cliff said, laughing as he lifted his head out of the water. "Under water. In my mask!"

"How many colors?" I asked, as he squirmed out of his mask. Once again he swam over to me and clutched my neck for support.

"Bunches," he yelled, well, as a kid would yell.

"Blue?" Nathan asked.

"Yep," Cliff answered.

"Red?"

"Yep!"

"Purple?"

"Yep! Bunches!"

Nathan swam over to us, so close that I could see the blood pulsing through a vein in his neck. "You can always see a rainbow," he said to Cliff.

Cliff's face worked its way into a question, "How?"

"Cry and then smile," Nathan said.

Cliff briefly gave it consideration. "No, you can't," the kid yelled suspiciously.

"Watch," Nathan said and he set his eyes so close to the water they began to fill up with tears. He then lifted his head and tilted his face to the bright sky, smiling and squinting his eyes together at the same time. "I see a rainbow," he said in the same tone that moments ago Cliff had used. It occurred to me, in that instance, that Nathan, in aging, would never shed his boyish sense of adventure, nor would I ever want him to.

Cliff let go of my neck, pressed his eyes close to the water as Nathan had done, then lifted his head to the sky.

"Keep your eyes open, just slightly," Nathan said to Cliff. "Do you see the rainbow?"

I watched Nathan and Cliff contort their faces into rather silly and similar expressions and it was here, then, that I realized that I could have fallen in love with Nathan anywhere; it didn't have to be Manhattan, didn't have to be at the end of the Seventies, and what I always wanted from him—a life together—could have happened anywhere, any time in the world.

"I see a rainbow!" Cliff yelled and then returned his eyes close to the water to experiment with it again.

On the plane back to Manhattan later that evening I was wide awake from the excitement of the day, awake, too, from the luminous sheen the day seemed to give to everything in my sight now: the slick shine of the vinyl flooring as we walked into the airport terminal, our reflections in the enormous glass windows, the way the airport lights twinkled on the dark runway. After we had said our goodbyes to Tad and the dolphins, we exchanged addresses and phone numbers with the Lamberts beside our cars. We followed their car down the gravel driveway, and as Wayne turned into the highway, Cliff stuck his head out and yelled back at us, "Merry Christmas! Ho, Ho, Ho!"

That was the first and last time we ever saw the Lamberts, though many times throughout the years, I have tried to seize the hope and joy I noticed in Cliff that day, noticed, too, in all of the Lamberts. On the plane Nathan slipped into a silence—there was no need to verbally confirm our happiness with each other. Nathan opened his book, a science fiction novel, and read until he fell asleep. I felt, then, as I still do even now, lucky to have had Nathan in my life, a life full of so many different kinds of rainbows because of him; he had, after all, bequeathed to me a meaning for every color. How do you thank someone for the joy they bring to your life? I thought, looking over at Nathan beside me, his cheek slipping down slowly in search of my shoulder, is loving them the only way? I wondered, then, how Nathan and I—two gay lovers—could make our lives together become more of a family. Family, I thought, such a limited religious concept to so many people. Wasn't my father no longer my family because of the brutal, disregardful way he treated me, even though we were related by blood and genetics? Wasn't Nathan's mother more of a real family to him, even though he was adopted? Wasn't family merely a sense of love and responsibility to one another? Didn't our family—Nathan's and mine together—extend well out into our lives, into the way we kept our home, the way the postman sorted our mail into the same box, the way our neighbors recognized us together, the way our friends were so important to us that they became our responsibility—our family, in many ways?

"Stop thinking so much," Nathan would have said to me if he were, well, inside my mind, which, of course, he very much was. I finally drifted into a light, conscious sleep, but awoke when I felt Nathan shudder.

"We were crashing," he said. His skin was pale and clammy and he ran his fingers around the collar of his T-shirt as if to send air down to his skin.

I looked abruptly around the darkened hull of the plane, then realized Nathan was only referring to his dream. "No," he said, and squeezed his eyes together. "That's not right. The planet was exploding. There wasn't room for both of us." He opened his eyes and looked at me, as if we were to be parted forever in just a moment. "Only one of us could escape," he said.

"I'm not going anywhere without you," I said, reaching above his head to turn off the bright, recessed spotlight which was making him look so uncomfortable. "And you've been reading too much."

Nathan went back to work the next day, there were some drawings he wanted to finish and several end-of-the-year forms he was worried about. I had taken the week off and I puttered around the apartment a bit; in the evenings Nathan and I met friends for dinner. Toward the end of the week I decided to refinish the kitchen cabinets, and I took the cabinet doors off their hinges and began to strip off the layers of enamel that had for years hidden the carved details of the wood. This annoyed Nathan to no end—he hated to see things in a state of flux. The smell of paint remover bothered him, the paint shavings and newspapers on the floor bothered him, the dust bothered him; even the sight of my carpenter's belt on the seat of a kitchen chair bothered him. All of this only led to another one of our ongoing fights about the fact that my tools—screwdrivers, jigsaw blades, chisels, sandpaper blocks, and a nail gun—were always so visible throughout the apartment. New Year's Eve, as we were dressing to go to Jerry's party on the Upper West Side, Nathan flew into a tizzy about a putty knife I had left on the floor that I had been using to pry open the lid of a can. He accused me of being inconsiderate; I accused him of being anal retentive. Look, I pointed out to him, he had thrown my clean T-shirt in the hamper before I had even had a chance to put it on.

Once we got out of the apartment, we both apologized to one another. Jerry's studio apartment, that evening, was full of men, packed so tightly when we arrived, it seemed as though we were walking into a beer blast at a gay bar. I have never been comfortable in crowds and I worked my way to the table that served as the bar, slipped behind it, and kissed Jerry on the cheek, helped him fix drinks, and settled into an adaptable space of my own. Nathan edged his way through the room toward an open window, pausing to speak to his friend Martin, who at that moment was trying to make his way to a bowl of nacho chips.

Later, when the crowd had thinned out after the realization that a new year had set in, after all the party hats and noisemakers had been used, abused, and tossed into the trash, I noticed Nathan sitting in the windowsill, holding a plastic cup, talking with Curtis, another friend of ours. It was then, seeing him across the room in the light that the candles threw off from their positions on the bookshelves—his sharp, patrician profile, the way his Adam's apple bobbed as he spoke—that I felt my stomach leap through a dizziness. It was, of course, another moment of my recognizing the joy of being with Nathan.

I was helping Martin throw some trash into large black garbage bags when he said, "A bunch of us are going to the hospital tomorrow to see Hank. About noon. Why don't you guys come with us?"

I looked up at him, startled and confused. "Hank?" I asked, my heart feeling as if it were about to jump out of my chest. "*Hank Watson?*"

Martin nodded. "He's over at NYU. I thought Nathan told you."

I shook my head, trying to conceal the wave of shock—part fear, part anger—that was making me breathe too rapidly now, the sound of my own air echoing in my ears.

"Now his doctor thinks it's toxoplasmosis."

I tried to listen as Martin explained how a neurosurgeon had drilled a small hole in Hank's skull for a tiny sample of brain tissue for a biopsy, but the details, as maddening and horrifying as they were, only made me grow more furious at Nathan. When had we stopped talking about things? Hadn't we both realized that there was no way we could escape this epidemic forever? Or had we never talked about anything at all, basing our relationship only on a string of good-time adventures? Or were we now so independent of one another that we weren't really a couple? Something more like roommates who had sex with each other? I was so angry at him for keeping this from me I was ready to stomp across the room and begin a war, ready to pull him aside and throw a nasty little tantrum. But even more than that, I was horrified that this was happening now to Hank—*and Nathan hadn't told me.*

"When did this all start?" I asked Martin, calmly looking him in the eyes.

"He was in the hospital the same time you were," Martin said. I nodded, aware, now, why Nathan would probably not have mentioned it to me. We were, then, fighting our own battle. But then I was hit with a sudden thought— another chain of possible infection, another reason for us to be worried, another reason for Nathan to keep quiet. Hadn't Nathan and Hank carried on their own little affair, back during the days when none of us were worried?

I felt my eyes tearing now from frustration, and I lifted my eyes up to the ceiling and squeezed them as I fretfully smiled, now dwelling on the rainbow of colors, blurry and ironic at the edges of my vision. Nathan must have noticed me, because it was then that he made his way through the room toward me. He knew, instinctively, that something was wrong, and he slipped his arms around my waist, pressing his forehead against mine. He was breathing very loud, then, a pushed out sort of breath through his mouth, as if he were out of breath. I could smell the sweetness of the alcohol on his lips. "You've had too much to drink tonight," I said, forcing myself to avoid a confrontation.

He ran the back of his hand along the side of my cheek, hearing the grainy sound of his skin against the stubble of my beard. "And you haven't had enough love today," he replied, drawing my lips to his with a kiss.

As it turned out I did not confront Nathan immediately about Hank; we were both tired on the cab ride home that evening after Jerry's party and I did not want to make Hank the antagonist of a quarrel. As it turned out I was unable to bring up the subject of Hank for some time. Our own war began that morning, January 1, 1987, in the emergency room of St. Vincent's Hospital. We did not know it was AIDS then, not that particular night, not that particular hour, but that is the time we trace it back to, to mark it as its beginning. Even though we both suspected it that night, a thought placed concretely in our minds, we denied it to anyone within our periphery as well as to ourselves; the thought of it, then, was so impossible to accept.

There were no warning signs; nothing, really, that Nathan or I first noticed. Nathan exhibited none of the presymptoms: nausea, night sweats, fevers, rashes, or swollen lymph glands. We were so familiar with the disease, so familiar, too, with each other's bodies, that the slightest perception of change would have alarmed us. I do remember a remark I had made at Thanksgiving at his parents' house that year; how I had complained that Nathan could eat and eat and not carry around an ounce of fat, and how I envied him for his metabolism. At five-foot-eight and still boyishly blond, Nathan seldom weighed more than 140 pounds; his skin had that thin, natural vascularity bodybuilders dieted for months to achieve.

But in the five years that Nathan and I had lived together I scarcely remember Nathan being sick. There were the headaches, of course; the nights he would come out from behind his desk, his head burning, his pale complexion flushed and his deep green eyes so tired I could sense sleep swelling them closed. We always believed the headaches were from tension, though; at times, I think Nathan often feigned a few—a routine had developed with Nathan shedding his clothes and lying face down on the bed. I would then straddle his thighs and massage his back and neck till I could feel the muscles and tendons soften like putty beneath my fingers. Some nights, the nights I really believed in the headaches, Nathan would fall asleep against my touch. Other nights, the ones I believed he pretended his malaise, he would roll over on his back and draw me into a kiss.

Was that denial, though, not noticing the headaches? The real ones? Nathan had always had a cast iron stomach, too. He could eat Mexican, Indian, and Brazilian dishes without even the slightest discomfort, where I was so obsessively worried every time diarrhea would strike me, analyzing every probable cause. So I was surprised on New Year's Eve when we came home from Jerry's party, and Nathan mentioned on the way up the stairs that he felt achy and I playfully pressed my hand against his forehead as he unlocked the door, only to feel the slick, burning flush of his skin. I found him some aspirin and we went to bed, but his fitful tossing kept lifting me out of sleep. Later in the night I felt him leave the bed and heard him begin heaving into the toilet. Food poisoning is what I immediately thought, and when the retching subsided, I helped him clean himself and convinced him that we should go to the emergency room. On the walk to the hospital—we lived only a block from St. Vincent's—we had to stop and start several times. Nathan was bent double with cramps and would have to lean against a wall and close his eyes to regain strength enough to continue. Standing there on the sidewalk, our breaths fiery puffs of moisture into the cold winter air, I kept going over and over in my mind the things we had eaten the day before. Had there been any fish? Salmonella in the chicken? Was the dip bad? At the front of my mind, though, was the suspicion that it might be something beside food poisoning; there was, after all, the fact that I had eaten everything Nathan had and I felt fine. Had the smell of the turpentine from the painting I was doing in the apartment made him sick? Could this have been caused from some kind of bacteria we might have picked up from the Florida waters? Or did Nathan simply drink too much at Jerry's party?

I have friends who feel it is inappropriate to summon up the metaphor of war to fight illness, particularly AIDS, but when the virus reveals itself it is like a war in the way it assaults the body, robbing first one soldier of the immune system, then another, till a break in the rank allows a contingent of villains easy entry for attack. The horrible thing about AIDS is its ability to lie dormant and undetected in the body for so long, assembling its villainous chain of nucleotides before making its presence known. In the early years of the epidemic there was considerable debate over whether one should even be tested for the virus. What good would it do, most of us believed, except bring about despair? There was no cure, no treatment; doctors were as mystified as their patients. And so when the body begins its war, each person's battle can be as different as one fingerprint is to the next; anything, then, becomes a potential weapon against the virus: a tablet, an IV tube, a small hand-held crystal, or, simply, a glass of water.

The first weapon is the hope that it is something else—something that does not allow it to be recognized as AIDS. By the time Nathan and I got to the emergency room that night, Nathan's temperature was 103 and his clothes were drenched from sweat; I held his head in my lap till an orderly wheeled a stretcher into the room and helped Nathan to lie on it. While we waited in a hallway for Nathan to be assigned a room, I kept nudging him into consciousness, fearing it was not sleep that was pulling him under. "Everyone's getting the flu," I kept whispering to him as I wiped his forehead with the corner of the sweatshirt I had been wearing. Already I was myself sweating from fear, but even then, I remember thinking, the worst thing that I suspected was that it could be—at most—what, an attack of appendicitis?

Once Nathan had been placed in a room, I felt comfortable enough to let him fall into sleep, but he was continually aroused for a battery of tests—why is it that just when the body craves repair and rest, doctors and nurses and interns appear to poke and prod, causing only more weakness and worry? Nurses arrived to take his pulse, his temperature, his blood, even to present a tray of food he could not eat. He was given sedatives and pain killers and hooked up to an IV to replenish the fluids in his body, but before all this was done he was wheeled away for X-rays. One by one things were dismissed or ruled out. It wasn't appendicitis, wasn't food poisoning, wasn't a gastrointestinal obstruction, wasn't, even, just the flu. None of the doctors or staff had any names in those hours; they arrived and disappeared the way travelers pass through customs.

Nathan's fever finally leveled off at 101, but late in the day a new doctor arrived, entered the room with an indifferent shrug and looked at Nathan's chart. Flatly he announced that the chest X-ray looked clear, except for a shadow that was probably the pulmonary artery, but he wanted to order a CAT scan to make sure it wasn't a lymph node. *Lymph nodes, lungs*—I remember thinking—weren't we here because he can't keep anything in his stomach? I followed the doctor into the hall and, here, grabbed the sleeve of his jacket before he disappeared.

"But what is it?" I asked. "What is going on?"

He turned and looked at my face, saw my concern, but just as quickly I noticed him shake it off, as if he knew what I was thinking but could not bear the emotional weight of it.

"It's too soon to say for sure," he said. "I want to be certain. The blood tests will be back tomorrow. And I may want to do a bronchoscopy."

I let go of his sleeve, watched his hand drop to his side, and though no diagnosis had been uttered the suspicion of it had been confirmed. The next day he came into the room and announced the results of the tests—there was evidence of pneumocystis in Nathan's lungs. Nathan looked first at the sheets of his bed, then over to me, but I looked away, feeling too awful to meet his eyes. I had escaped. Nathan had been caught.

"And the blood test came back positive," the doctor said, then cleared his throat with a cough. "Antibodies for HIV," he added, as if he felt a more precise explanation was in order. And then the doctor did a most remarkable thing. He sat on the edge of Nathan's bed, and in doing so, filled up the hollowness of the room. "My name is Ben," he said. "Ben Nyquist. I've been gay longer than I've been a doctor." It was here that I looked up at him, felt Nathan shift his eyes toward him too, and I realized he must be close to our age. "This is pneumonia and we can fight this. I've helped a lot of men through this. But I can't do it with just medicine and pharmaceutical tricks. You have to help me," and here he turned and looked squarely at Nathan. "You have to want to get well, you have to let me know what hurts, what doesn't seem right, where the discomfort is, what is happening to you. You have to tell me things you might not tell anyone else." Then he turned to me and I felt Nathan's eyes follow him. "And you have to encourage him to do it."

What he did in that moment was deflect the diagnosis of AIDS and tell me not to clutch so desperately to Nathan. He wasn't offering us a cure after all, only a way to make it through this first battle. The weapon he had given us was hope. "We're going to start with a Bactrim drip," Dr. Nyquist said.

That was the first assault of the artillery of drugs.

The battle of AIDS is more than just a battle for health; it is also a battle against pride, vanity, denial, and fear. At first there was no conscious attempt to keep Nathan's illness a secret; he was in the hospital the first few weeks of January, a time when people normally slip away from one another, recovering from the social overburn of the holidays. In those first few days the thought of telling people did not occur to us; we were, after all, dealing with the shock of the facts ourselves. *"Nathan is in the hospital,"* was all I would say when I got Brian, Nathan's boss, on the phone to tell him Nathan would be out of the office for a while. *"Intestinal problems,"* was all I could add when pressed for more details. *"No visitors, yet,"* I stressed, and then felt the enormity of it all descend on me and my voice grow thin and confused. *"He'll call you in a few days,"* I explained. *"Things are difficult right now."*

In many ways not telling anyone that Nathan had AIDS was our way of refusing to acknowledge the virus, a form of denial as it were; the most pressing concern was getting Nathan immediately back to health. In those first few days of his diagnosis Nathan and I had many issues to grapple with, what did all the tests and numbers and anagrams mean, what were the drugs doing, was a rash, for instance, a side effect or a symptom. Since we began living together I had always allowed Nathan an independence in the relationship; I never really tried to pin him down from moment to moment—to do so would have made me a jealous mess. But now I could not bear to let Nathan out of my sight, even as I was aware that fear gripped my every thought. I knew a hysterical partner would do Nathan no good, but knew my face could not discretely hide my underlying emotions, either. And Nathan knew me too well, could tell exactly what I was thinking and feeling. So I would silently watch a nurse tap Nathan's forearm and then slide a needle into his vein, watch him gag on a pill he couldn't swallow, hold him up as he walked to the bathroom—all without revealing my own discomfort as a witness. Only when he was asleep would I then walk into the hall, sit down in one of the chairs of the lobby and cry. I cried in the shower under the thick, warm spray of water, cried as I hurriedly dressed to return to the hospital, cried on the subway, cried when I entered through the doors of the hospital—but I never allowed myself to cry in front of Nathan. These are things we keep hidden from one another, the fear, the worry, the sorrow, too, that life was not going to be anything like what it used to be, or, for that matter, what it could be if things were not, well, so different.

"Are you ashamed of me?" Nathan had asked me the night Dr. Nyquist had broken the news to us.

"I'm not judging you," I answered. "Do you feel ashamed?"

"Yes," he answered. "And no." He was silent for a moment, as if he were checking his breathing, or finding, perhaps, a force for his voice.

"I don't regret anything," he said.

"Regret?" I asked, not expecting any answer, really, only needing to repeat the word. "How can you regret something you never knew existed?"

He said nothing else, but I watched, here, as fear reshaped his expression. He turned away from me, his face compressing into anguish. "You won't leave me?" he asked, almost inaudibly. "Will you?"

I was stunned by the question, though I should have known by then the battle against AIDS uncovers many layers of anxiety. "Nathan, what would I do without you?" I answered in a calm, even voice.

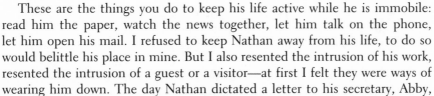

These are the things you do to keep his life active while he is immobile: read him the paper, watch the news together, let him talk on the phone, let him open his mail. I refused to keep Nathan away from his life, to do so would belittle his place in mine. But I also resented the intrusion of his work, resented the intrusion of a guest or a visitor—at first I felt they were ways of wearing him down. The day Nathan dictated a letter to his secretary, Abby, when she had shown up to check two different sketches Nathan had drawn, I sat watching them with a silent rage. But Nathan perked up when he began quizzing her about the status of a client's account, and I realized that this mattered to him. I called Brian at home later that night and asked if it were possible for someone from the office to stop by at least once a day. I knew he was still puzzled by all this intestinal stuff, but he allowed it to continue, knowing the truth would unfold sooner or later.

Nathan had been placed in a room which he shared with a fellow named Sam Karan. Sam, a few years younger than Nathan, was tall and elegantly thin, and looked as if he had been folded up and slipped into a hospital bed. He had severe KS, his body covered with reddish lesions the size of nickels, and he was continually coughing, a mild, gurgly underwater sort of cough that always made his presence keenly felt. Sam insisted to his every visitor—and there were many—from the beautiful young men who stepped cautiously into the room—to his mother and older sister who continually fussed about him—that they acknowledge Nathan's presence, include him in their conversations. Sam preferred to have the heavy plastic partition open to give the room more space, and by bringing us so willingly into his life, made us, really, see that we were not alone in our struggle.

On his sixth day in the hospital, just as things had begun to look better—Nathan's strength had begun to return and we had settled into a routine—he started running another fever, leaping from 102 to 103 to 101 back to 102. Nathan kept floating in and out of an exhausted sleep. I felt certain that the infection was spreading, or worse, another infection had set in, but when Dr. Nyquist arrived he noticed a rash on Nathan's chest—probably an allergic reaction—and he took Nathan off Bactrim and began Pentamidine.

That evening, before leaving to go back to the apartment, I sat in the lobby, not really ready to leave, my mind a heavy cloud of details, and I sat there trying to sort through things, wanting someone to just tell me what to do.

"I see you better?" I heard a voice ask, and I looked up and there was the Jamaican nurse who had visited me when I was in the hospital myself the year before with my own suspected bout of pneumonia. She was leaning over me, the whole large mass of her stuffed into a starched white uniform like a sausage, and over the tiny whites of her eyes the thick, painted lines of her eyebrows were wide and arched in surprise, her smile flattening out her broad nose. She carried a paper cup of coffee and as she sat down beside me I watched a thin stream of steam rise and disappear as she tried to smooth out with the palms of her hands the wave her uniform was making at her lap.

"You remember me?" I asked, surprised she even recognized me, thinking there must be so many people who pass through her life.

"You the student," she said and I noticed a gold crown at the back of her mouth.

"Student?" I answered in a way that revealed my depression. She had not remembered me after all; instead, she had confused me with someone else.

"The one looking and learning," she said, her voice announcing it like poetry. I gave her a shrug, indicating that she was wrong, she had mistaken me. "Sure you are. You the one with the mind that never close. Looking and learning. I seen you when you were here last. You the one who want to know all the why."

She took a sip of her coffee, fumbled with a napkin which was underneath the cup, then shifted her large body so that she could sit on the edge of her chair and lean in closer to me.

"What room your friend here?" she asked.

I was startled now that she could have remembered Nathan too.

"Third floor," I answered. "372."

"Ahhh, with Sammy," she smiled again, nodding her head up and down. "I stop by and say hello," she said, balancing the coffee cup on the tight spread of the fabric of her uniform at her lap. "All these boys. So strong."

I was not really ready for a conversation with anyone and I felt my eyes move away from her, out into a huddle of visitors in the middle of the lobby and then through the glass window, out into the traffic of Seventh Avenue. "This is not all pain," she said and I looked back at her again. "This is life beginning and ending, sorting out the problems of the body. But the soul is what you keep. Look for the soul."

She shifted herself again, as if ready to leave, but stopped and leaned in even closer to me. I smelled a hint of honeysuckle and soap, studied a line of bumpy freckles that painted her cheekbone, then I looked at her hospital identification tag, reading the fine print above her photo that read Dora Ferdinand. "Do you pray?" she asked.

"No," I answered, and I was not in the mood, either, to be preached to.

"I don't know much about God," she said. "Who does, really? But praying keeps me low, you know?"

"Low?"

"Level. Calm. If you don't pray to God," she said. "Then pray to love. Make God what you need Him to be for you. Pray that you keep the love of the soul, even after the body dies."

She stood and flattened out her skirt. "Pray," she said again before she left. "It's a good way to learn."

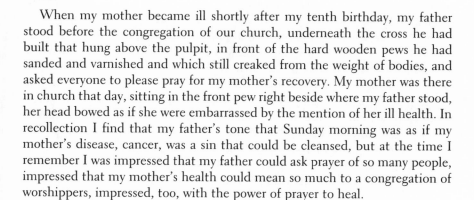

When my mother became ill shortly after my tenth birthday, my father stood before the congregation of our church, underneath the cross he had built that hung above the pulpit, in front of the hard wooden pews he had sanded and varnished and which still creaked from the weight of bodies, and asked everyone to please pray for my mother's recovery. My mother was there in church that day, sitting in the front pew right beside where my father stood, her head bowed as if she were embarrassed by the mention of her ill health. In recollection I find that my father's tone that Sunday morning was as if my mother's disease, cancer, was a sin that could be cleansed, but at the time I remember I was impressed that my father could ask prayer of so many people, impressed that my mother's health could mean so much to a congregation of worshippers, impressed, too, with the power of prayer to heal.

My mother's health did not get better, though; after school I would ride in the car with my parents for the thirty mile trip to the suburbs of Galena, to a parking lot of a large shopping center, where I would sit and wait in the car as my mother went first into a doctor's office, and then next door into a pharmacy. On the long ride home my mother would sit in the front seat coughing, lean her head back against the plastic cushions of the seat and close her eyes. Once, she asked to lie in the back seat; another time, we stopped and I watched her disappear into a ravine, then return pale and clutching my father's arm, settling back again into the front seat and looking through her purse for lipstick.

On those days I would wait for my mother, I would pray for her to get better. She did not get better, of course, the parking lot of the shopping center soon became the parking lot of a hospital, my father still suggesting that I remain in the car, out of everyone's way. I would sit on the hood and look up at the twelve story building, the largest I had ever seen, wondering which room was my mother's and would I see her if she came to the window and waved. Prayer and medicine both disappointed me as a boy, for they both allowed, I believed, my mother to die. Years later, when I fell in love with Will, prayer once again failed me when my father and his religion denounced me and my sexuality. "People do not pray," Will said to me one night. "They beg. True prayer should be divorced from God and religion." We were lying in bed that night, the covers flung to the floor and Will was stroking my cock, my heart pulsing out of control at the sight of his thick, silver-haired wrist moving up and down me. "To pray is to desire, but it is to desire what God would have us desire, or, rather, what man's vision of God would have man desire." His fingers crawled up my belly to rest against my chest. "True prayer," Will said, and rubbed a finger around my nipple, "is a demonstration of belief in something."

If prayer was to be another weapon I could provide in Nathan's battle to regain his health, then I would use it, employ it, even, if necessary, preach it. What I wanted was our lives to be restored to the way they were before Nathan was ill, but knowing that prayer could not, realistically, provide me with that, I prayed that we could find some sort of stability with the virus. Instead, I rocketed through the unsteadiness of my confusions, shuttling between the hospital and the apartment with whatever weapons I could find to bring to Nathan: a clean pair of pajamas, a comic book, a new pair of socks, a postcard that had arrived in the mail. By the end of Nathan's second week in the hospital, Sam had been released and sent into a home-care program, and that first night without him in the room I fell asleep in the chair beside Nathan's bed as we watched a rerun of "Laverne & Shirley." When I awoke during a commercial Nathan was in the midst of talking to me, but I only caught his last words, his voice groaning into a rasp of, "I can't do this."

I lifted my head, felt the tendons of my neck cramp with movement. "What?" I said, in a voice full of annoyance.

"I can't do this," he snapped back at me.

"You have to," I said. "I'm not giving you up that easily."

His face went through the contortion of a man frustrated with misunderstanding. "No," he said. "I have to tell people."

I stared ahead, watching the television screen snap into a beer commercial. "Are you sure?" I asked. "Have you thought this all through?"

"What else have I got to think about?" he answered. "I've got to get through this."

Nathan began by telling his mother first. The morning after he had announced it to her over the phone she was there at the hospital. I never knew exactly how much Nathan confided in his mother about his life, was never really certain myself if I knew all there was to know about him; I had long ago resolved that what I didn't know about Nathan I wouldn't worry about. But the morning Mrs. Solloway appeared in Nathan's hospital room I felt a fear that she would see Nathan's illness as retribution for the lifestyle he had chosen, or, even worse, turn to me as a source to place the blame. If circumstances were different I could certainly envision my father's reaction as such; I even could have expected that of my mother. But Nathan's mother possessed a liberalism that is rare in parents, due, perhaps, I've always believed, to Nathan being her foster child and not her natural one. Nathan was not really worried about what she thought; he was worried, instead, that she would hover over him too much. "You're doing it enough," he said to me the day he told her. "That's not what I want from her." What he wanted, simply, was for his mother to possess an awareness of his fight. What she provided, however, was another source of strength.

When she arrived at the hospital Mrs. Solloway began doing the thing that neither Nathan nor I could do; she began calling people. Nathan and I would give her names and phone numbers; her voice was calm and purposeful with every call. She was careful not to make her call sound as if it were a death alert; in fact, she orchestrated it both to inform the caller of the news and let them know they were needed in the struggle. She called Martin and asked him to bring some clean pajamas to the hospital for Nathan, and then called Jerry and asked him if he could bring some cookies because there would be people dropping by the room and food was always a great deflector. She had a long conversation with Brian and Abby concerning the best way to keep Nathan updated about the office but not overworked, and then she even called a client who had been particularly anxious about Nathan's drawing being unfinished. "No one is going to fire his mother," she said to me when she finished her call, proud, I believe, to have a new importance in her son's life.

Not everything was as easy and succinct to orchestrate. That was the same day that Vince called the hospital, and when he was connected to the room and I answered the phone, he said, surprised, "Robbie, what's going on? I've been trying your apartment for days. I finally called your landlord. Are you okay?"

"Vince," I said, glancing over to Nathan to let him know who was calling, feeling at that moment that I wanted to hang up because of the pressure. Nathan had been flipping through an old issue of *The New Yorker* and he stretched out his arm and I handed the phone over to him.

"Vince," Nathan said. "I need a favor. Can you tell this to Jeff and Denise, too?"

Friends helped us as if we were family; a network of support webbed itself around us as we moved Nathan from the hospital back to the apartment. Nathan and I were seldom alone now; Martin went out for prescriptions and Jerry would bring videos and magazines, Debbie and Andrew, our neighbors, took the laundry to the corner and brought food to us, Brian and Abby would come by with specifications and details for a drawing Nathan might be able to work on for about an hour in the morning. From California Jeff even called one of his actor friends in Manhattan who doubled as a barber and who showed up at the apartment one day to give Nathan a haircut. Denise and Vince called periodically, as much to check our progress as to make their presence known. It seemed as if there was someone with us every step of the way.

But it was Mrs. Solloway I was continuously aware of. It was always a shock to see her sitting on the couch as I passed through the small room that separated the bedroom from the kitchen; the sight of her sleeping or looking through her suitcase always unnerved me, reminding me that things were not as they should be. Manhattan apartments are tediously cramped, no matter how large they appear to be, and I sensed Mrs. Solloway's perfume in the fabrics of the apartment, her toiletries lined the bathroom counter beside Nathan's and mine, a stray strand of her long, grayish brunette hair could be suddenly detected as a beam of sunlight fell across a chair. When she was sitting with Nathan in the bedroom I would oftentimes find myself watching her every move, as if some sort of subtextual behavior was to be revealed to me in the way, for instance, that her fingers were folded around each other and rested atop her lap. I don't think it was the presence of a woman that really disturbed me, or even that she was an older woman, of a different generation; it was the presence of a mother that left me so uneasy, made me very much aware of the absence of mine within my own life.

Nathan had been born while his father was in boot camp in North Carolina, two months after his parents had been married in north Florida. Nathan's father had died while on a three-day leave in Seoul and a stray bullet from a prostitute's mishandling of another soldier's gun caught him just below the heart; his mother, despondent, turned to drinking and not much later flipped her car off Highway 53 one night driving home from a bar and was instantly crushed when the car landed in a ditch. His mother's mother had died several years before and his grandfather in Florida had no interest in raising a three year-old child on his own. His father's parents still lived just north of Tallahassee in the trailer park that his father had escaped by joining the military. There were already seven other children in the family, one as young as Nathan, and there were problems with the county child welfare officials over charges of sexual abuse. Nathan was shuttled between agencies and foster homes until he was four years old and adopted by the Solloways. Nathan had told me he had once made a phone call to his grandmother when he was a teenager, Mrs. Solloway reluctantly bequeathing the number after considerable whining on Nathan's part. The conversation was pretty uneventful, or, rather, pretty memorable, full of a lot of harsh sounding phrases like "Who?" "Nothing." "No." and "Really?" Nathan had been unable to make any kind of emotional connection with his family through that phone call, and it was Mr. Solloway who had explained that sometimes families are created out of a different bond besides blood, that love is sometimes stronger in these other kinds of families, a remark Nathan would remind his father of years later when he first announced that he was bringing me to their home in Hartford for a visit.

But in all the years that Nathan and I had been together, I had never been able to conquer the sheepishness I felt at displaying my affection for Nathan in front of his mother, and I always believed I sensed some discomfort from her when she was forced to think of us as a couple, even though there were never any outward signs from her as such. But now she took pains to touch me, to acknowledge my presence, holding my hand or placing her palm against my shoulder, slipping her hands into the water while I was washing dishes in order to graze her fingers across mine before lifting a plate out to dry.

"Did you help her?" she asked me one night after Nathan had gone to sleep and I was in the kitchen drinking a beer.

I knew Nathan had long ago explained to his mother about my own parents, and, now, blown back into a memory I squinted my eyes, as much as not to remember as to try to recall some affection for my mother. "I don't think I was a very good son," I said to Mrs. Solloway, attempting, really, to avoid the weight of her question. Mrs. Solloway was standing at the stove, pouring boiling water into a cup. "I was very self-absorbed," I added.

She laughed, a big, hearty, motherly laugh. "Most children are," she nodded. "Most grown-ups are too."

There was a silence, then, and I watched her dip the tea bag in and out of the steaming water. "It was frustrating," I said. "I didn't know what to do. I remember I once saw her without her wig. It scared the shit out of me. I couldn't look at her for the longest while."

She sat across from me at the table, still dipping the teabag. "My mother was not the strong, silent type," I said. "She always had problems, and always let you know about them—tightness in her chest, pains in her back, her joints swelling, what she had just thrown up. There was nothing I could do to make her feel better. Something else was always wrong. Now I don't remember if she was really that sick or just a chronic complainer."

I watched her lift the teabag out of the cup and twirl the string around the bag, squeezing out the last of the dark liquid. "It could have been her way of making you notice her, or making your father notice her. Were you an only child?"

I nodded, then said, "I never knew how much I loved her till she was gone."

She nodded, here, along with me, and then cupped her hand over the rim of her mug to keep the tea warm, a habit I had often noticed in Nathan. "I had a child before we adopted Nathan, born premature. She didn't make it. After that I didn't want another child. How could I? And then one day I woke up and thought that if I adopted a child I wouldn't feel as much pain as this child grew and left home, that I could go about being a parent but without the emotional attachment. I was wrong of course," she laughed, lifting her mug to her lips but deciding the tea was still too hot to drink.

"And just because a child grows up and moves away, the responsibility of being a parent is still there," she said. "I have this friend, Helene Thurston, who angers me every time she mentions her son—she expects her son to send her money and take care of her when she's old. That's not why we become parents—to expect in the future that the roles will be reversed.

"I remember the day I was first frightened by the thought that Nathan would one day leave me. When he was a boy he used to cut out pictures from magazines of all the places he wanted to go and paste them into a book. He was a real dreamer. I never discouraged him, though. But I never wanted him to leave home. Last year, when you boys got back from London, Nathan called me and I told him I had gotten his postcard. And then I asked him if he remembered that book of cut-outs he used to keep. He said yes and then I asked him where he was going to go next, where in the world did he want to go? I didn't know you were in the hospital then, but I knew something was wrong. He said, 'It's not the places that are so important, Mom, it's who you have with you on the journey.'" She placed the mug to her bottom lip and took a short sip. "We're never aware of how much we love until we're faced with losing it."

Time is what you fight with AIDS. It's a disease of inches, difficult to chart, at times, on a day to day basis, robbing you, as well, of any plans and dreams. When Nathan was hospitalized I realized I knew so little about HIV, the way the virus replicates itself within the body; realized, too, how little hope the doctors could provide, what a gamble, a crapshoot, medicine was, after all.

Why does one antibiotic work for one man and not another? Why does one man develop KS while another struggles with pneumonia? Now, at night, I would awaken after a few hours of sleep, my body tensing because my mind was rested, ready to resume its thinking. It was then, deep at night, that I could no longer fight off my hatred. I would get out of bed, move to the couch or a chair, try to read, but instead I would be focused, resolutely so, on why this was happening to us. I searched and searched through my memory for someone to blame, but my exercise was futile, between Nathan and myself there must have been over five hundred men we had each slept with, and so I would just sit there hating myself, hating my situation, trying, with all my conviction, not to blame Nathan, not to hate him for bringing this into our lives— this, this unexpected virus. And so I would find myself rigid with thought even away from the bedroom, and I would roll my neck to unwind the stress, stand and stretch and return to the bed, unable to sleep. Sleep, now, was no longer an escape for me; such was the way anxiety inhabited my world.

AIDS creates fear in surges; every gay man facing AIDS reviews, at some point, the sexual contacts he has had in his lifetime. It's not really to try to pinpoint the source of infection—there is seldom a way of knowing which encounter was the source. I believe this review, this inspection, is to reassure ourselves that the act of sex itself was not the cause of the problem— sex, after all, is what defines and unites gay men; it is their God and their religion, the way they dress and talk and sing and move down the street, the way they meet their friends and lovers, the way, too, they define their community. What was at fault was a virus—a retrovirus—no one could have predicted. A virus that could possibly be transmitted between two men during a sexual act. How had an act that could bring both life and pleasure suddenly become darkened by illness and death? The act of sex, I felt—no, I decided, finally—was not at fault. What had to be accepted, what I had to remind myself over and over, was that sex between two men does not cause them to die. There were ways, even then, to prevent the transmission of the virus; but hadn't Nathan and I been practicing safe sex for years?

I have often wondered why God spared me instead of others; wondered, too, really, if there even is a God, came to question Him more and more the clearer it was understood that I was not to die of AIDS. Is it God that is so judgmental, or His Christian followers? Is suffering the punishment of sin or is sin the punishment? Was Nathan suffering because he was in love with another man? Was evil the root of the hatred which could sometimes crack my poise as swiftly as a thunderbolt? Religion falters when it teaches that gay men should be failures, pariahs, unloved and unlovable outcasts. Society suffers, as well, by treating these same men as exiles; families disintegrate when their sons become expatriates. But if, to me, AIDS is not a retribution, is there some sort of meaning in the challenge it provides to both the infected and the uninfected? Is there meaning in suffering or merely meaning from experience? And how, in that experience, do I find the manifestation of God?

What saved me from death or harm, for instance, the day when I was four years old and fell off a swing set? What saved me, years later, as I narrowly missed stepping in front of a Manhattan bus? Why did my mother die at an early age while my father survived to haunt me as an adult? Is there some grand scheme to the way my life unfolds before me?

Nathan would have said that I was looking for too much meaning in things. Why, for instance, couldn't I just believe in God?

"Life is a journey of decisions," Will once said to me after I had shrugged my shoulders and replied, "I don't care, either one," when he had asked me one Saturday night if I wanted to go to a movie or out dancing. I didn't really care which one we did, I was eighteen years old at the time and blindly in love with everything about Will: his tall, slender, runner's build, the bookish eyeglasses he wore, the short, stubbly graying horseshoe pattern of his hair. All I wanted was to be with him, no matter what we did or where we went. Will, however, thrived on debate and confrontation. "You weren't put into the world to be pampered," he would say to me if he felt things were becoming too comfortable between us, if he felt, for instance, I was just floating along and enjoying our relationship, which was, well, just what I wanted. His intention was neither evil nor devious; what he wanted was for me to be able to stand on my own two feet. He wanted me to decide, for instance, that we should go out dancing, but only so that he could convince me to go to a movie instead. Thus was the illogical construct of our relationship, which, in his fashioning, he never wanted termed or defined as a relationship. "We're falling into a trap," he would say about everything from my socks invading his underwear drawer to the way gay life seemed to be defined by the late night disco schedule.

I grew to learn to argue with Will, and a couple of times he acquiesced to my decisions after willful pouting on my part, but I have often felt that the best thing Will gave me was the knowledge of the subtle things about gay life. I picked up a sense of style from him, from a balance of color, fit, and fabrics in clothing to why irises are so much more elegant than red roses. These things were never explained to me, however; at a store Will would pick out a shirt and tell me to go try it on. Standing in front of him in a tightly buttoned shirt with my hair all wild and curly and in my eyes, he would tip his chin down so his tiny brown eyes could look over the frame of his glasses. "That's better," he would say, not even adding a smile. And then we would end up at the barbershop or the shoe store. And I learned to accept these opinions of Will's as new facts of my life.

Which is why the day I heard about Hank's death I found it so upsetting; Hank had been Nathan's guide into gay life as Will had been mine, and I knew the loss of him meant that Nathan must feel as if his past had been lost too, the creation and history of himself called into suspect as it were, as if all those questions and things one wonders about as they stumble into gay life hadn't really happened at all.

They met on the beach in Harwich Port the summer before Nathan was a senior in high school. Nathan's parents had taken a house on Cape Cod for a month; Hank was rehearsing and performing in a summer stock production of *The Comedy of Errors* that featured a roaming chorus of jugglers and mimes of which Hank was one. Hank wore only red suspenders and skin tight black tights in the play, but his costume was his short but magnificent body, all tensed and ribbed and striated and furry about the chest. Nathan never saw that performance, but he did meet Hank on the beach. Hank had settled near Nathan's towel one afternoon, though Nathan had not even noticed him then, absorbed, instead, in reading a book of science fiction stories by Isaac Asimov.

Like Nathan, Hank had a fascination for things fantastical, and at one point when Nathan looked up from his book, Hank smiled and asked if Nathan had read *Foundation*, which was his favorite Asimov book. Nathan nodded but said his favorite book was *The End of Eternity*, because it was about time travel, and they fell into a discussion of other authors and books from Bradbury and *Fahrenheit 451* to Vonnegut and *Slaughterhouse Five*.

Hank was a restless spirit, never content to just lie on the beach, relax, and talk about science fiction. At first he invited Nathan to join him for long walks along the foamy stretches of sand, but by the end of their first week of friendship Hank was teaching Nathan the movements of mime. Their relationship was not consummated sexually that year; Hank suspected all along that Nathan was gay, and their talks would often skirt around suspected topics of interest, from bodybuilding to dancing to what was trendy and exciting back in Manhattan where Hank lived. Nathan, however, was falling in love with Hank, fascinated with him in the same way I was with Will, from Hank's passion for blue snow cones to the smell of his underarms that wafted through the ocean breeze when they would lie side by side on beach towels. Hank aroused the gay man in the young Nathan, but he also charmed that adventurous boyish spirit.

They kept in touch by letter and phone, but their paths did not cross till two years later when Nathan moved to the city to begin his freshman year at New York University. Hank, by then, was wildly into the gay life and his openness both frightened and intrigued Nathan. Hank took Nathan to his first gay bar—Julius's in the West Village—a dark, somber bar frequented by a non-threatening neighborhood crowd, the kind of straight-looking men you would expect to see at ball games or business meetings. But he also walked Nathan to the Hudson River piers and the Rambles in Central Park, explaining what all the looks and codes and signals between men meant. Hank knew all the stories of the tribe by then, passing along gay history like gossip as they walked through the streets of Manhattan and in and out of stores, explaining the kind of love they shared with Alexander the Great and the exploits of Oscar Wilde and James Baldwin, embellished, of course, with Hank's own history—the details of his own tricks, from what he did to the guy who lived above the deli on Second Avenue to what type of furniture the man on 17th Street had in his duplex apartment.

And then, one night, he took Nathan back to his apartment in Gramercy Park, dimmed the lights and gave him enough wine till he was relaxed, then undressed him and led him into the bedroom. It is not hard for me to imagine the two of them together, Hank running his hands along Nathan's arms as if to warm a chill and then settling them about his waist; Nathan tensing first his back, then his buttocks, then relaxing as Hank drew him into a kiss, his tongue warm and ardent, easily parting Nathan's lips. I know how Nathan felt as Hank edged him slowly down onto the mattress: nervous and suspicious, but also wildly eager and thrilled. I felt the same way my first night with Will; Hank was the first man Nathan ever slept with.

For Nathan, this was a combination of mysteries revealed and lust requited. Hank explained, however, after they had been together a couple of times, that he wasn't "into" relationships and didn't intend to be in one with Nathan. He enjoyed the excitement and spontaneity of finding a new trick whenever he was eager for one, relished, too, the potential danger of anonymous encounters. Still Hank and Nathan got together occasionally, for dinner or movies, and then began going to the baths together—Hank abandoning Nathan the moment he had undressed at the lockers, Nathan wandering around fitfully for hours till he ended up in Hank's embrace long after they had both used and abandoned other strangers.

Hank, eight years older than Nathan, always recognized that Nathan was becoming too attached to him, and instead of opening up the possibilities of Manhattan to an inquisitive college boy, he set about fixing Nathan up on blind dates with friends who were looking for boyfriends, just as Vince had done for me all those years ago. Hank took Nathan to the bookstore in the East Village where Nathan found a part-time job, went with him to the blood banks and the sperm clinic in midtown where he showed Nathan how he could earn some extra cash. They went together to the revivals at the Thalia and the pool at the McBurney Y, and in the summers took the ferry out for day trips to Cherry Grove and the Pines. It was Hank's suggestion, too, that Nathan, for a lark, take the anatomy drawing class Hank modeled for at Parsons. Nathan, however, was angered by Hank's nudity in front of a classroom of artists and strangers, becoming close to tears because Hank was so unsympathetic of Nathan's feelings for him. Nathan still held the belief that one day Hank would realize the error of his ways and they would settle into a relationship.

At first Nathan's sketches in the class were wildly cartoonish and full of fury, the body all out of proportion, bulky and muscular, and often attached to a tiny, freakish-looking shiny bald head. This was before Hank began wearing that inexpensive toupee that Nathan so hated; instead, Nathan would sometimes help shave Hank's scalp, a process that he found both ironic and erotic. At the end of the twelve weeks of the drawing class, the instructor politely suggested that Nathan try something like graphic arts instead of figure drawing, but Hank noticed in one of Nathan's drawings the way he had exquisitely detailed the contents of the classroom, the small desks and chairs and the concrete blocks of the wall in the background. And so it was Hank who suggested Nathan try his hand at drawing landscapes.

It was always easy for me to be jealous of Hank. He possessed a part and history of Nathan that I did not know, and when glimpsed, aroused an immense jealousy within me; I always felt so intimately excluded from their friendship. I often heard stories of things they did together after the fact—never invited to participate with them, always retold of the adventure. I felt, too, that Hank took advantage of Nathan's good nature, borrowing money, for example, when he couldn't scrape up enough funds to meet his rent, even though Nathan, himself, was struggling to meet his bills. In many ways I always wanted to believe that Nathan outgrew Hank, the way a child outgrows a toy, but I know as Nathan drifted farther from gay life and deeper into our relationship through the years, they saw less and less of one another because I did not care that much for Hank. I knew they would occasionally talk and get together, knew, too, they got together more often than Nathan told me about, even if it was just Nathan showing up for the jazz classes Hank often taught around town. Hank also was still friendly with Jeff and I was invariably told second-hand of his exploits about town. The times that Hank found work in an off-Broadway play or showcase, Nathan and I always went to see it and visited with Hank backstage.

This then, was what happened to Hank: He was first hospitalized for pneumonia, then eleven months later he was back again fighting another bout when a doctor diagnosed the presence of meningitis in his spinal fluid. He also had a bacterial infection of his left ear, and his T cell count fell below 50. After three weeks in the hospital he returned home with a hospital bill of over $15,000. I knew all of this from phone conversations with Vince and Jeff. Nathan and I never discussed this, however; we avoided the subject of Hank like we hoped to avoid the plague. The next year Hank developed an abscess beneath his left armpit that required surgery and was treated at the same time for another ear infection. He had begun, then, to feel dizzy and light-headed and had trouble maintaining his balance. He continued to work part-time at a card store on Seventh Avenue, occasionally landing a role in a TV commercial; the residuals he earned from dancing in a thirty-second spot for a fast food chain nearly carried him out of debt.

But his memory began to increasingly fail him and he became lethargic and confused, till a friend, Tom, finally took him to the emergency room at St. Luke's-Roosevelt. A CT scan revealed an infection similar to Toxoplasma gondii, even though it could not be confirmed through a blood test ordered by his doctor. When he slipped into a coma, the doctors began treatment for toxoplasmosis. After a biopsy of his brain could still not detect the specific protozoa that causes toxoplasmosis, another doctor recommended radiation therapy for lymphoma of the brain. At first Hank responded by partially awakening and even reached a point where he was able to swallow small amounts of baby food that his mother, who had flown in from Iowa, had been able to feed him. Eventually, the coma returned and a week later, still unconscious and living off life-support machinery, he developed a bacterial pneumonia and died two days later.

It was Mrs. Solloway who gave me the news of Hank's death, filled me in with the more gruesome details of his illness when I came home one Saturday afternoon from having taken a quick job of building a loft bed for an apartment in Chinatown, though the whole time my concentration had been on worrying about Nathan and I felt I had done a sloppy job with the assignment. Mrs. Solloway had taken the call from Jeff, who had called from Los Angeles and who knew Tom, the guy who had been helping Hank at St. Luke's, and she had repeated the story to Nathan earlier in the day. Mrs. Solloway had known Hank as long as Nathan had; she had met him that summer in Cape Cod and had, in fact, even seen him perform in *The Comedy of Errors*. It always made me feel so guilty that Mrs. Solloway had liked Hank where I had not; I felt so small and judgmental knowing that she was so accepting.

"He took it well," she said, looking down at me sitting on the sofa where I had landed to absorb all the facts of Hank. "I think he took it well. Don't wake him up just yet, though, he finally fell asleep."

I slipped into the bathroom and took a long, steaming shower, though at the end I was still agitated, wanting to wake Nathan and hold him and let him know I was with him in this new crisis. He was awake when I entered the bedroom and I slipped the towel on the back of the chair and began to dress. We did not speak to each other but I was conscious of him studying my body as I bent over to put on socks and then a pair of sweat pants and a T-shirt. It was then that I first recognized a microbe of hate growing inside me, a disgust for the way things had changed for us, almost as though Nathan should be blamed. But I refused to believe it, pushed the idea of it back down inside of me, burying it beneath the skin and tissues and cells of my body, hoping it would never be found again.

"I don't want that to happen to me," he said, his voice cracking the silence of the room like a misfitted floorboard. I looked over at him and met his eyes, which were fixed and determined but reddened by sleep or crying, or, perhaps, a little of both.

"Promise me that you'll pull the plug," he said succinctly. It was, I think, one of those first moments between us that we had ever acknowledged the possibility of our own mortality, and I looked determinedly through the top drawer of the dresser for my hairbrush, not wanting to imagine the possibility of Nathan's death.

"And what happens if I go first?" I asked, hearing a tone of bitterness creep into my voice.

His eyes narrowed, and he replied, "Don't be cruel."

"I'm sorry about Hank," I said.

"I'm sorry, too."

"We should have," I heard myself breathe in air, "helped more," I said and shook my head.

"How?" he asked and I heard, then, an edge of bitterness within his voice. "We can't face our own facts."

"I'm sorry I'm scared," I said, remembering, then, the day I had finally walked away from Will, angry and hurt because I knew he could not give me the irresolute attention I wanted, scared, though, to find myself a young gay man so vulnerable and lonely within the world. By the time I had met Nathan I knew that I could never expect the kind of love that I had wanted of Will to happen with any man, even though I still, resolutely, believed it to be possible. I looked at myself in the mirror and tried to calmly brush my hair, noticing, as I did so, the creases of tension across my brow. Moments passed between us like years till I finally heard Nathan saying, "I could never give him up, you know."

"I know."

"I can't make those clean breaks like you," he said, referring as much, I believed, to my father as to Will.

"I never expected you to."

And then his demeanor shifted entirely, as if all the tension that held him into place had evaporated. "I didn't want Hank to be the reason why you left."

"I remember the first night I met you," I said, looking at the image of Nathan sitting up in the bed that was reflected in the mirror. "Christmas night, remember? It was like a gift, you know. I felt so lucky that Hank brought you to that party."

And then I felt myself turning and moving toward the bed, hearing myself say, as if an echo shouted across a ravine, as I slipped into the bed beside him, "But I always knew it would be a fight to keep you."

Nathan had always been the one of us who cooked, but I soon found myself helpless with so much restless time on my hands, unable to stop worrying about the prospect of Nathan's health, unable, really, to concentrate on anything else. Unwilling to return to work and with Mrs. Solloway usurping the cleaning chores, I began roaming the aisles of the grocery store, bringing home heavy brown bags of cans and jars of gourmet sauces, protein-enriched breads, plastic wrapped vegetables, and vitamins and herbs. I knew nothing about cooking, nothing more than how to fry a hamburger or grill a cheese sandwich, or, perhaps, how to heat a frozen entree or reheat a slice of pizza. The kitchen had always been Nathan's domain; I had never cultivated the patience for cooking.

At first I began by cooking large pots of pasta, then progressed to throwing fruits, milk, ice cream, and protein powder into a blender to create shakes, then, more boldly, began to experiment with pureeing broccoli, asparagus, and potatoes into soups. Food was what would save Nathan, I had decided; we had, by then, lost too many friends already from the inadequacy of medicine. Nathan was amused when I would walk into the bedroom and say, "Try this sauce, I just made it," and that delight is what sustained me when I returned to the kitchen to cook something else. Food soon became a new weapon in our war, a hope that could be created out of weight and mass.

Nathan had been sent home from the hospital with a stash of prescriptions: Compazin for his stomach, Nizoral for the thrush in his mouth, Cyclovir for the herpes sore on his chin. Dr. Nyquist had also given him prescriptions for Halcion and Xanax, for help with sleeping and anxiety, and had also started Nathan on a four-hour cycle of a new drug that was just completing clinical trials—Retrovir, soon to be more commonly known as AZT. Whether it was these medications that made him better, my cooking, or my prayers, I am not sure, but he did grow stronger. Nathan's mother went back to Hartford, friends calmed down, I went back to work, and Nathan was faced with being a man who was HIV-positive. But as easy as it was for the two of us to believe that Nathan was not living with an illness but coexisting with a virus, everything, nonetheless, seemed funneled into one fatalistic question: How much time did we have left?

But it would also be dishonest of me to say that every moment of my life was full of despair and misery when Nathan was diagnosed with AIDS. If the truth be told, our lives together became more intimate with the recognition that he was ill and what time we might be granted together could be limited by his health. But there was a period when Nathan did get better, or at least seemed healthier; he returned to work and our lives took on a false normalcy. So when Vince first called with the suggestion that Nathan and I should meet him and Jeff for a weekend in the Pines that summer, I had given him an eager laugh. "Of course," I had said, trying to pitch even more enthusiasm into my voice. "It'll be fun," I added. "Like the old days." Even then, there had been too much wistfulness in my voice, for what I had envisioned were the days before Nathan became sick—the days when Vince and Jeff and Michael and Wes and Pat and I and so many others had cavorted so carelessly on the Island.

It was, I concluded, one of those blind agreements friends make to one another just to reassure themselves that they are still the strongest of friends, a promise no one ever really expects to be fulfilled. I hadn't expected us to ever spend the weekend together. We never planned it. As easy as it was for us to suppress the recognition that Nathan was sick, there was still the consciousness that that could change at any moment. Time is unmanageable in the fight against AIDS; everything is unpredictable, filled with worry, even if it is unexpressed. I could not even predict how our lives could change from week to week because of the uncertainty of Nathan's health. But Nathan had been doing better, I had convinced myself at that time; in the last few weeks he had added three pounds from the new weight gain supplement Ben Nyquist had recommended that I add to the milkshakes I created for Nathan.

But Vince and Jeff were on the other side of the continent in Los Angeles the night I had spoken with Vince on the phone, and I knew they were worried about Nathan's health, knew they were upset at not being able to be a part of our support network. So when Vince suggested a weekend in the Pines, my laugh was to reassure him that I appreciated the gesture, and that I still valued his friendship.

Time slipped between us, then, and when Vince called me on a Wednesday morning that horribly hot week in July and said we had to come out to Fire Island that weekend, I shrugged off the nervousness in his voice as due to our not seeing each other for such a long time. I thought he might have been frightened that I would decline his invitation, because it had been over a month since we had last spoken with one another; I'm sure one of the thoughts that must have crossed through his mind before he called was what if they can't come, what if things had become worse?

Jeff had just finished filming a TV pilot Vince had written, Vince urgently explained to me on the phone, and one of the network executives had mentioned that he and Vince could use the house he owned on Fire Island. It was all set, he had said. Could we be there on Friday? I answered hastily that of course we would be there, my days for the demolition company where I was working were flexible and I didn't want to reveal any anxieties to Vince, though I did stress the fact that the final decision rested with Nathan.

When I mentioned it to Nathan that evening I had expected some resistance, that he wouldn't want to go, that it would mean disturbing his routine, thus knocking him off balance. Nathan had become, in those few months since the onset of his illness, somewhat more sharp-tempered, responding to something with an immediate "No," or "Of course not," then twisting himself up into a thought while trying to flatten out the worried waves of his forehead. Nathan had cultivated a desire to no longer flee the city and I hated to see that his once adventurous spirit had been curbed or, even worse, defeated. But he surprised me when I had explained to him the plans to go away for the weekend to see Vince and Jeff. He nodded his head assuredly at me across the kitchen table as if he had been waiting for days for me to ask him the question, and then he had simply mentioned it would be nice to get away. The overhead light caught the side of his face and gave his long, slender face a fuller look, but as he moved back from his chair to leave the table, I noticed his eyes drift into a memory, and I wondered, briefly, if all this change would be good for him.

At first I had been excited about the weekend, too; it was, for me, a chance to spend some time with Vince and Jeff, get out of the city, give myself a break from all of my nervous energy and anxiety, and it had been over a year since we last saw Vince and Jeff. But when Nathan and I arrived Friday afternoon at the Sayville Ferry, I had found myself annoyed at everything. There was a line for the tickets, a line to the get on the ferry, and we had grossly overpacked—or, rather, I had insisted that we bring warm jackets in case the weather changed unexpectedly. I had carried a backpack and a suitcase, and two plastic shopping bags. One bag was filled with the kind of groceries we would not be able to find on the island: nutritional supplements, vitamins, and medicinal-smelling herbs. The other was filled with things to distract us if necessary: books, magazines, and the board game, Clue. What, I thought, would happen if we did not have any fun? When I had been packing I had also slipped in several cassette tapes of dance music and showtunes; if everything failed, wouldn't music certainly lift us?

Nathan and I could also not take our eyes off of a shirtless man waiting for the ferry, a man so tanned and lean and chiseled he had made me want to scream with rage at the way he willfully invited everyone to admire his body. Why hadn't we outgrown this, I thought—this desire to ogle and possess the flesh? The maddening thing was the man was soon surrounded by men who were as handsome and as unclothed as he was, and I caught myself scowling at their tilted-back smiles and partylike attitudes. Nathan had opened a book and begun to read, and I flipped through the Weekend section of the *Times*, but my anger kept pulling me away, resentfully watching the other men.

At the harbor in the Pines, more tanned, shirtless men with sunglasses pitched on top of their heads met the other men in an explosion of kisses and hugs. Across the boardwalk I heard a campy scream and when I looked in that direction I noticed another group of muscular boys. It had also been disturbing to realize that I knew no one in sight; I had been going to the Pines intermittently for almost eight years and no one even looked familiar to me, and it made me feel as if we'd taken the wrong boat by mistake. I had even been annoyed that the directions Vince had given us to reach the house made us have to tag behind a group of men in skin-tight swimsuits, the threads of the spandex fabric glistening across their asses like mica chips in sidewalk concrete. Nathan and I had agreed before we arrived there that we did not have to even attempt to maintain the gay "schedule" that weekend—the routine everyone follows in the summer: the beach, the afternoon tea dance, the nap, the dinner, the late night dancing, and the drugs. This was, he had stressed, simply an opportunity to relax. So I was even angrier when we arrived at the house and found ourselves walking into the middle of a cocktail party.

Vince waved to us from a second story deck but I had been unable to hear what he had said because of the volume of Madonna's "Open Your Heart" that was pumping out from stereo speakers positioned somewhere near the front door. A reedy young man with a light olive complexion and helmet of black curly hair met us at the door and introduced himself as Tony. He took a bag from each of our hands, and told us he would take them to our room, motioning us to leave our other bags on the ground and to go further into the house and up the staircase. Vince met us on the first landing of the stairs; Nathan reached him first, and I watched them fall into a hug. Vince was dressed in an orange T-shirt and plaid shorts, the effect of which made me think he was picking up too many fashion tips in Los Angeles; for years he always dressed in the de rigueur Manhattan black, a color that particularly suited his lean, clonish looks. And then Jeff was suddenly behind us, and as I kissed Vince on both cheeks, I watched behind me as Jeff lifted Nathan into a bear hug, squeezing Nathan so tightly I worried momentarily that his ribs would crack. What I had realized, in that instance, was that I was bothered by the apparent difference in their sizes: Had Jeff always been this big and striking? How long had Nathan looked this thin and frail? Jeff was dressed in a white tank top and short, tight disco shorts, and he looked to be a pneumatic curve of large muscles, as if he had been on a strict diet of steroids.

"We've missed you," Jeff said to both of us.

"Everyone in L.A. is so pretentious," Vince added. "I want to move to Bakersfield, but Jeff wants to get a house in Beverly Hills."

"*Beverly Hills?*" Nathan replied with mock surprise. "But I hear Bel-Air is so much more fashionable."

"I just want a home," Vince said. "I'm so tired of being subrosa."

Tony passed us on the landing carrying our suitcases and we had all turned and watched him climb the stairs to the second floor.

"He's ours for the weekend," Vince said.

"Ours?" Nathan asked.

"He comes with the house," Jeff answered.

"There's a videotape of him in our bedroom," Jeff said. "You'll have to watch it."

"The boy did a film," Vince rolled his eyes upward. "Sans fabrique."

"Very chic in our circles," Jeff said.

"Because we're stuck in television," Vince added. "Oh, for something more pithy, like film. Don't worry, I still have every intention of being a serious *artiste.*"

And then we followed them upstairs. The house was an architectural blend of high-tech structure and pastel colors. I felt so imperfect in those surroundings, noticing the coffee stains on my shorts, the frayed hem of my T-shirt, the dingy yellow tint to my aging white socks.

"But this we had to do," Vince had added, motioning to the party around us. "It was part of the bargain."

"We had to appease Nicholas, the guy who let us use the house," Jeff said. "Don't worry, the rest of the weekend belongs to us."

As we entered the large, airy main room of the house, a modified saltbox structure, Vince introduced me to a woman with a deep freckled tan and wearing a cream-colored linen pantsuit, and I stood beside her, politely trying to find a common subject to discuss other than the glorious lavender sunset that was happening beyond the glass windows and that I would rather have observed alone and in silence. The whole mood—the fading sunlight, the overamplified music, the rectangular lines of the room—made me feel as if I had stepped into a cubist painting. Nathan took a seat on the sofa next to Vince and Jeff, and I watched from the corner of my eye as Tony appeared and disappeared and then reappeared with a drink for Nathan.

I soon found my patience waning as I strained to hear a conversation about the comparison of the Pennsylvania impressionists to the dark somber painting of a New England landscape that hung over the fireplace of the house, and I excused myself from the freckled woman and found the room where Tony had placed our suitcases and lay down on the bed. When I awoke it was dark outside, the sliding glass door that led to a deck was open and a cool breeze drifted into the room. Nathan, or someone, had thrown a light quilt over me after I had fallen asleep, and I edged my way out of the bed and eased my vision back into the light that drifted in from the hallway.

A few minutes later I found Vince downstairs on a sofa reading. He lifted the book toward me when I sat down beside him. "Plato," he said. "Can you believe they have a copy here?" He placed the book on a glass-top coffee table, next to a crystal ashtray and small carved wooden box.

"I'm not usually this tired," I said, struggling to shake the sluggishness from my body.

"Tony left some dinner for you. You hungry?" Vince asked.

"He cooks too?"

"That boy is full of surprises, believe me."

"Where is everybody?"

"Tony took Nathan and Jeff dancing," Vince said.

"Dancing?" I replied. I remember that I felt the tension invade my body again, the thought of Nathan squeezing through the crowd of sweaty bodies to find some kind of space on the dance floor, the hobble he must be feeling from the pain in his legs, the sweat from his body possibly chilling him and making him sick. We had spent so much time and energy thus far trying to keep him well.

"Relax, Robbie," Vince said, then, and his smile creased into the deep dimple on the right side of his cheek. "This weekend is for you, too." And it was here that he turned to me and cupped my face with his hands, at the same time I felt myself leaning into him. My head drifted down to his lap, and his fingers glided through my hair and then rested on my chest.

"I don't sleep anymore," I said, comforted by the warmth of his body around me. Next, I closed my eyes, falling, at once, into a deep and peaceful sleep.

There is a certain spare tranquillity in the Pines that exists only in the mornings and which no other part of the day can even attempt to achieve, a magnificent emptiness to the beach, really, the sun bright but not yet intense, a coolness in the air that stings the cells of the lungs, accompanied by the hushed cyclic sound of the ocean waves. Years ago I used to love this part of the day simply because of its emptiness of gossip. Every trip I ever took to the Pines I heard a story about someone: the fan dancer who collapsed one night at the Sandpiper, the Esther Williams party one house threw, the heiress who was accidentally bumped into the sea at a too-too crowded tea dance. And, of course, who slept with whom and what, precisely, was so enticing or disappointing about their attributes.

There was a deliciousness to hearing these stories repeated; that was, I think, part of the allure of being a part of the Pines scene—the mythic quality to it all. Years ago I would sit on the deck of the house or on the beach in the morning and imagine what the day would bring: who I would meet, who I had promised to look up, what parties I had heard were happening, and how could I find a way to be invited. But the true joy of the Pines was the spontaneity of it all, following someone into the Meat Rack, meeting a new friend on the beach, or finding an old friend in the harbor who had an invitation to the exact party you wanted to be seen at.

That weekend in the glass house, though, that summer in 1987, I realized I wanted no plans at all for our weekend. That morning I had been aware that my life had grown empty of expectations, and I had felt, then, so disappointed in myself. Every day since Nathan's diagnosis I had faced a certain bitterness because of AIDS, growing into a monster unable to encompass plans. I had no idea, really, how to overcome that resentment; my time, instead, slave to the cruel spontaneity of an unimaginable virus.

"Tony'll do that," Jeff said when he found me in the kitchen that morning. I had been frying bacon in a skillet and blending pancake mix in a bowl. He came up behind me, lifted the weight gain supplement that I had placed on the counter, read the contents, and set it back down.

"You're up early," he added. He was dressed in an oversized gray sweatshirt and sweatpants, the effect of which hid his meticulously defined physique and made him, with his blond crewcut, resemble a sleepy polar bear who had just realized he was hungry.

"I slept too much," I answered.

"I know," he replied. He lifted the pot of coffee a little too high off the stove, as if he wasn't certain what it was, then tipped it over as though he had just discovered a toy and poured himself a cup. "Everything is bad for you," he said, reaching for the milk in the refrigerator with what seemed like a large gray paw. "Red meat. Sugar. Milk. Cigarettes. Coffee." And it was here that I had first detected a bitterness in Jeff's voice. Jeff's feet were spaced shoulder-width on the tile floor, his knees slightly bent, his buttocks shifted slightly back as if he were about to stretch to reach for something above his head.

"Want some now?" I asked him, tilting the bowl in his direction, realizing his stance was really more defiant than playful. "I can make you some now."

"No," he had answered, and lumbered over and sat at the table, looking out through the window at the empty beach, his chin resting on his knuckles. "I'll wait till everyone else is up."

I had been aware since I arrived that there was a clumsiness hovering about us, an inability to discuss things except in the vaguest of terms.

"Beautiful day," Jeff said. His face had already lost its sleepy edge and a windowless regal countenance had displaced his vulnerability.

"Yeah," I answered, matching his gaze out through the window. "The series sounds good," I said, trying to chart the conversation into a more personal territory, to show Jeff that I was interested in what was happening in his life.

"It won't happen," Jeff said. "It's too offbeat. But the exposure is good. So's the money. Vince is desperate to buy a house, but I want to take a trip. You and Nathan have to help me convince him to take a trip."

"A trip?" I asked. "Where?"

"I want to go to India."

"*In-di-a*?" I repeated, stretching my surprise out to three syllables. "Why there of all places?"

It was then that Jeff smiled, more wistfully than acknowledging. "It just interests me, you know. I mean, it's just a place of such extremes—poverty against all that exquisite architecture. And all those different languages and cultures bumping up against one another. It's someplace to just get lost, you know. It's so spiritual."

"Spiritual?"

"All those religions," he answered.

"Religions," I had repeated as if I were an echo. "Are you becoming religious now?"

"I was never not religious," he said. "I just never believed in God."

"And now you do?"

"No, not really. I want to believe in something, though. I want to know what faith is like."

"Wanting faith is probably more admirable than finding it," I had replied, perhaps, a little too breezily.

"Surely you must believe in something?" he asked, cocking his head to one side in an agitated, cublike manner

"Uncertainty," I answered. "I believe in earthquakes and hurricanes, pestilence, and plague."

"Is that why you're so unhappy?" he asked me and his face became aloof again. I felt, then, as a child does, watching his balloon ascend into heaven after it has slipped through his grasp.

"No," I answered. "It's because I want to believe that faith is possible."

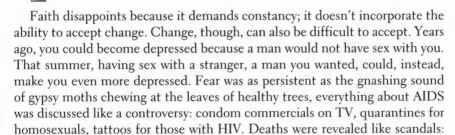

Faith disappoints because it demands constancy; it doesn't incorporate the ability to accept change. Change, though, can also be difficult to accept. Years ago, you could become depressed because a man would not have sex with you. That summer, having sex with a stranger, a man you wanted, could, instead, make you even more depressed. Fear was as persistent as the gnashing sound of gypsy moths chewing at the leaves of healthy trees, everything about AIDS was discussed like a controversy: condom commercials on TV, quarantines for homosexuals, tattoos for those with HIV. Deaths were revealed like scandals: Liberace, Michael Bennett, Willi Smith, Stewart McKinney.

That summer, I had heard the latest gossip of the Pines before I ever arrived for that weekend visit. At the gym I had overheard a story about a man having to be flown off the island by helicopter because he had developed pneumonia overnight, Nathan knew of a house where all of the occupants were HIV-positive, Jerry had told me the story of a bodybuilder who threw men he believed to be straight off the boardwalk because he was so angry about losing his lover to AIDS. Faith, then, that summer, had been believing in the power of distractions, the ability of a well-made Bloody Mary or a buff party at sunset to keep you from becoming depressed.

"India?" I had asked Vince while we walked on the stretch of beach that separates the Pines from the Grove. We had left Nathan and Jeff back at the house playing backgammon. It was early afternoon and there were clusters of sweating men on the beach, lying atop blankets and towels, radios spilling sound in every direction. "Why does he want to go to India?"

"He's perfected his body. Now he's worried about his soul," Vince answered. "I suppose we all are," he added, and it was here that I detected a note of bitterness in Vince's voice. "I remember when the body was the soul."

"A temple," I answered.

"A place to worship," he smiled. "And we all did so, quite religiously."

"I would have thought you would be jumping for a chance to go to India."

"I really want to get a house," he said. "I feel so rootless in California. Denise and I have talked about getting one."

"Denise?" I said, surprised at this revelation.

"She's giving up her New York apartment for good and she and Linda want to get a house. Jeff and I thought about sharing half of it with them. I think it would work."

I had nodded in silent response, taking in the row of squatty houses that lined the shore of the Grove, and as I did so, felt slightly disappointed that I been unable to find a vision of myself within Vince's plans.

"I remember the first year I came to the Island," Vince said. "I was seventeen and I came out here with my first boyfriend, Larry. I told my mom I was going to Atlantic City but we really came here. We held hands in public. I remember I felt so bold and proud because we were doing that, but my heart was just racing every time we passed someone on the boardwalk. We were staying at a house in Ocean Beach and we took a beach taxi to the Ice Palace. There was some kind of silly rule then that you had to have at least one woman dancing with every three men, but no one did. Larry and I even slow danced together, kissing and necking in front of everyone. We just believed we were invincible."

We walked over to a log of driftwood and Vince broke off a piece and tossed it back into the sea. I found a piece of smooth, dark green glass in the sand that I picked up and slipped it into my pocket to show Nathan later.

"Nothing seems invincible now," Vince said, looking to where he had tossed the piece of wood. "Except maybe my depression."

"Things are going so well for you," I had said, shocked to learn that Vince would ever admit he was depressed. In the years that I had known him Vince had possessed an infallible sense of purpose; he knew exactly where and what he wanted to do. When had Vince changed and why hadn't I noticed? Had I been too absorbed by the changes I had confronted because of Nathan to consider Vince?

"Everything is just so uncertain," he said. "Will the series happen? If it does, will they keep both of us? What if Jeff is replaced? What if he leaves me?"

"Leaves you?" I asked, shocked again by another revelation. "What do you mean leaves you? You just said you might buy a house together." Vince was walking, then, a few paces ahead of me, wanting to avoid the subject, I think, but at the same time knowing he needed to talk to someone. "Is he seeing someone else?" I asked.

"No," Vince answered and pitched his eyes to the sand. "I just found out I'm positive."

These, then, were the astonishing facts. Vince was healthy and had no intention of immediately beginning any sort of drugs or treatments simply because he possessed antibodies for a virus, or so he had stressed to Jeff. Vince had found out his diagnosis the week before—which explained the concern I had detected in his voice on the phone. Jeff had no intention of even being tested; to be uncertain, Vince had explained, was Jeff's way of believing he was not already defeated. Vince had wanted to be open about his serostatus, to find a support group and consider enrolling in a clinical study only after he had done some homework on the drug, but Jeff had stressed that they should keep anything that Vince should do private, between themselves. Hollywood, Jeff had said to Vince, doesn't understand the disease. Jeff was afraid it would work against them, both of them, no matter whether Jeff was tested or not. Wouldn't they both be turned down for work, he explained? Wouldn't they both be considered a risk? Jeff had agreed, however, that Vince could discuss it privately with his therapist. Everyone, I remembered that afternoon, has a different way of viewing their life.

Hope is really all we have, I thought while sitting on the railing of the upstairs deck, the sunset falling warmly against me. Behind me, Tony, shirtless and wearing baggy boxer shorts, was sweeping the deck and I listened to the rhythm of his broom against the wood, trying to blend the sound into the ocean waves, trying, really, to detect some encoded message, trying to find some sort of revelation to life. I hope, you hope, we hope, was all I could come up with—hope that if you have it that you will not get sick; if you don't, that you won't get it; if you're already sick, that you won't get worse. Nathan and I were hoping that Ben Nyquist would be able to get Nathan enrolled in a clinical trial at NYU Medical Center. Vince and Jeff were hoping to keep the momentum of their careers going. Weren't we all hoping that time would not give up on us? Weren't we investing, after all, in the possibilities of the future?

Vince and I had walked on the beach for hours that afternoon, going over every possible scenario of what the future could be like, the undercurrent of our fear and hatred of this new situation replaced by a dialogue of optimism and choices. For every possibility Vince had conjured up, I had an alternative to suggest. If Jeff left him, he could move back to New York. And, besides, if Jeff wanted to leave Vince, wouldn't it be better to let him just go? And what if Vince, himself, wanted to leave Jeff? Hadn't we both heard of those stories? I had reminded him. And wasn't it wrong to invest so much hope in a television series that might never happen? Or if it did happen, it could easily fail

178 / JAMESON CURRIER

simply because of ratings. Couldn't Vince find as much meaning in his life writing about his life as he could writing merely for income?

"I've been lucky," Tony said when he had sat for a moment with Nathan and me on the deck before moving on to one of his other chores. "Right place at the right time." Tony had grown up in a family of seven brothers and sisters in a factory town in Washington, left home to study at UCLA and paid for his schooling through whatever jobs he could land. For a while he was a bartender, then a pool boy; then he began doing some modeling on the side, ecstatic that the money was so good, and he had been living with his brother, Stephen, another model, in an apartment in West Hollywood. Tony had lucked into the houseboy job through a friend he "sort of had a thing" with—the same friend, he proudly said, who had gotten him the work in the video Vince and Jeff had seen.

The sight of Tony's lean, tanned skin against the pale fabric of his shorts was erotically magnetic that day, such a breathtaking distraction, and I had tried not to look at him, not to draw my attention to his body, but my eyes had not allowed me. Tiny circles of dark hair ringed his nipples; another puddle stretched up out of his shorts and floated across his navel. His eyes, dark brown, worked with a silent optimism. When he had stopped the sweeping, he sat on the wood beams of the deck, cleaning the grill with a soapy brush, water trailing off into the sand below the house. Tony was eight years younger than I was that summer and it occurred to me, in his presence, that I belonged, now, to an older generation of gay men. Of course he has hope, I had thought, then—the hope of youth, an invincible and unclouded future before him. The envy of it had made me shudder with lust, and I had wondered, briefly, what Tony might fear: Not finishing school? Finding himself unlucky? Not falling in love, or, perhaps, worse, finding unrequited love or love abandoned?

Nathan had fallen asleep in the deck chair behind me. Even as much as I hated our predicament, hated the way things had changed for us, I had never considered leaving Nathan, nor when I was in the hospital had Nathan indicated that kind of behavior was possible of himself. But we had both still felt fear, that fear of abandonment, of making it through life alone, without support or, worse, waking up expecting to find the person you had always trusted not there anymore. Part of the difficulty of life comes from our imagining what our life will be like—all the "what ifs." Contentment comes from understanding that there are things you will never understand. I know this now, but there are still days I forget this rather simple hard-learned lesson.

An amber hue washed over the planks of the deck, and I sat for a while and studied the hairs on my leg, amazed that they could now look so blond in this fading light. Ahead of me, over the charcoal-like plane of the ocean, was a fiery bouquet of clouds. A group of men dressed all in white—white T-shirts and shorts and linen pants and blowsy shirts—had walked onto the beach to the side of the house then. Normally, I would not have paid much attention to them, especially on such a weekend as this, except that I had noticed that each man carried a white balloon. I knew, then, exactly where they were headed, having once been part of a procession like this myself. One man reached into a box and tossed a clump of white dust into the waves, another man scattered a handful of that same dust across the sand, another nervously brushed away the ashes the wind blew across his pants. Then they stood in a small circle and released their balloons into the sky. I watched them travel skyward against the gathering of reddish-yellow clouds, suspended for a moment like a cluster of tangerines.

"Where do you think they end up?" Jeff asked. He had walked onto the deck behind me to watch the balloons climbing up through the sun. "Heaven? Hell? Purgatory? Syosset?"

"If I knew where they went, there would be no mystery to life," I said.

"Mystery," he said, slipping his large, bulky arms first around my shoulders then down to my waist so that I felt the warmth of him surround me. "Is that what keeps us going?" he asked, and it was here that he took my hand and held it in his own for a moment, and then brought them slowly up so that they rested together across my chest in a way that reminded me of Vince's embrace the night before. "This is what I don't understand," Jeff had said next. "I've been with him almost six years. And he still has no faith in me."

Vince had long joked that if it hadn't been for the play that brought them to Los Angeles, he and Jeff would no longer be together—that if they had stayed in Manhattan, they would have found themselves moving in different circles. Vince, for instance, said Jeff would probably be bartending in a Chelsea leather bar while he would probably be writing cranky opera reviews for an Upper West Side newsletter. Jeff, however, had never understood the humor in this statement; one night on the phone, in 1986, not long after they had first moved to California, he had complained to Nathan that Vince was becoming extremely bitter because of Jeff's new "gym" friends in West Hollywood. Vince saw Jeff's extracurricular activities as a threat to their relationship, though he had never tried to stop them. Jeff's love for Vince, as Jeff explained it to Nathan, was a selfless love, not a selfish love. No one person can control another, Jeff believed, and if they try, they are most likely doomed to failure. Why, then, was this so difficult for Vince to accept?

"We've talked about this over and over," Jeff had said to Nathan, which were the same words Vince used when I spoke on the phone with him a few days later. Only Vince had added the observation, "And it's a no-win situation."

Vince had explained that night that he and Jeff had fought over a guy Jeff had met at the gym, a short, bleached blond Scandinavian with the ridiculous-sounding name of Thor.

"It's just physical," Jeff had said to Vince, which Vince had said to me had made him feel like a troll. Vince, of course, was far from troll-like, could, in fact, woo his own sub-species of bodybuilders. Months later, when the situation was reversed—when Vince had been involved in a tête-à-tête with a film editor named Franklin who lived in the Hills—he had mentioned Jeff was so livid he was threatening to leave him.

"I forgive him his friends," Vince had said to me on the phone that afternoon, months later, when we had talked about this new scenario, "and he berates me when I have my own. Suddenly he's the selfish one, not the selfless one." Across the miles between us, I imagined him shaking his head in disgust, or slipping his sunglasses to the tip of his nose to meet my stare if I were across the table from him. "Now he's allowed to get jealous, but I'm not. It's not fair."

"You should feel flattered he's jealous," I had said. "It proves he still cares."

"I just don't understand gay men," he said. "Including myself. I thought I would have outgrown the pressure of wanting sex, not just with Jeff, but with anyone. I thought I would some day reach a point where it wasn't a driving force in my life."

"Is it sex you're after?" I asked. "Or intimacy?"

"It makes me feel good," he said. "What does that make it?"

"If you're so unhappy, why don't you leave him?"

I could hear the shock in Vince's voice. "I could never do that," he had replied. "Things are too deep between us."

What is the meaning of life when life disappoints you? Where does faith come from when you are all out of strength? How could I believe in a God when the view of God encompassed so much discrimination and destruction? How could I accept the false romanticism of religion when faced with the harsh disappointment of facts? I had always believed that the search for truth would be the best way to live my life. But the night I heard that Hank had died, my body went into shock, a tension invaded my shoulders and locked my muscles like a straitjacket. What could I learn from this except that grief comes as periodically as the waves of the ocean? Was truth now only to disappoint me? Make me afraid to go on living? A few days later, still worried and confused, I had stopped at a church on Carmine Street on the way home from work. I don't know what I had expected to find within the dank, musty air or that dark, hollowed out room. Certainly not God. Certainly not the truth. All I know is that I started to cry, my anger and anguish directed at some force far beyond myself. Was that from faith or from the lack of it? Was it fear that made me reach out to something beyond myself or the belief that faith could provide me with a sense of strength? Who heard me that night I do not know. Faith, I decided, does not save you from life. And life, I learned over the years, takes you through too, too many changes.

Oddly, it was Nathan who had lifted our spirits that evening in the Pines. The conversation at dinner had volleyballed through a variety of topics and moods. Vince would serve up a clever remark, Jeff would complain that he thought his teeth weren't white enough, Nathan would ask why white teeth were so important, and I would try to change the subject. Tony had wandered in and out of the room bringing dishes and clearing plates and wanting to know about the best Black Party any of us had ever attended or had heard about. The conversation was headed, at times, into that perilously nostalgic territory, which makes for great introspection but terrible table-top conversation. By the time we were eating dessert, Vince was listing all the things he had never done but would still like to try.

"I've never water-skied," he said. "Or snow-skied or tried paragliding."

"Too wild," Jeff said. "I'd love to try something more cerebral. Like having my chart done."

"You've never struck me as the cerebral type," Nathan had said to Jeff.

"Which is all the more reason to want to try it," he answered, flexing his bicep as he reached his hand down to scratch his back.

"I'd love to have my portrait painted," I added, watching Tony scoop up the plate in front of me. "Something real formal."

"But that's nothing like who you are," Jeff said.

"That's exactly the point," I answered. "To see myself in another way."

"I'd love to be photographed in drag," Nathan said. "I've never done drag."

"Never?" Vince asked, surprised.

"Not even as a kid?" Jeff added.

"Well, girls," Tony had interrupted, his eyes flattening into bright blue lines from his smile. "There are a load of dresses in the closet upstairs."

And then Nathan's posture had changed; his shoulders arched back as if he had been possessed by an enchanted sprite.

"Just don't stretch them out of shape," Tony had said, looking specifically, then, at Jeff. "And there's makeup in the master bathroom. Just clean up your own mess when you're finished."

The closet was an unexpected surprise—a rack of sequined ball gowns and cocktail dresses behind an unnoticed hallway door. On the floor was an assortment of spiked heels and sandals; in the back, garment bags full of wigs and hairpieces. We stood before the door like a group of Miss America contestants with a handful of gift certificates redeemable in evening wear.

"Did you know about this?" Vince asked Jeff a few minutes later, his hands on his hips in his best Bette Davis manner as he watched Jeff rummage through the makeup in the bureau drawers in their bedroom. Jeff, I had

learned from Vince, was much friendlier with Nicholas, the television executive and host for the weekend, than Vince.

"Not at all," Jeff had laughed, but his feet were squarely positioned for a
possible fight. "But I'm not surprised."

"You should shave," Nathan said to me while testing for a foundation
to match the color of his skin; my beard had the ability to become a dark
shadow across my face in only a few hours after shaving. Nathan and I were
as much of a contrast of complexions as Jeff and Vince were, and as I had
left the room I realized I was jealous that Nathan could go without shaving
for days without any visible sign of stubble; for a moment I had felt like I
had been banished from a game because, well, I had this adult "problem."
By the time I had returned, Nathan was adding a pale blue eyeshadow above
his eyes, Vince was trying on wigs and Jeff was fussing with a short satin
kimono he had discovered.

"Try this," Vince said and tossed me a heap of dark black curls. I slipped
the wig on and sat in front of the mirror.

"Oh my," Jeff said, noticing my reflection. "I never knew you were so beautiful."

"You have a sort of Ava Gardner type of elegance," Nathan had said, smiling behind me.

I made a face at myself in the mirror. "No," I had answered. "More like
Connie Francis on steroids."

I suppose a stranger coming upon on us that night, that summer, might
have thought we were four silly gay men, accompanied by one too excitable
houseboy. After seeing our desperate attempts at drag, Tony had decided to
join us—and we had pitched and rocked as a group down the boardwalk, Vince
screeching to a halt every time his heel snagged between two boards. Vince
was much too hairy to believe even possible in a dress, and I know I looked like
some PTA reject in the cocktail dress I had chosen. Nathan had dressed himself in an elegant ball gown and a Donna Reed type wig and was, perhaps, the
most passable of the group. But Jeff, I suppose, had been the oddest looking
of the bunch of us, dressed in the blue kimono, which he wore split open to
the waist, and a red beehive wig. To complete his ensemble he added a pink
feather boa that he kept snapping at Tony, who had dressed himself in a
leather miniskirt and a halter top.

The night had been gloriously black, the stars high and distinct, and we had
walked to the Pavilion where we camped on the steps, slinging bitchy insults
at the muscle boys and disco bunnies and whomever else dared to walk by us.
Before we had left the house, Tony had retrieved a handful of joints from the
carved wooden box on the glass coffee table, and we had lit them one by one,
chain-smoking the bitter reeds—Jeff taking short, quick puffs, Vince pulling

out a drag, Nathan trying to taste the air he held in his lungs, Tony moistening his lips before smoking and then passing it along to me, where I held it before my lips, watching the paper flare into a gentle, golden glow from my breath like a firefly suspended before my eyes.

We danced for a while underneath the stars, not the independent pelvic hopping thrusts of disco, but a giddy swing step, lindy-hopping in and out of each other's arms, passing between partners as if at a square dance. Later, deep into the night, or early in the morning depending on your sense of time, we had sat together on the chilly sand of the beach, savoring the lazy accomplishment of our adventure. Jeff held Vince in his arms and I had sensed, then, it would be impossible for them to give one another up. The bond that existed between them, I knew, had long since passed through that intense sexual heat; they were, quite simply, more than lovers; they were as Nathan and I were: companions, soulmates, family, the best of friends. Tony, feeling a bit left out, had rested his head in Vince's lap and the image of the three of them, all heads and limbs entwined in one another, had reminded me of some exotic many-limbed god. India, it occurred to me next. Something Indian. I had told Jeff on the deck during sunset that no one needs to travel that far to test the soul. Jeff had replied that he still had to find his soul before he could test it. Now Nathan, passing me the last joint of the night, had placed his head against my shoulder and I felt him sigh. "Do you suppose someone could mistake us for lesbians?" he asked.

"Never," I heard Vince answer with a laugh. "We're not butch enough."

For years I carried around a mental picture of Jeff's chalky, pumped up body wrapped around Vince's smaller, more compact and dark furry one, a crisp, starched white sheet entwined between their legs as they lay together on top of a futon in a starkly painted white room. Where this skewered picture came from I am not sure—perhaps from some sort of greeting card logic that was scrambled within my brain or, maybe, from the feeling I had that it was Jeff who was always protecting Vince, simply because he was the larger, taller, bigger one.

Jeff often jokingly blamed his body on his father, though, as he explained it, it was not so much the inherited genetics that had helped him develop such a striking physique. In seventh grade, Jeff had been beaten up in a fight on the football field when an older boy had called him a sissy, and Jeff had responded to the assertion by sticking out his tongue at his assailant. Jeff's father, appalled that his son was spending too much time with piano classes and choirs, had arranged for his son to have boxing lessons at the Y with a former light-heavyweight champion. The boxing did not toughen Jeff up; that came years later in high school when Jeff decided to try out for football. But it did introduce him to the heady masculine arena of the gym, the slamming metal lockers and damp smells of cheap deodorant and wintergreen oil, the tired leather of punching bags, and squeaking sneakers.

What Jeff's father did not realize, nor does any parent, really, is that toughening up a boy neither makes him a man nor changes his sexuality. Nathan, for instance, had never doubted his sexuality. He first realized there was something different about himself the summer he was eight and playing "Superman" with a friend. Nathan had not been playing the hero, but, rather, the victim waiting to be rescued, lying near the railroad tracks where he and his friend had walked. His friend, Richie, was "Superman" and they had worked out an elaborate scenario that climaxed in a daring rescue and a kiss.

"If Superman was good," Nathan said to me years later when we had first started dating, "good fighting evil, and I wanted to be rescued by Superman, how could I consider myself evil? I know it's screwy logic. Evil was what Superman destroyed. I wanted to be rescued. How could there be something wrong with that? I wanted to be protected and held and cradled in Superman's arms. I wanted to be Superman's boy. I wanted to go with him on all his adventures. Richie was really not very cute—a little chunky—but he was a conduit for my fantasy, a way to make it real. Our relationship was all up here," he said, and it was here that Nathan had pressed a finger against his temple. "I believed in Superman," he said. "I knew there was nothing wrong with me, that Superman could see I was a good boy because he had X-ray vision. I knew he would beat up anyone that didn't understand."

Nathan had laughed in a high cackle the night he had told me his story. "I always hoped that Superman would rescue me from Richie," he said. "I lived for Superman. Superman was my god."

I am a disappointment to my father's faith, or, rather, the unyielding view of what is right and wrong that my father interpreted from his Christian religion. As successful as I have been in escaping my father and his religion, I have never been able to escape the genetic imprints he left on my body. I see him every morning in the way my beard grows in. He is in my large, calloused fingers, the cleft in my chin, the thickness of my wrists.

But it was my mother I saw before me that evening as I removed the cocktail dress in front of the bathroom mirror. Nathan had fallen into bed when we had returned to the house, and I had undressed him and hung up his clothes before taking care of myself. Vince and Tony had stayed up late listening to a George Michael cassette and the cast album of *Follies*, but I had found a bottle of wine and retreated to the solitude of our deck, till I grew restless and decided to shower. It was then, in the bathroom, that I had caught a glimpse of my mother's nose, the line of her cheekbones in the makeup of my face. As I washed and rinsed my face I caught the color of her hair and the slope of her eyebrow. When my mother died, my father refused to pack up her belongings; her lipstick and mascara were still in the drawers of her bedroom dresser where she had kept them. One afternoon my father caught me playing in her make-up, trying on different shades of lipstick, and he slapped me across the face. His blow knocked me off my feet, my chin slamming against the counter of my mother's dresser on my way to the floor. My father refused to allow me to get stitches and for months I had an ugly scab at my chin, and as I dried my face in the towel that night, pulling the cloth roughly against my skin, I let it stop at the pale scar that still bisected my chin. Next, I had lifted my chin up into the light above the mirror, trying to compare it to the scar that still traveled across my right eyebrow.

In the shower I felt a palpable yearning seizing me again and I fumbled with the spigots, trying to make the water hotter. "Wherever there is love there is God," my mother would say to me on Sunday mornings, pinching the collar of my shirt, a shirt that was always too small for my neck no matter what age I reached. Why hadn't I remembered that when Vince had asked me on the beach, "What is the point of going on?"

What is the point? I had wondered, soaping my arms up with a mittened sponge. That afternoon I had stumbled through a host of reasons for Vince: Because I wanted him to go on, I had stressed; so did Nathan and Jeff, I felt sure. Wasn't the purpose of life—our lives as gay men—to prove we had more meaning than that of a microbe? Wasn't the way we chose to live our lives and the way we responded to circumstances what gave our lives meaning? Wasn't the meaning in the way we loved?

When I stepped out of the shower I saw the hazy outline of my body in the steamy reflection of the mirror. A patch of my stomach came into view and I looked down at the hernia scar buried beneath the hair of my groin. Had I inherited, too, the weaknesses of my body? Was my father also responsible for this? I had never possessed a boyish waist, another one of my features I believed too closely resembled my father's—but my waist by then had also been thickened by my own design, mostly during the year in college when I had stopped smoking and started eating too much. Beneath the hair of my chest, my skin was the translucent color of my mother's skin, a patchwork of blue veins so close to the surface it looked like the tattoo of a road map. I've always been amazed by the strange incongruity of my body, the straight long hair beneath my arms, the wiry curls across my chest, the spongy mass at my groin. By then, that summer, flecks of gray had begun to appear at my forehead and on my chest, while the hair grew darker and thicker as it traveled like wings up and across my back. All this aging, I had thought, even before I'm thirty.

The sun that day had burned a ring around my neck and forearms, and as I toweled myself dry I imagined that I must look like a real freak amongst the perfect men of the Pines. Why did being gay mean being so hyperconsciousness about the body? How could anyone simply love a body, I had wondered that night, if the soul has lost its purpose? What is worse, I considered, the body worshipped or the body mistrusted? How does someone conquer depression when the facts cannot be changed?

Nathan had once remarked that it was the bone structure of my face that had so initially intrigued him. In the mirror it was clear to me that night that I was neither beautiful nor ugly—a handsome somewhere in between, I had thought—more different, perhaps, than striking, more blue collar than sophisticated.

How does a man begin to explain the attraction of one man to another? Is it found in the thickness of the skin or the tension of the muscles just beneath the surface? Is it the rank smell of underarms or the way cologne clings to the hairs of the wrist? Is it the way he moves, the way he takes up space in a room, the way his breath belies equal part aggression, arrogance, and self doubt? How does one man fall in love with another man? Is it spontaneous, planned, or, perhaps, equal parts luck and faith?

Faith, I rolled the word over and over in my mind, a concept I kept going back to it again and again that weekend. What is faith? I had wondered, slipping between the cool sheets of the bed and curling up behind Nathan. Is faith merely an act of courage or is it only a guide. Or, perhaps, really more an act of optimism? Do we invest too much faith in faith? Was that, then, why my father's faith disappointed me?

Nathan had stirred into consciousness as I slipped my arms around him. In the darkness of the room, the blond buzz of his haircut seemed to drink in the light. "We should visit them," he had said, his voice syrupy with sleep. And I knew, then, exactly what he meant. Nathan and I possessed a relationship with Vince and Jeff that linked us far beyond the past intimacies of our bodies; we were, I believed, within each other's souls.

"We will," I answered. He turned and placed his lips against my neck, and fell, easily, back into sleep.

My father had once told me he found faith in the little silences of the day, in the shower underneath a warm blast of water, for instance, or seconds before waking up in the morning or falling asleep in the evening, looking through the mail, or the moment when the television was shut off. Perhaps that is another thing that I inherited from my father, that contemplative energy that grows within a deep, noiseless space.

I had been lost in that space the next afternoon, sitting beside Vince on the ferry back to Long Island, surrounded by our luggage, the humming motor of the boat vibrating into our bones, washing out the sound of the boat crossing through the water. Nathan and I were headed back into the city; Vince and Jeff were going to drive in their rented car to visit Vince's mother in New Jersey before returning that evening to Los Angeles. On the trip across the bay, Nathan and Jeff had stood on the prow of the ferry, watching the flat shore of the mainland stretch into view.

"I can't believe I overpacked," Vince had yelled with a light laugh at the end, waking me out of my pensive mood. "I remember when all I came out with was a swimsuit."

"I know," I nodded, giving him a smile.

He nodded back and looked over at where Nathan and Jeff stood against the rail, their faces lifted into the breeze.

In the parking lot, Nathan, so disdainful of goodbyes, had given Vince and Jeff a quick hug and a kiss on the cheek, and left in the direction of the bus, not waiting to see if I was following behind him. Jeff kissed me, searched his shorts for the car keys, then lifted the bags like a set of weights and started out across the parking lot. Again, Vince and I were abruptly left together and, it felt, at that moment, like we were two souls parting after being marooned together for years on an uncharted island.

"See ya," Vince had said, and it was here that he placed his hands against my shoulders, squeezing his fingers into my flesh.

He leaned his head against my neck, but I pulled his face up into mine, feeling his dark eyes sinking into the swarthy pores of my face. I drew him into a kiss. He pulled back at first, slightly startled by my intimacy, then slipped his arms around me tighter and pressed his lips back against mine. His mouth opened up to me, and I tasted, that day, the moist sweetness of his breath.

I gave him, at that instance, the only thing I could be certain of, the only faith I knew I really had, the passion of my friendship, the desire to want to see him once again, the only thing I had been certain of.

"See ya," I had yelled to him minutes later across the parking lot on my race to catch up with Nathan, my arms loaded again with baggage. "I'll see ya soon."

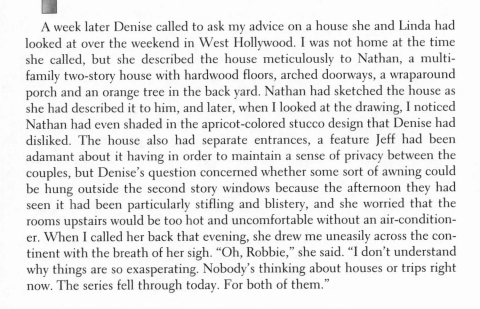

A week later Denise called to ask my advice on a house she and Linda had looked at over the weekend in West Hollywood. I was not home at the time she called, but she described the house meticulously to Nathan, a multi-family two-story house with hardwood floors, arched doorways, a wraparound porch and an orange tree in the back yard. Nathan had sketched the house as she had described it to him, and later, when I looked at the drawing, I noticed Nathan had even shaded in the apricot-colored stucco design that Denise had disliked. The house also had separate entrances, a feature Jeff had been adamant about it having in order to maintain a sense of privacy between the couples, but Denise's question concerned whether some sort of awning could be hung outside the second story windows because the afternoon they had seen it had been particularly stifling and blistery, and she worried that the rooms upstairs would be too hot and uncomfortable without an air-condition-er. When I called her back that evening, she drew me uneasily across the con-tinent with the breath of her sigh. "Oh, Robbie," she said. "I don't understand why things are so exasperating. Nobody's thinking about houses or trips right now. The series fell through today. For both of them."

Nathan always believed that I looked for too much meaning in insignificant things, when I always believed myself that I was perceptive of living in a time of unrivaled change. "Remember when we used phones with rotary dials?" I would remind him, "or the days before there were answering machines and videotapes?" It seems so odd to me now, though, stepping back and looking again at those years, how easily I could point out technological progress though I could be so unaware of sociological changes.

It was Nathan who had suggested that I go to Washington that weekend in 1987. It wasn't important for me to march, wasn't important for me to feel as if I were a part of a larger community. Nathan had wanted to spend a weekend alone with his parents in Connecticut and he thought it best that I get out of the city for a weekend, too. In the last few weeks I had seen Nathan grow weaker and weaker, at night he was unable to sleep because of nausea or fear; I had even heard that Nathan could seldom finish his work at his desk, often slipping away to lie down on a couch in someone's office. Every time I heard something like this from someone—someone confirming my own fears about the declining state of Nathan's health—I would slip into a silent hysteria. That hysteria would soon fade into a furious hatred, a hatred that I kept so checked and tacit within myself that I often thought I would some day explode.

That Saturday I had spent alone in Washington I had wandered through the museums that framed the Mall—the various wings of the Smithsonian, the Air and Space Museum, the National Gallery of Art. I wasn't really interested in connecting with anyone; I wanted, instead, to accept my solitude. I remember it felt good to be looking and moving, flowing, like a documentary film, in and out of the rooms, pausing before an impressionist painting or touching, briefly, a rock brought back from the moon. I had always believed that tourists at museums are often more interesting than the art itself and that day it had proved to be true once again; everywhere I went I noticed rooms not full of art or wonder but of cruisy, good-looking guys. It had been hard not to notice them, really, hard not to wonder what it would be like knowing just one of them in any sort of permutation: friend, lover, trick.

The day had not been without other anxious moments though. I had never been comfortable in museums, never knew what to do with my hands, feeling like a bull in a priceless china shop, and I had spent most of the afternoon with my hands shoved into the front pockets of my jeans as I had walked around, my shoulders hunched forward but my elbows jutted away from my body. I had always believed that that kind of posture pushed me into too pensive a mood—more so than normal. As my boots slapped against the polished tile floors, I had thought about how small my life was in the grand scheme of the universe—a tiny speck, really, in a large building in a large country on a large planet, in a big solar system and an immense universe. I had wondered how much my life mattered beyond the meaning I myself gave it. Would, for instance, a simple encounter with another man recharge it? Or change its direction or meaning? When I stopped to regard a series of French sculptures, a young man wearing black jeans and a white turtleneck caught my eye as we hovered around each other: from the rear I had been awed by the way the thin cotton fabric of his shirt stretched taut at his shoulders and then billowed out like a skirt at his narrow waist; when he was beside me I had noticed his strong profile; in front, I had studied his auburn bangs and large, brown eyes. I lost sight of him sometime later, scared, I think, by the fact that I could let him change my life; that I could bestow on him that power.

After a few hours my eyes and legs had grown tired and I walked back to the hotel near Dupont Circle where I had found a room for the weekend. I read for a while, then fell asleep in front of the television, much as I had done for years with Nathan. Sunday morning I got up earlier than I normally did on weekends, showered, and walked to a deli just off Connecticut Avenue. There was an air of expectancy about Dupont Circle at that hour, everyone seemed so electrified and purposeful. I had sensed it in the way the guy at the cashier handed me my change, felt it in the line that formed in front of the instant banking machine, witnessed it in the soulful eyes of a man setting up a T-shirt stand by the subway exit. I walked for a while, following the flow of the other walkers, down Connecticut to 17th Street and over to the gates of the White House. I had not expected to feel anything there, and I didn't, ignoring the President the way he had thus far ignored the epidemic.

The purpose of the march that weekend had been to demand increased funding for AIDS-related projects and to insist on an end to federal laws that discriminated against gay men and lesbians. AIDS activism had just begun to germinate; there had been a protest on Wall Street against the Food and Drug Administration and Burroughs Wellcome over the high cost of AZT; there had been, too, the vigil in San Francisco outside the old Federal Office Building. There had been angry voices since the beginning of the epidemic, but it was only, then, that they were first finding a collective voice. But I, myself, had not yet found an outward, vocal expression of my anger; I was, really, still moving, then, through denial and disbelief.

Which is why I had felt Nathan's absence all the more that Sunday morning. I had walked toward the Washington Monument; it was the most obvious thing to do, of course, having seen it towering above the skyline. Washington had always reminded me of some unknown European city, the buildings so low and federal-looking, the wide boulevards, the memorials and monuments, and that afternoon the lawn around the Washington monument had been bright green and cushiony, the sky so vast and open above me that I had felt, once again, like such a minute particle of the cosmos. As I came up over the hill I looked out at the Mall, which stretched down to the Capitol building. A crowd had assembled around something that was covering the lawn, and I walked in that direction, full of curiosity.

I had not heard of the NAMES Project Quilt then; now, of course, it is widely recognized as an ever-growing AIDS memorial, but that day it took me a few moments to comprehend what I was seeing: panels, six feet by three, stitched together into blocks of eight and then thirty-two. Volunteers, dressed in white, stood at the corners, handing out programs, brochures, and maps. That day, the quilt contained 1,920 names. Spread out, it was larger than two football fields and included the names of brothers, fathers, sons, mothers, daughters, babies, lovers, and friends. Even then, at its inception, it had been the nation's largest community arts project.

What had begun as curiosity quickly changed to amazement as I approached and read the first few panels. The colors had seemed so bright and saturated to me, charged like neon by the morning sun. I had followed the white canvas walkway that bordered the perimeter of the panels on the ground. Some panels were simple, containing only a painted name on plain fabric. Others had been more elaborately hand-stitched with designs or needlepoint, or with names spelled out in sequins or bordered by feathers. Some were personalized by clothing: a plaid shirt, gym shorts, boot laces, a leather vest, one, even, displayed a jock strap—others contained record albums, photographs, and quotes. The hardest for me to look at, though, were the ones which had contained only first names, the ones that read Mark, Bill, Mike, or Steve. Those were the names I had collected years before on scraps of paper at parties, bars, gyms, and beaches; the very same kind of scraps Vince had kept in the fish bowl in his apartment, dolling out names for me to call when I needed a date. Standing there I couldn't help wondering if I had known the man behind the name. Could it be a friend I hadn't spoken to in the past few months—someone, perhaps, I hadn't even known was sick?

I had been unable to keep my eyes from moving from panel to panel, the same way, I believe, it was difficult to look away from the aftermath of an accident. When I finally looked up I noticed I had not even made it a third of the way down the quilt. I was surrounded by other viewers: men and women mostly my age, their heads bowed, motionless, as if in prayer. The tableau reminded me of one of those large cathedrals Nathan and I had visited not long before on our trip to Europe, the ones with plaques and epitaphs lining the walls of the transepts where people are buried beneath the floor. But what had been viewed there, in Europe, with a calm sense of reverence, had been magnified, in Washington, with anger, shock, compassion, and grief. Footsteps moved so slowly and carefully their sounds could not be detected, the silence broken only by the amplified voice of a woman reading a list of names somewhere in the distance. Ahead of me a young man in a blue polo shirt and jeans had seated himself cross-legged on the walkway in front of a red silk panel that spelled David with silver block letters, his head buried in the palms of his hands. Though I had strained to hear, I could not detect any sounds from him, but I knew by the way his back heaved with short, jerking breaths that he was crying. Behind him, I was suddenly astounded by the sight of a woman pushing an empty stroller; beside her a man carried a baby less than six months old in his arms. On the other side of the panel an elderly woman with a cane touched the frame of her eyeglasses and leaned to read a name.

Behind each name was the story of a life, someone who had struggled with this disease and lost. Behind each panel there were other stories: Who made it? Who had helped? Why this color? This fabric? What did the design remember or represent? Who cried when it was finished? What names did they recognize as they walked by? That day each of us brought our own stories to the quilt, our views, opinions, knowledge, and experiences with the disease. We were suddenly and unexpectedly united, sewn together as it were, by our thoughts of families, lovers, friends, and co-workers: some dead, some sick, some worried. This had become our Gettysburg cemetery, our Vietnam Wall, our Tomb of the Unknown Soldier. But those wars were over—this one was unfinished. I remember the horror I had felt that day knowing the quilt would grow larger and larger, the end nowhere in sight.

And then I had been unable to look at it anymore. Something that moving, that beautiful became unbearably painful, painful at the thought that Nathan or I could one day be a part of it, our lives reduced to a name on a piece of fabric. I gasped for breath and walked away from the quilt, out of the crowds assembling in the Mall, over to the sidewalk, pushing myself through everyone, headed, I felt, in a direction no one else was going. Eventually I found my way to the tidal basin beside the Jefferson Memorial, looking out at the reflection of the sun against the water, trying to find some sort of tranquillity within myself. But my head felt thick and dulled and I walked around the waterside and sat on the steps of the memorial, wanting only, at that moment, to find some space of my own; no one else was seated in that portion of the park.

The workboots I had worn that day made my walking feel ponderous and as I unharnessed the knapsack from my back and sat it on my lap, I felt my feet swell and relax into the boots. I opened the knapsack and drunk water from the canteen I had filled at the hotel, then found the bagel I had bought earlier that morning at the bottom of the knapsack, unwrapped it and began to eat. The butter had melted and seeped into the pores of the dough and it gave the bread a sweet and salty taste. What I did to try to calm myself was to focus on the elemental things—the walking, the stopping to rest, the eating bread and drinking water.

Two girls, arms entwined around each other's waist, sat behind me and I watched them fall into a kiss. Suddenly, that corner of the memorial, which a moment before had seemed so empty, was populated with little cliques of tourists. A stocky young man lingered around the steps, then had seated himself beside me.

"Smoke?" he asked me, indicating the pack of cigarettes he grasped in his hand.

"No thanks," I answered, and I watched him use the lighter that hung around his neck on a cord. He had that lumbering high school football player look—thick neck and chest, pale doughy skin and red cheeks, brown hair cropped a bit too short. If the time and place had been different, I would have felt sure he was waiting for some buddies to show up to harass the crowd. Instead, he took a long drag off his cigarette, then pulled at his tongue with two fingers as if to remove a flake of tobacco, and leaned against the fountain ledge.

"Water?" I asked him, tilting the canteen I held in his direction.

He nodded and took the canteen, resting it on his bottom lip and pouring a quick, thick, drink into his mouth. He wiped off the lip of the canteen with the bottom of his T-shirt when he was done.

"I noticed you on the other side of the lake," he said, as he handed me back the canteen. It was here that I had caught his glance, his dark brown eyes wide and fiery with expectation. "Chris," he said, angling his body toward me and stretching out his hand, not into a handshake, but to place it firmly against my thigh.

"Robbie," I had nodded back to him, realizing his brash contact was that of a boy's. I looked at him again, searching for the lines on his face, but there were none, and I wondered at that moment if he had even made it out of his teens. His hand, flat against my leg, was balled into a fist and he lightly tapped my thigh.

"I've had about an hour of sleep," he said, somewhat proudly, moving his fist back to his own thigh. "I went to a club last night that was somewhere near here I think," he added, and looked out at the bridge in the distance. "The music was wild. *Real* wild. Lot of hot guys here."

"Yeah," I answered. "Lots to look at."

"I came all the way from Arkansas. *Fucking Arkansas.* I told my sister that I was just going. Not to stop me. I had to be here."

I watched him take another drag from his cigarette, and then I looked out at the water and the trees planted along the bank, aware, acutely, of all the places we travel because we are gay—to different towns and different bars, hoping to meet someone, to find someone like ourselves, hoping to find ourselves, too—another journey, really—traveling inside ourselves to try to figure it all out.

"You ever have a girlfriend?" Chris asked.

"*Girlfriend?*" I answered, a little too loudly, realizing Chris's question had knocked me back to a mental image of Marcy Telford, a smart, flirty girl I had been attracted to in junior high school.

"Long time ago," I answered, wondering, briefly, what Marcy's life had become. Married, driving her husband crazy with her nagging, I decided; she was always chiding me for never bringing her presents.

"She like really flipped out when she found out I was seeing this guy," Chris said, stubbing his cigarette into the concrete of the fountain. "He's really hot. Keith—that's his name. But he's married. Gina went and told my parents and then the fucking high school gets involved. And then his wife files a restraining order—against me. She's a jerk. He's a jerk. Gina's a jerk. I ended up staying at my sister's, only her husband gets real nervous having me around." And it was here that he looked at me again, testing me, I believe, tapping his fist against my thigh once more. "Why is it everyone gets nervous while I'm around?"

A young ball of fire, is what I had thought, but didn't say. A boy wound up with expectation and desire. He was wonderfully distracting from my gloominess at that moment. For a moment I had thought about asking the boy for a cigarette, just to keep the contact going, but instead, I reached for my canteen and took another sip of water.

"You come here by yourself?" Chris asked.

I nodded.

"I bet you could probably get any guy here you wanted," he said.

I remember I felt myself flush from his flattery but I found my smile somewhat weary, nonetheless. "I have someone."

"Oh," he said, in that of-course-you-do-and-I'm-so-disappointed tone. "Figures. All the hot-looking guys are taken. Or they're jerks."

It was then that I realized that I was attracted to him, impetuously so, simply because of his dismissal of me. Suddenly, he had become the unattainable one. "He went to see his parents this weekend. We live together in New York," I said.

"New York?" Chris answered, his eyes catching fire again. "New York City?"

I nodded and he looked me over once more, as if able to see me in a brighter light.

"I thought about going to New York," he said. "You ever go to the Saint?"

"*The Saint?*" I replied, jarred into a memory. "Not in a while."

"I heard the Chelsea Gym is really hot, too. And the Spike. You ever been there?"

"A couple of times," I answered. Why was it that people in other parts of the world knew meticulously what the scene was in Manhattan, more so than those who lived there? How was it that the pulse of New York—fashion, art, theater, music, gay life—was more apparent once you were off the island? I had been so concerned about Nathan's health and mood, scanning the newspapers for possible new drug treatments, that I had paid no attention to theater reviews, celebrity interviews, or gossip columns. I had not known what the next big musical was due to open on Broadway, had not known what Harvey Fierstein's next project was, could not tell you who the man was who sang "I Want Your Sex" on MTV, could not tell you, either, what the fashionable gay club was, or, even, what the guys were wearing when they went out. "You'd do real good there," I had said to Chris that afternoon, pushing myself into flirting with the boy. "The guys there would go wild over you. You have that look, you know?"

"Yeah?"

"Oh yeah, you could probably get any guy in the place," I said, playing the young boy's game now but feeling rather old at doing it. "I know some guys I could fix you up with, too, if you're ever in New York."

He flipped out a cigarette. "They as hot as you?" he asked, then lit the cigarette. He took a drag and exhaled to the side of me and gave me a wry, half smile. "Don't know how someone could let a guy like you out of his sight on a weekend like this," he said, his fist again on my thigh. "He crazy, or something? He a jerk?"

"No," I answered. "He's not feeling well." I remember that I had felt, then, whatever charm I had been able to muster instantly vaporize.

"Oh," Chris answered tensely, then had looked down at the canteen he had drunk water from. I watched the blood drain from his face, a light sweat formed on his upper lip as he took in the fact of what I had said. "You should have stayed with him," he said to me, with a chill that iced the air between us. I don't think he had intended to make me feel repulsive for coming to Washington. He stubbed his cigarette out briskly. "See ya," he said, and slipped off the steps and headed away from the memorial. I felt, then, an overwhelming frustration settle in my shoulders, till it was replaced by an anger burning across my chest so bitter I thought I had been slashed by a knife. Who, of the two of us, would be accused of homophobia here—him with his fear of me—or me with the hatred of his insincerity? And then I felt myself moving slowly, as if delayed by the stop-action lens of a camera: replacing the canteen in the knapsack, brushing the crumbs off my jeans, slipping the handles of the knapsack through one arm, then another. Standing. Walking. Crossing the street. I never made it to the march that day. I went back to the hotel. And into the bar just off the back of the lobby. A few drinks later I made it up to my room, armed with a bottle of scotch I had coerced from the bartender.

Later that evening the phone rang in my room. "Robbie?" the caller asked. It was Nathan.

"Hi," I answered, somewhat lightly, glad, really, to hear from him, trying to snap myself into some sort of sobriety.

"How was the march?"

"Good," I answered, but in a tone of voice that meant I had not wanted to discuss it any further.

"Are you alone?"

"Of course."

"I miss you," he said, and all at once I felt my misery at being away from him. "Remember when we were in Rehoboth Beach a few years ago?" he asked.

"Yeah," I answered. I felt, then, the blood return to my body. Years before, Nathan had handcuffed me to the bed in the hotel room we had rented in Rehoboth Beach.

"You couldn't move," he said. He had tied my legs, too, with rope to the bed frame. I had stayed that way for hours, Nathan kissing me, tickling me, rubbing lotion into my skin, jerking me off. This was not long after we had gotten back together, and it was his way, Nathan had explained to me, of making me trust him again. Outside the room was the beach. It was summer and we were only inches away from the nests of single gay boys scattered atop the sand on towels.

"Don't move," he said, that evening on the phone that he had reached me in Washington. "My lips are against your chest. Feel them?"

"Yeah," I answered. "Nice."

In my mind we were back in the hotel room in Rehoboth. Nathan had gotten me hard with his mouth, pulling away just as I was about to come, then suspending his ass just above my erect cock, teasing me by sucking on my nipples, till he slowly eased himself onto me.

"Hard?" he asked me on the phone.

"Yeah. You?"

"Feels good," he said. "You feel so good."

I had stayed in Nathan, that day, what seemed like hours, with an erection so hard I had often measured other ones against it. He held my balls in his hands, squeezed them as I fucked him, pushing them down between my legs so that the skin of my cock was tighter inside him. The smell of him, the sweat of us together, hovered around the room all day.

"Remember what you did?" I said.

"Yeah," Nathan answered.

"Do it again," I said. "Let me taste them." Nathan had squatted on my face and I had licked his balls, then sucked on them like candy.

"Feels good," he said, again, on the phone.

"Don't come yet," I said.

"I won't."

"I want to play with your cock."

"Go ahead."

"Making you squirm?"

"Yeah," he answered, with a nice, heavy sigh. "You?"

"Yeah."

"I want to kiss you," Nathan said, and I imagined the odor of him, the press of his face against the stubble of my cheek. Nathan had not left me alone that day at Rehoboth Beach, tied up in bed. He had washed me with a cool rag, lifted my head up to help me eat a hamburger, helped me piss into a glass to relieve myself. He denied me nothing that I asked for—within reason, of course, and which he could willingly accommodate me with—a different radio station on the stereo, a pillow to prop up my head, relieving an itch on my foot. I knew when Nathan and I got back together that he was out to make our relationship work; he didn't have to prove anything to me. Still, I had enjoyed the luxury of the demonstration. "Remember when I let you go?"

"Yeah," I answered. When Nathan untied me I had remained in bed, hoping to prove to him that I would not leave him, that I was not anxious to get out of the bed or away from him. "Fuck me," I had whispered into his ear, my arms slipping around his back. His eyes had widened and we had slipped into a kiss, and then I had pulled away and lay again on my back.

Nathan knew I did not prefer to be the one fucked. But that day, lying free, finally, of the bindings, what I had wanted was to be fucked by Nathan, testament, I felt, of a double sided trust that existed between us. I knew Nathan would not abandon me, and that I, too, would not give up on him. Nathan had started, first, by lifting my legs and pressing his lips against my ass. Then he rolled me over on my stomach and told me to relax, and he started to knead my buttocks, working his hands gently and firmly into the crack of my ass. He had covered his fingers with lotion and then had begun to slowly part the lips of my ass, rubbing the lubricant first against the hole, slipping first one finger into my rectum and then another. He did this again and again, pulling his fingers out and kneading my ass, getting me to relax so that there was no tension, no shock, every now and then slipping his hand around my balls and squeezing my cock. Next, he rolled me over and set the heels of my feet against his shoulders. He continued working his fingers into my ass, making sure I was still relaxed; then, deftly, he slid his cock into me.

"Remember how it felt."

"Yeah," I said. "Do it again."

I had become so relaxed that there was not the slightest discomfort when he entered me, my body drawing his cock in like a warm gulp of air. A man who has never been fucked has no idea how pleasurable the sensation can be, but a man in love fucked by the man he loves finds the exhilaration one of the reasons for being alive.

"Nice," Nathan had said. "It feels so right."

He began sliding in and out of me, in and out, slowly and smoothly, and I had kept the rhythm going between us. Then he paused, leaned down and kissed me, and I had tasted his smile in my mouth that day. And then he had started again, slowly and smoothly. I was already on the edge of coming but I had held it back, tensing the muscles of my ass to feel Nathan inside of me more sharply. Nathan had gasped and I felt sweat beginning to thicken the cells of his skin. He leaned further into me and his motions took on a harder, firmer thrust. And then I had felt the shift go through him—the transformation a man can go through from simply performing the physical act of sex to having sex with someone he loves. The clear skin of Nathan's chest had blushed, his neck had tensed and his breathing had hollowed out; he moved inside me buoyed by a desperation. I felt, then, that same passion overwhelm me as well, that shift occur within me, and we had stayed that way, in and out, in and out, till I had felt the jagged spurts of his come travel up from the base of his shaft and spill inside me.

"Robbie," he said, and that was all. We were never big talkers or moaners in bed. I could tell how Nathan felt about me simply by the way he looked at me, the way he touched me, the way, too, he held me when we had finished making love. Silence meant everything between us. We had rolled over to our sides—he was still in me—and we lay there for a bit, entwined. I didn't want him to pull out. And I made no attempt to leave the bed.

"Did you?" he asked me over the phone.

"Yeah," I answered, rubbing the meager result of my orgasm into the hair of my groin. "You?"

"Yeah."

There had been, then, that evening in Washington, another gap between us, neither of us wanting to let the other go.

"I need you back," Nathan said into the phone, the same thing he had said, too, that day in Rehoboth.

"I never left," I answered, feeling, though, that day in Washington, the geographic distance between us, him in Connecticut whispering into the receiver of his parents' phone and me locked up within myself inside a hotel.

"I'm not giving up," he said.

I knew he hadn't been talking merely about the two of us. "And I won't let you," I answered.

"Robbie," he said with a sigh. "I have a problem."

My body stiffened from worry.

"What must I do to make you happy?" he asked.

Another gap fell between us and I moved the phone from one hand to the other to give myself a second to think. And then I let out a sigh, not a sigh, really, but more a disgusted breath of air—disappointed because my voice could not articulate the rapid thoughts of my mind. "Nathan," I said slowly. "I want you to fuck me. *Again.*"

He didn't respond and we fell into another silence.

"You can't ask me to do that," he finally said.

"I'm not asking you to," I answered him. "I *need* you to."

That weekend in Rehoboth Beach had happened in 1981, shortly before we had begun to live together. That was the weekend that Nathan and I launched ourselves into a monogamous relationship, monogamous in a very loose sense of the word, really, more emotionally committed to one another rather than sexually exclusive; we began to call ourselves lovers, and what indiscretions either one of us entertained, we kept to ourselves. Unlike my first lover Will, Nathan had no desire to bring other lovers into our bed, no desire for threesomes or for comparison lists of who had had the better tricks or hotter sex. What was monogamous about us, though, was a psychological bonding, a combination of companionship, friendship, love, and sexuality. The way I had made this work was to root my trust in Nathan much deeper than my need for sex from him, knowing he wouldn't walk away from me or give up on our relationship. What Nathan had wanted, after all, was for us to work as a couple, a partnership that could extend beyond the perimeters of sex. Jealousy or disappointment, in sexual matters, was not allowed to consume us, therefore.

Nevertheless, I had found it impossible to remove the guilt I felt when I had sex with someone else while I was in love with Nathan. Temptation was a daily force on the streets of Manhattan. On any day, at any hour, it was possible to pass a handful of desirable men at any place in the city—Manhattan, after all, was and still is a smorgasbord of different types of men—a boulevard of beautiful immigrants, really, from such places as Iowa, Ireland, Italy, and Israel. How one handles temptation of each one of them, I believe, at least on my part, depends on the state of contentment and fulfillment one had achieved with their primary partner. But we were also young men, then—*young*, young men.

I remember the first time I tricked on Nathan after we had gotten back together—it was shortly before we had gone to Rehoboth Beach—and even though we had been professing an open relationship for months I was consumed by the guilt of my deed. I had been working in an actor's loft on the Bowery and the guy—a tall, handsome, well-built man who had had some soap opera parts—had spent the day parading in front of me in various states of undress, and throwing out suggestive remarks as I worked and I knew from Alex that the guy also worked as a hustler. I could tell that this guy was so eager for sex that it made me nervous while I worked—I had made it a rule to never do anything while I was out on a job and I had kept my check throughout the day, deflecting his remarks, as I boarded the wall where he wanted to create a walk-in closet. When I left I left untouched, but I was somewhat erotically rattled. It was still daylight outside, and I had walked down 8th Street and over to the park, where I had sat on a bench on the south side. A young guy who looked a lot like Nathan and who was walking a cocker spaniel passed me once, then passed me again, and before I knew it we had struck up a conversation and I was headed back to his apartment with him.

That trick was quick and ultimately unsatisfying, as soon as we had both come he was ready for me to go—he wasn't even interested in any sort of conversation, let alone an attachment. I had hoped at least for some sort of dialogue between us so that I could differentiate him from Nathan, make me want Nathan even more, really, than the craving to fool around on him. Ironically, the lack of dialogue between myself and my trick had that same effect, for back out on the street I had been instantly sorry for what I had become, and I had decided, then, that day, that I would just let Nathan think I was fooling around on him, wanted other sexual partners, that my desire for other sexual partners had been realized, even though it was something I no longer wanted to pursue.

It was the course of the epidemic that pitched us deeper into monogamy. I sensed, somewhere around 1983, I think, that Nathan was looking for other sexual partners. I remember, too, the first night I put on a condom before entering Nathan, or, rather, Nathan had slipped a condom over my cock; I had felt, then, so ashamed of myself, uneasy that I might be carrying something inside that was potentially harmful to another person. Sex between us had become quite passionless; anxiety accompanied every orgasm. We were, however, comfortable and content enough in our relationship to not need sex to define it. How we recaptured sex, though, had been through the re-creation of romance. Nathan had called me up at work one afternoon and had asked me out on a date. We were both in such deep psychological ruts—I had just heard that Wes had died—that I thought Nathan, going through one of his fits of anxiety, had finally flipped. He persisted with the ruse of asking me out and then asked me to meet him at his apartment—our apartment—and he had given me the address, which I had absurdly written down on a scrap of paper and folded and put into my pocket. I arrived home without shopping beforehand, without checking the mail, ringing the buzzer and announcing my name, fingering the scrap of paper in my pocket as I climbed the stairs. When Nathan had answered the door of his apartment—our apartment—he had candles burning on the tables and bookshelves. We ate dinner, which he had cooked, and listened to the stereo, making out afterward on the couch, still fully clothed, like two boys meeting on a first date might do. We had danced a bit, taking turns leaning our heads on each other's shoulders, then kissed some more in the candlelight, till finally neither of us could bear the weight of the clothes on our bodies. I suppose, in a way, we had successfully locked out the rest of the world that night; our escape from the epidemic had been an escape into our relationship.

When Nathan was in the hospital with pneumocystis, I had made an appointment to see Dr. Jacobsen; I had wanted to be tested for HIV. I had not been tested, myself, when I was hospitalized the year before, or, rather, my results had never been fully disclosed to me and my reasoning was that if Nathan and I were both sick, or both to be sick, then maybe we should just go out together—leap off a building or jump in front of a subway car, or take, concurrently, a bottle of pills. I felt certain that I could discuss the possibility with Nathan, or be ready for a reply, myself, if he were ever to broach the subject. Blood tests, then, took two weeks to get results back, and as I shuttled between the hospital and the apartment—not wondering about the result, really, just suspended until the suspected verdict was to fall—I had been convinced that I had done this to Nathan. I was the cause of his illness. I had infected him. This was provoked from the belief, then, that passive partners were the ones that were easiest to be infected. I had spent most of our relationship—years—fucking Nathan, before the concept of safe sex had been introduced and assimilated.

So I was stunned when I returned to Dr. Jacobsen and he had announced that I had tested negative. How was it possible that I had been spared this? Nathan and I had shared combs, razors, silverware, sheets, lubricant, clothes, and toothbrushes. I had tasted his saliva, his skin, his hair, his sweat, as he had mine. The day I had found out my result was the day before Nathan was to be released from the hospital, but I did not tell him that evening. I waited a few days, till we were settled back again in the apartment. Nathan had gotten up from a nap and was sitting behind his desk, checking some figures his secretary had brought him, when I walked into the room and said, directly, "My test came back negative."

I hated myself at that moment for the way I said it so casually, hated myself for waiting the few seconds for him to understand what I was talking about; when he did, I watched an angry fire overtake his eyes. He did not say anything to me, and I didn't allow him a comment. I left the room and went back to the kitchen, where I had been reading the paper, ashamed and guilty because I brought up an issue we had carefully avoided for weeks. A wall had been thrown up between us, a barrier neither one of us had had any choice in building, but one I was desperate to see knocked down but didn't know how. I wished, then, I had tested positive—and it occurred to me that maybe things would be easier if I were to become infected too.

"You have to be careful," Nathan had said, coming into the room. It was then, at that moment, that I knew I would someday have a life without Nathan, and I put down the newspaper on the table with a deliberate movement, feeling censured because I had somehow been spared. Why does one man carry antibodies and another man doesn't? Why does one man's immune system collapse and another does not even contain the virus? Not even science could answer those questions.

Nathan and I did not stop having sex after he became ill. Sex, or, rather, making love, became redefined for us. The simple fact, however, was that I was negative and he was positive; he was infected and I was not, an identity that I carried with me throughout my day—when I shaved in the morning, took a glass of juice from the refrigerator, brushed my teeth in the bathroom at night. Even when we both had had colds Nathan and I had never stopped kissing one another—deep, ardent kisses full of tongues and lips and breath and saliva colliding and mingling with one another. For a while, after he first became ill, Nathan would not kiss me on the lips, afraid of infecting me, and I, too, kept my passion in check, afraid of passing on some other kind of germs into him. Sex, then, became holding each other's hand as we watched TV, hugging one another in the bathroom, kissing each other on the forehead when coming into a room. Sex, too, was still the climax of an orgasm, but there had been a division between us, a separation between him and me, a sort of hands-off-while-I-get-myself-off-and-you-just-help-me-a-bit-by-just-watching-you-know type of attitude. Nathan had become too protective, too worried. We no longer had anal sex; no longer had oral sex, either. Everything, really, distressed us too much.

"It would be immoral for me to do it," Nathan had said when he had met me at Penn Station when I had returned from Washington. Seeing him for the first time after an absence of a few days, I had noticed the darker skin around his eyes, the stiffness in his walk, the tilt of his head as if it were too heavy for his body.

"No, it wouldn't," I had answered. "It's only immoral for you if I was unaware of the potential consequences. I know what can happen. I understand the risk."

As daring as my words sounded, when we reached the street I was suddenly afraid of everything: crossing the street too soon, the traffic moving too quickly, even our weaving around a cluster of businessmen wearing name badges. I had lifted my hand in the air to hail a cab, but felt, instead, like a man drowning and waving wildly for someone to help.

"Why?" Nathan asked me when we reached a restaurant in Chelsea where we had decided to go for lunch before returning home.

"Why?" I answered. "Why not? What's wrong with a man wanting his lover to fuck him?"

Fear clung to us like cigarette smoke, the smell of it seeping into our clothes, our hair, underneath our fingernails. In our past, when two men fucked, there was no concept that a virus could be passed between them, that it could lie dormant, undetected for years, then suddenly erupt and send the body into panic. Fear was consuming our relationship: my fear of Nathan becoming ill, possibly dying, fear of myself, as well, becoming infected. Fear. Fear. Fear. And more fear.

"Is sex that important for you?" he asked when our food came, though he did not eat much, moving a pile of shredded carrots around his plate.

By then I had grown annoyed with our conversation, angry that we kept talking about it, over and over, that everything in our lives now was tinged with such complexity. "No, you know that. I don't want to be afraid of you, Nathan. I don't want to hate you. I want to trust you—I have to trust you."

I threw my fork against my plate in frustration. "Don't you understand, Nathan? I accept whatever happens. If the condom breaks, the condom breaks. I don't blame you. You're not to blame." I had worked myself into such a restrained public rage that I could only breathe through my mouth.

Nathan dropped his jaw to speak, looking as if he were going to scream. "Robbie," he said, with an irritated force. "I don't blame you for any of this. What kind of man would I be if I did?"

And so the days passed between us respectfully; Nathan was never one to ask for help and I tried to believe there was a normalcy to our lives together, that picking up medication from the pharmacy was something that anyone would do, that calling Ben Nyquist to check his opinion on a blood transfusion for Nathan was not motivated by some unchecked hysteria. And then one morning in early November we lay in bed together, the sun breaking through a thick bank of rain clouds that had drifted over the city. A thin chill hovered in our bedroom and I slipped myself around Nathan to find more warmth. Patches of rainbows fell on the bedspread where the sunlight refracted through the small crystal prisms which Nathan had hung on the window grating.

In bed Nathan moved in closer to me and as I embraced him, I slid a hand down his stomach and realized he was hard. I held his cock for a moment, feeling the heat of it, then I slipped away from him and opened the dresser drawer beside the bed.

"Two," Nathan said. "I want to use two."

I pulled out the lubricant and two condoms, but he took them from me before I had returned to his side of the bed. He found a T-shirt on the floor and slipped it on to keep the chill of the air off of his back; I slipped between his knees and pressed my lips against his balls as they dangled above me. He slipped first one condom on and then the second one, then took the lubricant and rubbed it on his covered cock. I lifted my heels and placed them against his shoulders and he took the lubricant and rubbed it gently with his fingers into my ass. Our eyes met here and I could see, vividly, that his were full of fear.

"Relax," he had said, and we shifted our position a bit. I titled my head back, and my eyes, at that moment, were suspended in a rainbow of light. I held myself there feeling the colors burn into my eyes. I believe, then, I had a glimpse of heaven. I closed my eyes, relaxed, and felt Nathan move himself slowly into me.

"Robbie," Nathan whispered. "I'll take care of you."

Then I let go of heaven. And he did.

12

"Do you believe in heaven?" Nathan asked.

I looked up from the magazine I was reading, the November issue of *Spy*. Nathan had been watching "Jeopardy" on the TV suspended on the wall and a commercial for taco chips was being blasted into the hospital room at the same moment he had asked his question. Nathan seldom had existential thoughts on his mind; I knew his question must have been triggered by the living will we had had notarized by a volunteer earlier in the day and the concept of it—taking life away—had stayed inside him, festering, just as the virus had unknowingly for years. Before he had signed the document he had mentioned that he was anxious about having been away from work for over a week, anxious, too, over the possibility that he might not be able to return to work at all. My anxiety that evening, however, was from the fear that this time he might not be released from the hospital.

I was tired and agitated and conscious of being both that night, I remember, and I looked over at Nathan from where I was seated as if I wanted him to repeat the question, but my gaze was caught with a reminder, once again, of the hollowness of his face. Instead, what I really wanted to know was how could he believe in heaven considering the hell he had been living this last week, the way he looked lying there in the hospital, bleak and susceptible and needy. Even then I thought I must not have been much help to him, and I sat there silent, dumbfounded at my speechlessness and guilty of my own health, trying to suppress the continual headache that I seemed to carry with me wherever I went.

His eyes met me fiercely and he clicked off the sound of the TV, forcing me, then, to speak. "I don't know," I answered roughly, clearing my throat of an oily phlegm, backing down from his stare. "Do you?"

"There must be a point to all this," he said, his head wobbling sarcastically as if to acknowledge the IV bags above his head, the plastic tubing wrapping its way into the needle stuck in his forearm.

"The point is to get better," I said flatly, an image floating through my mind of Nathan being ill for years and years. "Why don't you try eating something?"

Nathan had been unable to control his nausea for almost a week, a gastronomical attack and a vomiting spree had sent him back to the hospital four days ago, the muscles of his back so weak Ben Nyquist was afraid that his back would break from the strain of retching. By then, that evening in his room, Nathan had lost six more pounds since he had been hospitalized again; his frame, beneath the sheets of the bed, poked up sharply like spokes of a tent.

What happened next was that my stomach growled, a loud and irritating moan, really, and Nathan cocked his left ear toward me, as if trying to listen to a foreign language in order to better translate it. I felt so reprehensible and so hungry at that moment—I had raced home as quickly as I could from a construction job I had taken downtown, showered the smell off of me, and then hurried over to the hospital, which was only a block from our apartment yet the distance seemed to take hours to traverse. As I walked my hair was still so damp that the December evening chilled my scalp. Food and eating were never on my mind; my goal, instead, was getting to Nathan as quickly as possible. Every step was heavy with fear and uncertainty that I would lose Nathan at any moment, that this was it. And so it was that every moment became precious to me, every moment away from Nathan was time I felt I had lost.

Throughout his hospital room there was food Nathan could not eat, or, rather, food that Nathan had asked for hoping to be able to eat and then found he couldn't: a bag of Pepperidge Farm Mint Milano cookies Jerry had brought the day before sat on the stand beside the bed; a glass jar painted with leaves of holly and full of candy canes was on the floor beside my chair where Martin had left it after retrieving it from his gym bag; the plastic container of sliced peaches Nathan's mother had gotten that morning from the Korean market on Seventh Avenue were still on the table that swung over his bed. It wasn't just that Nathan despised the hospital food—he was always complaining that it was too bland and never what he checked off on the menu—but that he couldn't keep any of it down. Eating for him meant an instant trip to the bathroom or the sink.

The doctors had no idea how to settle his stomach or bowels, so they sent him through a battery of tests, instead: CAT scans, T-scans, X-rays of his abdomen, chest, and skull. What wisdom we found arrived to us through visitors: Martin said peppermint always helped him feel better after he vomited; Jerry pushed for Nathan to drink vitamin supplements; Mrs. Solloway was convinced that salty food—pretzels and crackers—would contain his nausea.

I knew Nathan was annoyed by all this folk knowledge; it was, he felt, as if they believed he had given up, as if it was his fault that he could not keep anything down. The more someone pushed food on him, the more he pulled back, his eyes wild from the fury of his discomfort. And so it happened that I could not bear to eat in front of him no matter how hungry I would get. I could never even bring myself to leave Nathan's room, either, after I had arrived in the early evening. I would sit through the parade of visitors and nurses and doctors and interns, giving up the chair or a corner to whomever walked in, slipping over toward the window and sitting on the thin slip of a sill that hid the radiator or leaning against the wall till I could no longer stand, then sliding to the floor, my arms clutched around my knees until it was time to stand again, sometimes blankly zoning out, ignoring the conversation floating about the room, wanting only to be in Nathan's presence, not wanting to leave him alone, or, instead, fearing, really, that he was going to leave me.

And so I came to hate Nathan for this, hated having to wait there and be hungry, wait to hear news from a doctor or an intern, wait for someone to leave, wait for his mother and father to stop kneading their hands together, wait till Nathan needed something done, wait till he threw up and I would have to clean the floor or the sink or run a warm washcloth across his mouth and forehead, wait through the long hours of the night and the following day till I could return to the hospital, wait to attempt to be optimistic and hopeful.

I cannot say, honestly, that Nathan's illness brought out the best in me. I operated silently, instead, full of anger, wanting all of this illness to be over somehow—hoping, really, that this deviation to our relationship would just end. I couldn't see myself taking care of Nathan like this forever, already he had been in and out of the hospital more than twenty times in the last eleven months. Nathan had become quite vocal when he was in pain, and he would grimace and moan as he shifted himself in the bed; in the bathroom he let out anguished screams as streams of fluid broke out of his body. And each time he was hit with one of these agonies my chest would constrict itself with fear, my heart pounding painfully against my own chest. One night his father had drawn me out of the room—against my will, really—taking me forcefully by the wrist, his fingers pinching at my veins, and leading me out into the hall. "I thought people went into the hospital to get better?" he sternly asked me, the blood seeping to the surface of the skin of his face and staying there, his eyes bugging out in anger at me, as if I possessed answers and solutions that I was holding back from him, as if I were keeping Nathan from getting well.

I looked at Mr. Solloway, his hair askew around his face like a clown, his eyes, large and moist, like a child's. I had no answer for him, silently ragged with my own hysterics, and I walked back into the room hating Nathan even more for subjecting me to nights alone with his parents. How could he do this to me? I asked myself over and over. Wasn't he aware of how much I loved him?

Nathan's parents had been staying at our apartment since he had returned to the hospital at the end of November and I had been waging a silent war with them ever since they had arrived. If they had ever considered me a nice, worthy person or even an adequate partner for their son, I knew their opinion of me must have certainly changed. They wanted to know everything that was happening: Why was I working when Nathan was in the hospital? (We needed the money, Nathan's health insurance was late in turning around our payments; we couldn't even afford the prescriptions any more.) Why was he throwing up so much when he barely ate? (The fluid in his stomach created too much pressure, according to one doctor.) Why had he lost so much weight? (I don't know, I don't know, I don't know.)

At first I would walk away from them and their questions, into another room or the bathroom and shut the door, squeezing my fingers through my hair till I was calm. Then I began to purposely avoid them. After leaving Nathan's hospital room I would walk alone along Seventh Avenue, away from the direction of our apartment, taking a circuitous route through the Village, hunched up within the wool lining of my coat till I reached Sheridan Square, window shop through a few stores, and then head over to a bar on Greenwich Avenue.

The drinking began innocently, at least that's how I would like to believe it did—I would usually start with one beer at the bar, almost instantly high from the alcohol because I was so tired and hungry, so nervous about Nathan's diet that I was ignoring my own. My eyes would roam the crowd of men, not really cruising, not even wanting to cruise, actually, instead alighting for a few seconds on a profile, a wisp of hair out of place or the shape of some guy's arms, but feeling as passionless about all these men as I did of the Christmas trees and decorations that trimmed the bar counter in those weeks before the holidays. Finally, a buzz would lighten my mood and a sense of time would disappear, and I would stay and listen to the music as long as I could, before it all spilled into noise, and then I would find myself back out on the street walking again till I reached the apartment, quietly unlocking the door so as not to alert the Solloways that I had returned.

Most of the time, when I returned home the Solloways were asleep, or almost asleep if they were waiting to ask me more questions. I had given them our room to sleep in, given them the bed that Nathan and I had shared together for over seven years, the bed that I had made the headboard for at Alex's workshop, the bed above which I had hung a charcoal sketch Denise had once drawn of Nathan and I sitting together one evening in the Peacock Café not long after we had met one another.

Even if they were asleep, Mrs. Solloway would usually join me in the kitchen, politely pumping me for details till I could break away and flee to the bathroom. It was then, when she had given up on me and gone back to bed, that I would creep back again into the kitchen and have another drink. I had started to keep the whiskey bottle underneath the sink and I would pour myself straight shots, looking at objects in the kitchen—the salt and pepper shakers, the grain of the table top's wood, the cabinet door knobs, till I became calm again and my gaze reached a blurriness once more. Some nights I would tip the bottle to my nose and the smell would sink into me, and I could sense it seeping back out in the sweat of my skin. It was then that I remembered how, years ago, the odor used to cling to my father's shirts at night, how I used to walk by him with disgust, believing he was both a fool and a drunk. Did my father become a drunk because of my mother's illness? Had he, too, suffered from a lack of faith? My father would have probably been so pleased if he had known of Nathan's illness, a sodomite punished for his sins, and so I would clench my jaws together, hating him even more than I could possibly hate Nathan for dying on me, ruining our relationship, and in the process convince myself that my life was so miserable I was worthy of another drink if I wanted to stay alive.

And so I came to blame Nathan for sending me into an alcoholic stupor every night, blamed him for the pounding headache that would awake me in the morning when I would hear Mr. Solloway bang the lid of the toilet in the bathroom, blamed him for the misery my father's image continued to inflict on me, blamed him for the questions I could not answer day after day after day. I felt so bitter and useless in those moments, nothing I could do would make me feel better, if I took an aspirin and the headache went away, for example, I would only then want to have another drink. And whatever I could do for Nathan was never enough. No measure of happiness or good thoughts could keep him from getting sicker. Didn't I know the progression of the infection? Wasn't I just being realistic? Hadn't I already lost more people in my life than I thought I would have by this age?

And so I tried to ground myself, making lists of what to grab and take to the hospital for Nathan, things that I could hold in my hand and say to him, see, I brought you this, this clean T-shirt, this fresh, clean piece of clothing—smell it, Nathan, smell it—it can help you feel better right now. Nothing, however, could make him want to eat, and his lack of appetite—his lack of wanting an appetite—pitched me further and further into despair. How do you keep hoping when the person who has inspired that hope seems to have lost his own faith? What more could I give to Nathan to make him want to go on living? I expected at any moment that Nathan would announce that he was ready to die, that my lack of faith in his becoming well had shaped his own lack of faith, and his questioning the existence of heaven only seemed to confirm my conviction.

"My mother used to believe that everything in heaven was white," I said that evening in Nathan's hospital room, watching him click through the channels of the television, silently, the sound of the set still turned off. "You know, the Hollywood stereotype—white clouds, white harps, white angels. I always thought it was probably more gold, you know, like an autumn sunset—all those fiery, beautiful colors."

"Fire?" he echoed back to me with a nod. "I had a dream about fire last night." Nathan's dream activity had increased wildly in the last month, and he had regularly taken to explaining them to me as he could recall them. "I was in a city enclosed in glass," he said. "The planet was nothing but red and orange gases, like everything was on fire. I was a baby, I could see my eyes and feel bangs against my forehead."

As he said this, I watched his face flush with blood, as if he had talked himself into a fever. I moved from the chair where I was sitting, to the edge of his bed and rubbed my hand across his brow, but felt no fever, and let my fingers rest up within his hairline. "My hair was thicker," he said with a shy grin. "And my parents—my real parents—put me in this capsule like a casket that had a glass roof I could see through, like I was being buried alive. I could feel my whole body breathing, though, but it was using up the oxygen. I could feel molecules disappearing with every breath. Then there was a rumbling sound and I could see the planet below me as the capsule rotated and then I noticed I held a baby in my arms, that I wasn't alone in the capsule. I had escaped with a child who was younger than me, but for some reason seemed to be me as well, as if I had escaped with myself.

"And then the capsule landed near a river, and a woman with white hair took me out and I was swimming in a river, only the water wasn't moving. Then I saw a dolphin and it carried me to a wall where I climbed out and lay on a beach.

"And the sun was so warm and I felt myself drying out and my eyes became so heavy I thought I must be in heaven. That's what heaven was. Heaven was earth in my dream. I could hear cicadas chirping and grass growing and the water stirring. And then I saw you coming toward me in a boat—your hair was cut like it was when I first met you. And then you had the baby in your arms and I could see you and I started to cry because I was so happy.

"But then I tried to speak, but I couldn't hear my words and instead you started singing to the baby, and I felt myself lifted up again, this time like I had wings and I was soaring out over this planet and I felt myself flying closer and closer to the sun, and that's when I woke up, sweating so much I could feel the water in my T-shirt. What does it mean, Robbie? Is there a meaning to all these dreams?"

It was then, just as he had asked his question and I sat there, silent, unable to find a response or a meaning for him, that Dora walked into the room. She placed a plastic bag on the corner of the bed and pulled out a plastic container.

"So glum in here," she said, her voice pitching notes higher than usual, as if she were singing. "Someone must be hungry," she added to Nathan. She tipped the lid off of the container and held it up in front of Nathan's face. "Pudding. Just the way you like it."

Nathan smiled grimly, looked up at the TV momentarily, then back at Dora, as if she should have known better than to try to bring him food.

"I can't taste anything anymore," he said to her, casting his eyes back to the television.

She brushed off the alarm that must have swept across my face at that moment. "But you get hungry," she said, taking her puffy dark fingers and squeezing the corner of Nathan's lips affectionately. "Eat when you get hungry."

She pretended not to see me squirm in my chair, and she took a towel from the side of Nathan's bed and went over to the sink and rinsed it with hot water, aware of me sitting silently in the chair with nothing left to say to anyone. If there is a god, a goddess or some divine higher power or celestial being, I thank them all for sending us Dora. There was something so selfless about her—the way she moved across the room and ran the warm wet end of the towel across Nathan's face and neck, up and down one arm and then the next, patting his skin with the dry end of the towel as she did so, in order that he would not catch a chill. All at once I felt so ugly and culpable being unable to move from the chair I had returned to, defeated from not having been able to interpret Nathan's dream, unable to provide him health, really, hating myself for hating Nathan, hating Dora for doing what I could no longer find the energy or enthusiasm to continue to do.

And then she began to hum, withdrawing a tube of lotion from the pocket of the apron she was wearing over her uniform. She poured some into the palms of her hands and began rubbing it into Nathan's skin. A few moments later she was audibly singing, a heavy chant of foreign words as she worked over Nathan. I sat there wondering if she might be doing some sort of Caribbean voodoo spell, not at all inclined to stop her. If magic could cure Nathan, who was I to question it? And then she returned to humming again, and after her voice became softer and softer and Nathan had closed his eyes as if he had been hypnotized into sleep, she turned to me and said, "God tested Job too, you know. Took it all from him. Thought he was in hell. But one day he woke up a richer man. God gave him heaven on earth."

Is heaven a place of God or a concept of the mind? Does a lack of faith produce illness or does a disbelief in God produce despair? How can I believe in a just and loving God? Answers elude me as much as my belief that there is a God; all I know is that by the time Nathan came home from the hospital I had lost what faith I had had—hope no longer moved me through the day. Instead, I was propelled once again by fear, the uncertainty of everything, every millisecond of the day lengthened by the terror of Nathan becoming worse—the fear of losing Nathan, really. As much as I hated the scenario, hated what was happening, hated Nathan, too, at moments, I could not let go of my need for him, my need to know how he was feeling every waking moment of my day. Everything in my path—a phone call, a visitor, a cough, a fever—posed a potential threat from keeping life status quo, for if Nathan woke up one morning and did not feel any worse than the day before, hadn't something better at least been achieved? Having Nathan at home was harder than having him in the hospital. He had not returned home a stronger man; at best, he was mobile enough to make it to and from the bathroom by himself—that is, as long as no object obstructed the path he had to take because of the IV pole he now had to push along beside himself—and because of that we had been subjected to his numerous accidents.

We seldom had any time alone now; the Solloways had sublet an apartment on Perry Street, a few blocks away, and Dora alternated with Mrs. Solloway as Nathan's home care attendant while I was at work on day jobs; Dora had taken a leave of absence from the hospital, sitting by Nathan in the mornings and afternoons, easily doing the same things during the day that I could no longer do at night without a vile hatred rising to the surface of my skin—fetching a glass of water for him, cleaning his eyeglasses, helping him shave or brush his teeth, cleaning up the bile and blood of his vomit from the front of his pajamas. I could feel the fear in my touch, in everything that moved around me, as if I were claustrophobic and pushing against surfaces trying to find a better way to breathe, or at least more air, and I slept, now, on the floor beside our bed, not wanting to get tangled up in the IV tubes attached to a catheter that was implanted in Nathan's chest, not wanting to feel his body pitching in the bed, not wanting, either, to be too far away from Nathan should he cry out for me, waking up every time he moved in the bed, getting up and sitting with him every time he woke up from nightmares of fiery planets and spaceships.

My composure began slipping as Nathan began to slide in and out of mild states of dementia, and I moved now through heavy states of depression, as if I were carrying sacks of potatoes around wherever I went, wanting, at times, to just selfishly throw everything to the ground and run away from all of this horror. One morning, pulling myself off the floor, my body stiff from where I had curled it to maintain its warmth, I heard Nathan having a conversation with Hank, who had been dead, then, for almost eight months. Another morning he kept saying he was scared of a bird that had flown into the room, but overturning everything I could find, he would not believe me that one was not present, and only when he was back asleep did the belief stop haunting him. Another evening, coming home from work, I found him in bed squeezing the head of his cock, beet red in the face, and I kept asking him over and over, "Nathan, what's wrong, what can I do to help?" scared shitless myself, then, unable to do anything, really, till Dora appeared with a urinal and helped him piss.

And then one morning I woke and smelled a tart, bleachlike stench in the room, and I knew, immediately, as I got off the floor that he had urinated in the bed.

"I'm sorry," Nathan said. He was already awake, waiting for me, his eyes wide and moist searching out my reaction. "I couldn't wake you again." The planes of his face had sharpened and he was breathing through his mouth.

"I'll help you change."

I helped him from the bed and into clean pajamas, then sat him in the chair, moving quickly next to change the linen on the bed. When I had snapped the last corner of the fitted sheet into place, I heard him gasp, "Robbie."

When I looked over at him, I noticed he had already wet the pajama pants I had just helped him put on. I felt, then, my anger rise to the skin of my cheeks, though nothing in me could make me yell at him, though I stared furiously and repulsively at him. I know, though I said nothing, that he sensed my anger across the room because when I had finished with the bed he was crying.

"Help me go," he said, as I helped him step out of his soiled pants and into another clean pair.

"What?"

"It's time for me to go now."

"No, it's not," I answered, a bit roughly. At first, I thought his mind had slipped away from him again, but then I understood what he was talking about. Nathan had become obsessed with suicide in the last few days, worried that he was running everyone ragged—which he was—and he was struggling, once again, with the guilt of it. By then he had devised several scenarios in which he could easily depart—jumping from our fire escape, running a razor into his wrists, and a combination of medicines that he had discovered while reading a book Betty Rollin had written about her mother's illness.

"Dora said she could get the pills," he said.

"But we don't want Dora to get the pills," I answered, harboring a private thought that, perhaps, we should just speed up this deterioration.

I watched him contort his face with anger—by then he was so used to being treated with the immediacy of a baby, that he would pout like a child if he didn't get his way. "I don't want you doing this," he said.

"I don't mind it."

"Yes, you do."

"You'd do it for me," I said.

His face now moved out of its selfish need, and I watched him look around the room, gathering in the state of his belongings. "Then why won't you help me?"

"I'm not ready to let you go, Nathan," I said.

I watched him take it in, the weight of my statement, and he bowed his head toward his lap. "But I don't feel good, Robbie."

And then I hated myself for what I had to say next, knew I couldn't avoid the subject any longer, the thought of it annoying me like a bit of food caught within my windpipe, my body clenching itself as I tried to maintain a congenial tone of voice. "Would you feel better if you wore a diaper?"

"Okay," he answered, in his singsong childish voice without giving it much thought. Then, when the idea of it had sunk in, a few seconds later, his face squinted together as if he had been burned.

How can I hide my hatred, I thought, as I pulled a diaper from where Dora had hidden them in a dresser drawer. How can he not see it in me when I feel every shiver of his pain and embarrassment? As I moved him back to the bed, adjusted his hips, took the cloth and ran them around his legs, his eyes never left me, uneasy and entreating. How can I prove to him that I want him here, that what is happening now has no bearing on my love for him, when, in fact, my hatred of what is happening is mutating that very love as vilely as the virus within his body? I felt my teeth clenching in anger, holding in my fear, when I found myself leaning down and kissing him at his waist, my lips wetting the skin above the cloth of the diaper. I kept them there, rubbing my nose along the hairs of his navel, breathing in the joyous scent of him, yet at the same time wanting to pound him with my fists out of frustration.

How long can a person maintain his dignity as his body deteriorates? How long can a lover expect to remain composed and dignified as he watches it? Nathan's eyes grew larger, moister, and deeper as if what life he still possessed rested within those sharp green ovals. He continued watching as I straddled his body, rubbing my stubby, cutup fingertips against his papery skin. I felt him, beneath me, beginning to sweat, heard him breathing in and out, heavier and heavier, and it was here that I took in a view of the disgusting state of his body, wanting to make love, however, to the beauty that remained of his soul.

There is something you lose within yourself when you watch someone die, for as much as I would have liked to believe that Nathan was getting better, I knew, of course, that he was not. I suppose that's why I hated everything so much then, when, as I hovered over him, touching him as only a lover would, I heard him say, defensively, "Robbie, it's okay to let go now," but felt, at that same moment, his fingers grasp my wrist to hold me in place.

Vince once said to me that what he disliked most about Christmas was the waiting for things, waiting in line for the sales clerk to show you the merchandise, waiting in line to have it gift-wrapped, waiting to give it to someone or send it in the mail, waiting at the post office, waiting to buy scotch tape because you invariably run out, waiting for the day of the big party you've been invited to, then getting there and waiting for the stupid party to just end. Most of all, he felt, the holidays were just unbearably too long; what he disliked was the anticipation of Christmas—he once told me that one year, the Christmas he was six years old, he had opened all of his presents before his parents had even awakened. Nathan always felt, however, that Christmas Day had the potential to take on a magic and majesty of its own, despite whatever frustrations and anxieties the holidays as a whole could produce.

That year, 1987, I missed Vince's friendship as I moved about the city, missed his grumbling beside me in bank lines waiting to cash a check, missed his irritated snap over having to find a co-worker a present because he had just gotten one himself, missed the way, too, he would tighten his lips and jut out his jaw over hearing about a party that he had not been invited to. I missed most of all, I think, having someone to confide in about the status of Nathan's health. Vince and I continued to talk coast to coast on the phone; I think we spoke to each other almost every other day that year, Vince calling from the futon bed in the new, airy second-floor apartment he and Jeff had found in West Hollywood, usually catching me after I had finished cleaning dishes or changing bags on Nathan's IV infusion pole. But there was a certain distance between us that could not be successfully overcome through the phone, a reserved manner of avoiding true feelings as it were, as if bad things could not be happening in either of our worlds during the holidays, or, rather, certainly nothing more thwarting than what the season would ordinarily bring.

But I knew that Vince had been up for several rewrite jobs on screenplays that had been aborted by a studio when a director had been fired; knew, too, that he had lost his position as a script reader with a producer after a development deal fell through; knew that he was spiraling through his own depression, worried about his own health, spending more time on an analyst's couch and at a chiropractor's office than at his own desk writing. I knew this because of the phone calls Nathan had had with Denise; knew, too, that Vince must have known the truth about Nathan's health long before he ever dialed the phone because that was the way Denise always was with her friends—passing along the truths that neither of them could share with one another for, well, so many complicated reasons.

Yet in many ways I was glad that Vince was not there to witness Nathan's continual decline; wouldn't it just be a constant reminder of what could happen to him as well? Ben Nyquist had discharged Nathan from the hospital not because Nathan was getting better but because there wasn't anything else they could do in the hospital to treat him. The best he could do—all any of us could do, really—was to help ease Nathan's pain. Since we lived so close to St. Vincent's, Ben would often stop by on his way out for lunch or to run an errand. He and Nathan had hit it off with a shared infatuation of grade-B sci-fi monster movies, and he would often arrive at the apartment with a bootlegged videotape of something like *The Giant Spider Invasion* or *Reptilicus* for Nathan to watch.

Nathan, however, was in and out of clarity—one minute he was witty and lucid, the next he rambled on as if he were in a grade-B horror movie himself, ranting more vehemently that it was necessary to leave Krypton before it completely burned to ashes. "*Escape*," he would whisper when I would rub water on his cracked lips with the tips of my fingers while he was sleeping. "*We must escape.*"

There was, of course, no escape and no one was saying to me or to anyone that these were Nathan's final days, but even with my most shining optimistic belief that maybe Nathan could get better it could not keep that gloomy contemplation from hovering over me. At night, alone with my thoughts and too much booze in my blood, my hatred and despair would arrive in full force—

all I wanted was for Nathan to die so I wouldn't have to witness his pain, feel his pain myself, really—the only moments of respite I found were when he was sleeping, but even then I worried that he would not wake.

And then he would open his eyes just when I had settled into my own complacency and I would have to help him rush to the bathroom, before his rank stream of diarrhea hit the floor. When he was clean and back in bed again and asleep, I would leave him and return to the kitchen and drink. But something deeper, deeper and more faithful than the bottomless pit of hate I thought I had fallen into, was not willing to let Nathan go. And so the holidays became a double waiting game for me, waiting not only now, like Vince, for all this holiday madness to subside, but waiting, too, to see if Nathan would live through it. That Christmas we had not put a tree up in the living room—it would have only seemed absurd. Holly, mistletoe and red felt stockings were festive concepts we couldn't understand that year. Yet oddly one evening, when I had reached my first buzz, something strangely positive—as strange as the plots of Nathan's and Ben's movies—blinked in my brain like a light switch being flicked on and off. It was then that something in me decided that I would not let Nathan die during the holidays. *It just wouldn't happen.* I decided, huddled deep in the spell of too much whiskey, to give Nathan the best kind of Christmas present I could give—to give him the gift of another Christmas Day together.

Christmas Day, 1987, I woke up before the alarm went off, and, strangely, I felt as if my fear had disappeared with my dreams during the night before; my body lifted itself off the floor beside the bed as if pulled by some mysterious puppeteer's thread. Nathan was still sleeping and I stood over him a moment, then checked his IV bag to see if it was empty. His pump was still humming and I settled into the quiet of the apartment, amazed by my own sense of clarity that morning, as if a mist had been burned off my brain.

Dora had twisted a red ribbon around Nathan's IV pole to make it look like a candy cane and I evened out the curves where the ribbon had slid together, then went and plugged in a string of colored lights I had hung within strands of pine garland that I had used to frame the window three days before in a burst of wanting to feel festive. Outside the day looked gray and uneventful, but there, too, I could sense, by placing my palm against the cool pane of glass, an unexpected enchantment that the day could possess, and I felt, oddly, as I looked at the blank windows of the other apartments within the courtyard, like a kid playing hooky from school.

In the kitchen I put away the dishes and glasses we had used for dinner the night before. I had told the Solloways and Dora that I had wanted to have Nathan to myself on Christmas Day, that I had wanted to spend it with just the two of us together, and that I would prefer to give a large Christmas dinner the day before—on Christmas Eve—inviting Dora, Abby, Brian, Martin, Jerry, and our neighbors Debbie and Andrew. The Solloways reluctantly agreed, but Dora, I think, was relieved. She knew that with so many people in the apartment I often felt excluded from Nathan's attention, so she was all the more eager to see me spend more time alone with Nathan.

Nathan was awake when I returned to the bedroom and when I caught his eye he pointed to the bottom drawer of our dresser, a drawer we seldom used except to store our accumulated junk—sample cologne bottles, shoelaces, sunglasses, old batteries, Nathan's erasers and colored pencils. "Look in there," he said in his raspy morning voice as I moved through the room, and I wondered as I walked over to the dresser if today was to be intelligible for him. I opened the drawer and knew immediately what I was after—a small, gold paper-wrapped box I had never seen before.

"I thought we said no presents," I said, bringing the box over to him. Nathan shrugged his shoulders and gave me a devilish smile.

"We always say that," he replied. A lucid day, I thought. There is a God and he has blessed us with a lucid day. I had been worried, too, that last night's dinner and guests would have left him too tired, but his smile was as bright and strong as it had been the Christmas Day we met eight years earlier.

I sat beside him on the bed and carefully unwrapped the box, as if it were covered with the most priceless sort of paper, and wondered quietly to myself what the present could be. The box was no bigger than an earring box.

Inside were two plain silver bands—wedding rings, really. Nathan and I had discussed the possibility of wearing rings years ago, shortly after we moved in together, but we had both nixed the idea—neither of us wore any jewelry, not even watches, and at the time I knew Nathan had only viewed rings as an encumbrance to his, well, other subtly hidden desires.

"Mom got them for us," he said, and I instantly felt terrible for having made the Solloways time with us so much more miserable than necessary. I lifted a band out of the box—the smaller of the two—and slipped it on the finger Nathan had moved closest to my hand. He then took the box, fumbled with the other ring for a moment, twisting it in front of his eyes as if to catch the light, then lifted my hand up and slipped it on my finger. And it was here that he held my hand before his face, as if it were in itself a work of art that needed to be judged.

I did not shed any tears then, did not revel, either, in the extremes of joy and misery I felt at that moment; instead, I leaned over and kissed him, tentatively, as if it were for the first time, but breathing in, willingly, the sharp, sour taste of his breath.

"Did your mom tell you I'm taking you to the movies today?" I asked him as I took his hand in my own.

"Yes," he replied. "She was jealous."

"Dr. Nyquist is going to come with us," I added.

"Good," Nathan smiled again. "I hope he brings the pot."

"The pot?" I answered.

"I asked him to."

"You knew he was coming, too?"

"Of course," he said. "I told him I wanted the Colombian kind."

Ben arrived around noon that day. By then I had helped Nathan dress, not once but twice—he had fussed over the belt of the jeans I had helped him put on—saying that the waist felt all wrong, and he kept pulling and tugging at it. What was wrong was that Nathan had shrunk so much that the pants wouldn't stay up, even with the belt, but he was right when he said that the corduroy pants we had changed him into fit him better—at least to me they seemed to fit him better.

Ben had indeed brought "the pot" with him, though he did not know if it was the Colombian kind or not. He had gotten it, he said, through one of the hospital's connected pharmacies. "I would say this is being used for medicinal purposes," he said, rolling the grass into the cigarette paper. He lit it, took a puff, and passed the joint over to Nathan, whose eyes widened as he twirled it between his fingers.

"Prescription for a good time," Ben said, and we watched Nathan take a deep toke. For a moment I was worried that perhaps the pot might cause Nathan to have some sort of adverse reaction, and Nathan, looking at me, could immediately detect my concern. "Maybe it will make me hungry," he said and passed me the joint. I took it and brought it to my lips, immediately feeling as if I were a birthday boy who needed to make a wish.

We smoked some more, then watched a documentary on PBS, then the end of a King Kong movie. Ben and I, consumed by hunger, made sandwiches, and Nathan even ate a small portion of a bowl of oatmeal, more to keep in with the spirit of things than because his appetite had improved. Afterwards, we helped Nathan out of bed and into his winter coat, which smothered him up as if he were about to embark on an arctic expedition.

Nathan and Ben had decided in advance of Christmas Day that they wanted to see a movie that was playing at a triplex on West 23rd Street, a distance that I felt was too far for Nathan to comfortably walk. Ben and I helped Nathan down the stairs; by then Nathan had difficulty standing alone, but stubbornly refused to use a cane, though his pride did not prevent him from leaning against one of us or making us wait a few minutes on a landing to catch his breath. In the taxi to the movie theater I sat in the center of the back seat between Nathan and Ben. Ben stretched his arm across the back of the seat and I felt his fingers brush across the back of my neck and I placed, in turn, the palm of my hand against Nathan's knee, to remind him I was still beside him. When Nathan and I first started dating one another we would often go to the movies together, where, seated, he would hold my hand between the dark space of the seats, not to hide his affection, really, but to experience the thrill of being able to display it, privately, within a public space of the city.

Inside the cinema Ben helped Nathan buy a large popcorn with extra but-ter, a large soda and two boxes of candy. I stood at the corner of the lobby watching Nathan make his way proudly through the line, approach the counter, place his order, and pay the clerk, all the time feeling like a parent watching his child audition for a role in a big-budget movie. Ben fidgeted impatiently behind Nathan during this sequence of events; I knew he wanted to take charge, make things happen smoothly, but he knew—not as a doctor, I think, but someone who had been a part of this crazy epidemic for far too long—that we had to let Nathan set the pace for the day.

Nathan picked out a seat on the aisle and I sat beside him, once again posi-tioning myself between Nathan and Ben. For the first hour of the movie—about aliens who help the residents of a crumbling brownstone—it was hard for me to concentrate—not because of the pacing or the script—but from being consciously aware of Nathan continuously clearing his throat, as if phlegm had been lodged there that he couldn't get rid of, and because the refreshments he had purchased required constant monitoring by Ben and myself—holding things for him, running napkins across his face or lap, pro-viding him with extra hands without seeming intrusive. All this noise and shuffling about made the couple in front of us keep turning around, as if their frowns and hisses at us would make any of it easier. I remember growing annoyed with Nathan, annoyed with all the fumbling, guiltily wishing at that moment that the sick Nathan would just disappear. Luckily Nathan fell asleep during the last half of the movie. It was then that Ben switched his position so that his hand was draped across the back of my seat and his fingers once again searched out the nape of my neck. I remember feeling so odd at that moment, as he fingered my hair, as if being out on a date with a parent, yet not really certain if Ben's intentions were sympathetic or affectionate. The details of the movie escape my recollection now, but I remember the way Ben's fingers moved through the strands of my hair, how his thumb stroked the center of my neck, how he kept brushing his fingers against my skin even when the movie was over and the lights came back on, waiting for the theater to empty out and not wanting to wake Nathan until the last possible moment.

We walked down to Eighth Avenue then, Nathan balanced against Ben as I thrust my arm out into the traffic to hail a cab. The afternoon light had dis-appeared, and the streets were a mess of blurry, silvery lights. On the way home, the cab driver seemed to take delight in pitching us around the back seat as he swerved in and out of lanes, as if he were on a perilous, mad holiday mission to get us to a flight we had already missed. Nathan fell asleep again, his head cocked back against the seat, his mouth open to reveal the bottom row of his crooked bright white teeth. I wanted to apologize to Ben about ask-ing him to help with this, wondering what he had given up by agreeing to help, but every time I tried to think about what to say the cab would lurch and bolt around the traffic, and I would grab hold of Nathan, worried that all this motion would make him nauseous.

When we reached 13th Street, I opened the car door and hooked my hands through Nathan's armpits and lifted him out of the cab while Ben paid the driver. Nathan was still groggy and as he leaned into my embrace his head fell against my shoulder and his body shivered. I could feel the convulsions within him as he vomited down the front of my shirt. Ben didn't notice any of this until he was beside me and I could feel the wetness seeping through my clothes and against my skin, the stench making me dizzy and frightened. I know I was in shock as Ben lifted Nathan into his arms. The motion caused Nathan to vomit again, streams of mucus covered our arms as he was transferred between us. Ben lifted Nathan like a wrestler about to slam his opponent to the ground, but shifted Nathan's body so that it pivoted against his shoulder. I went ahead of them, fumbling with keys, holding doors open, rushing up the stairs by instinct.

"Help me get his clothes off," I said when we were inside the apartment. I could see the wave of shock moving over Ben, but he held Nathan up for me, watching me unbutton his shirt, slip off his shoes and socks. Nathan had also shit in his pants and the odor and filth seemed at that moment unbearable, but we sat Nathan on the toilet in the bathroom and took off his pants, Nathan looking at us with the trusting expression of a child. What lucidity he had had now seemed to be expelled along with his body fluids.

I began taking off my own clothes and throwing them in the corner, moving swiftly to the shower and adjusting the water temperature. Ben drew back against the door frame, not knowing what was happening, and when I turned to him and said, "Get out of those clothes," he began undressing in confused but deliberate actions. I stepped into the shower and stretched my arms out to Ben. He instinctively moved to Nathan, lifted him off the toilet and helped him step into the shower. The feel of Nathan's nude body in my arms when I caught him again by the armpits was a sudden tonic, and with his back pressed against my stomach I tipped us back together into the stream of water. His body shivered again and as I moved my face around to catch his expression I heard the gurgle of his smile. I looked over at Ben, now undressed and waiting at the side of the tub, and I nodded my head, indicating to him that it was all right to join us in the shower.

Ben stepped inside the shower and took Nathan from my grasp. I reached for the bar of soap and the washrag and began to wash the hard skeleton of Nathan's back. It made me immediately remember the way Nathan and I used to shower beside one another at the gym, years ago, watching men drift in and out of the door of the sauna. Most of those days I was only watching Nathan, the sight of his body unclothed never failed to amaze me. I reached around, now, years later, and began washing the hard, flat ridges of his stomach, the back of my hand grazing against Ben's pulpier skin. Ben watched my hand move across Nathan's body, washing the shallow caves of his neck and shoulders and armpits, then back down to his stomach, my hand slipping around his cock and the soft, fleshy sac of his balls. As I moved my hand and the washrag between the cheeks of Nathan's ass, rinsing away the traces of shit, Nathan leaned his head into Ben's chest. The spray of water kept hitting Ben near his ear, so he pressed in closer to Nathan.

Something in those moments made me want to kiss Ben, bury my face against his chest and say I'm sorry, I didn't mean to ruin your Christmas too, but instead I reached down and began soaping Nathan's legs, one hand grasping Ben's leg to keep myself from slipping. Ben continued to watch me, his eyes searching out mine, looking for a sign to show him how he should be reacting to all this, when I noticed that Ben had oddly tilted his body away from my view to conceal his erection. As I moved my hand up his leg to the small of his back, to keep myself from slipping, really, I noticed, then, within the hairs of Ben's stomach, two maroon lesions side by side, the size of shirt buttons. I looked up at him and watched him look away from me as if he were ashamed, and it was here that I tucked Nathan under the angle of my arm and moved my hand from behind Ben's back and embraced his cock. His eyes first widened, then he closed them as if to shut me out, but he also pitched his body closer to mine, and I moved my hand back and forth along his cock, slowly stroking it, using the water and the residue of soap as a lubricant, watching the heat of his blood redden the skin at his collar bone. He took the palm of his right hand and pushed it back behind me, bracing himself against the tiles, and it was then that he gasped and I began to move my hand harder and quicker against his cock. He gasped again and I felt him come and I angled Nathan's body and slipped to the side so that the spray of water would rinse his cock.

Ben opened his eyes then, and took control, and before I knew it the water was turned off and Nathan was being passed between us and dried, Nathan's eyes vivid and bright as though there was nothing else he would rather do in the world than be pampered by two men. Ben carried Nathan to the bedroom and wrapped him beneath the sheets of the bed. Nathan rolled over to his side, looked up at Ben, and said in a slurry voice, "Stay." I watched Ben sit on the edge of the bed beside Nathan, then I went back around the apartment, cleaning up the clothes and towels and mopping the water off the bathroom floor. As I rinsed the soiled clothes I heard the TV come on and the channels flip. When I made my way back to the bedroom Ben was lying in bed, Nathan sleeping in his arms.

I found a T-shirt in the bottom of Nathan's closet for Ben to wear and I carried it to the bed, holding it up before me like an offering to a god. Ben stared at me and all I could think about—again—was how could I bring him into all of this when it was clear he had his own dilemma? I stood beside him, blocking out some of the light of the TV, and watched him drape the T-shirt around his neck like a small towel, not wanting to disturb Nathan's sleep. I slipped into bed beside them, leaning my head against Ben's shoulder, my body slipping against him like a spoon on its side, my gaze directed toward the television set. They were watching *Breakfast at Tiffany's* and I stayed there for a while, watching the scene where Audrey Hepburn crawls up the fire escape to George Peppard's apartment, listening not to the dialogue but to the way Ben and Nathan breathed beside me.

I wanted to tell Ben how oddly romantic I found all this—a feeling I was vividly aware had eluded me since Nathan's diagnosis. I was caught up in the way Ben's hair smelled from the soap, the warm, silky finish of Nathan's skin at my fingertips, the generous way, too, Ben held both of us in his arms, the flickering light of the TV set bending about the room like candlelight. I think Ben understood it, for he sighed and turned the television set off with the remote and the room fell into a dim, breathing silence.

"Put your hand here," Ben said, indicating the patch of his chest just below where the back of Nathan's head rested. "When I was in high school I used to hang out at the baths a lot," he said. I could feel the sound of his voice at my fingertips, feel, too, the back of Nathan's neck against my wrist. "I always looked a lot older than I really was. Or at least then," he said, lightly laughing, my hand moving with the motion of his chest. "It was such a safe place to go, you know. I know that sounds stupid now. But what were we afraid of? Antibiotics? I would rent a room and undress and lie with the door open. I usually stayed all night, guys drifting in and out of the room. My parents weren't too worried about me when I didn't show up at home—they were very free thinkers. Even back then. And staying out wasn't just about sex for me. I just wanted to hold someone, you know. I would just ache for it. That's all I wanted. I can remember when I was a boy I was afraid of the dark and slept with my mom in her bed because she meant security. Then in college I had a roommate who let me sleep with him and we started a relationship. A very open one, mostly, because we were already living together. But then we really started to depend on one another in a special way. Even though we were both interested in other sex partners. By the time I was in med school I was so keyed up and wanting to make it that being at the baths was my one way of relaxing. I'm certainly not trying to play down all the sex I had. I did a lot of things. Everything. At least once. It's probably where I got into all this."

I could feel Ben's breathing lifting his chest up and down, and I pressed my fingertips tighter against his skin, sensing out his heartbeat. "When Peter was sick he had surgery and a catheter attached to an artery near his heart," he said, and I listened to his voice thin out and lift it's way up to the ceiling. "Like Nathan's." It was here that he took his hand and rubbed it underneath the T-shirt I was wearing, his fingers stopping at the point where the catheter must have pierced the skin. "Peter and I were together about ten years—he helped me get through med school those last years. I was at home one day and Peter's catheter slipped out and he panicked. He started pulling on it. He started bleeding. Real bad bleeding. I had a choice. Stop it or watch him die. I calmed him down and packed him with bandages and called an ambulance. There was blood everywhere. When I went to get tested—about a year after Peter died—I was positive. Of course I can't say for sure that that was the cause—I had never been tested before and the test hadn't even existed when Peter was sick. How can any of us say for sure what the cause is? I'm not a virgin and I'm certainly not a saint. But what was I supposed to do? Watch him die? I'm a doctor and he was my lover."

Ben tilted his head so his lips pressed against my hair. I felt his arm reaching out, slipping around my waist, then, to the center of my back. I closed my eyes, wanting to relax and I felt Ben's lips moving through my hair toward my ear. "He went quickly," he said. "Too quickly."

"I'm sorry," I said.

"Sorry?" he rolled the word through his mouth as if pondering the solution to a mystery. "No, I'm sorry. I'm sorry I don't even know if I'm underusing or overusing medication with my patients. I'm sorry I'm a doctor and I understand less every day."

"Having something at least gives them some kind of hope," I said, wondering why I felt so compelled to always appear the Pollyanna. "Isn't something better than nothing at all?"

"My patients are all dying and I have no patience anymore," he said, avoiding answering my question.

"It can't keep going on forever," I said, still trying to remain optimistic.

"Why does the body die so much easier than the soul?" he asked, "when the soul doesn't let the body give up so easily?" He moved his head away from me and I watched his eyes look around our bedroom, as if trying to reach a decision. "I don't know how much time he has left," he said, bending his head back down to me so that I could feel his voice against my skin. "Nathan's a strong man, you know. He could still live a long time."

That was the Christmas I was convinced that nothing greater would happen in my life than my love for Nathan, wanted nothing else, really, except for that love to continue. And so I lay there believing, really, that Nathan could possibly, just possibly, be invincible to all this. That he could live through this. If there was a God, I knew that he had blessed me with something special and rare in having that very love I gave to Nathan equally returned from him, though I could also not accept that this same God could even attempt to take it so brutally and resolutely away. And as I laid there, wrapped up in both Ben and Nathan, that late Christmas afternoon, I knew, woefully, really, that this moment would never happen again for any of us. "Do you believe in heaven?" I asked Ben, my question coming from some unacquainted source within myself.

I felt his body, in my embrace, tense with the question.

"No," he answered, as if he had decided the answer long ago. "Heaven will only disappoint you."

In the weeks that followed I believed that my love for Nathan could transcend the pain of watching him suffer. But nothing, I learned, could blunt the cruel hard facts. This, then, is what happened: On January 17th Nathan began to have respiratory problems early in the afternoon. Dora hooked him up to an oxygen tank that had been placed by his bed. Running home through a light flurry of snow that had the decency to melt before it landed on the sidewalks, I felt the bone-thin air cut through my chest like a knife. By the time I got home, around 6:00 P.M., Nathan was semiconscious, lying on his back, gasping for breath, his arms twitching in the air above him as if he were trying to grasp on to something. I sat down on the bed beside him and pulled his arms down, holding them at his side, thinking it might calm him, but instead, I was shocked by the coolness of his skin, so I began to rub the palms of my hands against his arms, hoping it might help his circulation. The gasping continued, however, and I sat there, oddly worried that a man who had for the last thirteen months battled a virus might suddenly strangle on his own tongue. Thirty minutes later, when the gasping subsided, Dora helped me roll Nathan over to rest on his side.

"Have you made arrangements?" she asked me, in a whisper, as if her voice would wake Nathan.

I looked down at my arm, where the dark fleshy pool of her hand rested. Was this how it was to end? I thought.

I looked at Nathan, felt a retched anger rising out of my stomach and I wanted to shake the life back into him, as if violence would restore me with an ironic inner sense of calm. It was then that he died, died right in front of my eyes, the last breath went out of him, his heart stopped and he was still. Nathan was dead at the age of thirty-one.

Dora sat with Nathan while I called the Solloways at their apartment, my hands covering my eyes when I heard the gasp of Mrs. Solloway's voice when she had understood the urgency in my voice. The police had arrived before they made it over to our apartment, and Nathan's mother, upon walking into the door, was introduced at once to the coroner. I had not mentioned to her on the phone that Nathan was already dead, had not told her that he had died minutes before I had placed the call to her; I had been unable to speak the words, "Nathan is dead," in that sequence or arrangement, to pronounce it as a fact, as it were, instead telling her when she answered the phone, "You should be here. You should hurry."

I heard her gasp, then, again, this time at the door—and I turned away from looking at her, not wanting to meet her eyes. And this was when Dora took her in her arms and buried Mrs. Solloway's head into her dress, rocking her back and forth as if a child who had come in from a fall on a swing set. Mr. Solloway sat heavily into a chair, slumping down, studying the carpet on the floor, and I gave the policeman Ben Nyquist's phone number to call as Nathan's doctor, as well as our address and other information that he needed for his report, as if I were an automaton. The morticians arrived not much later, greeted everyone solemnly, asked us if we wanted to view Nathan before they took him away. We all nodded no, and they slipped on white gloves and slid Nathan's body into a dark, airless plastic bag. We stood around the bed, watching in silent horror, till they carried the bag out on a stretcher.

It was here, then, with Nathan gone—dead and carried out of the apartment—that I icily told the Solloways I would make phone calls tomorrow and meet with the funeral director. Mr. Solloway looked at me as if I were deranged, as if I had planned this day for years. I couldn't comfort them—I had no sympathy or compassion left in my body at that moment, nor did I expect any in return to be given to me. What I wanted for them was to just leave so I could have a drink and a good cry and fall asleep, to forget that all this unhappiness had happened.

That was, in fact, exactly what did happen. They left, I drank, I cried. Close to morning I fell asleep and when I woke the light outside was again misty and overcast, looking as if it might snow. In my hand I held the prism Nathan had stolen years ago from a chandelier at the Ritz Carlton in Boston. How it got in my hand that morning is still as much of a mystery to me as how Nathan, himself, had first acquired it. And that was the beginning of my first day without Nathan in the six years and three months we had lived together.

I could not let go of my hatred when Nathan died. I felt, in those days after his funeral, as if my life had been demolished and I became almost unrecognizable to myself, always waking up out of a trancelike state, like a mindless robot blinking on hold, really, waiting to be programmed by someone else, waiting for a set of instructions on how to react. Vince had flown in from Los Angeles to help me sort through things and the day after Nathan's funeral he went around the apartment touching Nathan's clothes and drawings and books and records, asking with every tap, in a short staccatolike manner, "Do you want to keep this? What about that?" or "Let's throw this out." Vince was as haughty as a Sotheby's appraiser, wanting to get it all out of the way as quickly as possible. I could not part with anything, however—I was not ready to part with anything—Nathan's death was still too close to me and Vince's officiousness intensely annoyed me. I was a ragged mess against Vince's meticulously groomed character. I pouted and moaned as he tried to throw things away; even when I had worn down his brusque manner, everything Vince would try to put into a box I would pull out and want to keep, shrieking in a voice I had not used since I was child and had broken my arm. I could not let go of anything Nathan had owned or used—certainly not the dark green baseball cap he wore when it rained, not the long blue shorts he bought in Miami, not the drawings, either, which he sketched in a notepad during his last visit to the hospital, not even the plastic glass we had used as a urinal. Nothing.

"You have to get rid of this stuff," Vince said over and over to me, shaking his head at me like I had approached a reservation counter with too much baggage. "It's just stuff." My apartment had become a maze of medical supplies but I wouldn't even let him touch those, not even to send them back to the home-care agency we had used the last month Nathan was at home. I hated Vince in those moments, hated the way he could so casually dismiss the years I had loved Nathan, hated him for not being around to help while Nathan was daily growing worse and worse, hated him for being infected himself, hated him mostly for treating my memories of Nathan as though they were pieces of clothing I had worn to tatters and now had to throw away. Was all this hatred my way of being defensive, protecting myself so I would not be so hurt? If that were the case then I had failed miserably; everything was arduous to me, especially my hatred. By the day Vince left to return to Los Angeles we had only dispensed one small box of Nathan's things. "It's not your fault," Vince said in a warmer tone as we said goodbye at the door. "You can't feel responsible for Nathan. And you have to get out of here. Robbie, things have changed."

Things changed even more after Vince left. What he left behind was a realization of the huge empty hole within the furiously impassioned creature I had become. I was surprised, then, at how painful my loneliness could feel, what a manic frenzy it would produce at moments just when I thought I had the beast within myself calmed. In the last few weeks of his life Nathan had always been talking, no matter how badly his body and mind were deteriorating, and his words had forced me, like Vince's insistent pleas and orders, into a constant state of motion, a roar of thoughts pitched between my ears as I moved from task to task for him. With Vince gone, with the Solloways back in Connecticut, with Dora back working at the hospital, with Nathan gone, dead, there was nothing but a maddening silence and stillness left to me, and within all this emptiness I could no longer find ways to escape, to relax, and in that first week after Vince's departure, I picked up four different men on the street or at a bar and brought them back to the apartment, pouring them drinks, stripping them of their clothes, clinging to their bodies in bed as if at any moment we were to pitch downward off a cliff. I could not bear to talk in the moments after sex with these men, could not find words of praise or endearments for my partners, could not discuss hopes or desires or the future possibilities with any of them. All I wanted from them was the physical comfort their warm, fleshy bodies could provide for me in those moments, something, however, that none of these specific men I had picked out were comfortable with just giving to me.

And so they would leave, and I would drink and take one of the sleeping pills Ben Nyquist had prescribed for Nathan, and in the mornings the headaches would return. I grew so depressed I could no longer answer the phone, could no longer go to work, no longer do anything but eat and drink and sleep, and hardly in that order. And I came to believe that I was being punished for hating Nathan for dying, punished, too, for hating my father, punished for hating reliving over and over Nathan's death, and punished, as well, for hating the emptiness I had now allowed to invade my life.

I would like to say that my life ended when Nathan's did, but it did not; would like to say, too, that my life was reborn with his death, but it wasn't. Change isn't easy; it's a distressful, aching descent into acceptance. And grief does not explode from you like anger, but rather soaks into your bones like arthritis, always reappearing just when you thought you had it beat. What I had not realized—or forgotten, rather—was that Nathan was only one death of many from this absurd epidemic. In March, just after I had started back to work, just after I had been able to pull the strength to remain sober and calm enough to pound nails into gypsum board for seven hours a day at the construction site where I was working, Dora called and said that Ben Nyquist had died, or, rather, that he had jumped from the balcony of his twelfth story apartment on the Upper West Side.

Ben Nyquist dead? I thought. Had that been my fault too? Had I not paid enough attention to him? Had I neglected being part of his support network? Had I purposely avoided that responsibility? Was that a death I could have averted? Or was my ignorance—my withdrawal from other people—still the residue of grief from the loss of Nathan? And then Jerry called and said he had tested positive and here I was, trying to console him but knowing I wasn't successful at being optimistic enough with him, and then Andrew and Debbie mentioned that her brother was ill and Martin called and said that Frank from the gym had moved back to his parents' house in Denver.

What is the point of going on, I thought—to bear witness? To tell a sad story with an unhappy ending? How deep does sorrow go? Is there a limit to how much one person can bear? Is the lesson of life that it does not comply with our expectations of it? Life seemed to me at that time to be a badly created detective story, no clues or codes revealing secrets, no insights or understandings imaginable in a puzzle that could not be solved—in fact, one in which the rules could unexpectedly change with every character.

Anything that could have been easy—washing the dishes, applying for insurance reimbursements—seemed to take the most concerted, concentrated effort. I saw myself, instead, alone, moving though space, suspended, really, out in the vast emptiness of interstellar darkness, like an astronaut whose life line has been cut sharply in half and cast adrift from his spaceship. Even Dora could not make sense of it all. One afternoon in April I found my way to St. Vincent's, wanting to connect with someone, wanting to help out in some way, wanting to start working again—at anything—and wanting to distract myself. Dora tried to console my still growing grief. "God's plan is not always obvious to us," she said. What kind of God would plan a horror such as this, I thought? Who could believe in a God this hateful?

Is this when faith begins, when things are at their lowest, when the tragedy—no, tragedies—are so absolutely devastating and unimaginable that you lift your eyes up to an empty blue sky and ask, "Lord, what can make me feel better?" Or can faith even be possible from a God who provides no answers, only a question repeated over and over, *Why? Why? Why?* Or was the true question instead, simply: How do you get through grief? Or was grief a process which is never finished? Vince had mentioned to me during his visit that it often takes as long to get over someone as you were with them. If that were the case why does the memory of my mother's death continue to haunt me unexpectedly fifteen years later when I only knew her the first twelve years of my life? It was true, I will admit, that my yearning for my mother was completely different from my yearning for Nathan. Was the pain I still felt from losing her now tied up with the anger over my father?

Does God lead you through the slowly changing stages of grief—shock, denial, anger, numbness, forgiveness, acceptance—or is it that change merely happens from the progression of time? Time is not always your ally, certainly not at first, not in those first few days and months. But how could I even begin to grieve for Ben, for instance, when I hadn't completely absorbed the impact of Nathan's death yet?

And so time passed uneasily. Nothing seemed to unfurrow my brow, unclench my teeth. I walked, then, as if I were trying to grasp on to things in order to steady my balance, as if I were moving about on wheels. Everything in my path reminded me of Nathan; seizures of grief could be provoked by anything—a stray blond hair still remaining within a hairbrush, Nathan's favorite mustard discovered in the back of the refrigerator, an episode of a television show he had faithfully watched coming on as a rerun. Get a grip, I kept thinking, trying to calm myself, trying to sleep, jumping up restless within the night from a panic because I was still alone and my nightmare had not been a nightmare at all, but, instead, a cold, horrible reality.

How do I change? I thought in those evenings hunched over the kitchen table jiggling the ice cubes in my empty glass of whiskey. How can I change? How can I feel better? Or is that now impossible? How do I let go of sorrow—or at least let it not impede the progress of my own life? How do I get on with things? How do I live with death? How do I accept it and move on?

The secret of life, Dora said sometime that month, is accepting the change. And with every step forward there will be two steps backward but what I have to keep doing is just walking, walking and more walking, never stop, and don't look back until I'm ready. And so I tried walking, getting out of the apartment more, but the walking felt like I was on a downhill roller-coaster into madness. Suddenly everyone seemed sick to me, on the verge of illness, dying or dead, even my own good health seemed so tentative and suspect to me. My street—my deli—my bank—my subway stop—Manhattan—New York City—the heaven I had once known and cherished had now become my living hell.

I'd love to say that the pain of Nathan's death faded away and I was left with beautiful memories of our years together, but if I did so I would be ignoring the true story of how I survived. As it was in those months following Nathan's death, I was tugged into a deeper abyss until I had reached a point one day where I no longer wanted to climb out.

The sun had been screaming into the bedroom when the phone woke me up that afternoon, yanking me out of the first heavy sleep I had fallen into after a restless night of clutching my pillow as if it were a body that were to leave the bed at any moment. I knew right away I had a headache and that it was only going to get worse, so I had let the answering machine pick up the call, then heard the click of the dial tone on the speaker, which meant the caller had hung up without leaving a message. I had felt the heaviness of my eyelids trying to close again, but I was too exhausted to go back to sleep, my head throbbed as if a hatchet had been thrown between my eyes. I had gotten up, wobbled into the bathroom, took two aspirins and sat on the toilet until I had finally felt better.

Next, I had gone into the kitchen and made coffee, perceptively aware, that afternoon, of a city going about its business without me. A low hum of the traffic from Seventh Avenue hung about the room like whiffs of incense, the vibrations of an approaching subway shivered up through the floor. It had been one of those maddeningly beautiful spring days where the sun seemed to reflect off everything like mirrors, and I had taken my coffee and sat by the window until the glare and the heat of the sun made me begin to sweat. Then I had unlocked the sash of the window, slipped my hands through the window grates, and pushed open the window. I had looked out and up, over the exhaust pipes and tar flattened roofs, squinting at the sky. Not a cloud in sight, I recall clearly. When I had pulled my hands away and looked back inside I had noticed a violet patch of light dancing off the kitchen wall from where the light bent through the crystal prism Nathan had hung on the sash and which bobbled before me as if it were being tortured.

I have to get out of here, I had thought at that moment, knowing it was already the end of April and I had only marginally begun to get on with things, knowing I couldn't avoid the landlord any more, that I had to make things, well, work again for me. The mail, I had thought, then. The mail, I remembered, must have arrived—I could go downstairs and check the mail—that would get me out of the apartment for a while—let me redirect myself. In my drunken stupor the night before I had fallen asleep in my jeans and that afternoon I found a T-shirt on the bathroom floor and slipped it on, then put on my sneakers and walked downstairs to see if the mail had arrived.

There had been a flyer requesting a donation for the Lambda Legal Defense Fund, a postcard from one of Nathan's former clients, a bill from Macy's, and an overdue notice from Mastercard. But an envelope addressed to

Nathan was what caught my eye, and as I walked back upstairs I ran my finger beneath the flap and pulled out the letter.

"Closing," the letter had read. "Closing party." I had touched the paper, rubbed my fingers across the print to make sure that I wasn't misreading it. I sat down on the landing, winded, the air knocked out of my lungs. The Saint was closing. The end of it all.

Not possible, I had thought. It just wasn't possible. I stood and folded the mail in half, shoving all of it into my back pocket and walked back down the stairs and out onto the sidewalk. I remember I looked suspiciously at the block in front of me, as if I expected to discover that I had wakened in a foreign land. Nothing had seemed different to me though—on Seventh Avenue the old man selling record albums from a milk crate was still on the corner, the bodega and fruit stand were exactly where they had always been, the plastic arch of colored pendants still hung over the diner as if it were still their grand opening celebration. Something, however, felt terribly wrong and it was then that I had caught a chill. Panicking, I began to run down the sidewalk.

At first, I had only run across the street, over toward 14th Street, startling a flock of pigeons from the bread crumbs near the gutter of the sidewalk up to the window ledges of the building across the street. Then, something seemed unfinished to me and I continued, running all the way to Union Square, running across the traffic lanes to cut over to Broadway. I wasn't really running, you know, months and months of drinking had left me huffing and puffing too much, and I would stop every now and then and cough and then walk viciously with my arms swinging back and forth, till I had caught enough wind to start running again. I had cut through Cooper Square, down Saint Marks Place and around the corner onto Second Avenue. It was right where it had always been once I got there. The building had not changed since the last time I had so studiously regarded it years before. Why I had expected to find the burnt-out gutted shell of a building I am still unsure of even today; perhaps it had been that it was too imprinted within my own emotional instability at that time. But it was there, nonetheless, that day. And nothing had changed about it. Or at least I remember I could not convince myself that it had.

Vince had always said how much he hated the Saint, or, rather, how he had come to hate the Saint. So had Jeff and Hank and Nathan. But they had all gone as often as they could endure the routine that first year—pumping up at the gym, eating an early dinner, taking a disco nap, then waking up for drugs and all-night dancing, dancing until mid-morning, really, then stumbling out into the bright sunshine for breakfast at Kiev or Clyde's or Tiffany's. I had never felt part of the Saint, really, even though I had been there that opening weekend years before. I had never been a member, either, even though I had never had a problem getting in no matter how exclusive the party. I had always seemed to know someone who was going even when I had no longer wanted to go myself.

But it had always been there—a place on the map of gay Manhattan, a native landmark, really. One had expected it to be forever part of the city scene, just like Radio City Music Hall was always there for tourists and heterosexuals. The parties at the Saint had arrived like clockwork every season. Black. White. Halloween. Easter. Just as the invitations had arrived regularly in the mail. Talk of the Saint had sustained many conversations I had witnessed since I had lived in the city: the doctor with the fans, for instance, or the guy with the snake, or the night the man sat on a light bulb, or, of course, who had done what to whom in the balcony.

But there had also been something highly magical to the place: the cyclorama silhouette of the Manhattan skyline that sat at the lip of the planetarium dome, the wash of colors fading in and out like the crest of waves, the mirror ball suddenly descending from the ceiling and filling the room with a universe of stars. Even with a hundred people on the dance floor around you it had had the capacity to make you and only you feel as if you were special, something like being in the movie version of your own life. That's what the whole experience of dancing had been like back then. Even within a crowd of muscular, sweaty, shirtless, beautiful men, you, yourself, could feel like the most important star in the cosmos. Everything had existed entirely for you. And then it had become history. Gone. Just like that.

Looking back on it now after a span of many more years, I was part of that world but also not a part of it. It was part of my gay experience but not the defining notion of it. Still, the impending extinction of the Saint had left me shaken that day, another change I had been unable to accept in my mounting hysteria, as if I had expected the plague to end one day and we would all go out for a long overdue celebration at, where else, the Saint, of course. Now, even that was not possible. Things had changed.

Or had I changed beyond what the Saint represented? Had I stopped going dancing and no longer needed the Saint? Had my life become too middle class, middle-aged, and domestic to even want be there? Or had it simply taken too many horrible turns—too many of the guys I knew who had used to dance at the Saint were no longer alive by that afternoon. Had it been simply something I had had in common with other gay men but with the recognition, that day, that there was no one around to remember it with that pulled me through my furious misery.

A building, I had thought. Merely a building—and I took a long, last look at it and began to walk away. And then I looked up into the sky, squinting in the sunshine and caught myself instinctively looking over at the fifth floor window of a building on Seventh Street. That was the bedroom window of Gene's apartment, the one with the platform bed, and I had remembered the night he first took me there, my head bumping against the ceiling as we had tried to hurriedly undress each other. David and Sal used to live a few doors down, and the nights Nathan and I had gone there for dinner would always end with coffee and a joint; the two of us tumbling out onto this sidewalk, buzzing, anxious to find something else to do before we went home. Wes used to be a waiter at the restaurant on Cooper Square, long before I met Nathan, and as I walked by it that sunny afternoon I had noticed the awnings had been replaced, and I realized I was flipping through a brief history of myself, or at least a history of my life in Manhattan, aware that it could now be catalogued into chapters, some more voluminous or adventuresome than others.

Walking down Eighth Street as I continued my route back to my apartment, I saw two boys leaning against a building, their jeans slung low and baggy on their hips, their caps turned backwards, and I wondered briefly if they were college students, if they were gay, and if they were, how did they make it through the world? Was it, perhaps, easier for them because AIDS had always been a part of their consciousness, that they had never known a world without AIDS? Was there, then, something that they could teach me to make my life easier? Then a drag queen in a miniskirt and platform shoes crossed my path and I caught myself trying not to laugh. Platform shoes, I had thought. There was someone who still wore them. Maybe things had not changed after all.

At Fifth Avenue I turned into the direction of Washington Square, looking down at my feet on the glimmering asphalt, disbelieving everything about myself—my age, my sorrow, my past, caught up, really, as if I were in a weepier version of *The Way We Were*. It wasn't that I was so nostalgic; it was the thought that the world had changed without me, in a way I had never could have imagined it to have, the way, really, a world changes in a science fiction movie after an atomic bomb has gone off. In the park a beggar stretched his coffee cup out to me and I turned away from him, hearing, though, the thick sound of the rattling coins, wondering which of us had lost more, and not just in terms of money. The heaviness of surviving not only Nathan's illness, but also the deaths of Alex, Sal, David, Michael, Hank, Ben, and so many others had begun to take its toll on me. A young man in a blue tank top caught my eye then, blond and slender but with bulky muscles, and I realized I would never have a body like that, and then all at once I remembered Nathan's body, the tissues of my lungs squeezing themselves together—craving for a drink to help me escape my memories. Nothing was supposed to change this way, I thought, the city opening itself up to me but my life wickedly swallowing me up.

At Sixth Avenue the traffic seemed to float around me, moving as if without sound. My body felt as if it were slipping away from my mind and I found myself concentrating on the infinite space between the curb and the street, only a few inches in reality, but that afternoon an enormous void that I could only overcome with the accompanying pain of straining tendons.

I had tried to catch people's eyes as I walked down West 4th Street, but I found myself too seeped in remembrance. Everything seemed suddenly so sad to me—the buildings dark, dirty, and empty. There had been the black tie New Year's Eve party that I gone to in that building, the granite bathroom counter I had installed for a woman who had lived over there, the guy who had lived in the apartment across the street who I had a crush on, and on the cold winter nights of my first year in the city I would stop beneath his window and look up, wondering if he was home, and if he was, who he was entertaining. Jerry used to throw parties at the restaurant over there. Nathan and I had a subscription one year to that theater company. Phil had lived two blocks from here. His friend Ray had moved in to take care of him in his last months. Ray had stopped having sex six years before. *Six years*, I had thought. We had all expected this to have been over by then.

When I had reached Grove Street I stopped to decide whether or not to cross Seventh Avenue. And then I had realized that that was the very spot where Vince had been waiting to speak to me all those years before after we had introduced ourselves to one another in the waiting room of the Clinic. Vince's chain of favors had led me to an apartment, a job, a lover, and a circle of friends I might never have found on my own.

Thinking of him then, physically so far, far away, struggling with his own version of this nightmare, had left me feeling only more miserable and defeated. Steps later I had found myself in a bar sitting on a stool and ordering a drink, having found a crumpled ten dollar bill I had stuffed in my pocket the night before.

By the time I had returned home that day it was dark and the phone was ringing when I entered the apartment. Again I let it go unanswered and when the machine clicked on the line went dead again. I slipped off my jeans, keeping the T-shirt on this time, and opened the refrigerator door hoping to find something more to drink. There had only been a swig of wine left in a bottle and I tasted it, then tossed the bottle into the trash, wanting the taste of more alcohol. Again I felt myself panic, my chest tightening.

Then, I went into the bathroom and looked through Nathan's prescription vials that I had hidden underneath the sink. Hadn't Ben Nyquist prescribed some Demerol for the pain in Nathan's legs? I remembered. What had happened to the morphine I had gotten at the pharmacy on Eighth Avenue?

I brought some vials out and placed them on the rim of the sink, then lifted them up into the light to try to read the labels better, aware, in those moments, of the way the light above the sink was reflecting off the silver ring on my left hand that Nathan had given me. As I was sorting through the bottles I had noticed my razor behind the faucet. I lifted it up, then, thinking, knowing, believing what I wanted to do, the only thing I had left to do.

It was then, at that moment, that the phone rang again. What am I doing? I had thought, distracted at last from myself.

I walked into the kitchen and looked at the clock, then at the phone, then back again at the clock. Who could be calling me this late? I remember thinking.

I lifted the receiver gently, as if I had expected it to be more bad news.

"Robbie?" I heard a voice ask when I had said hello.

"Denise," I answered.

"I've been trying you all day," she said.

"I've been out," I had replied, listening to the static of the silence between us. "Is something wrong?"

"Robbie," she said and I had heard her sigh, not a mournful sigh, but a quick breath of air, so very far away, but one, nonetheless, full of expectation. "I need a favor."

"Sure," I had answered, not caring what it was, knowing, really, that if I wanted to survive I had to reinvent myself, I had to want to keep on living. I knew exactly what Denise was going to ask before she had asked me her favor. I knew everything about where my life was headed was uncertain, but at last I was standing in front of a new door, waiting, hopefully, for something, any- thing, to be behind it. "I'm here," I had added after what had seemed like a long space of time. "Tell me what you need me to do."

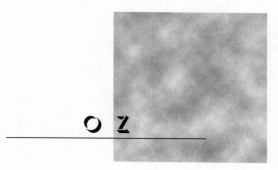

Vince once said that I became a Hollywood Boy the day I stepped off the plane and my eyes followed the shape of a young bodybuilder who had crossed my path. I always said that he remembered it wrong, of course; I had, by then, lost every shred of sexual desire and moved, instead, as though I was swimming underwater in the ocean, each step, each stroke requiring the most concentrated movement in order not to be sucked away by the tide. I thought the young man who had crossed my path that day was Jeff, or at least something of him reminded me of Jeff, perhaps because his height and bulk and coloring were similar, or that I was just magnetized by the size of his huge biceps and chest. I had, after all, expected to see Jeff at the airport along with Vince that day, though it was just Vince, alone, who had met me at the gate. "Darling," he said, sweeping up to me, taking the bag I carried out of my hand and kissing me dryly on the cheek. "Welcome back to Oz."

It was then that the bodybuilder passed by us again and my eyes followed his progression through the crowd. Later, months later, Vince said to me it was the moment he knew I was still alive. If I was strong enough to want to look at someone with desire, then I was strong enough to desire to want to live, he thought. He was right in a way, though sometimes it's obvious that your real soul resides somewhere outside of your body and not within your own mind, so easily detected by others and not at all discernible to yourself. Though I have often believed myself to be somewhat of a philosophical loner, I have never been a man comfortable with living alone, which was why after Nathan's death I felt that my own life should also have come to an end; things felt that they had spiraled so much out of my control, and which was why, when I landed in California, I partially expected my life to abruptly and willfully end.

I was rescued that year by a phone call from Denise; she and Linda were contemplating purchasing a seventy-year-old Greek revival house in West Hollywood that was in need of more repair than renovation. She called me and asked first for estimates on replacing patio doors, doorknobs, and retiling a bathroom floor, but by the end of our conversation she had asked me to come out and live in one of the bedrooms in exchange for the work I could do on the house.

I arrived in California with a host of problems that working on a house would not, in any sort of manner, easily repair; the hatred I had felt through Nathan's illness had now been replaced by an unmanageable sadness and guilt. For the first week I slept in my room on the second floor, time empty and uncertain, unable to unpack the suitcases and boxes that Dora had helped me ship ahead of my arrival, staring at the faded white walls and sweating through some undiagnosed discomfort that possessed me like a demon spirit. Linda and Denise left me politely alone, but Amy, their four-year-old daughter, kept peering into the room every morning. At first she was merely just a tiny, wide blue-eyed blond vision; she had inherited Linda's corn-fed midwestern genetics and, as the hours passed, I found myself lying on the edge of the bed waiting for her to walk by, smiling at her, not able to talk, really, but simply willing to look at her with the same wonderment she beheld me, and hoping that she would have the courage to step inside.

She did, finally, bringing along with her her dolls and crayons and toys, looking suspiciously at me from the edge of the bed, touching me and giggling as if playing a game of tag, running giddily out of the room with bouncy steps. The more discomfort I felt the longer she stayed; one afternoon, waking up from a fitful dream soaking wet, I saw her sitting on the floor beside the bed and looking up at me. Soon Linda and Denise had her bringing me muffins and fruit to eat and I found myself responding to her kindness with questions. "What's the name of your doll?" or "What are you drawing?" I would ask her in a groggy far-off voice that seemed to come from somewhere else in the room other than from my own body. She, in turn, responded with questions of her own: "Why do you sleep so much? Why is your face so scratchy? Don't you want to get out of bed?" Soon I began to follow her downstairs to the kitchen, sitting with her at the table while Denise and Linda placed plates of food in front of me that I could not eat, or, if I did, would send me hurrying to the bathroom.

I know I was drying out and letting go—booze and grief is a tough combination to overcome even when battled singularly, and it was hard in those days to recognize any progress with the daily misery I felt. I am still not sure to this day how deep of an alcoholic I was—all I know is that booze offered me an escape when I needed one. Sometimes, I would sit at the kitchen table and feel as if my head would explode; other times I would just moan or cough— most often my mouth would be so dry I would just sip at a glass of water or soda. Vince and Jeff would come over, usually in the evenings, and sit on the edge of the bed and watch TV with me, trying to draw me occasionally into a conversation, though all I wanted was to be just left alone, really, or so I thought—my body ached, of course, not to be left alone.

"I'm not sick," I would say defensively during commercial breaks, not wanting them to think that I had already died, believing I should at least say something. "I'm just tired."

Vince pretended as though he didn't hear anything I had said, chattering on and on about the gossip of the show we were watching or whatever the latest rumor was on a new sitcom in development, or who he had spotted on Rodeo Drive or in the steam room at the Sports Connection. Jeff, however, had become a quiet giant. His hairline had receded so far he now wore what was left buzzed so close to his scalp that from a distance he appeared bald; his flawless pale complexion now freckled and tanned by the Pacific sun. But Jeff had also become more introspective in the years since he had lived in New York. He would sit with his massive arms and legs folded into one another like a thick pretzel and want to know what I was feeling and why: Why did my shoulder hurt, for instance, trying to analyze its predicament as either a physical or mental manifestation of my grief or anxiety, or saying something absurd, such as I didn't love myself enough, or even suggesting that I try an herbal muscle relaxant to help ease the discomfort.

And then one day I was suddenly up and about, rummaging through the tools in the garage, thinking about repairing the warp in my closet door that kept it from closing shut all the way. That, actually, was easily enough accomplished in a couple of hours with the help of some sandpaper I found in the garage. When I had finished repairing the door, I found myself wandering outside through the yard barefoot, looking up at the house, squeezing my toes into the soil. It was a wonderful house with a sunken roof shingled green, crooked shutters once painted a dark blue over a previous white coat and now peeling, and a two-story back porch that looked more West Indies than West Hollywood. Cracked doors, window frames, and empty wine bottles were piled by a chain-link fence that defined the property. The outside of the house needed as much repair as the renovation Denise had suggested for the interior. It would take me hours just to clean the lawn, I thought that afternoon, suddenly eager to begin the task.

Everything I saw that day needed to be repaired or replaced; by evening I had hauled away most of the yard debris, burnt the rest in a fire in the back yard, and had an idea sketched out and ready to show Denise and Linda. I had drafted, on the back of one of Amy's drawings she had given me, plans for a top floor sundeck, opening up one of the second floor bedrooms into a glass-enclosed studio for Denise to display her paintings, and creating a bottom floor sun room at the side of the patio. This house, I knew, making lists of things that could be done and calculating the costs of each on a pad of paper in the kitchen when Denise and Linda returned that evening, could keep me busy for a very long time.

"I like her," Amy said, pointing to the picture I had placed on the bed. "She's pretty."

"That's Cinderella's fairy godmother," I said, wondering, at the same time why I couldn't remember the character's name.

"What's a fairy godmother?"

"Sort of like a guardian angel," I answered, realizing as the words left my mouth that she would probably not understand that concept either. "Someone who sort of helps you out and looks after you. Like your mother and Denise. But someone who isn't your relative. I can put it up over there so you can see it when you walk by my room."

"Okay," she said. She lifted the hammer off the bed with both hands and walked over and handed it to me. I found a nail in the plastic cup I had put on the dresser and I positioned it on the wall and hammered it into place. Amy watched me intently as I lifted the picture off the bed and slipped the back wire of it over the nail.

I had finally started unpacking the boxes in my room that morning, three weeks after my arrival, but had stopped when I had moved enough around to get to the crate I had made for the pictures I had shipped. Cinderella's godmother was the only picture I had been able to hang thus far; the others I had unwrapped and leaned, face forward, against the wall—most of them were drawings Denise or Nathan had made over the years.

"Is that you?" Amy asked, when I moved one of the smaller paintings from the pile against the wall and placed it on the bed to get to one of the larger ones in the back.

"No, that was my friend in New York," I answered, looking at the portrait Nathan had had sketched of himself the summer we had gone to England together and which I had framed when we returned home. I realized, as all those memories of him began rushing to the surface of my mind, that I was mis-describing him as just a "friend"—not even able to say his name out loud—when, of course, I knew he was much more than merely a friend, but realizing that it made no sense to try to explain my intentional mistake to Amy. Instead, I sat on the bed and lifted the sketch onto my lap, paralyzed momentarily by sadness. "Do you want to help me unpack some more boxes?" I said, trying to move on with the work.

"Okay," she said, her eyes as wide and curious as a kitten's.

I had not saved much memorabilia from my years with Nathan—mostly I had shipped out my clothes, books and work tools. I had given a lot of Nathan's personal effects to his mother—his eyeglasses, watch, wallet, the coffee mug he always drank from, and a lot of his drawings; the TV, stereo, furniture, and housewares I had donated to charities. Still, it was impossible escaping from my history with him as I unpacked. Amy pulled out of one box a pair of bright orange socks that Nathan had bought one year in Fire Island

and clutched them to her chest as though it was her favorite doll. Nathan was forever dumping sand out of them.

"They're soft," Amy said.

"Do you want to wear them?" I asked.

She nodded and I helped her slip them on her feet—they were so large and so cumbersome to walk around in she finally ended up wearing them as mittens.

"Do you want to see a rainbow?" I asked her. I had reached the shoe box where I had packed Nathan's crystals.

"Yes, yes, yes," she yelled and clapped her mittened hands together.

I moved through the tissues of the box and withdrew a crystal—the large one Nathan had stolen from the Ritz Carlton in Boston—and held it up in front of the sunlight from the window. "Look at the edges," I said to her, twisting the crystal in front of her eyes as if to hypnotize her. "See the colors."

She squinted a bit, peered into the crystal and then pulled back and yelled, "Yes, yes, yes," again. She raced around the room clapping her hands together. "Can I have it?" she asked.

My back stiffened with the question. I wasn't ready to give it up yet—didn't know if I ever would. "Why don't we hang it up by the window where you can always see it."

"Okay," she said, not at all disappointed, and ran out of the room.

By the end of the day I had finished unpacking and Nathan's collection of crystals—more than forty of them—were strung on threads and hooks on the side of the sills of the easterly window in my bedroom. There, I knew from my hours of sleepless tossing, they would catch the morning light.

"Don't you miss it? I asked Jeff. He was seated on a mat on the floor of his living room, his legs folded into one another, his hands resting on his kneecaps.

"Miss what?" he asked in between a series of deep breaths.

"Sex," I answered. Judging from Jeff's appearance it would be hard to believe that he had an arid erotic life. He was wearing a bright white T-shirt without sleeves, the effect of which overemphasized the development of his biceps, while the black spandex tights he wore made the folded muscles of his legs strain against the fabric like an overstuffed suitcase. I was seated beside him in clothing that thankfully boxed up my physique, feeling an uncomfortable tension in my hamstrings because I could not relax the muscles of my legs, or, rather, because they had not been exercised repeatedly enough to be as flexible and unconstrained as Jeff's more supple ones were.

"There's nothing to miss," he said, his expression losing it's calmness, however. "I channel that energy in other ways. Do you miss it?"

"I just don't want it right now," I answered, wanting instead, desperately, a drink. "I suppose I miss it."

I was fighting off a severe depression that evening—the night before I had had a dream about Nathan leaving me while I was in bed with him, swept away in a gust of wind through the window, the crystals clacking together like chimes. I kept reaching for Nathan's feet in my mind, clutching for the last remaining flesh of him, but my work was for naught—he kept slipping away, over and over again, no matter how many times I tried to reinvent the ending. The lack of restful sleep had left me sluggish and cloudy all day; by the time I had driven down to Jeff's apartment my whole body burned with a dull ache.

"It's not that I don't allow my body an orgasm," Jeff said. "I do. And usually a very heightened one. I've even had multiple ones. It all comes from within."

"Within?"

"Love thyself," he answered, detecting the uneasiness of my position and he sighed in a way that showed that he was more disappointed in me than disgusted. "Vince thinks I'm celibate because my sex doesn't involve other men."

"Or him," I said.

"We still have sex," Jeff said. "Masturbation. I know it's not satisfying for him. He just doesn't understand that I give him intimacy in other areas besides sex."

The truth, of course, was that Vince understood Jeff's bequeathing of intimacy and withholding of sex. What he didn't understand, however, was Jeff's adamant choice to remain in the closet, of not coming right out and stating publicly that he was gay. Jeff saw such a step as a limitation to his potential income; Vince, however, thought it would result in a boon of gay product endorsements—he had even volunteered to help Jeff manage them when they started coming in over the transom. The truth, of course, the real truth, was that Jeff had moved further and further away from acting and into teaching. He taught acting classes at a studio in Hollywood, aerobic classes at a studio on Kings Road, yoga at a studio on Sunset, and worked as a private trainer three days a week. Since I had arrived in California Jeff had decided it was his mission to teach me how to meditate, to find inner peace, or at least an inner refreshment. "Now, close your eyes," he said, and if I hadn't known the inflection of his voice for years I might never have detected its hidden irritation. "Relax," he said, as if he were beginning a chant, which, of course, was exactly what he was doing. "Let everything go," he said in syncopated rhythm. "Turn your attention to this point in time and space. This a time for relaxing. For letting go. For restoring yourself. Let the body relax. Become very, very comfortable. Take a nice deep breath. Relax your scalp. And forehead. Feel your eyes closed. Relax the muscles of your face. Your cheeks. Your lips. Relax your jaw and then the base of your tongue. Relax your neck. Then let your shoulders go. This relaxed feeling moves down your upper arms, easing the muscles through the lower arms into your hands, down through the knuckles and into your fingers. Feel the tingling sensation in your fingertips as your body relaxes more and more."

I tried to follow Jeff's instructions, mentally moving my thoughts along my neck and shoulders and fingers as he indicated. No matter how successful I was in getting my body to relax, I could not get my mind to do the same thing—my thoughts kept drifting back to Nathan and my remorse over losing him, and that evening with Jeff on the mat was his fourth attempt at teaching me to meditate. Thus far he had already loaned me books and cassette tapes on philosophy and inspiration and spiritual healing, none of which I could master or digest. That evening's meditation lesson, as Jeff moved further along to relax my body parts—my chest, stomach, groin, and legs—ended in a short crying spasm when Jeff reached the final point of the toes and I was still conscious of my tension. He unraveled his great, folded body and made me lie on my back and practice breathing till I was calm.

"Maybe Vince is right," Jeff said, pressing his fingertips so deeply into the tense spots of my shoulder that I clenched my teeth from the pain of it. "Maybe you do need to try and find a new boyfriend."

In the house I grew up in as a boy, my father would leave the light on in the second floor bathroom to prevent himself from tripping into something as he roamed the house in the late hours of the night. My father suffered from insomnia long before my mother died and he became a serious drinker. I remember hearing in my bedroom his heavy footsteps descending and ascending the stairs, his progress made noisier from the creaking of the weathered wooden planks which had been used when the farmhouse had been originally built sometime in the late 1890s. Twenty-two steps made up that creaky staircase, and over the years I have heard the wood cracking and buckling over and over in my mind when I myself have been unable to sleep. My father, for all the work he put into repairing his church building, never even considered repairing or even replacing or rebuilding the stairs of our house. I used to keep my bedroom door cracked slightly opened as a way to keep my own bearings intact, the light from the bathroom bending around the door as a splinter against my wall. After my mother died my father's roaming became more and more pronounced, up and down the stairs, over and over, and I would stare up at the ceiling of my bedroom, wondering not what would become of us, but of how tired I knew I would feel the following day.

From the extra money I earned running errands for my neighbor, Mrs. Crowder, or helping my father out at the church, I bought a ten-gallon aquarium for my bedroom, an extravagant purchase—or so my father thought—but once I had filled the aquarium with pebbles and seashells and a bag full of neons and guppies I had purchased at Woolworth's, the sound of the air pump blowing bubbles to the surface drowned out the sound of my father's nocturnal roaming and my sleeping became, in those days of my diminishing boyhood, a little more peaceful.

And so I slept in Los Angeles those first few weeks with my bedroom door cracked, again to give myself some sort of bearing as to where I was, but also once again staring at the ceiling as I had done years ago in my father's house, the orange night light Denise and Linda had left in the hallway for Amy spilling into my room and onto the floor like a puddle of dropped soda. Amy was not a sound sleeper and she would awake at night, crying, and wander from her bedroom into Denise and Linda's room where she would crawl into the bed with them.

Since I had arrived in California I had witnessed several discussions about Amy between Linda and Denise—who was taking Amy with her to work, for instance, or speculating on the cause of the child's flushed face or dirty fingernails. By the time I was back on my feet, unpacked, and beginning to paint the upstairs hallway and ceiling, there was a discussion, one morning with Linda—who had witnessed me persistently yawning as I leaned over a tray of paint with a roller in my hand—on whether Amy had kept me up during the night. I had tried to explain, in a rather drained and incoherent speech, that my sleep patterns were disturbed from matters other than Amy.

Amy never showed any signs of fatigue from her own inability to sleep, though she could fall suddenly into a deep, recuperative nap on the couch which could last for several hours. I would often stop whatever work I was doing, sit on the chair next to the sofa and pretend to watch television, but, in actuality, steal glances over at Amy, watching her sleep, wondering what the secret was to the way she rested so calmly—watching her breathing lift and expand her little chest, her eyes working beneath her eyelids, her mouth slightly parted to reveal the bottom line of her teeth, the silky yellow strands of her hair falling around her neck and sometimes clinging to the sweat of her skin.

And so our household fell into a routine of sorts as I became more adjusted to the family—Amy became my unofficial responsibility during the day after Linda left early to open the organic food store she owned on Santa Monica Boulevard, a sort of counterculture supermarket and café stocking incense, candles, paraffin, yarn, looms, clay, and new age paraphernalia—meditation tapes and self-help books, and vitamins, fresh vegetables, and baked goods made without any additives or preservatives. Later in the morning, Denise drove to Hollywood where she rented a loft on Melrose with another artist and which she had taken in order to develop her larger, more serious canvases. I cleaned up from breakfast, helped Amy bathe and dress and then took her with me to run errands, usually to the grocery store or gas station or hardware store. It was on one of our shopping trips, wandering down the aisles of the Pavilions, a large combination grocery store and pharmacy in West Hollywood, that Amy first spotted Mr. Peepers. Mr. Peepers was an oversized goldfish, not as large as the ones you can find in wishing wells of restaurants, but large enough to fascinate a four year-old from about a hundred feet down a store aisle. Mr. Peepers' name came from two enormous black eyes which, from certain angles, looked as though they were outlined in black so that he appeared to be wearing spectacles. "Robbie, Robbie, look—he's wearing glass-es," she said running up to the tank and pressing her hand against the glass when she noticed him.

I couldn't really pass him up, after all. I was, I will easily admit, so easily enchanted by Amy by then that it had become something of an obsession for me to want nothing more than to please her and make her happy. Why Amy cast such a spell over me had a much deeper genesis than merely as a distrac-tion from my grief. True, it was my desired escape from that grief that made me look so desperately toward her for some kind of joy or happiness—but I also found in her the same things that Nathan had found before in children—an inexplicable bonding that simply could not be explained away as an adult's imagining of the carefree manner in which a child sees the world.

And so we brought Mr. Peepers home and set him up in a large glass bowl in Amy's room, though Amy would often want me to carry the bowl from room to room to wherever she was in the house or the yard—usually wherever I was, for she now accompanied me on my chores, sat on the floor and colored in a book while I painted or worked. At first I obliged her—carrying Mr. Peepers and his bowl to whatever room she wanted—who wants to disappoint a smil-ing child? Then, I began suggesting that she take her naps in her bedroom with Mr. Peepers. Not long after that, I brought back to the house, one afternoon, a ten-gallon aquarium. Amy helped me set it up in her bedroom. We added blue and green gravel, a sunken treasure chest that blew bubbles, plastic sea-weed, and green plants. And so she finally felt comfortable spending more time in her room, even taking her naps there—magnetized and enchanted by the prospect of Mr. Peepers' new home.

"What about him?" Vince asked me the first day he had convinced me to go to the gym with him. It was about two months after my arrival and I was seated on the chest machine and Vince was jerking his head to the left, into the direction of a guy in a white T-shirt and blue running shorts working out on the stair master.

"What about him?" I replied, a bit annoyed, knowing where Vince was headed and not wanting to follow.

"See anything you like?"

"Nice arms," I said.

"He's a friend of a friend. I could introduce you."

I didn't answer Vince, such was the routine we had when we annoyed each other; instead, I took a deep breath and began working out harder.

"I think it's time you got out of the house," Vince said when I had finished my set. "You can't keep babysitting Amy forever."

"I like Amy," I answered. "I like spending time with her."

"You know what I mean. And you can't just keep fixing things all the time."

"I like fixing things," I answered him, standing up and wiping the cushion with a hand towel, conscious of the sweat on my neck and at the edge of my hair. "It's why I'm here. I don't need to meet anyone."

"You could be happier," he replied and sat in the seat I had just vacated. "When was the last time you had sex?"

I wiped the towel across my face, hoping to avoid the question. "None of your business," I said, in a tone I meant for the conversation to change. My mind had progressed so far from the desire for sexual partners that I found it frustrating to think about it. I stood beside the chest machine and watched Vince push through twelve reps. He had broken into a heavy sweat that day and the dark hair that was visible on his neck and arms and legs looked like it had been etched into his skin with a charcoal pencil. As he pushed through his last rep he contorted the swarthy features of his face into an excessive scowl. When he stood up from the machine the expression remained and I thought he was angry at me, till I immediately realized he was, instead, dizzy and trying not to show it.

"You okay?" I asked, catching our reflection in the mirror on the opposite wall. Vince's thinness surprised me at that moment; standing next to me— my shorter and chunkier physique—I noticed that day a stoop in Vince's shoulders I had never detected there before.

He nodded his head slightly, not wanting to disturb too much his regaining sense of balance, and it was then that he seemed to age before my eyes. I couldn't believe it, didn't want to accept the fact that things could be getting rougher for him. Two days before I had driven him to UCLA for a blood transfusion. "Want to work some on arms?" I asked him a bit too patronizingly.

He looked at me as if he had forgotten my name, then looked, bewildered, at his wrist. "I forgot my watch," he said, somewhat childishly. "What time is it?"

I looked up at the clock on the wall. "Almost two."

"No," he answered. "Time to cruise the steam room."

"I'll meet you at the car," I said.

I watched him shake the energy back into his body, then suddenly he turned and addressed me angrily. "I won't always be here to help you, you know."

"Fine," I said hastily, not wanting to provoke an argument, a streak of tension flaring up my back in its place. "I'll meet you in the steam room."

Had I expected then, that day at the gym, the progression Vince's infection would take, I think I would have become enraged much earlier, made the hatred I had bottled during Nathan's illness resurface and resound, lifting up my voice in alarm, walking out into the streets and screaming and waving banners and signs. As it was, my own composure was so often punctured by knives of sorrow that I had a difficult time grasping what went on in the world outside myself. But what happened, too, was I had Vince defeated before he even really began his fight with HIV. In my mind Vince had begun his trajectory into death the day I had heard he was positive.

But Vince was a fighter; he wasn't even interested in believing he was sick. In his first six months on AZT, he showed major improvements—weight gain, increased energy, and the resolution of a chronic fungal nailbed infection which had flared up. After a year on the drug, however, he had become anemic and leukopenic, so his doctor at UCLA took him off of it, and again his weight and energy increased, though that was when he had first detected what he believed was occasional lapses of his concentration.

Vince felt certain, by the time that I arrived in Los Angeles, that something was wrong with his memory. He would hand a ten dollar bill to a cashier, for instance, and forget what he had purchased or how much money had been exchanged between them. He once told me, one afternoon while he was over at the house, that he believed he was at the early stages of dementia. He said it in such a casual, off-handed manner, as if it were a joke, that at first I did not believe he was telling me the truth.

"I'm always dizzy," he said. "And there's a ringing in my ear."

"I'm sure it's nothing," I said, trying not to show my alarm. "I don't think it's related."

"I keep lists," he added, though, looking out at the valley beneath us. It was a hot and hazy afternoon, the smog level so high that it could make anyone forgettable.

"You always keep lists," I said.

"More," he added. "I make more of them and then keep losing them. It drives Jeff crazy."

"*Crazy?*" I asked him. "Crazy—upset, or crazy—funny?"

"Crazy—upset," he answered. "He gets crazy seeing all these yellow post-its around the house. I think it's part of his denial."

"His denial?"

"He can't accept any of this. He still won't get tested."

I knew, of course, of Jeff's decision to remain untested. Vince could not even discuss the complexities of a positive-negative relationship versus a positive-positive relationship with his therapist because Jeff was insistent on not being tested. Everyone has a different response to their potential mortality, I am well aware, but even I had been through the fear of getting tested—repeatedly so during Nathan's illness, only to emerge alive, negative, and guilt-ridden for surviving. Jeff, however, was not so eager to align himself with the AIDS community. It had more to do than just a fear of sex with other partners, or, rather, a fear of contracting a virus from someone else, which is how Vince described Jeff's self-imposed celibacy inside and outside of their relationship. If anything, the continuation of this unending epidemic had sent Jeff further into the closet. He was afraid of losing work, afraid of being blacklisted, afraid of being discriminated against by producers and casting agents and directors. He had become such a recognized face in TV commercials for an airline that there was talk, from his agent, that he could land a part in a series within a year. Rumor had already spread around town, however, about Jeff's lover and his AIDS-related work, though Vince, himself, did not consider it rumor; to him, it was fact.

Vince, on the other hand, had partially given up on his own Hollywood dream, his energies were now focused more on working part-time at a buyer's club of experimental drugs which operated out of a loft on Santa Monica Boulevard. Most of these drugs were not yet federally approved—many were newer, untested compounds which had not been through clinical trials or were only in the early stages of testing. The whole illicit notion of these products and their hopeful success provided Vince with the motivation to keep distributing them on the underground. He was always running off to meet someone, his gym bag weighted down by a bottle of pills or a bag of powder he was to deliver or the latest issues of *AIDS Targeted Information Newsletter*, *Antiviral Agents Bulletin*, or the CDC's *AIDS Update*. Vince carried such a high profile of AIDS information and treatment that Jeff would often become aggravated whenever they went to a restaurant or a movie and were inevitably interrupted by someone who wanted to know the latest on a clinical trial or a drug that was being used in France or sold in Mexico, for example. Vince, however, never even batted an eye when one of Jeff's new-age friends from his spiritual healing workshops approached them for information. Vince knew, or had heard of, every drug, treatment, or promise of hope or a cure that had happened thus far, from Chinese cucumbers to mixtures of deer antlers, licorice, peonies, and tortoise shells.

Vince had also become caught up in the AIDS activist movement which was rapidly spreading across the country like another epidemic, spending more time protesting and phoning and arguing then he did on any new writing projects or ideas. Even by then ACT UP had become legendary, import moved through the meetings—part town hall politeness and part coffee house casual—as if each move, each comment, each question, each discussion and opposing argument were being meticulously recorded by a historian for posterity. This was change, this was action, this, it was commonly known by everyone in the room, was a way to understand, or, rather, grapple with understanding the epidemic and fight back in some sort of fashion.

A great optimism still infused the membership of ACT UP that year, an air of expectation of challenge and change could manifest itself during a passionate debate over specific tactics of a forthcoming action—someone always able to interrupt and re-interpret the problem on a grassroots, down-to-earth, basic-instinct level. Every week a rash of open-palmed hands appeared in the air when the moderator asked for first-time attendees to identify themselves to the rest of the room. Even by then the membership had diversified beyond its core angry, young, and infected gay white male contingent—an uninfected, self-employed West Hollywood lesbian could easily have been seated next to a sero-positive church-going African-American wife from South L.A. There was an issue for anyone who wandered into a meeting to align themselves with—affinity groups dealing with medical treatment, housing for PWAs, clean needles for IV-drug users, women's issues, people of color issues, holistic treatments, health insurance reform, safe-sex education, and how to handle and speak to the media.

But that it was the actions—the protests and demonstrations—those in-your-face lie-down-on-the-ground street theatrics—that were the compelling force behind ACT UP. Everyone wanted to know when the next big action was going to take place. Everyone wanted to scream and confront and rage outside the meeting rooms—out on the streets, in front of buildings, blocking traffic, disrupting normal patterns.

And so I became caught up in the political zeal of the moment because of my friendship with Vince. It was Vince who pushed me out of the house and drove me to the meetings, Vince who repeatedly assured me that I needed to yell and be angry, Vince who believed, really, that perhaps I could meet someone in the fight.

I rolled my eyes in exasperation, of course; what I didn't want at that moment was to meet someone. But what Vince wanted from me, I knew, was my support—pure and unadulterated—for his own battle, which he would have gotten whether or not I was to become an activist. I was more burned out than angry that year; grief smothered me like a jacket I could not remove. But what I was afraid of, as Jeff explained to me one night while he was trying to get me to relax and meditate, was of openly bearing my soul to another being again. Not so, I answered him, tensing every muscle in my body as I responded to him—I could handle intimacy—I just wasn't ready for it again.

"Isn't that enough to make you angry then? That something has been taken away from you?" Vince yelled at me after Jeff had repeated to him the details of my reluctance.

And since I knew that Vince was right, I followed him out into the world again.

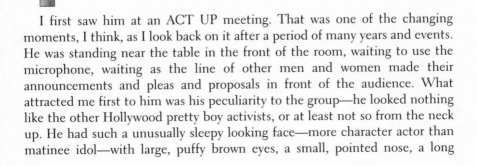

I first saw him at an ACT UP meeting. That was one of the changing moments, I think, as I look back on it after a period of many years and events. He was standing near the table in the front of the room, waiting to use the microphone, waiting as the line of other men and women made their announcements and pleas and proposals in front of the audience. What attracted me first to him was his peculiarity to the group—he looked nothing like the other Hollywood pretty boy activists, or at least not so from the neck up. He had such a unusually sleepy looking face—more character actor than matinee idol—with large, puffy brown eyes, a small, pointed nose, a long rectangular face that ended in a square jaw covered with the coarse black hair of a goatee, and a short-cropped receding hairline that appeared to be more fuzzy than hairy, but the day I first saw him he had disguised it by wearing a red paisley-patterned bandanna around his scalp.

He had one of those well-developed California physiques—not really as coifed and chiseled as the other Hollywood boys had, but bulkier and hairier—like a comic strip action hero, and the outfit he wore that night, a torn white T-shirt, a dark vest, over-the-knee-length baggy shorts with high-top workboots, and an earring in his left ear, gave him the appearance of some kind of giant street-fighting pirate. When he announced his name as Ian Steers when he reached the microphone that night in a deep, raspy British accent, I knew I was hooked on him; I could feel myself breaking out into a light sweat as I listened to him explain that there would be CD training for new members after that evening's meeting.

I couldn't concentrate on anything else for the rest of the meeting—Vince was seated next to me jotting down notes on a pad as one member blasted an insurance carrier about partner benefits, another diagrammed the floor plan of a pharmaceutical complex that was planned for a demonstration, and a handsome, compactly built guy described the expenditures of group's funds. All I could do was to look in the direction Ian had disappeared after using the mike, trying to detect where he was seated in the room, who he was sitting with, what he was doing while everyone else was asking questions or arguing over procedural matters.

After the meeting I mentioned to Vince that I wanted to go to the civil disobedience training, and that I would give him a call when I got home that evening to let him know how it was; he was already engrossed in a conversation with a guy wearing a red tank top and holding a coffee cup. But he interrupted his conversation and turned and gave me a look that was part surprise and part concern. "That girl's trouble, Robbie," he said in a loud whisper to me. "Take my word for it."

"I'm just going for the training," I said, though I know he could tell that was not just the case when I blushed and diverted my eyes from him.

"I could give you that training," Vince said, quickly excusing himself from his conversation and walking in my direction to the back of the room. "If that's what you want." When I didn't stop walking, he did. "Just don't be stupid," he said before he turned and left me alone. When I turned around to look at him, he had already been stopped by someone else.

As I walked away I reminded myself that Vince had disliked Nathan, too, at first. Over the years Vince usually disliked anyone I had dated or had expressed an interest in, unless, of course, he had set me up with them himself.

"Don't carry anything that can be construed as a weapon," Ian said, running his vision lightly up and down each of our clothing as we formed a semicircle around him. There were four of us who had stayed after the meeting—a thin, pale guy, a short older woman he introduced as his mother, myself, and a heavy-set man named Thomas who identified himself as a social worker. The mother and Thomas giggled at the same time at Ian's brutish, military manner of speech, while I was silently convincing myself that Ian had lingered longer looking at me than at the others. And then he stepped to the side of the group so that he was directly in front of me—my hairline came up only to the cleft of his neck.

"If you're beaten, don't fight back," he said, looking down and catching my gaze, and then he walked around me and took his forearm and clamped it about my neck. I immediately tensed up and opened my mouth in shock. His grasp was much rougher and firmer than I had expected for a demonstration of police activity. "Try to relax your body," he ordered me like a drill sergeant. "Go limp."

As I tried to do what he said I caught the bitter smell of his underarms, so sour I almost had to cough. It was a confusing and bewildering moment for me—trying not to concentrate on the pressure at my neck, wondering if he found me at all attractive in this position, and repelled at the same time by the odor of him. As I let my body collapse in his embrace he followed my body to the floor. "Get help from other demonstrators," he said, letting go of my neck. As I struggled with a dizziness as the blood returned to my head, I was aware of him talking with the other group members. As I stood up, he placed his hand at the small of my back.

"I didn't hurt you, did I?" he asked me, and it was here I detected the foul smell of his breath.

I shook my head, no, and tried to roll the tension out of my shoulders. Throughout the rest of the training, Ian kept touching me whenever the opportunity presented itself—on the arm or at the wrist, using me as his demo model as often as he could—and I purposely leaned into him as much as I could—to convince myself that the foul smell I was smelling really did come from his body and his mouth. But there was something, too, about his personality that began to nag at me the more I saw of it. As he explained the degrees of noncooperation with the police, there was a haughtiness present in his tone of voice—too cocky, too self-assured, I thought, and, after he kept referring to the time in San Francisco when he was arrested a little too often, I finally decided he was just too self-absorbed. By the time we were role playing getting arrested—with him once again the officious policeman—I was convinced he derived some sort of wicked pleasure at watching us be publicly submissive and on our knees before him. It wasn't that I felt he should have been more compassionate—certainly, the police nor the government weren't. It was, perhaps, that I expected him to be more of a teacher or a trainer than the show-off that he had become.

"Tell me why you are prepared to be arrested," he barked at the social worker toward the end of the class as though to impress us more with his command of the situation than for any sort of sincere response from us. When Thomas floundered and didn't answer him quick enough, Ian started yelling at him, "People are dying. Every day. Every second from AIDS. Don't you care?"

Thomas, himself, seemed to be either so repelled or so frightened by Ian that he could only muster weakly a, "Yes," as a reply.

By the time Ian had dismissed us and I went to retrieve the gym bag that I had left on a chair on the other side of the room, I had decided that I wasn't really attracted to him in any kind of fashion. I just wanted to get away from there. But as I walked through the doorway, Ian was waiting on the other side for me.

"There's another action in three weeks," he said. "My affinity group is starting up next week if you want to join."

I nodded and answered, "I'll try," believing that I had no intention of doing so, but feeling guilty because I was letting someone's personality get in the way of, well, the politics of the moment.

"Unless you're afraid of getting arrested?"

"No, not really," I answered, though I felt my heart start to beat faster from the silent fear of it.

"You wouldn't believe how difficult it was to get arrested at the FDA," he said in a boisterous sort of manner. "I helped set up the banner that said 'Federal Death Administration' and was setting off smoke bombs and still couldn't get a cop to come near me. I finally had to go let the air out of the tires of the squad car to get them to come at me." He was following me out of the building, leaning his face down towards me. I kept turning my head away from him and trying to walk slightly ahead of him, panicky of catching another whiff of his breath. Outside, the Santa Anna winds blew relentlessly down from the slopes of Hollywood Hills; above us, I noticed two palm trees leaning into one another like giants whispering secrets.

"But the worst of it was," Ian said, matching my steps, fumbling to keep his vest from flapping too wildly in the wind, "I had to pee the whole time. For someone this big I have a bladder the size of a subatomic particle."

It was such a funny and unexpected self-deprecating remark—and one that caught me so off guard—that I had to stop in my tracks and let out a laugh, something like a high-sounding hiccup. Perhaps I had misjudged him, I thought, at the same time this strange noise emitted from my throat.

He stood beside me and squared his shoulders and looked off into the distance of the parking lot. "I sort of need to unwind," he said. "I've been rushing around all day." And it was here that he lifted his arm and smelled his armpit. "I didn't even get to shower at the gym and I'm sure my breath is still reeking from the garlic I had for dinner."

I stood beside him and said nothing to contradict him. "Do you want to get a drink?" he asked, his facial expression all of a sudden a bit too childlike squinting in the wind.

My body tensed at the thought of a drink—part of me wanted to continue with Ian, to try to figure him out, another part of me wanted nothing to do with him. And then there was my fear of alcohol. I couldn't drink again. When he saw my hesitation he rubbed a hand along my back. "Come on," he said. "Follow me to the Abbey."

"He's hot," Ian whispered and nodded in the direction of a dark-haired guy with thick eyebrows seated at table behind us.

I looked over at him, nodded at the recognition of his rugged, western look, and then glanced around the courtyard of crowded café tables. Mostly everyone there was hot, I thought, buffed and blow-dried to within an inch of perfection—but it was odd for a companion to point that out, or, rather, a person that you assumed you might be having a first date with. It had left me feeling imperfect and somewhat disappointed, and I wanted to leave, but I held myself in place, repeating to myself Vince's belief that I was not being social enough.

"Do you think my shirt's too small?" he asked.

I assumed he was fishing for a compliment, so I made an attempt to play the dating game and answered, "No, it looks great. It shows off your body." Too bad it's cutting off the flow of blood to your brain, I had thought to myself. Ian had spent the last hour talking about the audition he had had for a movie earlier in the week, a part that if he got would send him to New York for about a month. I didn't have to work very hard to keep the conversation going that evening—Ian was a one-man dialogue all unto himself—he talked about how he had found his agent, how he had started acting and what he felt was his best role to date—a cameo some years before on "Magnum, P.I." I didn't dare ask him about Tom Selleck, however, for fear that it would draw the spotlight away from him. But he did start talking about Selleck himself—commenting on how much sexier he was in person than on film, how tall he really was, how it was impossible not to watch him while they were filming. "He'd probably be one of my top guys if it wasn't for that voice," he said.

"Top guys?"

"One of the hot ones, you know," he said. "Fantasy man. I can't believe I got to meet him. He was much too nice, though."

"Too nice?"

"I'm a push over for those really macho-looking guys—the Tom of Finland clones, you know. The ones that act as tough as they look."

"Sure," I nodded and gave him a weak smile, feeling defeated once again. Just when I had had enough and was ready to excuse myself from his company and leave, he reeled me back in when he said, "I'm not usually this self-absorbed. I always appreciate a guy who listens well, though."

He didn't stop talking about himself, however, or the guys he was attracted to. We split the bill for two decaf coffees not much later and, as he followed me back to where I had parked my car, he said he lived right around the corner and asked if I would come over for just a second and tell him what I thought of the audition videotape he had assembled from the films and television shows he had been on.

I didn't think much of the request; by then I was so convinced that he was not attracted to me that I casually shrugged my shoulders and said, "Okay. Why not." I wasn't a bit tired—the dry wind had made the evening alive and romantic.

Walking against the wind was actually more relaxing than sitting and listening to Ian's comments about the guys around us at the restaurant, and Ian had become much more normal-seeming to me on the path we took to his house. His house was one of those white, two-story California Ranch houses, set close to his neighbors' similar homes, but once he unlocked the front door and we had stepped inside, his behavior changed again as if he had been given a mood altering injection. We were still by the door when he took his palm and clamped it at the back of my neck and pulled my face toward his. He leaned down and roughly began kissing me, his tongue aggressively parting my lips. I was taken aback by the suddenness of it all, the semi-violent demeanor he approached me with and the foul taste of his mouth. I drew back from him, but he only pushed himself further onto me, slamming me up against the closed front door. "Do you like my body?" he asked in a heavy, clipped whisper. I nodded in reply, too shocked to answer with my voice, really, but more surprised that he could even detect a response from me—he was that close to my face. "Yeah?" he asked. "Let me hear you say it. Tell me how much you like my body."

I know he was trying to pull me into another game of role playing—the master and his submissive—but the whole effect seemed to me to be of someone who had watched too many porno movies, yet I was also a bit frightened of laughing at him, or laughing him off, afraid that he might become as quickly psycho as he had been assertive.

When I didn't respond to him quick enough vocally, he started kissing me again, moaning through his mouth, or, rather, groaning and growling through his throat in an animalistic manner, the sound erupting as he shifted his mouth over mine. I wasn't the least bit turned on by it, but something shifted mentally within me. I hadn't had this kind of sexual experience in some time and I was snared by the thought that I must seize this moment— what if this were never to happen to me again? Could I let this opportunity go? His hand began rubbing my crotch and I began to untuck his shirt but my movements seemed slow and lethargic compared to his more deliberate, mock-brutish ones. His shirt came off, then mine, then my pants, then his. We had moved exactly four steps to the floor, and he rolled on top of me, my body disappearing beneath his larger one, his cock hard and bricklike as he rubbed it against my stomach in order to feel the friction.

I was pinned beneath him and he reached down underneath himself and clutched my cock, my body feeling the cool air as he lifted himself slightly away from me. Whatever was happening was not very stimulating—I couldn't get hard no matter how much he pulled at it and chanted in his groaning sound as if he were about to start some sort of tribal act. It just wasn't working for me—nothing—the smell, the taste, the aggressiveness, the role-playing, his me-me-me attitude. I closed my eyes, trying to focus on something that might be sexy, but I couldn't concentrate—he was working me too hard too quickly to get any kind of physical response. Finally, I wedged myself so that I could turn myself over beneath him, to try to get away, but when I realized I was on my stomach and my ass was positioned just at the head of his cock, his groaning escalated even further. When, a few seconds later, he had me pinned beneath him again with his hands against my wrists, I pushed up with all my strength and knocked him away from me. I stood up quickly and said, "This isn't working for me."

He gave me a quizzical look, as if I were the most stupid person in the world, but I reached for my clothes and hurriedly began to get dressed. He lay on the floor, playing with himself, as I did so, and when I had put my shoes on he looked up to me and said, "Step on me."

"What?"

"Step on me," he said, still stroking his cock. "Put your foot on my stomach so I can shoot on your shoe."

Now it was my turn to give him a look like he was the most absurd person on the earth. "Dream on," I said and opened the door, hearing, I'm almost sure, him get off on even that as I hurried to the sidewalk.

What was it that hadn't worked for me? The smell? The personality? The borderline kinkiness? The fear of becoming infected? Hadn't I also assumed, after all, that Ian was positive? Was I afraid of intimacy or was it just one of those times when sex just doesn't work between both partners? Or had I lost my desire to want to have sex?

And then suddenly I couldn't walk anymore, my legs folded up beneath me, my energy vanished and I found myself sitting on the curb of the sidewalk, my head between my legs as if I were trying to stop from throwing up, my shirt flapping in the wind. All I could think about was how much I wanted a drink. The tears came not long after that, short and fast, squeezing themselves out of my eyes as if they were from some sort of unbearable pain. What else did I have left to lose? I thought then, if I had lost my sexuality? What else could God take away from me?

Time seemed to stop as I leaned into my lap and cried. Sometime later, I pulled myself up, the tension exhausted from my body. I found myself remarkably calm though my path, internally and externally, was no clearer to me than when I had stopped. Walking back to my car I saw two guys leave the Abbey and lean into a kiss when they reached a parked car, restoring the evening back to its romantic windiness. From their silhouettes I could tell that they were the perfect WeHo gay clones—muscular, skimpy clothing, freshly cut hair—

but nothing stirred within me as I watched them pass by. It was then that I realized that I wanted to be back home with Amy and that desire possessed me as I drove back to the house, the street lamps, however, casting long shadows across the roads as though I had found my way into a film noir script by mistake, desperate, confused, and challenged.

And then one morning while I was replacing the faucets in the upstairs bathroom, Amy came in holding something in her hand.

"Look, Robbie, Mr. Peepers fell out," she said, her palm wide open and her eyes bright and dancing; she loved Mr. Peppers with a keen, unfocused purity.

My back stiffened as I understood what she had said, and I turned sharply to look at her hand.

"Honey, give him here," I said, quickly drying my hands on the towel nearest to me. "It's not right to play with him like that."

She handed him over to me, her blue eyes becoming frightened. "Why?" she asked in a tiny, far-off voice.

"Mr. Peepers is only supposed to be in the water."

"Can we put him back?"

"No, honey, not really. Once he comes out of the water he gets sick and he can't go back into it." I could feel, then, my pulse going wild, the blood throbbing at my temples with fear. I had no idea how to describe death to a child; I hadn't been able to accept it myself, after all.

"Is he still sick?" she asked.

"Sort of," I answered, wishing, at that moment, that Linda or Denise were around to pick up the slack. They would know what to say, wouldn't they? How easy it would have been for me then to just say, Go ask your mother. "Show me where you found him," I said, instead.

She walked out of the bathroom and I followed her into her room, and she pointed to the floor where the goldfish had been found. I looked at his aquarium and noticed that Amy had tossed in one of the extra crystals I kept in a box on my windowsill, in order to see how it would look in Mr. Peepers' home, and the resulting polluted water where the metal hook had quickly rusted must have made Mr. Peepers want to jump out of the water to safety.

"Amy, something's happened to Mr. Peepers. He's not going to be able to swim anymore."

"Why not?"

"Well, Mr. Peepers died."

"What's died?"

"When somebody dies, he can't move anymore," I said, squatting down to her height, showing her Mr. Peepers' immobile body in my hand, watching her face move into confusion. "He can't swim. He can't think. He can't breathe. He can't see. His body stopped, honey." She hung on to my every word, open-mouthed and growing teary eyed in front of me. I let out a large sigh and sat on the floor, bowing my head to look at Mr. Peepers.

"Can we put him back in?" she asked.

"No, honey. He won't swim anymore."

"Why not?"

"When you die you don't come back," I said, watching grief merge into the soft, pure spaces of her face, straining with understanding.

"Did Mr. Peppers know he was going to die?" She sat on the carpet beside me, staring at the dead goldfish I still held in my hand.

"I don't think so, honey," I answered, then shook my head in bewilderment. "I don't know."

"Is Mr. Peppers sad that he died?"

"He's not alive anymore so he doesn't know," I said, confused all at once by her simple, childlike logic. "But it's okay to be sad because we miss him because he won't be with us anymore."

"Where will he go, Robbie?"

"Well, we can bury him in the ground in the back yard if you want to."

"Can I keep him in my drawer?"

"No, that's not right, honey. We need to let go of him. We need to put him away some place. We're supposed to bury him when he dies."

"Okay," she said, and as she said that she looked so tiny and fragile to me. We took Mr. Peepers downstairs to the kitchen and I found an empty pop-sickle box in the trash and we put him inside; Amy watched my every move with an unbearably sad expression, staring at the process the singular way that children stare when they first encounter death—part afraid and part curious, full of both wonderment and sorrow. I led her outside behind the patio and we dug a large hole with spoons and buried the box. As we did so, I tried not to make too elaborate a deal of burying Mr. Peepers, but knowing at the same time that I had to provide a sense of closure for the child. I shook my head, then, believing I would make a horrible father on my own, wishing Nathan were here to know what to say to a child.

"Am I going to die?" she asked me as we covered the box with dirt.

"We all die at some time," I said. "But people don't die till they get very, very, very old," I added, not wanting to frighten her. "Many, many years older than Mr. Peepers."

She seemed to weigh my words again, then asked, "Will I see Mr. Peepers again?"

"Maybe," I said. "If you grow up to be a good girl you'll see Mr. Peepers in heaven."

"What's heaven?"

"It's the place we all go when we die, Amy," I said, suddenly exhausted by her endless source of questions, not knowing how to cut my own disbeliefs into acceptable answers for a child. "It's a good place," I added. "But you don't want to go there till you die."

"Why not?" she asked.

"Because you're here, honey, with me. You want to wake up in the morning and be with your mommy and Denise and in your bedroom. You want to be here, Amy. This is your home."

"Okay," she said, though I could tell by the tone of her voice she was not thoroughly convinced.

"I bet when we go see Santa Claus we can ask him to get you another fish."

"Does Santa live in heaven?" she said, suddenly wide-eyed and happy.

The logic both confused and amused me. "Sure," I answered. "He can live there if we want him to."

She had taken my hand as we crossed the lawn, and all at once I wondered why I couldn't let go of things as easily as she had, why Nathan still lingered so acutely within me. I thought that I would get over him in time, though with each passing day I realized that that was not to be the case. He was too much a part of me and I found I missed everything about him. I missed the way he would read the newspaper at the kitchen table, folded vertically as if he were still on the subway, missed the way he would dance while listening to an album, moving so uncharacteristically unrestrained about the entire room like a showgirl to make me laugh, missed the way, too, he would kiss me before he would fall asleep.

"Can I ride on your shoulders?" Amy asked me that day as if death had resolutely been accepted.

"Uh huh," I had answered, lifting her easily into the air.

Denise always believed that Christmas awakened the child within herself, a dormant, festive spirit resurrected on Thanksgiving by watching parades and cooking turkey for a gathering of her friends, a feeling, Vince once remarked to her, which must have been created by that "Leave-it-to-Beaver"-we-must-be-perfect mentality every dysfunctional family of our generation possessed. When she was a girl Denise would wait impatiently in the days that followed Thanksgiving for her mother to bring down the box of ornaments from the attic and her father to take herself and Melanie and her brother John shopping for a tree at the makeshift nursery assembled in the parking lot of the shopping center near the highway. Everything about the season held a magical possibility before her, from the arrival of the Sears catalog in the October mail to the first sighting of Mrs. Darrow's electric candles in the house across the street the day before Thanksgiving. Denise had always believed Christmas awakened layers of delight not ordinarily seen; when she was a child, for instance, Denise's mother lavished a joy toward her daughters that was contagious, infusing wreath broaches or socks with holly designs with an excitement and tenderness she didn't ordinarily possess.

Denise once mentioned to me that what she missed most about the East

Coast was the change of weather, the delineation of four distinct seasons, but what it robbed most, she felt, was Christmas from feeling like Christmas—the sharp, icy breath of fresh air after shopping in overheated Macy's while wearing a winter coat, for example, or the flurry of snow which could happen a few days before the holiday—just enough to whip up the belief in the possibility of a white Christmas. Christmas in L.A. has a surreal quality to it, the apostasy of a religious winter celebration so incongruent to the balmy weather that actually occurs during the month of December; the absurdity of it only heightened by colored lights and ornaments strung in ficus trees, fake snow sprayed on window panes and houses decorated with Santas in red velvet outfits while the temperature hums along mildly in the seventies.

Denise, however, had set her own traditions in place her first Christmas in Los Angeles—decorating the rooms inside with white candles and pink poinsettias, stringing green lights and threads of popcorn and cranberries around a purposely fake silver tree, while outside a simple wreath of fresh pine garlands and mistletoe hung a little more elegantly on the front door. On Christmas Day she once again assembled those friends who were closest to her, but it was Linda and Amy who had changed the focus of Christmas, changed the occasion from an assemblage of friends to a more intimate celebration of family.

This intimacy left me feeling disconnected that Christmas of 1988, even though Denise and Linda had made a great effort to include me. That was the Christmas that I had stayed upstairs in bed when I had heard Amy's footsteps thunder down the steps, froze when I heard her laughter wiggle its way through the air shafts upon discovering her gifts under the tree, felt a miserable ache in my chest as I was unable to shut out the sound of wrapping paper violently torn away from taped boxes. I could not bear to witness Christmas that year, could not bring myself to watch Amy's spontaneous glee when I was so aware of an unhappiness within me which I kept as guarded as my memories. Something that morning had paralyzed me—a loneliness so empty and profound that I had been incapable of responding when Linda had appeared at my door to invite me to join them downstairs. I measured time, then, from the moment since Nathan's death, and all I could understand that morning was this was my first Christmas without Nathan. All I could imagine in those moments after Linda had withdrawn from my door, was how much pleasure Nathan would have drawn from the experience of this family. I even tried to imagine his joy washing over me, the way he would have helped Amy assemble her puzzle, how he would have cut her turkey into odd little shapes, how he would have taken his own saliva and cleaned the smear of chocolate from the corner of her mouth.

By the time Vince and Jeff arrived that afternoon, I had showered and was seated downstairs in front of the television, feigning an interest in the Etch-a-Sketch Denise had given Amy and which she had positioned within my lap like the stand of an easel. I sat there wanting to be somewhere else, really, wanting to be outside fixing the railing or upstairs finishing the tiles of the bathroom wall, engaged in a normal day, away from all this silly, needless holiday chit-chat with Vince about George Bush and the nominees for his cabinet.

Let it go, let it go, let it go, I thought, silently retreating further into my shell, shutting out any attempt to socialize as Vince assumed command of the kitchen preparations for dinner, and Jeff drew Linda into a conversation about the role he had auditioned for last week for an upcoming episode of "Murder She Wrote." *I am ruining Christmas,* I thought, as my sullenness continued through dinner, picking at the plate of stuffing and candied yams and turkey, turning over a heap of string beans with my fork, not eating anything, though, just licking the tongs of the fork occasionally, as if my pretended action would not make anyone suspicious of my behavior.

As it was, everyone did ignore my moroseness. Later, years later, I learned that Denise had warned everyone to ignore my desolate disposition. And it was true that Vince and Jeff made no acknowledgment of my mood that day; I remember I even played a game of Trivial Pursuit with Jeff and soundly lost, reciting my answer, "I don't know," in a defeated monotone before even attempting to recognize the question.

But it was then that Denise came by and asked if I wanted to help clean the dishes. And I was thankful at last to have a task to do, a purpose to channel my pent-up energies. Even after I had finished cleaning that evening, I stayed in the kitchen running a damp towel over the surfaces of the table and the counter and the top of the microwave—just to keep myself busy while we had guests in the house. Denise and Linda were in and out of the kitchen, wrapping things in tinfoil and plastic wrap, carrying on conversations with Jeff or Amy in the other room. And then the phone rang and Linda motioned to Denise that it was Mrs. Connelly calling. I looked around the room at that moment, perceptively aware that something was missing, and watched Denise move toward the phone, remembering, achingly, the role her mother had played the Christmas I had met Nathan.

Denise had only recently revealed the truth of her relationship with Linda to her mother and which Mrs. Connelly thoroughly disbelieved. But Amy had been a source of confusion for Mrs. Connelly for years, especially when Denise would remark that she had taken Amy shopping for clothes or to her first dentist's appointment. Mrs. Connelly had long ago stopped asking who Denise was dating but now she was convinced that if Denise were telling her the truth about her relationship with Linda that it could easily be corrected by a variety of doctors and Denise's permanent return to Kentucky. When I heard Denise begin her sentences with an anxious-sounding, "No, Mother," I left the kitchen and wandered into the unfinished room where we had put up the tree, dark, now, except for the strands of tiny green lights circling its conical shape, and sat and watched the lights blink off and on the silvery branches, and then felt guilty for not making any ornaments for the tree. When I was five my father gave me a woodburning kit for Christmas and out of the rectangular strips of thin balsam wood, I carved a dozen ornaments for my mother, burning out the details of toy soldiers and drums with the help of my father, then painting them with colored magic markers my mother had borrowed from the church's supply closet. My mother proudly hung those ornaments every year till she died; afterwards, my father preferred to spend his energy decorating the church instead of our home. The ornaments probably didn't even exist anymore, I remembered that night. For all I know he had burned them with my other things—but not long after I had met Nathan, I found some store bought ones which oddly approximated my crude, childish designs and I bought them for the tree Nathan and I would always decorate for the season.

"She won't even ask if Linda is around," Denise said, her voice startling me as she came up from behind; in her hands she held the red felt stocking which I had stuffed with candy and small toys for Amy and which had been lying empty on the floor when I entered the room. I knew Denise was determined for me not to be alone too long that day. "She still can't let go."

"Let go?"

Denise laughed and came over to the couch, sitting tentatively on the edge of it beside me, as if she were to get off at the next bus stop. "That I'm not around to spend Christmas with her."

I laughed with her over the idiocy of it all, the way we can sometimes drive ourselves crazy over things we cannot possess. Then Amy ran inside the room, shaking her head as her eyes adjusted to the dim light and made out our figures on the couch. "Robbie, Vince said that my Etcha is his. Go tell him it's mine."

I laughed again, and could feel Denise's smile widening beside me. "You go tell him I said that he's ruining a potential Picasso," I said.

"What's a Peek-ah-toe?"

"Just go tell him," I added more sharply, almost parental, and with that she had bolted out of the room.

I heard her laughter as she tried to repeat my message for Vince, and Vince teasing her saying there was no such thing as a Peek-ah-toe.

"It's too bad we don't have the opportunities to be parents that most people have," Denise said, and I knew she was referring to our sub-genre of the species. "Vince'd be a good father."

"Jeff, too." I added. "But he'd probably spoil the kid and let Vince take credit for it."

"Nathan would have been a good father," Denise said, and at the mention of his name we both worried that she had made a mistake of drawing him into our conversation.

"When he wasn't too busy being a child himself," I had added with a laugh, trying not to audibly spill into a sour mood.

"Did you ever think you'd have a kid?" she asked me, leaning back into the couch.

"He had names picked out."

"No, you, Robbie," Denise said. She turned to me, and I could sense her stare searching out my eyes, but I was looking away from her, out at the tree, fascinated by the rapidly changing forms of lights. "Did you ever want a baby?"

"A baby?" Again, I laughed. "Not by myself."

And then it was her turn to laugh, but I joined in with her, enjoying my own joke. "Too much responsibility raising a kid alone," I added. "You and Linda have a nice arrangement."

Amy's squeal bubbled into the room, and we both turned and looked in the direction of the sound. I knew Vince must be tickling her. "How much do you think a child understands at that age?" I asked.

Denise's hand drew up to her chin, as if she were about to affect her mother's pose, but then she moved her fingers into the dark mass of her brown hair, then ran the tips of her nails against a few of the top frosted strands and twisted them together. "I think she knows we love her and love each other," Denise said. "Though I don't think she has a clue to the mechanics of things."

"I had no idea at that age how things would turn out," I said, folding my arms across my chest as if to protect myself from my memories. "I find it hard to believe that children are that sophisticated at that age."

"They are brighter than we were," she said. "At least I think so."

"There's more to know, I guess," I added. "I think we were sheltered a lot as kids. They kept secrets about the way things really were—communism, Vietnam, sex, *hom-o-sexuals*."

"If Amy learns that being gay is all right," she said, "and then her children learn the same and their kids and their kids. Won't it be accepted someday? Totally accepted?"

"Maybe so, but for every child that learns it's okay, more are taught that it's not."

I felt her tense at the thought of the contradictions I had raised. "I don't understand why we have to deal with so many issues," she replied, sharply. She stood up and walked to the tree, adjusting one of the red glass ornaments which had tilted itself into an awkward position. Her mood changed as she caught the reflections of the lights and the silver and the glass in her hand. "I'd love to have another kid just to be able to give them Christmas," she said, cupping what looked from where I sat to be a prism of changing colors.

"Another kid?"

"I've been thinking," she said and nodded at me shyly, withdrew her hands and then mysteriously left the room.

My first year in California I had come to believe my body separated me from other gay men, a body I could hardly understand or seldom seem to keep healthy, a body I could neither shape nor sculpt to the perfection many of my peers so easily achieved themselves. Much of this may have had to do with my self-consciousness and often low self-esteem when I walked into the gym on Santa Monica, though it may also have resulted from a lack of motivation and an absence of discipline in wanting to achieve what I also perceived as an often frivolous and irrational goal. Whenever I went to the gym with Vince or Jeff, I was so vividly aware of how imperfect I physically had become: the lumpiness around my waist, the thighs that wobbled a bit too much, the skinny forearms that ended in large, calloused fingers. Around me, the tanned, hairless West Hollywood boys stretched and pumped in their bright spandex shorts and tank tops, wiping the sweat carefully away with their short white towels, their biceps cresting into peaks with a casual but calculated flex of their arm. Times had changed without me; that was the year an aerobics boom had happened, the same year the sex bathhouses had turned into health food and juice bars or trendy clothing stores selling skimpy clothes for exorbitant prices, the same year that perfect bodies of young gay men seemed as easily manufactured as a skimpy clingy Calvin Klein T-shirt.

And that was the year, too, I first noticed my body beginning to pull away from me, the hint of its youth fading into a series of lines around the eyes and the steely string of muscles from my thighs to calves aching at the end of the day from a combination of weariness and supporting what I believed was too much weight for my frame. I suppose I wanted to mistrust my body—imagine that its heartburns and charley horses were the result of something more serious, something which could move me into that other category of gay men—those who struggled with infections and the onslaught of exotic diseases—the rumor had it, after all, that that year fifty percent of the population of gay men in West Hollywood were HIV-positive.

But the truth was I was undeniably healthy myself, increasingly so, rebounding steadily from the abuse of cigarettes and booze, having cast those addictions aside with my continental shift. When Nathan died I was at the apex of those addictions, yet at that point in my life I ironically looked and felt fitter than I had ever been before. Now, I could not stop eating nor retaining water, in spite of the fact that I sweated uncomfortably in the California heat. What energy I had once found from booze and cigarettes I had been unable to replace. In its wake a growing depression, lethargy and apathy had rooted itself, as much a result of grief, I believe, as from the affects of withdrawal.

Often at the gym I would stand with my head folded into a book or a magazine, not really reading but frozen nonetheless into an antisocial stance. Vince would find me, as he had done so for years, eager to make a campy comment or a joke about someone he had seen or something he had witnessed, hoping to draw out an equally catty response from me, something like remarking over the coiffure of some young Adonis, "Did you see her? She looks like she waxed those locks into that position." Now, however, his comments usually failed to provoke a retort; seldom, either, could I grin or even offer the slightest reaction. Instead, I would only lift my eyes up to meet his, trying to shade their fear and confusion by directing their attention to the object of his remark. "You're not even gay anymore," he said angrily to me one day when I had once again failed him.

Not gay anymore? I thought as I watched him stomp away from me. Was it really true? Did I no longer belong? Blend in? Had I separated myself from everyone? It was true that I was not having sex anymore with other men, but I was also not eagerly pursuing that goal that year. But didn't the fact that I had slept with men for years count for something? Didn't I still socialize with gay men, albeit rather dully? Didn't I live with a lesbian couple, after all? Didn't that count? Wasn't I here, at that moment, reading a gay newspaper? In a gay gym?

Or was Vince, instead, referring to my loss of humor? My lack of merriment, the withering of my spirit? It was a fact that I had become more dour than merely pouty; hate over my predicament of losing Nathan no longer seethed out of me or fermented inside me, instead, I had resigned myself unhappily to its change. I was, that year, just twenty-nine, but possessed, at times, the cranky demeanor of a bitter old man of seventy whose life had not turned out the way he had imagined. Or was I resentful, instead, of the cluster of Peter Pans around me who refused to grow up, resenting in its place my own willingness to let my life be determined beyond the physicality of my body and face? Had I come, therefore, to hate gay life or to hate its sometime shallowness? Was I misjudging others or had I come to despise myself?

Vince stood before me that day waiting for his hateful remark to elicit an uneasiness in me. It worked, of course; I looked frantically away from him, out into the room of gay clones biking, running, lifting, sweating, trying to find something—anything, really—to say that could prove him wrong. I walked over to him and nodded my head toward a blond guy on the chest machine and asked, "Do you think it's bottled?" Vince arched his eyebrows and looked out into the room where my gaze had landed. It was then that he turned back to me and took the paper I was reading, an issue of *Frontiers*, and briskly thumbed through the pages till he landed on an ad in the yellow pages toward the center. He tore the corner of the page out and handed it to me. "Do me a favor," he said. "Call him. He's a friend of a friend who owes me a favor. He's not cheap. So I'll arrange to have the first four visits on me."

"I had no idea it would be so expensive," Jeff said, thumbing through the small notebook Denise had handed him and which he had spread across the solid thickness of his thighs, "just to find the perfect man."

"The perfect father," Denise corrected. She was huddled close to Jeff, leaning into him, really, her hand clasped at the heavy muscle of Jeff's tricep where his T-shirt ended, her fingers testing its firmness, as if it were a perfect melon she had to memorize to use as a barometer to judge others.

"No one's perfect," Jeff said, tensing his arm where Denise's fingers rested, as if he knew she were measuring him. "Believe me, Kens do not exist."

"Kens?" Denise asked. She looked up at him, her eyes first meeting his sky blue ones, then shifting to regard the tightness of the skin around his eyes.

"Barbie's boyfriend. The perfect man."

Denise laughed, her voice echoing down the stairs to the floor below. "Unfortunately, they don't list virtues," she added, looking back down at the notebook. She had spent the morning at the sperm bank with Linda, filling out forms, finding out procedures, talking with a doctor and nurses about the ease and difficulty of conceiving a child via artificial insemination. Linda had treated the appointment as natural as a new distributor approaching her in the store to begin stocking a new product, asking a series of well-informed questions, like what infections the donors were screened for, what tests had been conducted on the sperm itself, what was the success rate of impregnation of both the doctor and the clinic. Denise, however, had been unprepared, startled with every word, from "speculum" to "pipette" to "cervical cap," and she was soon seized with the possibility that something could go wrong. Afterward, Linda had dropped Denise off at the loft she rented for painting and Denise had spent the day sifting through the catalog of possible donors, calming herself with the knowledge that if Linda was so unruffled about the idea of foreign fluids entering Denise's body, then Denise should be too. Denise and Jeff were seated in the small, cement stairwell outside her loft—Jeff had helped Vince carry over folding chairs in the back of Denise's Jeep for a meeting of an ACT UP affinity group which Denise had agreed to let take place in the loft. "How can I tell that someone 6'2", blond, left-handed and Methodist is honest and not a bigot?" Denise asked, leaning into Jeff again.

"You can't even tell if he's straight," Jeff said.

"No one's straight," Denise answered. "At least not to you."

"Well the fact that he's donating sperm might be one factor that he's at least a liberal," Jeff added. "Unless he might have some bizarre science-fiction power complex to replicate."

"Great," Denise smirked. "I could give birth to the next Napoleon. Are you sure I should have a liberal donor? I want to make sure family values are represented as well."

"If there were a gene for family values then we would all be happy instead of just gay," he said. "So you better just have the doctor mix them all up. I hear they will do that," he said, closing the notebook. "That way no one can assert parental rights without generating a lot of red tape and the kid won't grow up feeling compelled to locate his father."

"I wish I could look into the future and see that this guy was the right one. Or that one. Or that someone could tell me this is the one for you, Denise. This is the right one."

"No one can make your decisions for you," Jeff said.

Denise lifted the book from Jeff's lap and clasped it upright against her breasts, as if its contents of perfect men would spill to the floor like a tipped carton of milk. Above them a spray of laughter burst out the open door of the loft like the burp of an opened soda can. "What are they doing in there?" Denise asked. "Why was this so important?"

"Anarchy," Jeff said, standing up and stretching his arms out above his head as if he had just awoke. It was then that Denise regarded Jeff's physique as if she had never noticed it before, the perfect symmetry of it, really, the way with his legs spread apart and his arms outstretched he appeared as if he were an Atlas. "They're planning to deface federal property," Jeff added. "Vince said that they were worried about the meetings being bugged."

"Bugged?" Denise repeated, shocked, standing up to measure her height against Jeff's. "Aren't they scared?"

"Scared?" Jeff answered, moving back toward the doorway into the loft. "I hardly think so. Vince is always excited about the possibility of being arrested."

The day Denise began to seriously consider who her donor should be was the day she began to dwell on her own imperfections, or those physical qualities about herself which she found so unappealing when she studied herself long and hard in her bathroom mirror that evening; she had convinced herself that her chin was too long, her nose was too angled, her fingers too stubby and her thighs too short. All she needed, she told me later, was a concert pianist and track star with a square jaw who was over six feet tall—was that too much to ask in a man? "And a dormant hair color," she added. "I'd like to at least pass on my hair."

Denise was a little taken aback by her own calculations, however, when Linda interrupted her manic inventory activity and suggested that she look at the donors who listed volunteer work as an activity.

"*Volunteer work?*" Denise responded, "Why volunteer work?

"Because it shows they care about something," Linda replied as if it were an obvious admirable quality not to overlook, and, well, because she knew Denise well enough to know that Denise was focusing perhaps too much on the way someone looked, which, of course, she was.

Denise once remarked that if she had known what a challenge it was for her to become pregnant, she would never have attempted it at all—she would have easily have abandoned any expectations or hopes of having a child through artificial insemination. Her first insemination, she once told me, ranked right up at the top of her list of most embarrassing moments, not quite edging out for first place, however, the time she tripped choreographer Twyla Tharp while learning a dance combination during a Broadway chorus audition. She and Linda had gone together to the doctor's office that morning—Linda had arranged to take half the morning off from the store and the worry about getting back to work had left her unusually tense and edgy, the uneasiness spilling over into Denise's own mood. Denise had always relied on Linda to exert such a rational control over things, but she moved that morning with such an unnatural jerky rhythm, as if she were an electric toy whose batteries were running out, that Denise wondered if Linda had changed her mind about a baby.

In the examination room, the doctor, a lesbian named Martha Spears, was a bit too cheerful, or so Denise thought, talking Denise and Linda through the insemination process in a sing-song voice, as if she were demonstrating a process to a class of first graders.

"It's so beautiful," Dr. Spears said when she had finally made Denise recline on the examination table and had looked at Denise's cervix. Denise had rolled her head over and had given Linda a surprised look, which Linda had equally returned—a pair of arched eyebrows lifted at one another—no doctor had ever commented on the attractiveness of Denise's you-know-what before—and certainly not before a witness. It was then that Denise had mouthed "Are you sure?" to Linda, which Linda had dismissed with a flattening of her lips and a slump of her left shoulder, which had only made Denise convinced that the idea of a baby was perhaps something they should reconsider.

Denise had undressed to only a bra that morning, then tied a crinkly blue plastic hospital apron around herself, her legs elevated by stirrups when she had positioned herself on top of the starched-white butcher's paper that covered the examination table. The room was cheerless and spare, white walls, a green vinyl chair, the smell of day-old disinfectant tissues in wastebaskets, and the temperature so cold Denise could feel her nipples contract. "The timing seems perfect," the doctor said when Linda clasped her hands around one of Denise's hands. "A perfect day to make a baby."

"I've mixed several together like you wanted," the doctor said, drawing up almost all of the sperm, which had been thawing in a dish of warm water at the side of the examination table, with a plastic pipette. Denise has often recalled that it felt like such a strange, chilly procedure, even with the doctor's bubbly demeanor, as the doctor squirted sperm into her cervix.

The doctor explained that Denise should remain still, feet in stirrups with the speculum inside her, for at least twenty minutes. Denise tried to relax while she remained motionless, but felt muscles she had never been aware of in her body before tensing into shapes that made her want to itch and scratch and contort herself.

"Try thinking about the sperm moving into you," Linda said to Denise. Denise had looked up at her and had tried to visualize the movement of the sperm into her body but it failed to comfort her, her thoughts kept being interrupted by the sight of her stomach in front of her eyes—she thought she looked so overweight in this awkwardly reclined position, her stomach swollen, her back sticking to the vinyl top of the table where the edges of the paper ended.

Linda, however, had aggravated the embarrassing moment by walking around the examination table, peering at Denise's cervix like it was the White Rabbit's hole, then disappearing with the doctor into another room to view the remaining sperm beneath a microscope, leaving Denise alone with her feet in the air and the chilly feeling inside her.

"They look like boiling rice," Linda said, hopping back into the room when she returned without the doctor. "The way they all jump around in the water."

"Boiling rice is hardly a positive visualization," Denise said dryly, wondering if flexing her toes could prevent a floating grain from reaching her ovaries.

"Okay then, bean sprouts."

"*Bean sprouts?*" Denise responded. She looked up to the ceiling, the only place she could look to comfortably, and said, "I think we've been lesbians for much too long if the only thing we can say about sperm is that it reminds us of bean sprouts. Either that, or you desperately need a vacation from the store. Maybe you should be doing this."

"Well, what would you say they look like, then?" Linda asked, an annoyed tone creeping into her response.

"How do I know?" Denise replied. "All I can see are my legs in the air. And I can barely see them over my fat stomach!"

And this was where, Denise later recalled, that Linda had placed her head on Denise's stomach, lifting up the crinkly blue plastic apron and pressing her hair and ear against Denise's belly.

"Such power," she said, suddenly easing the moment. "To think that we can do this."

It was all Denise really needed to compose herself—the knowledge that she wasn't engaged in this baby making process alone. She couldn't help but notice, however, that when she got up from the examination table and shook the stiffness out of herself, that there were two elongated craters on the white paper where her buttocks had been.

Linda and Denise were to repeat the insemination process again at home the following day, the sperm kept frozen by a huge metal tank of liquid nitrogen. Denise, pulling the car up to the sidewalk where Linda waited with the tank, thought, in that instant when she mentally studied the makeup of this aberrant scene: What if she went through all this and she did not become pregnant? The tank, after all, looked like a milk can. A *stupid-looking milk can*, Denise thought. A milk can for a cow on her back with her legs up in the air.

The next day Linda inseminated Denise at home before Linda went to work. It was rushed and awkward and anticlimactic, Linda hurriedly trying to get it all done before she left the house; all Denise remembered was the gooey sperm running between her legs like maple syrup on pancakes. The following weeks went by like an aerobics class—sweaty and dizzy and a bit too rattled to focus on one thing for more than a second. Soon enough, however, Denise woke up one morning and had dropped three pounds and felt incredibly better. Her euphoria evaporated when her period returned a few hours later and she called Linda at the store to inform her she was not pregnant. It was then that Denise realized that this silly, awkward, embarrassing little procedure had the ability to instill in her a profound and piercing depression such as she had never believed possible.

"You seem tense," Mitch said.

I nodded in response, unable to say anything, conscious of the faint smell of his aftershave and his moist breath against the flesh of my neck creating a wave of goosebumps. We were lying on Mitch's bed, fully clothed, his body wrapped around mine spoonlike, enveloping it, really; he was a good six inches taller than myself and at least thirty pounds heavier.

"This is all we have to do," he said. I nodded again, or, rather, I imagined that I nodded. Here I was, another person believing I was tense, strung out, unable to function. I realized, though, that I had lost control of my body, tightening it as if afraid of enjoying Mitch's presence even though an erection strained against the waist of my jeans like I hadn't felt since I was in high school.

Wasn't this the purpose of a surrogate? I thought, trying to relax myself by opening my mouth and taking slow, quiet breaths. To make me get hard? To make me feel sexy? To make me want to have sex? To make sex comfortable,

enjoyable? I smiled at the paradox of the situation that I knew only I understood at that moment, the logical illogic of it all—Mitch had thought that I
was impotent, or at least that's what Vince had led him to believe when he had
arranged the appointment after I had finally acquiesced to his badgering.
Mitch's mission was to make me want to have sex, *gay* sex, to be able to express
myself sexually, doubtlessly, with a man when the truth was I had always
thought I had too much sexual feeling, too many thoughts of sex. I mastur-
bated every morning in bed before I got up and again in the evening after I
had shut my bedroom door and was pretending to read, my head full of the
images of men I had seen throughout the day—on TV, at the gym or the store,
the UPS delivery man, the guy in the car next to me at the gas station, objec-
tifying each and every one of them into an erotic detail. Sometimes, in the
afternoon, if I was bored I would jerk off in the bathroom while Amy was
taking her nap. The unfortunate thing, some people thought, was that I was
doing this all by myself. And the truth was, I could sometimes agree with
them; but the expression of it, now, with Mitch, another man, left me feeling
oddly iniquitous and cheap.

Not that he was cheap, of course. As Vince explained, Mitch was well
compensated for his services. When I spoke to Mitch on the phone two days
before to schedule an appointment, he made a concerted effort to stress the
legitimacy of his practice.

"I have a degree in psychology from UCLA," he said, as if academics and its
textual wisdom could better solve any sort of sexual dysfunction. "I'll make it
very comfortable for you," he added in a softer whisper, as if he suddenly realized he needed to balance the erotic nature of his services as well. "I have an
hour free on Thursday between seven and eight."

Nothing will happen, I told myself on the way over to Mitch's apartment. I
had jerked off an hour before I was to arrive, to prevent anything from happening. So I was disappointed, really disappointed, to find Mitch so attrac-
tively sexy. I had convinced myself that Vince had set me up with one of his
young West Hollywood buffed-muscle-boy activists, someone who probably
doubled as a hustler or a porn star or both. So I was startled when Mitch
opened the door and I discovered a much older man than I had expected,
someone whom I imagined to be closer to fifty than forty.

But there was, nonetheless, something highly appealing to him. At first I
thought it was the short style of his hair, one which revealed the silver in his
scalp like fibers of wool. Then I thought, perhaps, it had something to do with
the running slope of his nose juxtaposed against the squareness of his jaw. But
I knew, of course, it was more the aggregate of him than anything else—the way
he looked, moved me into the room and guided me toward the sofa. He was
causally dressed, more so than I had counted upon even if he had been a younger
man—a maroon sweatshirt without sleeves showed both his defined arms and
the damp strands of hair beneath them, and a pair of old khakis, threadbare at
the knees had paint splattered about the thighs. He had the demeanor of some-

one assertive—part father, part coach, part drill sergeant. As he waved me inside the room, I caught myself forcing my eyes away from him, glancing instead at one then another of the furnishings of his Art Deco bungalow—the Hurrell portrait of Vivien Leigh which hung above the sofa, the glass coffee table cluttered with Erté statuettes of semi-but-elaborately clad dancing chorus girls.

I'd forgotten, truly forgotten, what it was like to be so drawn to someone. Knew it dangerously so at that moment, however; knew, too, that if Mitch possessed any smidgen of the psychological acumen that he professed to have, he could have easily taken advantage of me. It wasn't until he scratched his jaw that I realized he reminded me of Will—a bulkier, more well-fed pumped up version of him. *Will*, I thought, realizing the waters of time which had flowed beneath my bridge, wanting to know, at that moment, what had become of him. It was as if Will had suddenly returned into my life after an absence of decades, and what I wanted most of him was to be able to explain to him what had happened to Nathan, why I was here looking for help from a sex surrogate when all I really wanted was to find someone else to love.

Mitch mentioned that we would begin our session with breathing and desensitization exercises. *Desensitization exercises?* I thought. From a sex surrogate? Shouldn't we be doing sensitization exercises? Already I was confused. Already my hard-on was painfully creeping against the fabric of my pants because of my previous hour's attention to it.

And so Mitch had me stand in front of him taking deep breaths—him staring at me straight on, me still averting my eyes. I stood there trying to remind myself of the clinical nature of my appointment. Trying to deflect my emotions. There was nothing romantic to it, after all, nothing remotely intimate with having a man, a stranger, breathe as you did two inches away from you. Intimacy is what I wanted; romance was exactly what I needed. I wanted a date at a restaurant with a candle on the table top, a man asking me questions about who I was and how I had come to the ideas I believed in. But what I needed, of course, truly needed was a surrogate for Nathan. Under no circumstances could I afford to expect that from Mitch after the end of our four sessions. And the realization of it trapped me in a spiraling misery. Mitch countered my degenerating mood by placing his hands on my shoulder and telling me to do the same to him, which I did. Something I didn't understand about myself was making me stay.

The odd thing was he asked me so little about myself, all he wanted from me was physical response. "Touch me here," he said, placing my hand against his chest, then moving it up to his neck and his cheek. "Put it here," he said, taking my other hand and bringing it against his waist, as if we were dancing.

We hugged each other in various permutations and then he took me into his bedroom and had me sit on the edge of his bed. He had me massage his shoulders—we were still fully clothed—then he massaged mine. Towards the end of the hour we had assumed our spoonlike positions and he asked me if I wanted to come by again tomorrow.

"I can't," I answered.

"The more we see each other the easier this will be," he said.

"Next week," I said. "I don't want to use this up so quickly."

I felt him nod against my shoulder, and I wondered if he expected this to continue beyond the four-time commitment. A few minutes later, I sheepishly said goodbye, awkwardly offering my hand outstretched for a handshake.

He took it and smiled back at me, the first genuine response I felt that I had attained. On the sidewalk to my car, however, I was already planning ways on how to cancel the next week's appointment.

How gay should a gay man be? According to Jeff, Vince believed that a gay man could never be gay enough, a source of irritation which always existed between the two of them, and a divergence of opinion which could usually be counted on to provoke an argument with almost anyone Vince knew. Vince believed that being gay meant being politically out as well as socially and sexually active. Jeff, however, refused to believe his sexuality defined him to a specific group. It wasn't that Jeff refused to act politically—he would and could where and when the instance mattered to him—and on a few occasions, mattered to Vince. The one ACT UP meeting Jeff had attended with Vince, however, had left Jeff with a negative image of activists—he felt that too many men in the room were too personally motivated to work collectively as a focused group. "There's too much therapy going on," he told me later. It was true, I often admitted, as well, that some meetings could easily digress no matter how strict the overseeing monitor was with Roberts Rules of Orders—a raised hand could suddenly grant a member a chance for acting out a rambling and often lengthy free-floating hostility.

Still, I believe, Vince always thought he could defeat the system by belonging to ACT UP, beat the odds against own death, too. "Where is your anger?" he once yelled at me when I had hesitated about accompanying him to an action. I felt so little in that moment, as if my lack of anger could cause his death, and he must have detected how upset he had made me, for he backed down on his pressure, convincing me, in a much softer and more polite tone, to join him because it would make it easier for himself to be there. One of the reasons I was there at all, of course, was because of Vince.

"I don't feel guilty," he said to me one afternoon when I had confronted him about what I considered was a particularly unlawful action. I was particularly cranky myself that day, I remember, brooding over my recent first encounter with Mitch, the circumstances of which I had kept secretive from Vince. "How else are we going to get their attention?"

I was sitting on the edge of our neighbor Larry's pool, who had agreed to let me use it once a week to give Amy swimming lessons, trying to sort out whether or not I should go back to see Mitch again, annoyed with Vince for arranging it in the first place and putting me in this awkward position. Vince was in the shallow end of the pool, helping Amy float on her back. He hadn't shaved that day and dark stubble of his beard and mustache along with the haggard look of his eyes made him look like an agitated terrorist.

"But it isn't civil disobedience anymore," I said. "It's vandalism. There's a big difference, Vince. It'll catch up with you."

I watched his face move through a thought, or attempt to store the information, and as I waited for him to say something I was struck by the combination of vulnerability and anger he now possessed. More and more Vince had been unable to process thoughts, taking longer to respond, his speech slow and sluggish as if his mouth were filled with food. Vince had always been able to understand the emotional component of being chronically ill, but he had come to feel that he had been robbed of his most vital asset, the cognitive speed of his mind, and this intellectual crippling is what angered and paralyzed him most, made him, really, fight back even harder. When I noticed his body freeze into place, as if panicked by his inability to think clearly, I eased myself into the water beside him and slipped my hands beneath Amy to take his place. Amy twisted her body up when she noticed I was standing above her. "I was floating, Robbie," she said.

"I saw that," I nodded to her, keeping my eye on Vince. He snapped out of his sluggishness when he remarked, angrily at me, "I didn't do it for your approval."

The evening before, Vince and three other men from ACT UP—Paul, Warren, and Stuart—had splattered red paint and handprints on the walls and walkways outside the Los Angeles County Board of Supervisors hearing room, stenciling "AIDS UNIT NOW" and plastering the marble pillars with posters to protest the treatment of AIDS patients at County-USC Medical Center and demanding a fifty-bed AIDS ward be created immediately. Earlier that week the four of them had also splattered the Health Department's headquarters with similar slogans, though they and other members of ACT UP denied taking credit for the action. Vince's own low profile after the event had nothing to do with his commitment to activism—or a lack of it—or so he told me that night on the phone, his voice giddy with the thrill of the accomplishment of his illegal mission. It was the sudden notoriety the action had caused in the media. "Jeff would kill me if he saw me on the news," he whispered, clandestinely, to me through the receiver, a remark which struck me particularly hard because of its absurdity.

That afternoon, the afternoon I had confronted Vince, he had managed to walk to the edge of the pool where I had been sitting, his body creating a ripple of light through the water as he moved. Amy had jumped up, clamped her thumb and finger to her nose and dived under water, a wave hitting the waist of my swim trunks as she disappeared as low as her inflated yellow plastic vest would allow.

"You should stay out of the sun," I said to Vince, trying to soften my own reproach, looking at him squint as he sat on the lip of the pool.

"I'm fine," he said, snapping briskly at me as if a drunk roused into action. He cleared his throat in two beats before continuing, adding with another snap, "Don't placate me, Robbie."

"I'm just concerned that it'll catch up with you. That's all," I answered. "It's one thing to be arrested and released. It's another thing to be sentenced to jail. That's the last thing you need right now."

"I find it ironic that you could think that a government which cannot get its act together to respond to an epidemic, could nonetheless assemble enough petty evidence to send an activist to jail. Doesn't make sense to me." He smiled as he said that, too, thrilled more by the speed of his retort than its theoretical content. His face soon crashed through another depression, however. "Unfortunately," he added, "there's nothing ironic about dying."

My second appointment with Mitch was spent in his bedroom watching porn movies, or, rather, lying once again on his bed, fully clothed with Mitch entwined around me, the two of us watching a tape of highlights of porn movies, bits of scenes with guys sucking and fucking each other, and then a compilation of come shots. "I want you to get so worked up that you could come in your pants," he had announced to me at the beginning of our session and we did not speak to one another again once the tape began. That's exactly what happened toward the end of the hour, I had gotten so worked up from watching the tape, fantasizing about Mitch, his hand on my crotch, groping and kneading and massaging it, that I came easily. Back on the sidewalk on the way to my car, I cursed myself again for showing up for the appointment, feeling both needy and sleazy, determined that this was exactly what I didn't need.

That was the same week that Denise became so worked up from her own logistical problems. It was her second month at attempting artificial insemination and she had used an herbal ovulation predictor kit that Linda had brought back from the store to determine the best time to inseminate. On the morning that it turned blue, indicating that the time was near for insemination, neither Denise nor Linda could arrange to get the tank until that evening. By the time Linda got home with the tank, Denise was too anxious and hungry to keep still, so they inseminated her that evening, after Denise had relaxed from running two miles on her treadmill.

That was the same month, too, that Vince had become convinced that the police were monitoring his activities. He was worked up, then, over the idea that he had been purposely videotaped at a demonstration in the Board of Supervisors' hearing room which had occurred after his graffiti drawing excursion. At first, I believed his paranoia was another manifestation of the enlarging scope of his dementia, because he seemed to harp on the fact, interrupting any conversation which we might have, his brown eyes skittish and distracted, repeating over and over, "I saw him. I saw him. He pointed the camera right at me. I know he was pointing it at me."

And then the idea of it seemed to drop away from him, but a few days later at an ACT UP news conference outside the Hall of Administration, he was convinced once again that he was purposely being photographed by the police. I wouldn't have paid much attention then, either, except for the fact that Stuart had made a similar passing comment to me as well when I had spoken to him on the phone one evening—that he believed that a particular cameraman did not have press credentials, but was someone from the government or the police who was monitoring their activity.

When Vince heard that theory he became even more worked up, so much so that at the next meeting he introduced the idea of consulting an ACLU lawyer. "I have enough trouble trafficking suspicious drugs back and forth to people who need them," he said before the membership. "I don't need the cops harassing me for vandalism."

The clothes came off very early during my third appointment with Mitch. When I arrived at his bungalow, he led me directly into the bedroom and we removed each other's clothes, then lay together on the bed, naked, facing one another. Oddly, he didn't seem surprised that I had an erection before we finished undressing; he ignored it, really, concentrating more on us achieving our parallel reclined positions in front of one another on the bed.

"You need to trust me," he said, his eyes connecting to mine. "Nothing I will do is unsafe or risky."

I nodded back to him as shyly as I had done the first time I had seen him.

"Tell me what you find sexy," he said.

You, you, you, you fool, I thought. Did he not perceive that I found him attractive? With an erection sticking boldly out at him? Or did he expect that from all of his clients? Still, I was tongue-tied, he must have known that it's hard for some people to express verbally what they find so visually attractive about someone. "I'm not too particular," I said, shrugging my shoulder, and as the words came out I felt they sounded wrong, as if I were cheap or didn't care who I slept with as long as I slept with someone.

He nodded. "I'm drawn to younger men," he said, adding a high little laugh. "That's natural when you reach my age. But I also like guys who are different than myself—more ethnic or exotic—latinos, Asians, blacks. A sexy man is a sexy man, though—however the package works."

I felt somewhat defeated that I was not his ideal type but I kept my disappointment to myself. He rolled over on the bed, away from me, and stretched his arm out and reached and opened the drawer of a nightstand beside the bed. It was the first unrestricted glance I could take of his unclothed body without him noticing my perusal. He had a lighter complexion than I had imagined, two spongy-looking scars visible at the back of his left ribs, a birth-mark at the right side of his back. The shape of him was bulkier than I had imagined, too, as if a young man's physique had been covered with a layer of pale, padded rubber. His ass, however, possessed a beautiful shape, rising up in the air as if it belonged to a younger man.

He withdrew a notebook from the top drawer, rolled over, and resumed his position parallel to me, the book placed evenly between us. Before opening it, he reached over and touched my cock, his fingers playing with the head. "Does this bother you?" he asked.

I shook my head no.

"I don't want you to come till I tell you. Hold it back if necessary," he said in the tone of a doctor, then withdrew his hand.

"Touch me here," he said, and he took my hand and placed it against his own cock. It was semi-erect and warm as I lightly clutched my palm around the shaft.

He twisted his body so that he could flip open the notebook and I felt the movement make him grow stiffer in my hand. He flipped through a few pages, both of us looking at photographs of male nudes clipped from porn magazines, videotape jackets, brochures and advertisements which were pasted or taped in a random assortment to black, scrapbooklike pages.

"Too young?" he asked me when he stopped at a photograph of an Italian looking boy with wild, curly black hair and full lips so beautiful it was breath-taking.

I smiled and nodded and added, "Much."

"Show me who you find hot," he said, tilting the book in my direction.

I reached up and flipped through the pages, realizing as I did so, Mitch's hand was back at my cock. I stopped on a page where a photo of a blond guy posed in white briefs, his hands positioned at his pelvic bones like a champi-on swimmer. Mitch smiled, "He is sexy," he said as if to confirm my choice. "What do you like about him?" he asked.

I was surprised that I had to verbalize it; I had never done so before, so, instead, I pointed to the parts of him that I admired—the V-shaped slope from shoulders to waist, the long blond hair and blue eyes, the tip of my index finger finally resting along the chest of the model. "Here," I said, my finger at the point of his heart, as if I had chosen a good, honest man.

"Close your eyes and keep him in your mind," he instructed. I did as Mitch said and he began lightly stroking my cock, twirling the tips of his fingers against the sack of my balls. "What's his name?" Mitch asked.

"Nathan," I answered immediately, before I had a chance to think about my answer or could change my mind.

I heard him flipping through the pages of the notebook. "Look here," Mitch said and I opened my eyes. "Like him?" he asked, pointing to another model with a similar physique, but a darker complexion and a rougher look because of his dark hair, dark eyes, and the day-old stubble of beard on his face, some-one, in fact, who might have reminded me of myself in my younger days.

I nodded, though not particularly taken with this guy as the previous one.

"Now imagine him with Nathan," Mitch said.

I shifted uncomfortably. Mitch must have sensed my uneasiness. "Imagine this is Nathan's hand," he said, giving my cock a squeeze.

This is not working at all, I thought, feeling whatever sexual mood I possessed immediately evaporate from my body. I wanted Nathan out of my mind. I wanted to have sex with other men. I wanted a relationship. I wanted a relationship with Mitch. Something in me had snapped off and I thought about just jumping up off the bed and leaving the room. It was then that Mitch leaned down and kissed my forehead, a gesture that felt so sincere my eyes popped open and I heard him whisper, "Was he your lover?"

I nodded, squeezing my eyes shut and all at once I felt myself gasping for breath. Mitch didn't ask me any more questions. He pulled himself closer to me, the heat of his body now intruding against my own, and he stroked my skin at the shoulder as if I were a pet who needed affection.

After a few minutes he rolled away and we were back looking at the note-book. "What did your first boyfriend look like?" he asked. I wanted to respond, *You, you, you,* you fool, again, but held it inside me. "He was a teacher." I said.

"Older?"

I nodded.

"Was it just a crush?"

"More," I answered, consciously aware that I was holding my details close to me. "We lived together."

"You must have broken his heart," Mitch said.

Hardly, I thought.

"Did you love him?"

"Yes."

"And you got over it. You found space for someone else."

Space for someone else, I repeated in my mind, in just the same way—the same intonation, the same flat accent, as Mitch had used. *Space for someone else.*

"I used to have a boyfriend who looked like that," he said, pointing to a young, pouty teenager with brown hair and irises so dark they looked black. "He could make me do anything for him. I used to cook for him, do his laun-dry. I was about twenty-three, right out of the Army. He was eighteen. I even drove him to San Francisco so he could see one of his old boyfriends." Mitch tilted his neck back and grinned in recollection. "He had one of those heads that just rotate. If they weren't looking at him, he was looking at them," he said, with a laugh arising out of his stomach. "It was frustrating to walk down the street next to him. He was so busy cruising and being cruised I would just go nuts. He was trouble right from the day I met him. He didn't last more than four months. But I learned a lot about what to expect from a guy if you want him to stick around. And how to feel when it was over. How to move on. I didn't know it at the time, but it was the best thing that could have happened to me."

"Lie back," he said, and he returned his attention to me, jerking my cock till I came. When I left I was eager enough to want to see Mitch the next day, but I cautiously reminded myself I needed to wait another week.

On my fourth appointment with Mitch I was decidedly more aggressive. When he suggested we begin with a shower, I began undressing him in the bedroom. But it was in the bathroom, under the warm, flowing spray of water, that his body became so fully real within my hands, the body that I had imagined for weeks touching and pleasing. I lathered him up with soap, racing my hands about his chest and stomach and then lifting his arms toward the ceiling to feel and scrub underneath them, twisting him to lather and rinse his back and buttocks, twisting him again for the groin and legs. He grunted and groaned as I massaged my hands and the soap against him, even bracing himself and clearing his throat as if to catch his balance. I felt myself smiling, really smiling, thrilled by the capacity of pleasure to astonish the body. I wondered as I felt his skin, silky and sleek beneath my touch, if I was capable of making him feel as good as the way he made me feel as I held him. He stopped me, though, not long after he cleared his throat, and moved me back into the water and began to soap up my body.

I did not, however, give up my attention on him. As he washed me I reached for his cock, keeping it lubricated with soap as I rubbed my hand back and forth around it. But I was surprised, nevertheless, when I felt him tense his body and reach down to stop my hand. When I looked down, I noticed his come beading off the hairs of my wrist and washing down into the bottom of the tub. I came, myself, a few seconds later, and as we dried and dressed again, I realized the hour was almost up. I had made up my mind in the shower that I wanted to see Mitch again, would keep seeing him for a while or as long as I could afford these sessions.

"If you want, I can arrange a three way for next time," Mitch said. I was sitting on the edge of the bed, pulling on my socks.

"A *three way*?" I replied, startled, my intoxicated expression flattening out seriously.

"I could get my lover to join us."

"Your *lover*?" I responded, dumbfounded. I stood up, moving quickly to the door. *Lover?* I thought, deflated both by the concept of word and the realization that I would not be able to attach its meaning myself to Mitch. I couldn't say anything else, and I stopped by the doorway. I was wounded, really wounded again. How had I let this happen? How had I let myself feel something for Mitch in such a short space of time? Feel this deeply, too?

Was I this insecure? Or just this stupid? He was a surrogate, after all, a *professional sexual surrogate.*

"I'll call you if I can work it out," I managed to say and left him while he was putting on his jeans. I shook my head back and forth on the whole drive home, pretending I had to brush my hair away from my eyes in case another driver caught sight of my misery. It was only when I was back in my own bedroom that I found a calmer space in my head. I knew I would never see Mitch again. But as I lay on my bed—my eyes alighting on the few possessions I had dragged across the continent to reaffirm my identity and who I had become— the paintings, the crystals, the small shelf of books—I knew I had already recovered what I had hoped to find through Mitch—the recognition that I could still want someone else in my life.

Denise had failed to become pregnant on her second attempt at artificial insemination, her period once again arriving on schedule, and the following month she had cervical mucus before she expected it and panicked. Denise had convinced herself that morning in the bathroom that she was ovulating early and that if she wasn't inseminated as soon as possible, her chances of becoming pregnant that month would be lost as well. She tried reaching Linda at the store—they were not scheduled to pick up the tank from the doctor until the following day—but Linda was busy with a customer and then, the second time Denise phoned, Linda was in the back supervising a delivery. After that, Denise called Dr. Spears but the doctor was with a patient and promised to return the call. Denise waited patiently for an hour, but when the doctor hadn't called after thirty more minutes she had tried again, only to be told by the receptionist that the doctor was with another patient and that Wednesdays were the doctor's busiest clinic days.

When Denise finally got Linda on the phone at the store, Linda decided that the herbal ovulation predictor kit that they had been using was unreliable, so Linda said that she would call Dr. Spears for advice. Linda, too, was unable to reach the doctor that day and on the way home she was worried that she was somehow failing Denise and so she bought another brand of predictor kit that the doctor had recommended from their first visit.

That evening they tested Denise again and she was negative. The next morning and afternoon she tested negative as well, but the doctor returned their phone calls a few hours before they were scheduled to pick up the tank. The following day Denise was still testing negative, but it turned blue over the weekend and Denise, for the first time since the process began, felt injected with passive tranquillity, waking up on Sunday calm and caught up with herself, ready, really, to want to try again. They stayed home that afternoon, even though they had talked about driving to Santa Monica. I took Amy out to see a movie and Linda put on a Holly Near CD, gave

Denise a massage with a sweet-smelling oil, and then inseminated her.

That was the month that Denise decided she wouldn't do the pregnancy test until her period was officially at least two days late. She had decided she wasn't going to drive herself crazy over this, she told Vince on the phone; she wasn't going to get all excited just to be disappointed again. But during the time they were waiting to see whether Denise was pregnant or not, Amy came down with the flu and the whole household fell ill, first me, then Linda, and then Denise got the 48-hour bug—sore throat, fever, chills, nausea.

Linda, however, was convinced that nausea was not a symptom of this particular flu, and she knew, just knew, that Denise was pregnant. When Denise thought her period might be late, she tried a home pregnancy test at her loft instead of working on a painting, her energy still sapped by the recent bug. When she watched it turn positive she held it up in front of her, stunned, then went and showed Lyndon, an artist who also worked at the loft with Denise, and made him read the instructions to make sure she had not made a mistake. She went to the pay phone downstairs and called Linda at the store, and Denise met her back at the house for an early, celebratory supper. A few hours later, however, while watching "Roseanne" on the television, Denise got her period. "At least I'm alive," she said when I found her in the kitchen later that night eating a frozen yogurt pie Linda had made for Amy, trying to ease herself out of another spiraling depression.

And then in July a letter arrived for Vince stating that misdemeanor charges had been filed against him and three other members of ACT UP for allegedly spraying graffiti on county buildings. Vince denied the charges, of course, in spite of the fact that a county employee—a sanitation worker who had witnessed the action—had picked out Vince from a videotape. Vince had been the easiest one to pick out, he learned later. His dark, wiry hair and mustache and those Clark Gable-like ears had been an easy marker for someone to identify. Two nights after the letter arrived, a county attorney interviewed on the evening news said that she had every intention of prosecuting the case, and had so far compiled a 165-page report against the four activists who were charged. Vince, however, had seen the story as vindication of his sanity—proof that he had been purposely videotaped and photographed—that it hadn't been his imagination nor caused by a slide into dementia. In fact, he added, the three minutes allotted to the story on the news was worth every ounce of suspicion and harassment which had happened. "The important thing is to keep the real issue before the public," he said. "This is a war against AIDS, not graffiti."

Jeff, of course, saw the story differently, even though he feared it could again open his own life to suspicion. "It seems silly," he said, "to spend so much time over a little paint."

A week later the charges were dropped after a sequence of embarrassing newspaper articles and television reports pointed out the foolishness of the police department for wasting so much time conducting an investigation of a graffiti incident. "The real criminals are the Board of Supervisors," Vince had remarked to one reporter when he had agreed to be interviewed. But when Vince saw himself on television later that day, all he could think about was how horrible he looked. For the first time, he said to me later that week, he thought he looked like a man who was battling to maintain his health. Jeff, however, had been annoyed once again that Vince needed to continue to make his fight so publicly visible. They had argued that evening and Vince had retreated to the bedroom. Vince felt, he said to me a few days later, as though he had reached a state of complete psychological confusion; all he wanted, at that moment, was to just die. On his bed, his head on the pillow, barely aware of the breeze from the window, he couldn't shake the escalating depression Jeff had incited, believing that his former self—a healthy, alert, and happy entity—had somehow been stolen from his body, and he was overwhelmed by despondency. But Jeff had entered the room, knowing his argument had been too rough on Vince. "You know I think you did the right thing," Jeff said. "Even if I still think the method you used was wrong."

"I know," Vince answered, rousing himself off of the bed, knowing he could not make it through any of this without Jeff's support. "I know."

It was Vince who had suggested that Denise try Clomid, a fertility drug that regulated ovulation, photocopying her pamphlets and articles and leaving her notes and phone messages that it also increased the probability of having twins. Linda, however, was adamant that Denise not take the drug; she had always been suspicious of both prescription and over-the-counter medications, suspicious, as well, of anything unnaturally packaged or preserved. Amy, for instance, was never allowed things such as Captain Crunch cereal or Fritos or Robitussin for Children (too much sugar, too much MSG, too much expectorant). Over the years Denise had learned to accommodate Linda's eating habits by adopting most of them herself, but she always felt, she once confided in me, that one of the reasons why Amy was so prone to sore throats and colds was because of the more unnatural natural food and herbal potions Linda often concocted and made her daughter take.

Linda promised to be more attentive to Denise's cycle if Denise stayed off Clomid, and the following month they ordered the tank for the fourteenth day of Denise's cycle to be absolutely sure that they didn't miss her ovulation. But when Linda called the doctor's secretary to arrange to pick up the tank, the doctor herself got on the phone. Problems had occurred with payments from Denise's insurance and the doctor, in her most firm, babylike voice, needed to know how they were to be resolved. "I don't usually accept insurance for this service," Dr. Spears informed Linda, "but I negotiate the process for my patients as a favor to them for as long as I can. I've reached my limit on this, however. I can't let you have a tank without payment."

Linda was furious at the doctor for berating her for something that she had not even known was a problem, but she kept her anger inside, chanting it away, really, as she drove across town to pick up the tank and to leave a check with the doctor. By the twenty-first day of Denise's cycle, Denise still had not yet ovulated and the tank had to be replaced—the liquid nitrogen stopped freezing after seven days—and Linda was once again forced to leave another check with the doctor.

Finally, on the twenty-third day, Denise started to get cervical mucus. Their wait was cut short that month when Denise got her period eleven days after insemination, her flow unusually heavy the following two days, so bad, actually, that Linda was worried that Denise might be hemorrhaging. Denise had believed she had somehow miscarried. When Denise got the doctor on the phone, Dr. Spears affirmed, "Perhaps it was a miscarriage," in such an unconcerned, disaffected manner, that Denise slammed the phone down on her and vowed never to go back to that clinic. Vince, however, described it as a possible menstrual miscarriage when Denise had called him for advice; he had searched and found an article in one of the medical journals he kept stacked on his bookshelves.

The following month Denise and Linda decided to skip insemination, not because Denise felt defeated or depressed, though she was by then certainly worn down, but because they had planned a vacation to take Amy camping outside of Seattle, and the logistics and expense of lugging the tank around with them, coupled with the unresolved insurance problems and the doctor's insouciant manner, had convinced them to take a break from attempting to conceive a child. The break, of course, did not remove the possibility of having a child from Denise's thoughts.

"The earliest would be May," Denise had said to Linda the afternoon they were driving to a campground near Olympic National Park. Amy was asleep in the back seat of the Jeep, clutching a doll to her chest.

"For what?" Linda had responded quickly, before the realization of what Denise was thinking had become obvious to her. "It's not really that far away," she then added.

"You're being a bit too optimistic," Denise said. "Even more than I am."

"I'm on your side, Denise," Linda answered. "You seem to forget that sometimes. I want the baby, too."

"I'm sorry," Denise apologized. "I just wish there were an easier way."
"There are other ways," Linda said. "I don't know if they are any easier."

"How would you feel if I asked Jeff?"

"Jeff?" Linda said. "For what?"

"To be a donor. We have all the tools. We know how to do it. It would save the expense. And Jeff's perfect. Physically so beautiful, you know. I'd love to have a boy that would grow up looking like him."

"But Vince is sick, Denise."

"But Jeff isn't."

"That doesn't mean he isn't infected," Linda said. "You're crazy to even suggest it. To even think it. This whole thing is making you crazy. Jeff won't even be tested because he's certain what the results will be. And I don't think, even if he convinced himself that he were out of danger, he would do it unless he was absolutely certain, which we all know he's not. Because he doesn't want it confirmed. It seems a bit irresponsible to me, Denise. It's bad enough that we have had to rely on sperm from people we don't know."

"That doesn't mean that we can't find another donor," Denise said.

"I won't fight you on finding a donor we know," Linda answered. "But we could also consider adoption."

"There's Lyndon, he could do it," Denise said, not willing to regard the possibility of adoption just yet. "Or Lyndon's boyfriend, Barry. I'm sure we could work out something with them. Or what about Robbie?"

"But he would have to get tested again, too."

"He would do it if we asked him to."

"We have to consider legal matters, too, if we get someone to be a donor for us."

"I don't think Robbie would challenge anything we wanted."

"Would this make you happy?" she asked Denise, which was the exact same question I asked her when she posed the situation to me when she returned from her vacation. I had been putting new shelves into the upstairs hall closet and had scratched my arms against the wood and had gone to the bathroom to rinse my arms and hands in the sink. I had left the door open when Denise had wandered up the stairs. Instead of entering Amy's bedroom, she had stopped by the bathroom door.

"Would you consider being a donor for me?" she asked me directly, without easing into any sort of conversation.

I could tell she had been somewhere else in the house brooding over asking me this question, had worked up enough nerve to just walk up the stairs and deliver it to me point blank. I knew of all the problems with the doctor and the insurance, and what details Denise had neglected to tell me, Linda or Vince had relayed to me the unknown facts. I even knew about Denise and Linda's conversation in the car as well; Linda had felt me out about the notion of being a donor before Denise had started to work up her courage to ask me about the possibility. Still, when I looked up at Denise, I felt myself blush as though I had no forewarning of her request, and I turned away briefly from her to dry my hands on a towel.

"I'll pay for whatever tests we need to have done to make sure it would work." She stood before me, tiny and fragile-looking, like a China doll tottering on a ledge, her eyes puffing up as she waited for my answer, her fists balled up at her side. "I'd be good to the child, Robbie. I'd be a good mother."

"I don't doubt that, Denise," I answered. The weight of her question had only really sunk in and I was frightened by whatever answer I could give. "Would this make you happy?" I asked her, instead, feeling so oddly huge and cumbersome so close to her.

"Yes," she answered me without hesitation. "I think of you as family already."

I never believed I had the power to create life, never assumed that I could genetically pass on my characteristics and thoughts and looks and personality to another generation, never understood that a fluid released from my body could change a succession of lives beyond my own. That fluid had always seemed a product borne of something else—at once dirty or passionate, at times simply a discharge, something merely to be wiped away or cleaned off after its release from the body. The possibility of my fathering a child involved a lot of conditions, a succession of discussions and meetings and tests and contracts which often professed to contain more passion and power than the belief I could muster that my sperm could somehow be successful in making Denise pregnant.

At first, I had resisted Denise's suggestion of becoming a donor by avoiding discussing it any further with Denise. At the forefront of my mind was the knowledge of Nathan's death. I had always assumed, for instance, that I was, in part, responsible for infecting him, in spite of the fact that I continued to test negative for HIV. What if AIDS were not caused by HIV but by some other unknown or undetected virus? I had wondered. What if I carried other diseases genetically inside myself?

Denise said she would accept the advice of whatever her new physician would recommend—a gay male doctor she had been referred to at USC. "And after all, Robbie," she said to me one day when I was obsessing on the risks I presented to her, "I haven't exactly been a virgin myself."

The whole concept of fathering seemed so removed to me when the day arrived and I shut myself off in the upstairs bathroom. I had, by then, been tested for HIV, seen Linda's lawyer three times, and signed two agreements potentially limiting my parental claims, financial responsibilities, custody and visitation rights. In the mirror my nipples stared back at me like innocent, unblinking eyes and I turned my gaze away from them, back to the magazine I had propped up on the back of the toilet tank. My father had always considered masturbation as the devil's gateway and I'm sure he would have considered this insemination-by-donor process as trespassing on God's territory, but I realized as I looked down at myself that I had no sense of sinning that day, no sense, either, that I was tampering with God's plan. I clutched my cock, nursing it, really, believing that the guy I had turned to in the magazine—the hairy Naval cadet on page 38—was somehow present in the bathroom, himself caressing my nipples into tight, erotic points on my body. He seemed, of course, so at odds with the purpose of my masturbation—to help create a family, so much so, actually, that it took me longer than I had expected to reach an orgasm, conscious too much of the import of the result and the necessity of coming into the condom, which I had to gently unravel from my cock and leave for Linda, who would within an hour suck the come into a needleless hypodermic syringe.

I stayed in my bedroom until I heard Linda leave my bathroom and run down the stairs. When I was sure she was gone, downstairs in their bedroom attending to Denise, I went back into the bathroom with the intention of showering, but instead found myself standing in front of the mirror which I had hung on the back of the door, noticing my stomach hanging over the waist of the shorts I wore. How had I ever ended up like this? I wondered. I had become so heavy. Was I eating too much? Or was this just age, creeping like a trail of ivy at my waist?

My hairline had receded too, I thought, and the gray was clearly obvious now, especially on the sides. Oddly, however, I noticed I had somehow grown into my face—once upon a time, so boyish, it now seemed caught up the with the body aging beneath it. It was then that I tilted my face toward the ceiling, the way I used to do years ago at a bar, hoping the spotlights would catch the bones of my cheek, hoping to create some mystique to an otherwise confused, aging young man.

What I saw before me that day, as I looked down the slope of my nose at the image before me, was a rather sexless figure, I thought. It wasn't that I was not attractive—there were the features that had always been there, that I had always believed were part of my attractiveness—it was just that the aura of me, the sexuality of my body had disappeared. Or was it simply that I had finally and completely lost my self-esteem? The truth was I could never believe in my features the way others had throughout the years. I could never believe, either, in the way I had noticed other gay men regard themselves in the reflective surfaces of our culture—primping in front of the mirrors at the gym or a bar, their hands racing along the sides of their hair or testing the smoothness of the beard at their jaw. I had always looked away from my reflections there, however, for what I often saw was a man burdened by too many things, most of all thoughts of himself instead of others.

How could I regard myself, then, if I fathered a child? When Vince found out that I had fathered a child with Denise, as I felt certain he eventually would if it came to pass (and if he didn't already know), would he still believe I had abandoned gay life, when, in essence, I felt I, myself, had embraced it even further? As I looked at myself in the mirror, I tried thinking up possible reasons and scenarios of why I did it (discounting the real reason, of course, because Denise had asked and wanted me to); the best answer I could fabricate, I decided, was that it really wasn't my sperm but Nathan's—sperm that I had had flown in from the clinic he had gone to in Manhattan back during the days when we first met. I knew, of course, in practicality and reality, such a method could never exist—my imagining as foolish as Nathan's science-fiction films and comic book plots had been.

The irony of all these thoughts was that in the end they proved to be inconsequential. The experiment with my sperm that month failed to impregnate Denise, as was the case the following month as well, but Vince, once he had found out that I was the donor, urged me to continue, and my sperm was tested and retested for its potency. But that was also the month that Denise's new doctor told her that one of her fallopian tubes was blocked and another filled with scar tissue. The scar tissue was removed and it was discovered that her cervical mucous was fighting against the sperm, interfering with her chances of pregnancy.

Once Denise realized that her body was not her ally in achieving her pregnancy, she never let her disappointment overwhelm her; instead, she thought of becoming pregnant as a new battle to win. Denise's mother, however, was thoroughly horrified when Denise began to explain her options, which more and more seemed to point in the direction of in vitro inseminations. Mrs. Connelly suggested that perhaps Denise should spend her money on therapy and counseling instead of visits to doctors and sperm banks. In fact, Mrs. Connelly had been so vocally distraught by this new turn of events that Denise and Linda drew up another agreement that transferred the rights of potential guardianship of their potential child to someone other than Denise's mother. Denise had wanted, if the child was to occur with my help, to allow me the choice of parental rights should anything happen to one or to both of them.

Jeff once said that he believed most gay men developed their bodies as a surrogate for developing their souls, that the bulk, muscle and definition of their physiques bequeathed them a self-esteem which faith and spiritual enlightenment could not provide them. Vince, however, believed that gay men overly-developed their bodies in order to avoid developing their responsibilities, refusing to grow up and take a place in society and commit to relationships. All I learned, that year, was how important my body and my relationships were in defining myself as a gay man. That was the year my body continued to physically disappoint me, the year I gained close to fifteen pounds, the year, too, I almost sliced my thumb off trying to remove an excess portion of a post of the deck I had started building in the back yard. That was the year Amy battled first measles and then chickenpox, Vince was found wandering around the L.A. County Museum of Art one day when he had blacked out, completely forgetting who he was, the same year that Jeff refused to do a scene in a music video because it required him to do full frontal nudity. That was the year, 1991, that Denise began in vitro inseminations in the spring, and after three unsuccessful attempts she finally became pregnant, twenty-seven months after her first attempt with insemination. Through it all I had continued to be the sperm donor. The day that she called me from the doctor's office to tell me the news it was a scorching day in late June; I had been outside working on the new stairs for the deck, but had had to stop and rest because the heat had gotten the better of me. As she laughed over the phone it was impossible not to share her happiness, but there was a cautiousness I detected, as well, as if she were afraid to be too happy—after all, she admitted later in the conversation, there were still months and months and months ahead. She still had the pregnancy to go through.

When I hung up from her I felt a giddiness I could not yet understand. A *child*, I thought. I could be a father. A *gay* father. Even though I had long ago removed myself emotionally from the act of conception, the awe of it, the power of the idea of it, certainly, becoming a gay father, moved me in a way I had not experienced since I had loved Nathan, bequeathing me a future, really, I had never expected to own again in my lifetime. Back out in the yard a new strength infused my work, my body moved with vigor, self-assurance, and happiness, a strange aura of sensuality floating around me. I felt as if I were an invincible young man of nineteen again, arriving in a new city to start a new life. I felt as intoxicated and omnipotent as the day, more than fifteen years before, that I realized I was undoubtedly gay and that was how I wanted to live my life. Looking skyward, I shouted out a laugh, as if I were thanking God and mimicking him both at the same time. It was then that I realized Nathan's hold on me was finally easing itself. And it was then, that day, I created a space for someone else.

15

These are the stories I could tell my child. In the briefest, most concise manner, I could say that Paul was born in Maryland and died in Los Angeles, Stuart lived on Robertson for over ten years but doesn't anymore, and Warren was a devoted fan of the movies. I could, however, embellish them a little more: Paul moved to L.A. after he graduated from college at Johns Hopkins, Stuart was born in San Diego, and Warren always preferred San Francisco to Los Angeles. The truth of these stories, however, emerge with the more specific details I add. Paul fell in love with a man and died of an infection of the brain normally associated with birds. Stuart never wanted to settle down with anyone till he met Clint but was stopped short by a sudden heart attack while waiting in an emergency room to be treated for dehydration. Warren watched movie after movie after he went on disability; that is, until he went blind and was reduced to only listening.

These stories, then, are impregnated with anger, more so than those stories I was a part of in the years before them, the years I moved about with as much bewilderment as with disbelief. I can clearly recall the day I drove Stuart to Orange County where he chained himself to a desk in Senator Seymour's office, can easily remember the day I handed out *Silence=Death* buttons with Warren outside the Academy Awards, can vividly recount the time, too, that Paul and I carried placards while President Bush addressed graduates at Cal Tech. Governor Wilson's veto of a bill outlawing workplace discrimination had also created a ripple of protests within my community of gay friends that year, and no one—not Paul, Warren, Stuart, nor even Vince—had to convince me to march or yell or demonstrate. I marched to the Hollywood Bowl, protested at LAX, rode a "freedom ride" bus to Sacramento, sat down in the middle of Avenue of the Stars outside the Century Plaza and blew a whistle and shouted till the police forced me to move. "This is what keeps me alive," Vince told a reporter that day, a sentiment I had always hoped to match but could never justify with the same amount of urgency because I considered myself incriminated with health. I marched because of what I had lost, what I was losing, and what I wanted to keep.

An electricity of uncertainty always heightened my support no matter how I gave it. There was always something more to it for me than just being a participant of a demonstration, something more than just the exhilaration I found from blending my shouts into the growing chant of a mob, something more than being visibly recognized by witnesses as attached to a cause, something more than the simple moments of intimacy which could happen when a fellow marcher, for instance, would draw by my side, smile and cement his friendship with the casual disclosure of the decline of his T-cells. I was there most of all because of my friendship with Vince—Vince, the dark and beautiful, brooding playwright who had abandoned his noble craft to assist the dying and fight the system for change. I was there to help him. And, of course, to remember Nathan.

There was always an uneasiness which haunted me at these events, however—that someone could collapse from exhaustion or that a rumor would fly through the crowd like a fact and an angry riot would ensue. I wasn't afraid of being arrested; my greatest fear was that something could get perilously out of hand, that no matter after how many weeks and weeks of planning something could go awry, a spontaneous disruption could take place that had not been discussed in advance or sanctioned by a vote, the repercussions of which would result in charges or casualties that could never be changed or rescinded. Somebody will be hurt from this, I always thought, though Vince often reminded me that we were there to be militant, not violent, a distinction too many people often blurred.

But fear never prevented me from finding my place in the crowd nor from hearing my voice within their chants; my energy never failed me—day after day I felt it necessary to summon up a never-ending rage. Everyone in my gay world was fighting on some level or another, learning how to cope, relearning how to live. I went to meeting after meeting and action after action. I know, now, that it was hope that kept me going, the same hope that I had known years before during Nathan's struggles but strengthened, then, by the collective sound of others. The dynamics of mob rule had nothing to do with the creation of my energy. It was the individual stories that kept me going, an army of fellow activists and friends who kept me sustained and active and angry and out-front and coming back and yelling and shouting and fighting to make things better.

These are the stories I must remember, then, the stories I must repeat to myself over and over before they are lost not only from myself but from history as well, the stories I must repeat to whomever shall pass through my life: the way Warren, dressed like an Ivy Leaguer in a white button down shirt and chinos, stood before the rag tag jeans and T-shirt membership and raged on and on one evening about Burroughs Wellcome's AZT monopoly and how we had to support the action organized by the New York chapter and that the prices had to be scaled down, the way Stuart, whose profile I always thought belonged in a sepia tinted photograph, wore a baseball cap on backwards, not as a statement, as was the wont of gay fashion, but because he had lost his hair from medication and radiation therapy, the way, too, when Paul, his asymmetrical Ichabod Crane-like frame had become perilously too thin, was arrested, paradoxically, at an AIDS convention for overturning a table, screamed at the security guard who handcuffed his long, bony wrists, "You're incarcerating a dying man."

I discovered that these stories ended no differently than the others, of course; that summer Vince and I drove down to Castle Park, a suburb of San Diego, for Stuart's funeral. I tried to find the words to say to his parents that their son was a good man, that he fought the good fight, but the words choked at the back of my throat and I sat on a flimsy folding chair in the upstairs room of a funeral home which overlooked a strip shopping center and buried my head in my hands unable to block out the annoying flickering fluorescent light which crept in from the hallway. Anger, I knew, then, was not an appropriate response to summon up, so I simply sat there and felt miserable.

I had last seen Stuart speaking at an ACT UP meeting a month before he died, his skin flushed cinnamon colored with worry, even through the makeup foundation he wore to hide the lesion on his left cheek and chin, as he strained to detail the side effects he had experienced from taking DHPG. Stuart had been one of the original founders of the L.A. chapter. A graduate of San Francisco State University, he had worked as a Postal Service carrier before he went on disability; later, he served on the board of directors of Health Access, a network of California organizations working for a statewide health care system. His symptoms first began in 1987, back in the year that Nathan was first falling sick as well. Stuart was only twenty-seven that year and he once told me that very early on he learned three important things which he credited with his long term survival: his T4 cells were very low, his immune suppresser T8 cells were high, and it was clear to him that the medical establishment had no idea what was going on inside his body, a story I had heard many men tell me before.

At his funeral Vince told the story of how Stuart would volunteer for things nobody else would try, dangerous stuff, like Compound Q and Viroxan, but that the skepticism, the fright of the fight, was what had kept Stuart alive. "He was a little crazy, for sure, I think," Vince had said with a wry smile. "But crazy in a good way, like the way on Halloween he would always dress up as The Ghost of Elvis Presley and hand out candy corn in prescription drug vials."

It has taken me a long time to remember how confusing those first few years in California were for me, how many stories were caught up within each other at the same moment, each coloring and defining the other. I've wondered lately if I should have clipped more newspaper articles or magazine stories to remind myself of how everything changed again and again and again in my life. All I have, really, is the sudden burst of recognition of those changes when memory is precipitated, for instance, by a song that comes on suddenly on the car stereo, a song that was rooted so distinctly in that time, something sappy or sentimental, usually, like a Michael Bolton or Natalie Cole ballad, or a song that was played over and over till it had its own meaning for me, something like Whitney's Houston's "I Will Always Love You," the theme song of a movie I never saw but whose story I reinvented in order for the song to ring true to me.

I have no problem with recalling the basic plot of those years; it's the details that overwhelm me, pull me out of orbit, and send me spiraling into a depression. In the simplest of ways this was what happened: Jeff died and Kenny was born. In that order. One. Two. Death. Birth. Neither the completion of a story, nor the beginning of another, really. Too much happens after birth. Not enough is done after death. The details of both, however, are entwined in each other. Jeff got sick. Denise gave birth.

A week after Thanksgiving Jeff was helping Denise to assemble her fake silver Christmas tree when he squatted to retrieve one of the branches from the box, a position he had often assumed in the gym for years carrying a tremendous amount of weight at his shoulders. As he lifted the branch out of the box and stood to snap it into place on the trunk of the tree, his vision, which had been becoming poorer during the last few weeks but nothing to be alarmed about, or so he thought, suddenly got horrendous. Everything became a blur and he felt a tightening at his chest. Scared that he was having a stroke he took a few steps and collapsed on the floor in the grip of a grand mal seizure. Denise, frightened, called an ambulance, but by the time the medics arrived, almost an hour later, Jeff was fine and attributed his collapse to some kind of freak accident or a reaction to something he might have eaten. Jeff, of course, looked no different than he had before his accident. At thirty-five he was over six feet tall and at 215 pounds was impressively built. When Jeff saw Vince's doctor the following day he was referred to a neurologist, but a week later, after another seizure, this time in Denise's doctor's waiting room while Denise was having her routine sonogram, her doctor suggested that Jeff, once he had again recovered, should be tested for HIV.

Things got worse, of course. An AIDS expert, after consulting with specialists and conducting a battery of tests, concluded that Jeff had full blown AIDS; exploratory brain surgery revealed that he had progressive multifocal leukoencephalopathy, an untreatable brain infection usually fatal within four months after the onset of symptoms. Jeff was hospitalized for a variety of successive illnesses, but in February he had a turnaround that his doctors couldn't explain, as if somebody had switched the channel on a TV set and a completely different program was showing. Vince always believed it was Denise's pregnancy that sustained Jeff. That Jeff's illness and Denise's pregnancy coincided is undoubtedly the reason why Denise's memories of those months are almost entirely confined to doctors' visits for herself or with Jeff. We all knew the ravages of what AIDS could do to a body, knew what to expect as the virus mutated into illnesses and weakened not only the man in which the virus harbored, but the souls of those who aided and comforted as well. But Jeff looked magnificent and healthy; it didn't seem right. Instead, Vince's face seemed to carry the strain of Jeff's illness more than Jeff's body, and Denise, her own body changing more and more every day with the growing weight of the baby, could only force questions out as greetings and good-byes: "What should we do? What should we do? What should we do now?"

Denise, in fact, became a worried flurry of questions as her pregnancy overwhelmed her: Why should she have an amniocentesis? What if the baby didn't turn? What if her pelvis was too small? Should she even be having routine sonograms? Denise sank into a depression long before the baby was born, and we all huddled into little groups, worried, discussing—even with Jeff—that her depression, her despondency, would somehow psychologically deform the child she was carrying. Whenever she was at Jeff's apartment, Jeff would do things for her no matter how at ill he felt himself: propping her feet up with a cushion, offering her juice or fruit, offering her, even, the lotion he used to keep his skin from dehydrating.

Denise questioned her own doctors as well: Why did she feel so weak? Why was she getting cramps? Was it normal for her blood pressure to escalate so rapidly? Little things began to bother her: the sound of the lawn mower two houses down the street, the poor TV reception, even the way the kitchen tap water smelled too much like chlorine. Once, when Linda discovered Denise crying in the kitchen, Denise told her that the reason was because she had no idea how much salt she should be having during a pregnancy, though Linda knew better than to believe that excuse: Denise had just hung up the phone from talking with Jeff.

Denise's pregnancy gave Jeff something to think about besides being sick, gave all of us something to think about instead of focusing our worry so explicitly on Jeff, or, at least, prevented us from vocally expressing our worries so resolutely—all of us, except Denise's mother, that is, who constantly questioned Denise on whether or not she should be hanging around and helping someone who, well, you know was not well. Our days—Linda's, Vince's, Denise's and my own—were devised to quietly keep track of Jeff, looking to see if pills were missing from his bottles, examining the contents to be sure he wasn't skipping his medication, or touching him at the neck when we greeted him, the hidden purpose being to see if his skin felt as if he was running a fever.

But we all seemed to wander through lethargic movements, too, knowing we had to do this or clean that or go there, relishing at times, just the solitude of driving alone in a car from one house to another, the radio tuned into the *Way-ee-yave*, the new-age-cosmic-chord music station that Linda had insisted we always listen to. Linda seemed to move more into herself during Jeff's illness, or, at least, curiously, so measurably away from Denise, as though willingly allowing Denise to share more time alone with Jeff. Only Amy, now almost six, seemed to move into warp speed, always zooming in and out of a room with a doll or a toy, throwing her dress playfully over her head to hide her eyes and giggling, not even videotapes could keep her still. At times she would pout or storm out of the room, upset because her mother would suddenly give more attention to Denise's needs than to the child's wants. Amy, once again, became my escape and refuge as I tried to pick up the slack within the household; and besides, I knew, it was so much easier to notice her shoes were untied than to call Jeff and inquire when he had last taken his medication.

It was Jeff who suggested the demonstration at the Oscars that year, Jeff who had never demonstrated at all before—though it wasn't like he hadn't been supportive of causes: He had been. Jeff's nature had always been to be more of a contributor than a participant. At first Vince's feathers were ruffled by the suggestion; activism, after all, was Vince's domain in their partnership, and anger had become one of Vince's more defining traits. What did Jeff know about protesting or demonstrating or civil disobedience? Vince wanted to know when he told me of the suggestion one evening on the phone. Then he changed his tone, suddenly worried that this was Jeff's way of giving up, of not getting on the wagon and fighting for his own health. Jeff had been closeted professionally for years, steadfastly so; wouldn't being seen at a demonstration end all that? Wouldn't that mean an end to his career? Wouldn't that mean, then, that Jeff was giving up? When Denise asked Jeff the same question a few days later after all of us had discussed Jeff's motive behind his back, Jeff replied, "I want to be arrested. It's time to be seen, not seen through."

I don't know why I am still alive, or how, but I hope by somehow reviewing the stories of my life and the stories which intersect them that I will stumble onto some kind of understanding or meaning or lesson I must carry forward through the rest of my life. Most of these stories do not exist in the world separately, isolated or detached, but are rooted in specific times and places and sentiments of history. The story of the demonstrations that year at the Academy Awards where Jeff was indeed arrested is rooted in years and years of Hollywood's unfavorable portrayal of gays and lesbians in film, heightened, as well, by a continued unresponsiveness to AIDS, a host of closeted performers, and a sequence of unflattering portrayals of gay characters in recently released mainstream films. Kenny's birth, on the other hand, is tied up within the history of the city itself, the history of the nation, really, though it is now difficult to find the truth in the facts of what happened, difficult to separate what happened from what seemed to happen. What seemed to happen, in fact, has become its own story in its retelling. Denise had gone to her loft that morning to find some slides of her paintings to send to a gallery in South Beach which had written her and expressed an interest in mounting a show of her new paintings. She had been running late that afternoon, had not paid any attention to the weather or the news, her focus only on getting the slides in the mail before she forgot to do them or got too busy to remember otherwise. Her due date was not for another two weeks but she had had an anxious feeling that morning when she got out of bed. She had attributed her uneasiness to Jeff, but she checked in with him before leaving the house that day, and her mind had wandered back to the gallery in Florida, wondering if she had time to complete the new painting she had started before the baby was born.

She had known nothing of Rodney King except what had filtered into her consciousness from overhearing the news as it drifted out from television reports or the car radio that month. Cops beating a black man who was resisting arrest. A trial in Simi Valley. Nothing, however, about the pervasive racial uneasiness which existed throughout the city.

She had been looking at a page of slides when she heard the sound of glass breaking on the floor beneath her, followed, a few seconds later, by an alarm going off downstairs which she thought must have been from the jewelry store on the corner. She went to the window and noticed a gang of boys running across the street. She thought it odd that there was no traffic on Melrose—it was so close to rush hour—and in the distance, out of the corner of her window, she thought she could detect the gray funnel of smoke rising from a fire. Denise and Lyndon had never felt the need to have a phone installed in their workspace—and they hadn't wanted the expense—and Denise's first thought was to go downstairs to the corner and call 911. At the moment Denise was working her way down the stairs she felt her first contraction, disbelieved it, rather, thinking it must be a reaction from her growing fear of the moment. At that instant Linda was on her way to pick up Amy from a friend's house and bring her back home—Linda had already dispatched me to check on Denise at the loft. Later, much later, Denise would describe the assemblage of events as if it were scenes from a movie, the way she clutched her stomach upon reaching the bottom of the stairs and pushed open the glass door, the sound of sirens in the background cracking loudly in her ear as she stepped outside, the way she had turned her head back and forth as she rushed with quick little steps out onto the sidewalk and in an instant recognized my car as I turned the corner and waved her inside.

My participation in the story of Kenny's birth that day removed, in part, my participation from Jeff's death that evening, the events now, in recollection, seem spaced so far apart in some vast, deep sky that I believe, at times, they must have occurred on different planets. Looking back I can scarcely believe that the events had come so close together. Denise, at USC, being helped through her breathing patterns by a nurse because her frightened doctor had left the building, en route to check on her house in Bel-Air; while Jeff, a few miles away, collapsed on his floor from the shock of another seizure. Vince had been at the apartment that afternoon, had seen Jeff walk out of the kitchen with a glass of root beer in one hand and suddenly crumble to the floor. The glass had not shattered, not even when Jeff dropped it and clutched the sides of his head with his hands. The glass had just tinkled, really, as it hit the carpet—though the soda had puddled and seeped about Jeff's body like blood. Vince had known then that that was the end of Jeff, but he had tried to revive him anyway, first, with mouth-to-mouth resuscitation, then, by beating his fist against Jeff's chest. He called 911 but could not get an answer; he got no answer, either, when he called our house, leaving only an urgent message for one of us to call him back as soon as possible. He could not move Jeff from the floor—even then, after dropping close to twenty pounds, Jeff was too heavy for Vince to lift or carry or push or drag. He ran to the house next door but no one was home; then began shouting out the window till a neighbor looked out and ran across the street to help. Consciously, Vince had known nothing more about Rodney King than Denise had; had not been prepared to find more crises at the emergency room than he believed could be possible. When he and his neighbor, a forty-seven-year-old woman named Sheila Gold, arrived at Cedars-Sinai, a doctor had pronounced Jeff dead in the parking lot while Jeff was still in the back seat of Sheila's car. Vince had then waited patiently for two hours until an intern arrived with a stretcher to take Jeff to the hospital morgue.

When Linda arrived at USC later that afternoon with Amy she had said there had been a frantic message from Vince, but no one had answered the phone at his apartment when she had called him back. Kenny was born when I was turning onto Sunset Boulevard that evening, I believe, on my way from the hospital to Vince's apartment. I had waited at Vince's apartment for over an hour until the phone rang—I knew it would be Vince retrieving his messages. "Tell me where you are," I said when he recognized my voice. "Robbie," he said, though I did not let him complete his sentence—I could tell from the sound of his voice exactly what had happened. "I know, Vince," I said, squeezing the receiver of the phone in my hand. "I'm on my way to you right now."

The news had been full of stories the next morning: A mob had torched the guardhouse outside police headquarters, fires had been set inside city hall, Koreatown had been looted and was burning. A truck driver had been hauled from his cab and kicked, smashed in the head with a fire extinguisher; a man driving home from soccer practice was hit by a bullet and killed; two men riding a motorcycle were shot; the riders in a stolen car had died when it flipped over after a high speed chase by cops. Buses and trains had stopped, schools were closed, the highways were clogged with people trying to get out of town.

I can remember clearly how upset I had been that morning as I watched the news on television, not because those stories existed so closely around me but because I had felt so entirely removed from them; I had stayed with Vince at his apartment that evening, and had waited until the last possible moment the next morning to call Denise and Linda and tell them about Jeff's death, as if the horrendous news of the riots would somehow displace my own sad news about Jeff. Linda had stayed at the hospital with Denise overnight; she had arranged for her brother to pick up Amy and watch her for a few days. When I called Denise's room Linda answered the phone, and I asked first about the baby in a horrid, fake-cheery voice—a boy, no name yet, everyone doing fine, Linda had responded in an exuberant manner. I felt so removed from the idea that I was a father, the force of it failed to register. "I can either tell her about Jeff or you can," I said, losing my repose, hearing as I did, a gush of air escape my own lungs.

"Oh," she said, not really an answer to me but a whimper, rather, the soft high-pitch of a whine which sounds more like the beginning of a sob. "Tell me what happened."

So many stories, I remember thinking as I repeated the story of Jeff's death as I knew it. Birth, death, destruction, unhappiness. How does all this happen so closely together? Now and then when I think about these stories I realize how much more powerful things were in my life other than my belief in God. God does not prevent death, I had realized that morning when I had left Linda on the phone to get Vince because she wanted to speak to him. Nor does he create life. Nor can he bequeath immortality. Nor can he decide what memories I shall retain, or what stories history will forget. Nor can he be judgmental, really. Nor should he be. Is God's purpose, then, to make you simply feel so powerless as things spin so chaotically out of control around you?

What I learned, that morning, from all those stories, was that strength is not always drawn from other people, or other stories, or from the way the world works, or from religion or a belief or disbelief in God—sometimes it simply must come from yourself, from somewhere, some place deep within yourself, from a belief in yourself, really, that you, alone, are the source of your own power or lack of it, that its shape and force is determined only by you. As I watched Vince with the phone against his ear, his eyes unblinking, a coldness set within his blue-stubbled jaw, I knew I had to find a way to keep on going— to fight and be angry and helpful and, well, alive, and just keep doing. I had to find myself.

"Vince," I said, when he had hung up the phone, my mind already defeating any potential obstacle the world had to toss in my path at that moment. "Go get dressed. I'll drive you over to see the baby."

After my mother died when I was twelve years old I told myself that I would never forget her, that she would always be with me as a part of who I am, a fact I repeated to myself in the same boyish manner when I had heard, in the early years of the epidemic, that Alex had died. By saying that I would not forget them I could keep them resolutely alive, their spirits, voices and features still ringing inside my mind. Alex was the first person close to me that I lost in the epidemic, and I dismissed his death as a fluke, really, a freaky and unexpected casualty. By the time Nathan died I could count more than forty friends, acquaintances, dates, and tricks I had lost to AIDS, my I-won't-forgets had turned into some sort of mournful mantra, my solitude invaded by a world of ghosts.

When AIDS first began and the losses began to mount, I believed, truly believed, that an end was in sight, a light could be seen at the tunnel's edge. The end was something possible and attainable, the talk of an epidemic merely alarmist and histrionic, the disease would be swiftly vanquished by science and medicine. That concept changed as the death toll continued to climb; soon I found I could grieve for men I had never met. And something inside me changed as the years passed by and more and more died, a numbness took hold of me, as if a washrag had been wrung of all its water and had been left outside in the hot air to dry, its consistency changing to a stiff, parched cloth, its color fading with age and from the brutal elements of nature. I'd always thought that change in feeling had something to do with the intensity for which I had felt over my lover's death, but the truth was I later learned that it was the added psychological consequence of experiencing multiple loss— death after death after death. By the time Jeff died, the passionate hatred I had felt because of Nathan's fate was now more of a low burning flame. Perhaps that had to do with the deaths of so many others I knew in between their two deaths, perhaps it had to do with the passage of time, perhaps it had something to do, as well, with my becoming a father. Whatever, the absence of such hate did not diminish the force of the loss.

In the days following Jeff's death, Denise was perceptively shaken, as if she had fallen asleep in a field of poppies and awakened in a different world. She couldn't focus, moved to tears at the sight of Kenny's soiled diapers, unable to breast feed or hold him in her arms, as if she had realized a part of herself had died with Jeff, which, of course, it had. Linda had taken time off from the store, and it was she who moved around the house, an old stoic in a young woman's body, giving an order and meaning to the chores ahead of us, a great walled fortress around our sorrow. It was a delicate, impossible balance for her to maintain—her inner realm punctured at some point, too, by sadness. Linda began to amend the casual displacement that had always marked her personality, however, coming into a room now and hugging someone from behind, as if the contact of a body against another body could somehow dissolve the sorrow present within her mind.

We did so little to put a closure to Jeff's death, for one thing the new baby occupied a great deal of our attention, but none of us were willing, either, to let go of the memory of Jeff; at times we even tried tricking ourselves into thinking it had never happened. Denise, at first, had created some sort of solace in her mind by believing that Jeff had lived long enough to sense that Kenny was being born. Vince, of course, had his own daily challenges because of his steadily declining health, using it as a weapon, too, to keep Jeff's parents from arriving in town. "There's no more harm for you to do," Vince said to Jeff's father when he had called the apartment to inquire about the funeral and the whereabouts of his son's belongings. "You've done enough damage. And he hasn't left anything behind."

The truth was he had left plenty behind—a treasure chest filled with years of memories and gifts; concrete, physical reminders of his life—a scrapbook of his print work, videotapes of his commercials—one for a bank still aired years after his death. We did not allow ourselves a funeral for Jeff, however; the immediacy of the riots worried us and we decided that Jeff wouldn't have wanted one anyway. As much as Jeff had thrived and prided himself on his tapes and roles and scrapbooks, he personally liked to live away from the spot-light; he always, for instance, took a back seat to Vince's more public person-ality—maybe not always and not willingly, really, but in the end, especially near the end, he had settled into routines and a comfortable life of close friends, wanting, more than anything, a peaceful psychic existence.

If I were making up Jeff's life, or making a story out of it, would it take the turn it took? Of course not; how often can one bear to hear *how sad* or *what a shame* or *such a pity, he was so young and beautiful*? I wouldn't end it that way, either, if I had the chance to revisit the experience. Jeff, of course, would have been appalled at the idea of a group of us assembled to mourn his loss, though he had, a few years before, sat down with Vince—not long after Vince had found out his HIV-status—and helped Vince plan his memorial. Throughout the process, as Vince often recalled, Jeff would shake his head and repeat, "This is too, too weird. I would never want to orchestrate how someone would remember me."

And so Jeff's body was sent from the hospital to a funeral home and cre-mated; an obituary was listed in the *Times, Daily Variety* and *Hollywood Reporter*; the phone rang and rang and rang; explanations and condolences were offered to callers and receivers. In our conversations small details were remembered about Jeff's life, oddly mixed in with details of the riots and Kenny's birth. We mentioned that we would let everyone know about a future memorial service, but we only said so in order to keep grief a little more at bay.

Time, however, did not move easy for any of us, though we tried to func-tion normally, go on about our day-to-day business in the world. And so the afternoon I was walking along Melrose after seeing Denise at her loft, about two weeks after Jeff's death, out on an errand to photocopy Jeff's death cer-tificate to send to his creditors—a task which I had volunteered to help Vince with—I was consciously aware of my internal voice chanting *I won't forget, I won't forget,* when I was startled to see pairs of empty shoes lining the sidewalk of an alley that led to the entrance of a small theater. At first I thought it must have had something to do with the riots, but as I followed the shoes—black ballet slippers with the toes and sides worn down to a soft white stub, brown and white two-toned character shoes, thick, yellow construction workboots and a pair of shiny black patent tap shoes, I knew that they must have belonged to Warren. I had heard that he had died a day or so ago, Vince had mentioned it in a passing conversation, and the theater is where he had often performed his recital-like shows. Along the path of shoes flowers had been tossed singly or in small bouquets—daisies, peonies, yellow freesias, red and pink roses, some already faded and dried or with their petals broken off and stirring on the cement—creating a trail like Hansel and Gretel's right up to a small sandwich board outside the door of the theater, where notes and cards and photographs and red ribbons and a pair of glass beads were taped and pinned and stapled to its sides. More flowers surrounded the board, flowers in glass wine carafes and shoeboxes and white plastic tubs, giving the whole assemblage the effect of a shrine.

Warren had begun his career in the Ballet Trocadero de Monte Carlo, but he had only lasted a season with the company because he decided he wanted to pursue a more Gene Kelly-like dancing persona than as a drag queen in tutu traipsing about en pointe. He was an exquisite and athletic dancer—everyone said so—and he had developed a cult following on a gay cabaret circuit which stretched from San Francisco to Los Angeles to New Orleans where he performed the shows he choreographed with a small troupe of friends, many of whom, themselves, performed in drag. The one time I saw him perform he did a flamenco with another guy while they were both atop short stilts and wearing only black pants. It was a vivid, exceptional piece of theater—the audience suspended in the belief that the two dancers were bound to topple over.

But Warren had been most noted for his activism, or, rather, the combination of his activism and his dancing. He had performed at benefit after benefit, fundraiser after fundraiser, had been as open about his HIV-status as about his sexuality. Warren had been a member of ACT UP/LA for almost four years, one of the first to join the Los Angeles chapter, and there was little doubt that it had energized and lengthened his life as it had Vince's. They had both participated in several early landmark demos, from the Board of Supervisors sit-ins demanding the opening of a special hospital ward for AIDS patients to being arrested at the Federal Building protest demanding the government relax restrictions on the use of experimental drugs. Warren had also helped organize the foreign travel restrictions protest at the International Conference on AIDS in San Francisco and spearheaded actions at LAX, Sacramento and Woodland Hills against Wilson's veto. The last time I had seen him was at the protest outside the Chandler Pavilion on the afternoon of the Oscars, and my memory of him that day was of him handing out red ribbons to the crowd and wearing dark sunglasses because even then the minimum amount of sunlight irritated his declining eyesight.

"To Warren. May you be in a better place with angels dancing on a cloud," one of the tributes on the sandwich board read. Another story to remember, I thought, then, staring down at the envelope in my hand that contained Jeff's death certificate. But what I felt was nothing, nothing left in my chest except an impossible emptiness, but I had realized, too, in that moment of vacantness for Warren that letting go of Jeff would be as impossible as letting go of Nathan. My mother's death taught me that there was nothing logical to the way death strikes, nothing logical, either, to the way one reacts to it; grief comes in a variety of forms and manners and expressions. Nathan, however, had made me realize that when death happens there's nothing that can ease the process for a survivor except the passage of time, nothing more necessary to recovery than the ability to sit quiet and wait and let time do its own healing. And so I stood in front of that sandwich board that afternoon for a long while, and when some time had passed, I turned and left the alley, knowing, as I made my way back to the sidewalk and joining the other people walking along the street, that I had remembered Warren with the only logical possession I seemed to maintain in the randomness my life had assumed—I had left behind, for a moment for Warren, my sense of time.

I have always maintained my belief that Jeff was Kenny's true father, not in the physiological or biological sense, of course, but in the spiritual sense, perhaps, I think, because their lives are so closely linked together chronologically, and because Denise so needingly one day transferred her friendship with Jeff into a relationship with her new child. But there are times when I look at Kenny and wonder if he is really mine, wonder about the probability of bedroom experiments and the power of genetics, the strength of one sperm over another to reach the final destination of insemination, even though I know, undoubtedly, that I am his biological father. Because I had signed away my strongest and most immediate parental claims on the child, how-ever, I neglected the emotional responsibility of being Kenny's father—a child was too much caught up in my own still vivid history of Nathan. It wasn't that I was so afraid of holding Kenny in my arms or caring for him; each time I did, however, as I felt my skin draw up against the baby's skin I felt the pain of the more unencumbered joy I knew Nathan would have found from the same experience.

But Kenny was also created out of the dynamics of our friendships, our own stitched-together family, our own history, our own position in time. Denise had named him from Jeff's earlier reference to finding the perfect man— Barbie's universal longing for Ken. But there is, I believe, now, as much of the history of Nathan in Kenny as Jeff, Linda or even myself. Our stories, although personal, are also the stories of our community. The details are the differences which set them apart, give them distinction and individuality, the same details which provide and justify a family for Kenny. This is how the homosexual world will alter the larger heterosexual one, the power of one story to stand apart from another.

Jeff once told me that the image he retained from his first seizure, as his mind lost consciousness and descended into blackness, was the figure of a woman in white, a breasty, blond woman dressed in a sheer, see-through teddy nightgown, he said, a woman who had appeared in an issue of *Playboy* sometime before 1970. "My father's revenge," he added. "She was the woman they kept flashing on the screen when he sent me through electric shock therapy." Jeff had spent hours after his seizure trying to restore his psychic wholeness, wondering daily what the image of the woman had to reveal to him not only about himself but his relationship with others.

Jeff had long before abandoned any belief in God, though he still maintained a faith, he said, believing, instead, that his sexual spirit created within himself his own truth—his own gay soul—believing that a gay spirit possessed no gender barrier, believing, too, that as a gay man he possessed something more than a carnal nature, something more than an aggressive mind with an embarrassed cock attached to it. For Jeff, being gay was about discretion and desire and love, not confrontation or declaration. He always considered himself a man who was gay rather than simply a gay man. A gay man, he believed, defined and limited and excluded him too much. Still, the presence of the woman within his mind seemed to once again be a test for him—a collision of his internal spiritual peace against the harsh reality of his history.

"I can't die with anger," he said to me one evening, seeking my alliance during a heated discussion with Vince. "Just because I'm different from my father."

"Then you forgive him," Vince said, not wanting to force Jeff into another confrontation with his family, but to force them into an acceptance of Jeff's life.

"I can't blame him," Jeff replied. "That would mean his God was superior to my own."

"There's more than one God?" I answered, confused by Jeff's logic.

"My father only turns to God when he has a problem, for comfort and absolution," Jeff had said to me. "The God he believes in is a political one, not a religious one; his God is unaccepting of homosexuality—that's not the same God, the same power I embrace. Virtue has nothing to do with sexuality."

And this was when he had turned back to Vince, as if to put a stamp to the end of their argument. "Just because I am not always as open and visible as some other gay men does not mean that I am any less proud of who I am. I was tortured—*tortured* because of something I instinctively possessed. I don't have to be out there in everyone's face to prove something I already know about myself."

Vince, however, was unwilling to let the conversation end. "But who will know it unless you show it?"

"I'll show it to prove my love for you." he replied. "Not because I need to receive some sort of reward for doing it."

I am full of stories to tell my child, stories of love and horror, hate and joy, stories of coming out, stories of first kisses and last wishes, stories of fighting for self-respect and dignity every day of every year. There are thousands and thousands of stories I could tell Kenny about gay pride, of course, how, for instance, millions of gay men and lesbians march openly and proudly down the street in parades every year in cities across the world. As many times as I have seen it or walked in it in recent years, I still come away with an unsettling sense of awe. This is what it feels like to me to march: It's not magnificent, really, more astonishing and implacable, to see that I have come for the same issue that a topless dyke or an Asian drag queen has come for, for instance, or to feel united with a wide, diverse spectrum of people, or to see how important it is to be out and open in society—yet so conspicuously aware, as well, of who I am not—what specific differences set me apart from so many others, even those who can also identify themselves as homosexuals.

There was a lot to be proud of that year; socially and politically, lesbians and gay men were more visible than ever before, the battle half-won by openly gay judges, cops, actors, teachers, and athletes. That summer, the summer of Jeff's death, the small contingent of our family marched with ACT UP in the pride parade in West Hollywood. The morning had begun with the slight tremors of an earthquake and there was a shakiness present as we assembled: Linda and Denise had argued over a hat for Amy to wear, argued, too, if Kenny wasn't just a bit too young to be outside for so long. Vince, however, had demanded that we all go together, though we had fought over whether or not to bring the cane he sometimes now needed to use. In the end, I agreed to carry a long umbrella like a walking stick, to use if necessary as either support for Vince or as a shield from the sun for the children.

Neither was needed that day, however. Amy took particular delight, I remember, from wearing a necklace of multicolored freedom rings and blowing a whistle repeatedly—much to her mother's annoyance, of course—and the three of us, Linda, Denise and myself, took turns carrying and checking on Kenny, pulling an assortment of lotions and drinks from a knapsack I carried on my back. Around us contingents of parents, professional groups, military veterans, women on motorcycles and dancing men on floats marched and paraded behind banners and posters while others waved from the curbs and reviewing stands along Santa Monica, a heady excitement tickling everyone. Everyone has their reason to march or attend, I thought. Everyone had their story, their reason to carry placards or to cheer for someone.

The day I arrived in California, a hot, smoggy day in July almost four years before that parade, Vince had taken me directly to Griffith Park from the airport. It was of those scorching afternoons, bright despite a blanket of haze, as blistering in the shade as it was in the sun, heat rippling off the cars in the Observatory parking lot. We had hiked along the trails toward the summit of Mount Hollywood, a breeze finding us every now and then when we stood squinting at the milky film of air trapped in the city below us. The details of the geography were so foreign to me that day, as unfamiliar as the day, years before, Vince had unraveled Manhattan for me from the deck of the Empire State Building. That afternoon Vince had handed me his sunglasses and I studied the places he had pointed out to me in the distance, the vista of buildings in the Los Angeles basin turning soft and wavy from the haze of the heat.

"On a clear day you can see the Pacific," he said, and then his voice broke into a windy laugh. "But if you're lucky you can just make out the edges of the freeway."

In spite of the haze that day, the panorama views were exhilarating, as Vince knew they would be, and there was a moment, an echo, really, when I was seized once again by the enormity of the stories below us, and my luck of having Vince and Jeff and Denise and Linda in my life to rescue me. But it was also clear to me, a palpable ache, really, that I had left Nathan, or the memory of him, behind in another city.

When does a story become finished? I asked myself the afternoon of the parade, as I handed Kenny back to Denise. Does a story end when someone dies or when someone is forgotten? I wondered, realizing, as I did so, my own answer would assert that someone remains alive as long as the mind still vibrantly believes them to be so. I remember looking up at the reviewing stand of spectators and then out and over them the slope of the Hollywood Hills behind them, the ground, in patches, brown and a little ragged looking between the buildings. Some day, I thought, this will all be over. No more parades, no more AIDS crisis, no more riots or protests or demonstrations— we will just exist, my gay brothers and lesbian sisters, as an accepted, healthy part of society. What we will have will be only our history and our stories, then: how a riot in a bar in New York City could turn into worldwide marches for pride, how there once was a terrible disease and a brave group of men and women stood up and fought and died so that others might live and be free. No heroes, really, just story after story after story.

That was the year that 150,000 people in America had already died of the same disease, and I knew, at that moment, as I returned my attention back toward the parade and reached my arm out to drape around Vince's shoulder, that my own story was still unfinished. And one day my friendship might simply be recalled as a small, somewhat insignificant footnote of a much larger and unfortunate devastating plague. But these were the stories, I knew, that I must tell my child to tell his own. Stories to repeat and repeat and repeat again. Stories, which like their tellers, must never consider themselves finished.

By all accounts I should be dead by now and unable to tell these stories. That I lived through such an unsettling era of gay life and be able to recount those times still amazes me, though I do not consider myself a survivor. I have made it thus far, I sometimes believe, simply from a combination of luck and fate. Some may see my stories of loss and despair and death after death after death as such bleak and sad tales, and many days I must remind myself, too, of the enigmatic gifts I've received from such uncertainty, bitterness and loss. I would never say that AIDS was a good thing, of course—that there had been a purpose behind all this pain and dying and loss and grief. But I would also be wrong to say that AIDS did not make some changes in my life that I would not have made otherwise, exposed me to experiences and emotions and events that shaped and molded my consciousness in a way that I could never have imagined as a young man.

In the days following Jeff's death, Vince became more and more politically active. He had campaigned against Ross Perot, campaigned against George Bush, campaigned so insistently for Bill Clinton that he had gone back to New York with a contingent of Los Angeles activists for the Democratic convention. It was a heady experience for Vince; he loved being the center of attention, loved being interviewed by the press outside Madison Square Garden, loved blowing whistles and shouting in the street and stopping traffic as if it were his right to do so. But it wasn't enough that Clinton had gotten the Presidential nomination. It wasn't enough for him that Clinton had shown compassion for people with AIDS while he was campaigning for support at a fundraiser in Los Angeles. Vince had been there that evening, of course; Jeff had bought the tickets in advance for a whole table of us, not to show courage or faith in the political process, but because he had wanted to do it for Vince. Jeff had died before the fundraiser and Clinton's election had become a crucial necessity to Vince. Things had to change, Vince had decided. Bush had to be defeated. The religious right had to be stopped. At times I believed America's growing hatred and intolerance was what was keeping Vince going. By August of that year Vince was adamant that he protest at the Republican convention in Houston, but I had also witnessed, by then, a vibrancy slip away from Vince not long after he had returned from New York, as if he had realized, for certain, back in Los Angeles, that Jeff was no longer to be there for him, a memory instead of a reason for returning home.

And so Vince, in private, became the lethargic antithesis of the angry, defiant public Vince. Vince stopped going for blood transfusions, stopped seeing his therapist, stopped going to his HIV support group. I felt him slipping away from me every day the Republican convention grew closer, and I began to suggest that we attend more actions and protests together, all with the hope that Vince wouldn't give up his own desire to stay alive. We had marched to the Mexican consulate in L.A. to protest the recent gay murders in Mexico. We protested outside a Beverly Hills fundraiser, protested outside airports and schools and insurance companies and doctors' offices and every place I could find to get Vince out of the house and away from the idea of dying. All I know now, years later, was that it was such a confusing period for all of us. All of this marching and yelling over gay rights and AIDS injustices didn't seem to be carrying us anywhere at the time, meaning anything to me at all, really, except how to avoid my true fear. If the truth be told, politics had no power for me outside of the need that it provide Vince with a will to go on. At one of the last ACT UP meetings I had gone to with Vince, six members' deaths were announced. And I had just sat there numb, unable to summon up any sort of anguish or anger. All I really wanted, instead, was my heart to carry me someplace else.

But the unfortunate thing was that an apathy had settled in with Vince as well. Nothing Vince had done had stopped Jeff from dying—no amount of shouting or protesting had prevented it. But Vince had also told me that he felt that Jeff had defeated himself—that Jeff was dead because he had not tried hard enough to keep his body going. *Not hard enough?* I had thought when I had first heard Vince's illogical notion. Jeff had worshipped his body, had spent years perfecting his physique; an artist had once chosen him to model for a wax figure for an exhibit at the Museum of Natural History in Manhattan. But Vince theorized that Jeff believed that he would not get well, could never become his healthier self again. When the surgery had failed to diminish the severity of his seizures, Jeff had stopped all other pharmaceutical treatments against any other potential infections, stopped exercising and meditating and visualizing his health. All Jeff wanted in those final weeks was to retreat from his anxieties—anxieties which included worrying about Vince, or, rather, who would take care of Vince if and when Jeff could not. The implausible thing was that none of us believed that Jeff would die before

Vince. Vince, after all, had been infected for years and was still making it. But Jeff, of course, had been the reason he kept going.

The horses were upon us before I had even recognized their presence, their hooves spitting against the pavement like shots out of a pistol. I remember perceiving Vince crouching, tilting the placard he had carried above his head as if to shield himself from the flash of an atomic bomb. I had not realized anything that was happening at that moment other than Vince shifting his position. The policeman's club had only grazed against my back as he waved it through the crowd from atop a horse, but the shock of its impact was enough to force me to my knees from fear. As I looked up over my shoulder, I saw the Astrodome rising above the scattering protesters, illuminated against the summer night like an alien spaceship.

"George Bush you can't hide, we charge you with genocide," a chorus of heavy-throated voices had continued to chant even though I had fallen to the ground. I remember that Vince had grasped my wrist, his placard angrily tossed in the direction of the police. All at once I felt myself rolling across the cement, my head dizzy. And then we were briskly moving across a field away from the demonstration, fleeing the scene like extras in a science fiction movie.

"Are you okay?" Vince had asked me when we were standing beside one another, panting—Vince leaning into the cane he used for support, my eyes searching for the small lump beneath his T-shirt where the catheter rose up out of his chest, worried it could possibly be leaking blood, though it wasn't.

I had nodded and responded mechanically with, "How about you?" He had nodded back at me to indicate that he was fine, though I didn't believe him, and I had realized, then, that the fear at my shoulder had now become an ache at the back of my head. I was tired, dehydrated—the early morning flight we had taken from L.A. had drained more energy than I had anticipated. If I was feeling so cranky I knew that Vince must be ready to collapse. Above us a helicopter roared into view from behind the Astrodome, a spotlight searching the crowd below as if to pinpoint an escaping criminal. Though we had separated from the majority of activists, I could still hear the noise of protests—a violent, sing-song chant of "We're here! We're queer!" rising up over the booming bass tones of Pat Buchanan's voice from inside the Astrodome. A haze of red smoke crept into the sky like fog from the fire bomb members of Queer Nation had ignited; overhead a burst of red, white and blue fireworks crested the stadium.

It was then that the moment was over, however; the moment of feeling like such a viable, determinable architect of history humbly perished. Vince turned away from the scene and weaved his cane like a blind man between a row of parked cars and I followed him, realizing as we made it to a parking lot, that I had no idea where to go next.

"Let's wait by the gate," I said, then, steering Vince into the direction of one of the exit lanes. Why hadn't I rented a car? I chided myself. Why hadn't I made Vince use a wheelchair? I tried not to show my panic—but why had we separated from the others? I knew we could find a ride back with someone—hadn't that always been possible wherever we had gone?

"We were lucky," Vince said as he slowed down his pace, his steps now more a painful, zombielike shuffle.

Lucky? I remember thinking, such an odd choice of words from someone so potentially militant as Vince. Lucky because we weren't beaten to a pulp? Because we weren't arrested? Because we got away without revealing our names? Wasn't the purpose of a demonstration to cause unrest? To be arrested? To create discomfort for others? To show up in order to be seen? Heard? Felt in that place where profound human emotions are supposed to rule?

The truth was, of course, we had retreated, abandoned our mission, left the other activists to defend themselves. Behind us, before we had departed, I had seen a horse step on the arm of a lesbian wearing a T-shirt that read "Find a Cure" and who had been peacefully lying on the pavement as part of a massive die-in. As Vince and I walked further away I had wondered, momentarily, if she needed help. But what could I do though, really? I couldn't drive her to the hospital. I couldn't drive the police away from her. All I could do was shake my head and scream from the pit of my soul. Was that it, I had wondered at that instant—was it our luck, then, that we were still alive?

Traffic was heavy in and out of the parking lots that evening, the lights of approaching cars impeding our vision with a tortuous and random assault. How easy it would be to die from a simple accident of a car, I had thought— how one little mistake from some unknown person behind a wheel could just wipe out our existence as we wandered along like some type of migrant holocaust survivors. *Survivors?* I thought. Was that it? Were we lucky, then, because we had made it this far? Vince remained silent as we continued our journey, his concentration on maintaining his energy. "I could rest a bit," I said, when we had reached one of the exits. The truth was I was stopping for Vince. My real dread, however, was that I didn't know how to get out of there, how to get back to the hotel. Vince calmly nodded at my suggestion, oblivious to my growing jumpiness, following me to a wall near the parking attendant's booth where we both took a seat.

What I have tried not to forget about that evening in Houston, or those years in California with Vince as well, was that I never stopped believing that the fight would keep him alive. But what I recall, too, was that the battle was exasperating on every level it was fought. At the rally that evening, Allen, a guy from ACT UP/Houston, had explained the logistics of the march's route from Herman Park to the Astrodome. Afterward, he had mentioned that the Republicans had just passed their anti-abortion, anti-gay platform. It had infused everyone around him with a rote hostility—a frenzied howl rose up into the air—a bizarre pep rally on both sides had begun. Fear, hate, anger, death. What I had thought about at that moment was not about fighting. Instead, I had stood there wondering, raising my hands to deflect the volume of noise away from my ears, if this was what being gay now meant? When could I laugh again? When could I be happy? When could I relax? When could I love someone the way I wanted to—the way I used to love long before all this mess had infected our lives? Was this what it meant to be human and alive in the Nineties? Another battle? Everything always so complex?

While Vince was sitting on the wall next to the empty attendant's booth that evening, gathering up more energy, waiting, really, for me to make the next step, I had moved toward the oncoming traffic, twisting my chest flatly toward the headlights of the cars and waving my arm up and down in a classic hitchhiker's fashion, hoping that the T-shirt that I wore—white with ACT UP printed in large black, bold letters on the front—would encourage someone to pull over and offer us a ride. The traffic avoided us, ironically, as if we had some sort of plague. After a few minutes, I noticed an old green van which had been at the rally in Herman Park, and the driver pulled over beside us and the passenger beside him rolled down the car window. Two men, or, boys, really, leaned their faces toward us and smiled. They were dark-skinned with wide, white flashing smiles. As we approached their car, I recognized both of them from the march.

"My friend, here, was too tired to make it all the way," I had lied next. "Could you give us a ride to someplace where we can call a cab?"

"Sure," the passenger replied, jumping out and sliding the van's side door open.

I helped Vince to his feet, and as I did so he said, "I forgot my cane."

"It's in your hand," I said, and he nodded back to me as if it were just a simple mistake he had made. When we were seated inside the van I was aware, once again, of just how thin and fragile Vince had really become. I could tell by his expression that he had lost his sense of place—another side-effect of his dementia—so I introduced ourselves to the two boys, Jack and Pedro, and as I had reached out to close the car door, I noticed a thick, smoky smell within the van, something so deep and heavy I knew it was more weighty than the smoke of a recent cigarette or joint. As we drove away, I asked the two boys a few questions about the rally, which unleashed a barrage of hyperactive explanations from them. Pedro, the driver, emerged as the loudest of the two, explaining how they had helped burn the effigy of Bush, which was now smoking in the back of the van behind our seat. A dead body, I had thought and almost laughed at the absurdity of it; Vince and I had traveled all this way from California to participate in a demonstration we had abandoned only so we could hitch a ride in a van with a mock dead body in the back seat.

Pedro said they would drop us off at the hotel before they returned to the offices on Montrose where they were headed. Riding back to the hotel, trying to keep my balance as the van jolted from every imperfection on the highway, I felt an odd tranquillity return. That summer, with the aftermath of Jeff's death, Denise's pregnancy and Kenny's birth, there had never seemed to be enough time to devote solely to Vince. Now, in the van, I could sense the span of years which had bonded us so strongly together; I could trace our friendship through a history of intimate moments, from an evening hunched over the candlelight of a Greenwich Village café to a silent walk together along the beach at the Pines. Those intimacies were there for me long before AIDS crept into the landscape I recognize now. But then, that evening in Houston, I had become so vividly aware of the moment I was living in—aware of what I mustn't forget.

The sad truth was that I had never felt comfortable at demonstrations, as if my own health had made me an impostor within my community. It wasn't so much that I felt excluded from that inner circle of zealous, angry boys; it was that I could never possess, under any circumstances, that out-there, in-your-face attitude. It seemed an awkward response for me to be shouting and demonstrating when what I felt was full of remorse. I had always believed, instead of demonstrating, that I should return to volunteering, picking up prescriptions for someone, delivering somebody a hot meal, which was why, perhaps, I had found such a comfortable rapport with Vince since Jeff's death. I had made Vince my responsibility even though I would have denied the fact of it to anyone, Vince included. Perhaps that was the difference between Vince and myself. One of us was a leader, the other a follower. But it was simpler than that, I knew. One of us was infected. The other was not.

On the radio Maureen McGovern was singing "The Morning After" and the strident ballad made me nostalgic as the van moved through the streets of Houston. Nathan would have hummed along; Jeff would have known all the words; in earlier years, Vince would have lip synched it and I would have laughed at the imitation. When Vince leaned his head back against the seat, I looked at the back of Jack's head, just barely making out the corner of his smile in the dark. Then I looked over at Pedro, driving, but from where I sat I could only see the back of his head and the white tops of his knuckles clutching the steering wheel. Next I looked down at my own knuckles, hairier and puffier than the boy's, and felt suddenly so aged and anxious sitting in the backseat.

Outside, the cab passed the marble fountain that had been dyed red by ACT UP, the water glowing in the night like blood from a giant wound in the earth. Vince leaned his head forward and asked how I thought Ian Steers had looked tonight. "Okay," I answered him, though I knew he looked worse than when we had last seen him in San Francisco a month or so before—his face now gaunt, the eyes hollow like a spooky skeleton mask. I knew Vince was making comparisons, wanted me to make comparisons as well. Everyone who ever visited Vince at the apartment for drugs or therapies which the buyer's club offered was always commenting on the darker sides of change. Ian had been positive for over eleven years and by then was distinctively showing it. Vince had only known he was positive for five, but his doctor had expected him to die last year.

I would never have acknowledged Ian's decline to Vince; such was the protocol which had developed between us. I, of course, had had my own history and unfortunate times with Ian. But I still refused to play that gossipy, bitchy game that even the sick boys liked to play. Never mention that things were worse was how I operated, always try to find something, well, positive to say if something must be said at all—look for the silver lining behind the dark rain clouds on the horizon. It's what I had done with Nathan, after all, even as much as I had seethed quietly inside with hate and anger over the fate of our situation. Fourteen years ago when we met I would never have imagined that Vince and I would have to hitch a ride in Houston because Vince was unable to, well, walk without support.

Even Jeff had been disappointed by life in the end. In his last week he had mentioned to me that he wished he had loved stronger. *"Stronger?"* I had replied.

"More visibly," he clarified. "I think I was too subtle about how I felt about things. Somewhere my passion just evaporated."

The death of passion, I contemplated over and over, a new phrase which I kept deconstructing in my mind ever since Jeff had revealed it to me. If passion was not enough to keep ourselves living, what exactly could then?

When the van reached the hotel, I thanked the boys and checked on what they were doing tomorrow. Vince had stubbornly decided to exit the car on his own and I had allowed him as much independence I could bequeath out of my peripheral vision. Pedro distracted me with a hug and by the time I had unraveled from his embrace and said goodbye, Vince was already at the revolving door, unable to match his steps with the rotation and the assistance of an officious doorman. I took Vince by the elbow, removing the cane from his hand and led him to a side door, the sound of laughter and a cool breeze of air floating toward us as the doors opened automatically before us by remote. A man and a woman in formal clothes bypassed the revolving door to exit our opened one. As they passed us, they failed to even acknowledge our existence, the woman moving so close to Vince I thought she would knock him over. Why should they acknowledge us? I thought in that instance, other than to show a politeness which they obviously didn't possess. Were they blind to a sick man and his friend simply trying to make their way through the door? Or were they just too self-obsessed to register anything but their own giddy moods, living in the clouds, oblivious to the way life really was for other people? The tragic mistake, I decided, was that America had made us invisible as much as we had designed it for ourselves. Hadn't we created ourselves as separationists with our gay ghettos and gay meccas and gay magazines and gay-owned businesses and patronage? In the elevator to our room we were suddenly joined by a politician and his entourage of four clean-shaven white-shirted men with small button-sized earphones, and I became perceptively aware in those moments of our personal brush against history and politics. Vince coughed loudly and deeply, drawing attention to himself, and we all silently regarded one another uncomfortably as the elevator ascended. All I knew, as we inched our way slowly between the floors, was how much I missed

L.A.—or, rather, how much I missed the family I had made for myself in L.A. and which Vince was an integral part. That thought, that ache, must have occurred to Vince as well. As the men exited on the floor before ours, Vince had asked me, as the doors were parting, loud enough for the men to hear, of course, "When did hate become a *fam-i-ly* value?"

Jeff had been adamant about creating a family—not a traditional, nuclear one (certainly not the kind of family made up of a man and wife and 2.5 kids with a house and a car in the suburbs), but a family of friends, a close-knit core of friends who checked in with each other every day, worried about one another, helped each other out in difficult times, were there to celebrate special occasions with one another. Jeff had shied away from creating such a family out of just his theatrical friends or sex partners, though he had hoped to incorporate people with those interests into his life. In fact, Jeff never demanded that these friends be gay men or lesbians, though that's how it had turned out, after all. The family he had chosen was Vince, Denise, and myself and those who were closest to us—Nathan, Linda, and Amy. Jeff had learned very early in his adult life that people can come and go rather easily from someone's life—a characteristic, he said, he had experienced too often from the succession of tricks he had invited out for second dates but never for a third.

Jeff had been adamant about maintaining his new family. It was Jeff who had inspired Denise to begin drawing, Jeff who arranged for Denise's first show at the Farrell Gallery in West Hollywood, which led to the Museum of Contemporary Art acquiring one of her paintings. It was Jeff who had kept Vince from returning to New York on his own after Jeff had captured the spotlight of success from Vince's play, Jeff who got Vince hooked up with an agent at William Morris, Jeff who arranged and paid for the loft on Melrose for Denise, Jeff who paid for Vince's medications when Vince's insurance company balked at the bills. It was Jeff who helped Denise find a house, Jeff who discretely loaned Linda money to make the down payment for her store and café, Jeff who suggested that I come out to California after Nathan died and sent money and a plane ticket before I could even anticipate making a decision. It was Jeff who had silently held us together, nurtured us, sheltered us, became, in essence, the silently devoted and protective father of our family.

At times I believe that Jeff picked us because of the troubles we had with our own, natural, families. Jeff's father had been as cruel to Jeff after discovering his homosexuality as mine had been to me. Denise's mother had been an irritation since Denise had left Kentucky; Mrs. Connelly was never satisfied with who her daughter wanted to be or what she wanted to do with her life. The truth is that no one chooses their family. Families include gay children, gay parents, gay siblings, gay spouses. Family values are hardly the sole province or the decision of the heterosexual white, suburban middle-class. But these values, these All-American family values of caring and nurturing and acceptance, are what Jeff was hoping to assemble when he constructed his family of friends.

Death within a family reverberates uneasily whether the family is a traditional one or not, of course. Jeff's death had shaken us all, Denise, particularly; once, while helping her change Kenny's diaper, she said she was oddly grateful that she now had the baby to deflect the shock. A loneliness had settled into Vince, however, that none of us could help him shed. Nor, do I believe, that he really wanted to discard it—the feeling, it seemed, gave him something to cling to even as much as it made him want to give up so much else. No matter how many lovers he and Jeff both had had during the course of their own love affair, no matter how much they had both changed and grown into distinct and different men, they had been unable to erase their own ardent relationship to one another. "Everyone is after me," Jeff said the night that he first met Vince at a disco in the East Village. "What I need is someone to stick around."

"I can't watch anymore," Vince said and clicked the remote of the TV. We watched the picture fade to a small dot as it had years ago at the beginning of "The Outer Limits." I half-expected an announcer to say, officiously, "Don't touch that dial." Instead, we both stared at the blank screen, stunned by the growing homophobia which had been recapped for us on the evening news. A reporter had noted the demonstration outside the Astrodome, but the clip had been of Buchanan, repeating the sound bite of his declaration of a "cultural war." And then the camera had panned across a sea of applauding delegates inside the convention, only to alight on a middle-aged cheering couple who waved a sign which read "No Queers or Baby Killing." *Aliens*, I had thought sitting in a chair in a strange hotel room in Houston, so far away from where I wanted to be. Are we that strange to them or they that strange to us? Where was the alliance that was supposed to exist in a democracy such as America? One nation, under God? If we were all God's children, where, then, was God in this picture?

I left the chair and unlocked the sliding glass door of the hotel room which led to the terrace outside our room. A blast of hot air met the stale, air-conditioned particles as I stepped out onto the deck. Immediately, I felt my body begin to perspire and I slipped my T-shirt off and tossed it onto a plastic chair, my arms outstretched as if to be crucified by the thick, humid air. The view was nothing from our hotel room—a parking lot, a loading dock, the stucco back wall of another building—and two floors below, a giant air-conditioning unit sat noisily atop another wing of the hotel. Again, I had thought about being back in L.A., settled into a more mundane routine, lying on the couch in the living room, Amy singing the alphabet song as she ran in and out of the room, Denise rocking Kenny in her arms, a small blue towel draped over her shoulder so that his spittle would not ruin her blouse, Linda behind us gathering up the newspapers or Amy's dolls from the floor, Vince napping in the recliner in front of the television.

I sensed Vince adjust his position on the bed so that he could see me outside on the terrace. Lately, Vince had become afraid of remaining alone; the aftershock of Jeff's death had nonetheless left its toll. I had taken it upon myself to fill up his day with people—a home-care nurse alternated with a buddy from APLA during the days; in the evenings I jogged down to his apartment, showered, fixed him dinner and slept over, leaving in the morning to work in Linda's store before returning to the house and checking on Amy and Kenny.

The truth was that I hated being away from Amy and the new baby, but Linda had wanted a leave of absence from the store to help Denise settle into a routine with Kenny, and with both of them at home, I had volunteered to start working more at the store to make it all possible. Being at the house, then, had left me feeling rather awkward, boorish and just in the way all the time. But it had also helped clear my time and create an accountability for Vince, even if, at times, all I felt I could offer him was the simple comfort of being present as a companion. In some bizarre way it felt that this new-found intimacy we had progressed into was something Jeff had bequeathed to us. The bizarre thing was, I knew, this new intimacy between Vince and myself was the first time since Nathan's death that I hadn't felt the misery of fate against me. Our relationship had reached a new intricacy—part brother and companion, part lover and friend, part carepartner and patient. Taking care of Vince, being able to take care of him, being with him, sleeping with him, infused me then with an odd exultation I felt ashamed to express to anyone as a fact.

On the way back to the hotel that evening, Vince had mentioned that he wanted to go back to L.A. in the morning, three days before we were scheduled to return. He had no interest in any more demonstrations or rallies or press conferences. "Home," is how he really said it to be exact. "*I want to go back home.*" The thought of it had made me shiver. Those had been Nathan's exact words when he was ready to die. Outside on the terrace I heard a siren move through a street I could not see and I shuddered and worried that it could turn into some freaky kind of metaphor for our lives ahead. Walking back inside the room, I shoved my palms into the pits of my arms, squeezing them together to feel my body's warmth, the sudden chill had made me step out of myself, or, at least, out of my thoughts so quickly I had almost expected to find Nathan in the bed.

I wasn't disappointed to find Vince, however. *Vince, Vince, Vince.* How much you've been through. How much we have been through. He had fallen asleep at his perch on the bed, and I untangled his fingers from the IV tube which I had hooked him up to when we had returned to the room from the demonstration. I stood beside him for a moment, listening to the hum of the generator which we had carted with us from Los Angeles. All this to stay alive, I had thought. To fight. I placed my hand against the machine to stupidly feel its pulse, then removed it and sat on the edge of the bed and unlaced my shoes.

That afternoon when we had arrived at Herman Park to assemble for the demonstration, a woman from Michigan, a member of Mother's Voices, had told Vince the reason why she had shown up in Houston was because her daughter had died the week before. "She got it in high school," she said. "A fucking high school in *Mich-i-gan*." Vince's face, throughout the woman's outrage over the fact that the CDC's prevention campaign failed to mention either the words "condom" or "sex," remained more reverent than vengeful. "Reagan," he had said, when the woman had finished her ranting. "Reagan ignored it for years."

"Bush is no better," she had added. "And it will only get worse with the religious right."

I don't think we can entirely blame the Republicans, I had thought, then, but I did not mention my thought to anyone, either. To do so could have possibly initiated my own lynching at the hands of the two thousand activists who surrounded me. But I had ignored it for years. So had this woman, I bet. So had Vince and Jeff and Nathan and Alex and Hank and Michael and Warren and Stuart and Paul and Ian and everyone else I knew. We had all been slow in responding. We had all believed a plague was impossible. What we had failed to remember, of course, was that we were not fighting with each other. What we were fighting was a microscopic virus which could enter and destroy the body.

I ran my fingers through what was left of Vince's hair, watching him sleep. How do you say goodbye to someone who is already gone? I had wondered once again that evening. I had never been able to solve that riddle. No one tells you it's not easy to let go. No book, no class, no guru or higher power or twelve-step course can make it any easier. Families are there to help you cope. Families and lovers, I thought. Weren't Vince and I both? Hadn't our history made us that to one another? I knew that Vince was not trying hard enough anymore. Something in him had died when Jeff had died. I slipped off my jeans and as I moved through the room I caught my reflection in the mirror above the desk. A bruise had formed on my back where I had been struck on the shoulder at the demonstration. I looked at it briefly, touched my fingers against it and winced. I'd love to remember that bruise as a sort of merit badge, something that I had earned in our great fight, but at the time I felt it only as another pain I must silently endure. Then I turned off the lamp and got into the bed beside Vince, curling my body around him as if we were lovers. *The death of passion,* I had thought, feeling the warmth of Vince move into me. No, not death. Maybe just the deep pause of a moratorium. I knew I would fight as long as Vince needed me to fight, even if I felt like time was running out on us, even if I felt like a burned-out, scarred, and empty shell, I would still do it for Vince. I took a deep breath of Vince's body, letting the smell of him drift into my blood. I knew I was ready again. I knew I was ready for my heart to soar. Passion suspended, I thought next. I embraced Vince tighter and did what I knew how to do in such moments—imagining us as we should be: *there, home, alive.*

Vince's hand felt warm and healthy, his veins puckered to the surface of the skin, though his body smelled rank and repulsive as the unwashed odor of him moved across the bed into the direction of my face. I had sat there for a long while, holding his left hand, twirling it back and forth in front of my eyes, grasping it, clutching it, stroking it, weaving my fingers in and out of his, but all the while staring at his mouth and looking for some kind of movement at his chest, wondering how, when the body loses the consciousness of its brain, it can still retain the knowledge to keep air moving in and out of the lungs.

A vacuous bearing had seized the hospital room all afternoon though I had willingly imposed most of it—I had turned off the television set, turned off the bank of fluorescent lights above the empty bed next to Vince, closed the blinds so that only the gurgle of the respirator broke the silence of the room. Soon, too soon, really, I would ask the nurse to unplug the respirator to allow Vince's body to move into its own, final, silences.

But I couldn't really do that, I recognized, sitting there, staring at his body for some sign of remission. Was this just too much of my fertile imagination at work, believing I could detect Vince's face moving through faint expressions—a flutter of the eyelids, an arch of the eyebrow, the flare of a nostril, knowing, of course, that there had been no movement within the muscles of his hand as I had held it for almost an hour. This was it, I knew, though I didn't want to accept that fact; I had been here too many times before—but this was one which I didn't want to have to passively accept.

This was Vince dying, Vince leaving, Vince's struggle coming to an end. "It's okay," I said, my voice breaking at it's highest pitch, remembering, as it did, that someone had once told me that hearing was the last sense to go. "It's okay, Vince. It's okay," I repeated, foolishly, in a lower tone of voice. A nurse shuffled into the room, looked at me holding Vince's hand, looked at the pained expression which must have washed across my face, then came to the bed and felt for Vince's pulse.

As she stood beside me I felt a panic race into my body, that somehow this nurse would determine when and how Vince would go. I felt my body tense, a jolt of anger flashing into my brain, and I became jealous of the moments of Vince's which she was stealing from me, just me, but I kept myself in check, guarded, not wanting her to touch Vince anymore, silently willing her to leave the room. Just when I was ready to sourly snap at her to get the hell out of the room, she had abruptly turned and left of her own accord.

I gasped out loud, just to let out the force of the emotions I held inside me, then tried to disguise it by clearing my throat, then wondered who I was trying to fool? Vince? Hardly. I had never been able to fool him. He had always been able to guess my moods—from the disgust I had felt after a bad date to the frustration I had felt when things with Nathan were not working out to the joy and pride I had felt the night I first invited Vince and Jeff over for dinner at the apartment Nathan and I had taken together in the West Village. And so I wondered, that afternoon in the hospital, if Vince could somehow, subconsciously, detect my own confusions then as well: my distress, my unwillingness to let him go, my fear of being alone.

All I wanted was his hand to squeeze mine in return, even if it were to just give me some sort of sign to go ahead and let him die. All he wanted of me was to help him die painlessly. Wasn't that the only set of final instructions he had given me to do? All I could remember sitting there, was an afternoon we had spent at the gym, years before, in Manhattan, where Vince had told me that if I wanted bigger biceps then I would have to work out with heavier weights. "No pain, no gain," he had said, repeating that often quoted phrase. What gain did I get from this pain? I wondered, flipping his hand in front of me. What do I learn from this one?

What a stupid thing to remember, I thought, how shallow and insincere to be thinking about a body in the gym while Vince lay in front of me dying. But Vince had always loved the gym, loved to cruise the locker room, loved to be around other gay men even after he had settled down with Jeff. "Get a look at *her*," I could hear Vince say more than once when we were walking on Hudson Street or Santa Monica Boulevard, and my thoughts would immediately stop their internal machinations to look wherever he was looking at at that very same moment.

Vince, of course, never stopped looking, and it had nothing to do with being disenchanted in his relationship with Jeff. Quite the contrary, Vince worshipped Jeff, took as much pride in Jeff's body as he did his own, particularly when Jeff elicited the lustful glances from other men. Vince went out of his way to make the dynamics of his relationship with Jeff work—sometimes to the extent of dangerously bending rules. But Vince also worshipped the beauty of the male body, whether sexually, visually or esthetically, "No harm to just look," he often whispered to me. "It's only natural." Vince believed that being gay was centered within the mind. But he also felt that a gay sensibility must be psychologically achieved—appreciating the finer details and qualities and characters of the male form and the gay personality had been something that had to be learned, not inherited. In the early years of his awareness of his infection with HIV, Vince had been able to learn, too, as other gay men had, how to handle the mental impact of being considered chronically ill—and had been able to deal with the resulting depression effectively and get on with his life. But his life had become immersed in the details of the disease—moving first from a volunteer to an activist to a carepartner—and he reached a point where he was continually reminded of his own pathology, day after day after day, second after second. With every thought, every step, every action, he found himself encountering obstacles larger than he could ever have imagined otherwise.

Vince had been able to look upon the deterioration of his body as a sort of advanced state of aging. Thirty-six years as a gay man, he once said to me, could translate into about seventy-two years in gay time. How had this happened? I asked myself, over and over, for what seemed like the thousandth time. How could a virus, so small and undetectable to the human eye, be able to invade and overcome such a much larger body? How many days had I looked at Vince's body, his face, peered into his mind, too, and not been able to detect that something so sinister was lurking beneath it?

Another evening in another hospital, I had thought, then. Here I am again. When will it end? Will it end? The thirty-ninth or fifteenth or seventy-eighth passing is no easier than the first. And so I hated the moment the nurse reappeared in the room and stood silently behind my shoulder.

"If you can't handle it, get out," Vince had said one day to the boyfriend of a man who had purchased some drugs through the underground buyer's club Vince had worked for. The boyfriend had worked himself up into a state of hysterics in his friend's hospital room. "This is the way things are," Vince had added, in almost a furious scream. "Deal with it." I had come to the hospital with Vince—we were on our way to a dinner party in Silver Lake—and I thought it was no way to talk to someone's lover, certainly not someone who was fighting their own battle, whether infected or not.

But Vince was right, of course; this was the way our lives had become, the way the roads had led us, how fate had dealt its cards. I often wondered, then, if it made us collectively stronger in spirit yet individually weaker in body? Perhaps yes, perhaps no. How one dealt with fate individually was determined by the temperament of the individual. But Vince, himself, had never recovered from the impact of Jeff's death—no matter how hard he fought, the loss had simply overwhelmed him—his spirit, then, had seemed defeated.

And so it happened: Vince's body, or what stubbornly remained of it, refused to surrender without a fight. But was there a limit to the punishment the body and its soul could take? What one individual could bear? When Vince had been diagnosed as HIV-positive years ago he had signed a living will so that his dying would not be artificially prolonged under any circumstances; it was a choice not so much to lessen his own suffering, but to diminish that of those who were a part of his life. The month before, as his mind began to further deteriorate, Vince had relinquished to me his power of attorney.

The last two months of Vince's life had been marked with increasingly violent nightmares. Often they involved Jeff or other old boyfriends or tricks, wielding bloody instruments in front of him—knives, guns, saws. Waking up from these nightmares, he would wake up and cry out from the pain he felt in his head. Vince had been suffering searing headaches for almost a year, and, finally, after one of his dreams he had me drive him to the emergency room. There, he had undergone a battery of tests. A doctor had ruled out any presence of HIV within the brain, but Vince had been left with only twenty-seven T-cells. He checked himself out of the hospital, but checked himself in two other times, and by the time of the third round of magnetic resonance imaging, a doctor finally discovered a substantial amount of fluid surrounding Vince's brain, confirming what was already suspected—that Vince, indeed, was progressing through the stages of dementia.

Then, and only then, did a doctor finally take a small biopsy of his brain tissue, draining the fluid from Vince's brain in an effort to relieve the pressure within Vince's skull. By then Vince had lost close to fifteen more pounds in one hospital visit alone, a total of five intravenous piggybacks hung on a multihooked pole beside his hospital bed. He was barely coherent when CMV destroyed the retina in his right eye, leaving him blind. Twenty-nine hours later he had slipped into a coma. "You need to make a decision," the doctor had said to me when I had returned to the hospital that morning. "There's a probability he could live in this state for a long time. He's a strong man."

A *strong man*, I thought, repeating the phrase over and over, the same phrase Ben Nyquist had said of Nathan in his final days. Is that how I would remember this day, this moment—that I must kill Vince, terminate him, pull the plug according to his wishes. How could I do this without any sort of attachment to the crime? How could I live with myself after this, knowing how I had acted in these moments? That I had *killed* a strong man.

And so I had called his mother in New Jersey, trying to seek some kind of escape from this responsibility. She had barely understood what I had said and when she did she explained that she was too weak to travel herself, offering only the phrase, "Of course, of course," as the best kind of absolution she could provide. When I had reached his sister, she grilled me with questions, "Why had I waited so long to call? Why hadn't I taken him home to die?" She knew that nothing else could be done; she had visited Vince two months before when he had come to the hospital for a brain scan.

When I had explained the situation to Denise and Linda on the phone, Denise drove to the hospital, leaving Linda behind to take care of Kenny and Amy. She had appeared in the room, clutched Vince's hand, leaned over and kissed his cheek and then turned to me and started crying. I found myself comforting her, trying to get her to calm down, when here I was feeling myself like a traitor or a murderer—the friend whose purpose was to kill another friend. "I don't want him to see me like this," Denise had said, sputtering out her words. I was surprised she had even shown up at hospital; after losing Jeff, I hadn't expected her to find the strength to make it. I walked her to the door and told her to wait outside for a while. She never returned; instead, she fell asleep on one of the small, hard-shaped plastic chairs placed at a nook in the hall.

Dying, Vince had oddly become more sexual to me, the more attention he demanded, the more he needed to be touched or lifted or moved. When the paralysis hit him, I lifted him out of chairs and into cars and offices and beds. I went back and held his hand again, stroking it, grasping it, kneading my fingers in and out of his.

And so he died that day. The nurse came in, an intern came in, I signed some forms, the life support system was dismounted, turned off, and pushed to the corner. Denise drove me home, I called Vince's mother and sister again, called a funeral home to check some details, and then lay down on my bed and fell asleep. That was the beginning of Labor Day weekend in the summer of 1992, the perfunctory end of fourteen years of friendship.

I have seen God more than a thousand times in my short life thus far, seen Him carrying candles in vigils and distributing condoms to students, seen Him wearing red ribbons at benefits, marching in AIDS walks and dancing at fundraisers; talked with Him in support groups, with therapists and in the basement of churches and synagogues. I have heard Him in speeches and prayers and demonstrations; smelled Him in hot meals delivered to home-bound patients, tasted Him in kisses and tears and sweat at funerals and memorials and wakes; touched Him at doctors' offices, pharmacies, video stores, and laundromats; felt Him, even, through the love of Nathan and in my friendships with others. Why, then, do I continue to disbelieve in the possibility of Him when I am continually aware of his presence all around me?

Not long after Nathan had died, Dora said to me that she believed that for everything God took away He would introduce something else to take its place. At the time she said that I knew she was trying to be optimistic, trying to lift my spirits, trying to let me know that my life would go on without Nathan, and looking back on things now it's clear to me that the doors which were closed with Nathan's death were reopened by Denise's invitation to live in California. Still, I didn't attribute this to God's intervention or from some divine plan; in fact, I had grown rather disenchanted with God, my religious views more ethically grounded by teachings of experience than metaphysically invested. I had almost become an atheist by then, and if not an openly declarative one, I certainly no longer prayed to any sort of omniscient being.

The fate of my arrival in California I have often explained to myself as the cyclical ability of nature to repair itself. In essence, my fate had nothing to do with God, or so I had come to believe.

Tony's arms were locked around my waist when I awoke, his head rested against my chest, his breath rising and falling in warm bursts against my skin. Sunlight broke through the window that morning, as it did most mornings in California, sending tiny pieces of rainbows through the crystals hanging near the window and landing on the walls, the bed, the furniture, and the clothes discarded about the room. I remember thinking, then, how right it felt to be holding him, and how nothing had really seemed right in that respect since Nathan's death, how, at last, it seemed comfortable to hold a man again. I was thirty-two at the end of that summer and was possessed that morning by a certain tranquillity and pleasantness, as if all the old and slightly tattered but nonetheless erotic pieces of a huge boyhood puzzle had been finally successfully located and reassembled.

The night before, Tony and I had gone upstairs to my bedroom, talked a while, gusts of warm, Pacific air billowing in through the bedroom window, interrupting the noise of the other guests who had come over to the house after Vince's service and which drifted up the stairs to my room. Tony and I had rambled sporadically through the details of our lives since we had last seen each other—the summer of 1987—when he had been a houseboy at the house on Fire Island where Nathan, Vince, Jeff, and I had spent a weekend. Tony had returned to Los Angeles and had become involved with a television producer, moving into the producer's house in Malibu, but was burned a few months later when the producer brought home a "newer" model, a blond surfer type just in from Florida. Tony had then moved to an apartment near Silver Lake which he shared with a bartender at Studio One, and decided to go back to school to get a degree in history with an eye to becoming a lawyer, studying part-time at UCLA and working for a landscaper who tended the estates in Bel-Air and Beverly Hills. Tony continued to do some occasional modeling, mostly catalog work, but he hated the scene, hated the attitude, hated being harassed and propositioned by everyone from the photographer to the stylist, and when he was shut out of national print campaign when an agent discovered that he had done a series of porn films, he had decided not to look for another agency, instead, only taking work when he was referred by one of his other contacts.

That evening in my room I had only the lamp on by the nightstand and the course of the wind through the room rattled the lampshade, creating ripples of light against the wall and ceiling. I lay on my bed watching Tony eagerly talk to me as if he had never told his story to anyone before. He was seated in the chair I kept near the window, and I could easily analyze my fascination and attraction to him; his pouty, youthful Mediterranean looks made him seem as if he were posing for Caravaggio, and for a moment I imagined myself as an artist, looking intently to memorize the details of him—the large curls of black hair, the brown doelike eyes, the square, athletic jaw, and a classic nose somewhere between hawkish and sleek. I could easily understand why he had been hit on by so many coworkers; he possessed one of those seductive ever-changing mannish-boyish looks. What I didn't understand was why he had followed me upstairs to my room. Tony had shown up to the service with Lyndon and his friend Ralph, who was also one of the members of Vince's buyers club, and when Tony had approached me at the funeral home he had greeted me first with, "You probably don't remember me."

Of course I had remembered him, though I didn't tell him the specifics of my recollection. In fact, I had remembered a great deal about him, more than he probably realized I knew. The weekend he had been our houseboy in Fire Island, Nathan and I had watched one of his videos. In it, Tony had engaged in a three-way—fucking and being fucked by two men at the same time, much larger and more muscular than he was. Tony, I remembered as he stood in front of me at Vince's service offering his hand for shake, was also amply and thickly endowed, and I blushed as I accepted his hand and recollected this fact about him. "The Pines," I said to him. "A couple of years ago." Nathan had never felt comfortable about us watching porn videos together, but as he became progressively more ill it was one of the few things we could safely share together. Nathan had not found Tony as intriguing as his fellow screen stars. I had been smitten with him, however; perhaps, in part, from some sort of perverse voyeuristic logic—I knew he was in the same house as I was at the same time I was watching him on film. But on film he had also possessed such a joyous and spontaneous attitude toward sex that I had been unable to keep him from popping up in my fantasies for weeks.

"I don't do that anymore, you know," he said to me, that evening in my bedroom, referring, I think, to the film work he had once done. Vince had mentioned that weekend in the Pines that Tony was also available "for hire" or for "special occasions." "Haven't for a couple of years," he added. "Everybody's seen them though. A couple of magazines printed a lot of photos from them. I can be trimming a hedge on Roxbury and somebody'll drive by, stop, back up and stare at me. At first I used to think they were looking at the houses, or that it was one of the places on the maps of the stars. When I realized it wasn't that, it turned annoying real quick. They'd start talking to me, as if I were their fucking best friend. I gave up a lot of that when Stephen became ill."

"Stephen?"

"My brother. He died last year. I spent a year-and-a-half taking care of him."

"I'm sorry," I said.

"I saw Vince one day when I went to pick up some medicine for Stephen at

Ralph's. Vince remembered me from the house. We talked on the phone occasionally—if he was there when I called Ralph—he was always suggesting something else for Stephen to try."

There was an awkward pause after that, and Tony looked around my bedroom, his eyes coming to rest at the hooks of crystals by the window. "You collect these?"

"Nathan did," I answered. "They're what I kept."

His eyes, then, glanced over to the portrait of Nathan which I still had hanging on the wall by the door. "He was one of the first guys I knew who was ill."

I was struck by the mystery in his voice, then, as if he were about to reveal a story to uncover a side of Nathan I had never known. Instead, his expression seemed infused with sadness and I watched him shift himself slowly in the chair, as if to push back his memory. Tony proved to be a welcome distraction to my grief over losing Vince—the mere sight of him so pleasant and fixating, but my eyelids felt as if they were fighting their own battle with gravity—the pressure of Vince's death still on my conscience—and, as it became harder for me to keep from falling asleep, Tony made a movement to leave, to put his shoes back on—that's all that had come off thus far. I asked him to stay a while longer if he wanted to, which he responded to with a nod.

"Should I set the alarm?" I had asked him then. "In case both of us doze off."

He didn't seem surprised at my suggestion, didn't seem alarmed or disappointed, either. All he did was shake his head no. "I have a job in Bel-Air around noon. That's all," he said, shoving a hand shyly into his pocket. In the light of the room, I could see his face moving through confusion, not knowing whether to stay or not, wondering what to make of my request, wondering if my intention was sexual or not, and how and if he should respond. I knew he was confused because my request itself was full of its own bafflement. On one hand I was wildly attracted to Tony; on the other I felt it would probably not go anywhere beyond an evening romp together and I wanted to believe that I had matured beyond the need for something as impersonal as that.

"I just need some company, that's all," I said, hoping I made it clear that my intent was not entirely sexually, though not entirely asexual as well—instead, just loaded with paradoxical passive-aggressive contemplation.

He nodded again, aware, though, that he may have monopolized my thoughts. "You're a good listener," he said.

It was my turn to nod, and I did so, but I shifted uneasily on the bed, wondering what to do next, but knowing, then, that something between us would happen. It was like a visual distortion, really, a wrinkle in time and I could leap ahead, see him without his clothes on, lying in the bed beside me. Déjà-vu before it happened, or, perhaps, I was remembering, instead, a scene from his video, or how I had felt when I saw it and had imagined myself within it.

"I could give you a massage if you want," he said. "Help you relax." And it was here that his face broke into a mischievous smile, brightened at the left side by a pair of deeply-set dimples.

I was surprised by the offer, surprised that he had come upstairs to the room, surprised that he had stayed so long, surprised that he was not so eager to leave. Suddenly I realized I was wide awake again and full of amazement. I responded by nodding timidly to his suggestion, and in the dim light I could feel his smile warming the temperature of my body. I bashfully began unbuttoning the white dress shirt that I still wore but he stopped me, brushing my fingers away, slowly completing the job himself, still possessing that magical grin. He took the ends of my shirt in his hands, slipped them over my shoulders, untucked the ends from the chinos I wore, and then folded the shirt lengthwise and draped it over my chair. I slipped the T-shirt I wore over my head and as he approached me I stopped him. His face flashed through confusion again, till I began to unbutton the shirt he wore. He unbuckled my belt, slipped off my pants as I worked at his shirt. I did the same to him till we were both standing in our underwear. His body was more muscular and defined than it had been years before, and he possessed a self-assurance unclothed that he did not own before when he had been seated in the chair.

"Lie down," he said, not so much as an order but as though an invitation to an adventure. "On your stomach." I did as he said, and then felt him straddle my hips, his knees digging into the mattress on either side of me. His hands began first at the back of my neck, lightly kneading the tension away. All at once I felt instantly exhausted again as he began to press harder against my neck. His fingers moved out further and further along the flare of my back, cupping my shoulders and rotating them as if they could be lifted out of their sockets. He worked his way down both sides of my spine, and I knew when he reached my ass and worked his way beneath the top of my underwear that if he turned me over I would not be able to hide my erection.

But then he massaged first the left leg, the thigh, the calf, the ankle and then the foot, tapping the sole first before pulling and kneading each toe. He did the same with the right leg, and when he had finished he worked his way back up to my thighs.

When he turned me over I noticed that his own erection diagonally protruded out of his briefs, the head of his cock peaking out above his waistband. My embarrassment lifted momentarily, though I still found that I could not make the next move. He took both hands and began massaging my chest, working in a clockwise fashion till he reached the nipples which he pinched and twirled between his fingers.

I groaned quite naturally, surprised by the loud sound of my voice echoing off the walls in the room, wondering at the same time what I had done to deserve this kind of attention for free.

"I'll stop if you want," he said, working me over, though, with that same contagious smile. I lightly laughed as if it were the most absurd question in the world, shook my head and whispered, "No." He reached down and slipped my briefs off, one hand suddenly working at my cock, the other kneading my balls.

I felt myself breaking into a sweat then, and he took his hand and licked the palm of it and returned it to my cock to make the friction slicker. I came not long after that, with an extreme and anguished moan that seemed to emanate somewhere acutely buried beneath my chest. I reached up then and tugged at Tony's underwear, pulling it down to where it hugged his thighs like a rubber band. He was bigger but more precisely knit than Nathan—a body which seemed to be defined by an endless repetition of exercises, a physique which demanded to be photographed, viewed, and looked at. I lay back and watched him masturbate while he continued to look at me; when he shot on my stomach we both grinned at the same time. After a moment, I reached over and found my T-shirt and wiped my stomach dry.

He laid down beside me but turned away from me and this was when I rolled over and took him in my arms. And then he began to cry—in short, sneezinglike spasms. I wondered, then, if I had done something wrong, or if I had been too selfish throughout the sex. "Sorry," he said, and he stopped as abruptly as he had started, then he rolled over, stretched out both legs and pointed his toes, then sat up straight at the waist, a perfect right angle, the skin, thin and taut against his stomach muscles. The whole effect seemed as if he were moving through a series of meditation exercises.

"Are you okay?" I asked him, somewhat worried. I had felt with him a sexual playfulness and intimate contentment that I had not found in some time and I was confused with what I perceived to be his own uneasiness.

He lay back down again, his head nudging up against my chest, his feet tucked up underneath him. "Yeah," he said, and I felt him nod, felt his hairline move up and down against the cleft of my neck. "I'm really more than this, you know. This is not just who I am."

As he curled his body tighter against mine, he seemed to want to hide himself as much as possible, as though he were ashamed to be the embodiment of such physical beauty, and that by rolling himself up into such a tight little knot, his attractiveness would somehow be diminished. I realized, then, that I had misjudged Tony, or, rather, I had judged him by the way he looked—or I had expected him to act and respond as sexually as I had found my attraction for him to be. But it was then, too, that I understood that he must be a bit too much as I was—unable to divorce the emotion I so often imbued to the physical act of sex—unable to disconnect the power of one body to astonish and excite another. And it was then that I knew, from a feeling somewhere deep within my chest, as profound and earnest as my earlier anguished moan had been, that Tony was a good and honest man. He was a man who only wanted to connect with someone beyond what sexual moments could be shared—just as I did—but without losing the eroticism of that initial physical attraction. I grazed my hand along the knots of his curled spine, the tips of my fingers nonetheless overwhelmed by the satiny feeling of his skin. "I never expected any of this from you," I said to the tense, compact figure he had become. "But that doesn't mean I didn't want it, or didn't imagine it, or didn't hope it would happen." And then I let my hand stop it's roaming against his body, and spread it out, fingers wide, against a portion of his back "I'd like to get to know you better," I added, feeling as the weight of my words sunk into him, the muscles of his back relax and expand.

And so that next morning—as I shifted the weight of him against me—I felt his cock, once again hard and fleshy, bounce against the hairs of my leg. He wasn't really awake yet, but not really asleep either, more in that limbo consciousness where the libido responds naturally to the senses. Instinctively, I ran my hand along the contour of his ass, over the cheeks to let it rest within the cleft of him, realizing, as I did, that my own erection had found its way against his thigh.

He had the body of a dancer, thin-jointed with long, stringy muscles, his olive skin coated with coarse, wiry black hair and a dark tan line that framed his ass like a bikini. He was twenty-four that year and that morning I was unable to keep my hands away from his body. Touching him, I finally felt free of the responsibility of Vince's death, free from the grief which had remained from Nathan.

And I had felt, too, that morning in bed, as if I had been somehow blessed, that, perhaps, God had finally given back to me something of what he had taken away. I did not expect anything further from Tony, his presence in that brief time had served as a sort of rejuvenating tonic, the inspiration that there was still more life ahead for me to live. Tony responded to my touch that morning by leaning up and kissing me. Before the morning was over I had fucked him and he had fucked me, the floor littered with lubricant, condom wrappers, hand towels and the wadded sheet from the bed. As I watched him leave the bed and go into the bathroom, turn on the shower and the sound of the water change as he stepped inside the tub, I found that I did not want him to leave my presence so soon—afraid that I would never see him again, afraid that the joy that I felt in his presence would never return. I felt, too, a protective jealousy wash across me when I realized that there must be others for him—that I was only one of many who probably continued to be such an easy sexual conquest. Or was I simply reading too much into this too quickly? Was I too willing to jump too far ahead—to expect an emotional attachment and relationship with him after only one evening and the morning after? What if Tony didn't feel as passionate about this as I did? What if this was just commonplace for him?

He's a porn star, after all, I reminded myself and rolled out of bed, picking up the debris off the floor, *this is nothing unusual for him,* feeling a little deflated as I let this awareness sink in and then consume me. But Tony didn't disappear right away; he had stayed for breakfast—a rather noisy one with Kenny, Amy, Linda, and Denise moving skittishly about the kitchen. Amy was particularly pouty because she didn't like the taste of the new cereal Linda had brought back from the store for her and only after Linda had promised her another slice of an orange would she even agree to try it. Amy was making a commotion because Denise was giving her full attention to Kenny and she felt excluded. Denise was seated at the opposite end of the table, trying to keep a messy apple paste more in Kenny's mouth than on his bib. I felt sort of sheepish trying to accommodate my overnight guest with coffee and a toasted bagel during all this commotion, though Tony, himself, bonded easily with Amy and created his own spotlight in all this morning lunacy when he showed her he could juggle three oranges at once without dropping any of them.

After breakfast I drove Tony to his apartment on Flores Street, one hand on his thigh as I drove along the route he directed me to follow, tapping my fingers against his jeans to the Bonnie Raitt cassette I had put on the stereo. "I should only have to work till about five," he said, when we had stopped in front of his building. "We're transplanting some trees up on Laurel Way today."

I nodded, uncertain if this was an invitation for me to suggest something later, but Tony proceeded with his own agenda before I had a chance to initiate my own.

"I could cook dinner tonight, if you're free," he said. I was looking out through the dashboard of the car, at the street sign ahead, but I could feel the intensity of Tony's eyes measuring my reactions. "Something simple. My apartment's not the neatest in the city, that's for sure. But it's comfortable. We could maybe rent a video, too."

"There's so much to do," I said, shaking my head as if I were about to reject his offer, looking out at the road ahead of me, scared a bit of witnessing the concentration he was exerting toward me, remembering, as well, how well he had, years ago, made dinner for a group of us on Fire Island. What did he want from me? I had wondered, then, years later. I couldn't help him out financially, couldn't help him out career-wise. Could he simply need the companionship, just as I did? Why would someone like him be searching in the first place—wouldn't it just be offered up to him? "Could I bring something?" I had added, then, and turned and looked at him, watching his face break into a smile. He was so handsome it was almost disbelieving. But something about him struck me as if he were a boy who had somehow lost his way, and he had turned to me like a tourist with an open road map—all at once eager and needy, as if my agreeing to have dinner with him was in, itself, an extraordinary reward.

"Sure," he answered and reached for the car door. "Wine, I guess." He turned away from me and looked up through the window of the car. "I'm up there," he said. "3S. About 6:30?"

"Okay," I answered, but before I could ask him why he was being so nice to me, he leaned over and kissed me on the cheek, the stubble of his skin rubbing against my own. "See you later," he said. I blinked my eyes in astonishment and waited a minute before I drove away, watching him walk up the sidewalk to his building, leap up his steps two at a time, unlock the front door, and disappear inside, but checking the street first to see if I had stayed to watch him do it all.

◼

Does believing in fate mean believing in the inability to determine the course of your own life? Does fate decide the events of your life or is your life determined by how fate shapes the events around you? Does God determine fate or does He only offer a way of dealing with these events? Or does modern religion even incorporate the philosophy of predetermination?

All I know is that my mind has been riddled with "what ifs" since that day I left Tony outside his apartment. What if Tony hadn't had to work that day? What if I hadn't gone to Vince's apartment and spent my day packing up his things? What if Linda hadn't shown up with Amy and Kenny to help? What if Denise hadn't brought Vince's sister, Julia, by the apartment to look through Vince's things before taking her to the airport? What if Denise hadn't decided to start sorting through Jeff's stuff and Linda hadn't offered to drive Julia to the airport instead? What if Amy hadn't gone along too? What if Denise hadn't said she would keep Kenny with her while she was at Vince's? What if Vince hadn't died and I hadn't met Tony? What if Jeff hadn't died? What if Nathan hadn't, either, and I had never ended up in California?

I suppose I could keep beating myself up over and over for the rest of my life, but the chain of events happened because they happened, whether or not they were from cause and effect, I can only still wonder about the "what ifs." I left for Tony's a little after six o'clock, leaving Denise behind in Vince's apartment, still looking through Jeff's collection of records and playbills, Kenny sleeping soundly on cushion of towels Denise had created on top of the bed. Denise had said she was finally ready to look through all of Jeff's stuff, decide what to keep, what to pass on, especially since it was so necessary now to close up their apartment, what with Vince gone now too. That was the reason why Linda had readily volunteered to drive Julia to the airport, to give Denise this space to sort through all those memories, and Amy went along with Linda, too, because Denise had insinuated that she would probably be doing this all evening. Linda left behind the bag that had bottles and food and diapers for Kenny and Denise had said that she would just eat whatever she could find in the refrigerator, or if there wasn't anything, she would order take-out. Linda had also volunteered to drop off some of the boxes I had already packed up of Vince's stuff at a thrift store on Vine Street on her way back from the airport, and I had carried about four boxes and put two in her trunk and two in the back seat, mostly of Vince's books and magazines he had wanted to be donated.

I arrived at Tony's about a quarter to seven. I had lingered in my car a few moments, lingered some more on the sidewalk. I didn't want to seem too eager; didn't the dating etiquette still demand of you to be coy and nonchalant on a second date, after all? But I also arrived with a bouquet of flowers, and apologized for being late—so much for that rationale. Tony had changed into linen shorts and a black T-shirt, his hair still wet from a quick shower; I could still smell the soap on his skin when he answered the door. The dinner that evening was as simple as he had promised—salad, spaghetti and parmesan bread; afterward, we watched a movie which Tony had picked up at the video store—*Soapdish*—and in which Jeff had a cameo role in one of the TV studio scenes.

It was close to midnight and we were lying on the couch, sort of watching "Saturday Night Live" and lightly making out and feeling each other up, talking between it all on a random selection of topics—still full of questions for one another—when someone buzzed Tony's apartment from the gate downstairs. We both jumped up off of the couch as if we had been caught doing something we shouldn't have been doing. Tony nervously laughed and I know I gave him one of those I should have known you'd have someone chasing you in the middle of the night looks but I couldn't help it—it seemed the right response to give at the time. Tony even seemed jittery enough as he headed toward the door for me to believe that it could have been one of his old boyfriends hunting him down. When Tony asked who it was through the intercom, the reply which came back was a breathy scream of "Robbie." I knew right away that it was Denise and that something was wrong, terribly wrong, my heart jumping into my throat as I reached for the front door.

As I leapt through the spaces of the stairwell, I first thought that something must have happened to Kenny. How Denise ever found Tony's apartment I couldn't figure out during my race toward the front gate, except that perhaps she had been able to piece together bits of information I had fed her throughout the day—that Tony lived on Flores, just above Fountain, and not far from Sunset in the building with the white terraces. That he was a friend of a friend of Lyndon's. That he had met Jeff and Vince in Fire Island. Later, much later, she told me she had seen my car parked on the street in front of what she thought might be the right building, so she knew she was in the right area; she had found the right apartment because it was the only one with the first initial "T" on the gate buzzer system.

When I got to the bottom of the stairs, Denise was standing with Kenny in her arms, rocking him nervously back and forth as if she were an amateur actress pretending to look like a distraught mother. Denise had always had a tentative demeanor about her, but that night she possessed an uncharacteristic weeping hysteria as she pressed her lips against Kenny's cheek in a rapid series of kisses. I looked at her, looked at Kenny, and I could tell that he was sleeping. Then I looked back at Denise's face but she was averting her eyes away from mine. There was a flushed color to her cheeks that I could make out even under the dim lights of the street lamps, as if she had just stepped off the treadmill after running ten miles. But there was also a teariness to her eyes and her bottom lip kept jerking and stiffening as if she were trying to speak but couldn't find the strength to force out any words. I knew the situation was out of control for her—behind her I noticed a squad car with the lights flashing and a policeman standing beside the car.

"Denise?" I said, moving my face closer to catch her attention. By then her head was wobbling so much it seemed as if she had palsy, and I slipped my arm around her waist and drew her into me.

"Oh, Robbie," she said, more a gasp against my chest than declaration. I pulled back from her and made a move to take Kenny from her arms, but she wouldn't allow me to take him from her.

"We have to go," she said and then whatever scrap of perseverance she was still clinging to finally escaped her grip and she started crying, really crying, as if suddenly allowed to do so for the first time in her life. At the same time a rapid succession of nonsensical sounds came out of her mouth as if she were trying to sing a set of lyrics she had long forgotten.

"Denise?" I asked, trying to calm her again by pressing her against my chest. "Go where?"

"Accident," she gasped, somewhere between all those heavy breaths and phrases. "I need help."

This, then, was what happened: On their way back from the airport Linda had dropped off the boxes in Hollywood, stopped at Pavilions for groceries and was headed along Melrose en route back to the house. The back seat where I had put the boxes were now filled with three bags of groceries: milk, cereal, soda, paper towels, diapers, and the frozen yogurt popsicles which were Amy's favorite. At the corner of Melrose and LaCienega, Linda had missed the short left exit lane onto LaCienega and had stopped to make a left hand turn at the stop light when a speeding car headed along LaCienega ran a red light and plowed into the side of Linda's car before she completed her turn, sending it over the curb of the sidewalk and through the chain link fence of a parking lot and into a parked car. When Linda's car hit the parked car, the impact was so sudden that Amy, even wearing a seat belt, was thrown from the vehicle through the windshield. The police said the speeding car was going eighty or ninety miles per hour. The other car, a Honda Civic, crashed into street lamp pole after bouncing off of Linda's car. The driver, Darren White, also known as David Wade and Davis Wayne, was taken to Cedars-Sinai hospital after the accident. The police told me the night that I went to identify Linda and Amy that White-Wade-Wayne had been arrested two months prior to the accident, at the same location, and had been charged with driving while intoxicated, reckless driving and driving without a license, and was later convicted of impaired driving. White-Wade-Wayne died within an hour of reaching the hospital; his girlfriend, Gloria, who had also been in the Honda, died at the scene of the accident.

Witnesses, including a dentist who was driving behind White, told the police that White was speeding and had run a red light just before the crash, narrowly missing hitting another car. The police later found four empty beer bottles in the wrecked Honda. The groceries in the back seat of Linda's car had remained intact and in place until the car caught fire in the parking lot where it had come to a sudden halt. Amy had died upon impact, but Linda had died only after the car caught fire, unconscious and trapped in place by her seat buckle and an inflated airbag. The dentist said he saw the Honda broadside Linda's car and watched Amy fly into the air; he pulled over to the curb and called 911 for help on his car phone.

The police didn't ask Denise to identify the bodies, only the belongings collected from the scene—Linda's earrings and watch, a silver band which Denise had given her for her thirty-seventh birthday, Amy's watch and the locket which she had been wearing that day, and two cans of baby peas and carrots which had survived the fire, rolling over the pebbles and debris of the vacant parking lot to stop inside a small crater. The coroner took me down a gray hall, flakes of paint forming near the ceiling like scabs, and showed me the bodies and described the accident while looking away from the bodies and at the report on his desk. Linda's face had been badly burned and they hadn't even wiped the black ashes from her skin; Amy's skin, however, had been washed and cleaned, though razorlike lesions puckered to the surface. The coroner had said that Amy had been the first to die, her body had not been burned at all, the collision is what killed her. Her neck had been broken by the impact against the plate of glass and she had not felt more than a millisecond of pain. The explosion had killed Linda. A man walking on Melrose had tried to get Amy to breathe, but seeing that she was already dead had tried to get Linda from the car but had not been successful. He had been hospitalized from the explosion, his chest and neck charred from the fire. The coroner gave me the man's name on a slip of paper, in case I wanted to contact him.

After dropping Denise back at the house after returning from the police station, I drove by the scene of the accident much later that evening, or, rather, as the red haze of morning was beginning to stretch out in the sky over the valley. How odd, I thought, that I had never given the intersection of LaCienega and Melrose any sort of assessment until that day, still refusing, however, to give that industrial-looking retail strip of upholstery and rug businesses that dotted the corners any sort of significant meaning to these events. I moved through that site, that evening, with a purposeful intent of uncovering clues or reasons or hints of explanations as to why this had to occur. I found, instead, only pieces of glass and pebbles and rocks where Darren White's Honda hit Linda and Amy, as if the whole horrible thing had been politely swept away and hadn't happened at all. *But it had*, I knew, studying, instead, the way the chain link fence had already been bent and mended back into place. I felt a scream begin to boil inside my body, till the pressure of it made it explode out of my throat in a cough. I realized, then, how much I hated having to accept the cards which fate had dealt to me, hated it with a passion I had been unable to direct toward anything else in my life.

Reaching out and touching the fence, I caught sight of the silver ring I still wore on my left hand, Nathan's Christmas gift, then let my hand fall away as my eyes searched through the debris at the edge of the fence for some sort of sign of Amy and Linda, as if I had become my own ghost, every minute detail of my life held up within my memory and examined for its sheer foolishness. How do I accept *these* deaths? I asked myself, when I have already witnessed the death of a generation of my own. Is there someone to blame for these two deaths? What lesson was I to learn from these?—that life can just end, abruptly and unprepared? In other ways besides AIDS? What chance did I have against fate, when all it dealt me was disappointing cards? And why should I let my heart be stirred again, only to have it potentially shattered?

Or do I just make believe that things will go on as before when, of course, they won't? What will *this* loss mean? Do I open up my sorrow again? Share my feelings? Or is it now my turn to be the pillar of responsibility?

Tony was waiting at the house when I returned, sitting on the couch and holding Kenny, draped in a dishtowel, in his arms. "He needed to be changed," Tony said to me, on seeing me walk into the room and finding him there. "There are no diapers in the kitchen."

I nodded and took Kenny from him. Tony looked up at me, trying to gage my reaction. I know he expected more emotion from me, more outwardly visible sorrow, perhaps, or at least more passion to want to draw him into my orbit. But I had nothing left within me then. I wanted him to just disappear, not ready for any further complication in my life.

"Denise fell asleep," he said.

I nodded at him, but answered rather coarsely with, "You didn't have to stay," hoping the tone of my voice would make him want to leave.

"She seemed too rattled for me to leave," he answered, not a bit rattled himself.

"This is hardly the way to begin something."

"It's okay," he said and waved his hand in front of his face as if he were shooing away a fly. "I'd like to help." Then, as if embarrassed by his admission, offered up, "Consider it a favor."

A *favor*, I thought, suddenly amazed to hear the sound of that word again— had fate thrust that word upon me or was God, instead, delivering me a sign? I nodded again, looking down at Kenny sleeping in my arms, then back at Tony. "Could I ask another favor?" I said, trying to be a little more congenial in my tone of voice but worried nonetheless that I was not succeeding at it.

"Sure," he replied, his face lifting with eagerness. He stood up from the sofa—no, jumped up, really, as if he were about to be sent on a mission, thankful, I think, of feeling like he was necessary and needed.

"Breakfast," I said, realizing my tone of voice sounded more like an order from a list of things, instead of a request. "I need to make some phone calls," I said more softly. "Could you stay and help us with breakfast?"

18

There is always something to talk about when one is falling in love, and Tony kept me talking during difficult times, asking me my opinions on politics, psychology, children, and men, but helping me, really, in essence, to release the demons of grief and loneliness after witnessing so much death back to back. We spent whole days and evenings swapping stories and revealing passions—my trip to Europe with Nathan, his trip to Barbados with his ex-boyfriend the producer, his fondness for artichoke hearts, mine for mocha chip ice cream. But what he wanted from me was to know, really, what I was thinking about as things happened in the world around us. What did I think about Clinton's speech, for instance, or had I heard anything about the new drug trial starting up at UCLA, or did I want to go out to a movie or stay in and rent one. What he was gauging in all this was how my temperament was healing, or, perhaps, if it were healing. But what I wanted from him—no, needed from him, I know—was more than the distraction his conversations so easily provided me. What I needed was what occurred between us between the conversations—the satisfaction he gave me that I could be someone who was still considered desirable.

And he did that, of course. Sex was a large part of the intoxication I felt over Tony, a large part of the escape I so needed from my grief, especially in those first few weeks after Linda and Amy's accident. Quite simply, he made me feel wanted after years of living through a self-imposed drought. I could try to convince myself that I adored him for the questions he asked me or the way he helped take care of Kenny or the concern he showed for Denise—and later, years later, I can detect that quality easily within my memories of these times and they certainly heightened my desire for him then—but the truth was when I noticed his eyes dilating at the very notion of sex, all restraint fell away and I easily succumbed to the desire he so effortlessly provoked in me, even though I was panicked with the profound guilt that I should not be feeling so elated while Denise was spiraling herself through such uncomfortable misery. At times, I believed I was moving too fast with Tony; on one particular day we had sex four times, the virility and sexual exuberance he unleashed in me was an astonishing but welcomed surprise. I had fallen for him as rapidly as I had for Nathan, a dangerous thing I tried to remind myself over and over, uncertain, really, what Tony's own intentions were, but even more—somewhat scared about being hurt at a time when I, myself, was feeling so needy. At times I knew that my action—that unbridled lust I felt for Tony—was perhaps exactly what Tony did not specifically want from me—but I always expected the passion to play out with Tony in a few weeks, that this was a fire that would burn out quickly—that one day he would simply be bored with me and be ready to leave. But I also knew—or, rather, felt it instinctively in his movements and the patterns of his questions—that what he expected out of me was something deeper—a commitment of sorts—a subject we had avoided specifically discussing, leaving the existence of it, instead, to an implied albeit tentative decision thus far to simply spend as much time as possible together. In other words, as boring or as sexually shallow as I felt I could sometimes be in his presence, Tony had no notion of wanting to move on to someone else. What he wanted was some place to belong which, of course, I willingly offered up to him.

How someone so attractive could not be so self-absorbed, I have never understood, but then I never professed to understand the nature of gay men—or men, for that matter—but Tony seemed to be a rare find in a town I often felt was full of chattering narcissists and driven materialists. Not that I wanted Tony to be completely lacking in egotism, after all. He knew, for instance, that he could easily distract me from my thoughts simply by the way his T-shirt would ride up his stomach to reveal the line of furry brown hair that bisected his waistline, an image so sexy to me in a city where everyone shaved their body hair that I would have to pull my thoughts away from him and into others in order to keep moving throughout the day. And he was as sexually driven himself as he made me feel; he could easily initiate an afternoon in bed as I could yield to it. And it wasn't that he was without an edge, either. At times he could sink into a moody depression himself, not wanting to be around anyone, and he would leave me alone where I was busy doing something out in the yard or in the garage to go sit on the front porch and read a book or a magazine, albeit, still within the conscious geographic realm of where I was working. And Tony said right up front that he did not want to go to a gay bar with me, even though I had never suggested it and had long progressed through the desire to do so myself with someone I was dating. He explained, in that boyish quality I had come so quickly to admire in him, that he didn't want to be tempted into ignoring me—a quality of his which I was so perceptively aware that he shared with Nathan. The longer Nathan and I were together, the harder it became for us as a couple to confront the evening randiness of unattached gay men.

Any other guy might have been jealous of the time and attention I lavished on Kenny, too, but Tony wasn't threatened; he moved through life with his own needs and plans. What he wanted from me was merely the intersection of my time with his, whether it incorporated other players or not was immaterial to him; he was simply grateful for the time that we could spend together, the way I had so easily found space for him in my life. "I need you," he said to me one morning on the phone a few hours after I had dropped him off at his apartment on my way to take Kenny to see his doctor for a routine examination. He was upset I hadn't invited him to accompany us, my thinking was that he needed some time on his own. "I don't want to go through my life alone," he succinctly corrected my decision.

And so Tony became the protective spirit for our little household, in many ways an anchor for the rest of us to tie our moorings against. It was an uneasy time for Denise, then, and as much as I tried to help her find a map back into the world I floundered when I came up against her lethargic soul. She couldn't focus, couldn't concentrate, and frequently lost her train of thought in mid-sentence. She had stopped painting, stopped going to her loft, instead holding Kenny in her arms wherever she moved about the house, as if he would blow away if she loosened her grasp on him, but unable to feed him or change his diapers, reluctantly bequeathing him to me to do so, hovering about us, her eyes unmoving from where her child was till he could be restored to her arms. And then she had trouble sleeping at night—eyes wide awake in a panic; during afternoons, she had trouble staying awake, falling asleep only if she was aware someone else was in the room with her. After Linda's and Amy's death she had been unable to look into anyone's eyes very long without her inward pain bringing tears to her eyes, and so she seldom left the house, seldom spoke to anyone anymore, sitting, instead, in front of the television set with Kenny in one arm and the cable remote control in the other.

It was Tony who broached her out of her shell, though; Tony who lead her out into sunlight when I had been so confused on how to even greet her in the mornings as I reached for a cup of coffee. He had shown up at the house one morning with a camera, an old Leica that had belonged to his father and which had to be peered down into like a telescope, the image focused with knobs on its sides—and he had convinced Denise to pose with Kenny outside on the lawn. He had demonstrated the camera for her, then: the way he had to load the film in the back in the shade, the way the two inverted images came together in the viewer. A few days later, when he had brought along the photographs he had developed—a stack of large eight-by-ten inch black-and-white photographs—Denise had placed Kenny in his crib long enough to look at the photographs. A smile broke out on her face as if she had been handed an expensive heirloom. "They're beautiful," she said, drawing her finger to the points where the lens had unfocused the background like a smear of grease against a pane of glass. In a strange, inexplicable way, those posed, flat, shiny black-and-white prints had helped her back into a three-dimensional world. I was in the kitchen, then, pulling out dishes from the dishwasher and placing them in the overhead cupboards, stealing glances at Denise's reaction to the photographs. When I looked over at Tony to see if he had witnessed what he had so easily achieved with her, he seemed to be radiating what I could only define as goodness, as if he were an angel sent down to reassure the righteousness of a doubter.

"Should I open the window?" Tony asked. He had dried himself off with a towel I kept draped across the back of the chair in my bedroom to prevent us from having to dart through the hall to the bathroom so often after sex. We had come upstairs after I had drawn Tony into a kiss when he had asked me a question about my father which I hadn't wanted to answer, after I had deflected responding to one of his earlier questions about why my father preferred not to work with electrical tools. I had been working in the garage building a cedar planter to put out on the deck I had finished in the back yard; Tony was sitting on a stool watching me fumble with an electric drill and wanting me to talk about my boyhood in Georgia, after he, himself, had revealed his own dysfunctional path growing up in an overpopulated family in Washington.

At the window, Tony lifted the bottom frame open with a tug and I felt a breath of air brush into the bedroom, strongly mingling together the stale smell of Tony's too-strong cologne with my rather dank underarm odor before the wind dispersed them both. Tony reached up his hand to stop the swinging movements of the crystals hanging on threads near the windowsill that he had disturbed, and, as I watched him cupping them with his hands, I once again regarded the natural and unselfconscious way he carried his naked body, at once sensual and sensitive, as though a cat stretching after a long nap before mischievously disappearing into the night. Dusk was settling in the room then—we hadn't turned on any lights as we had rushed up the stairs laughing and groping each other like little kids—and as Tony leaned up and angled himself against the wall and looked out the window into the yard, I studied the way the pale light ended against his skin into a vertical line of shadow along the length of his body, like a photograph slyly revealing the backside of the moon.

"Whatever he did must have been awful," Tony said, moving back across the room to where I sat on the edge of the bed.

"Who?" I asked, not really concerned about his question, more interested, really, in the way his flesh felt in my hands as I reached up and cupped his buttocks in the same delicate way he had handled the crystals by the window. I was still hungry for sex even though I had just come, hungry, still, for the feel and smell of him in my arms.

"Did he beat you?" he asked, rocking himself deeper into my embrace. I pressed my face against his pubic hair, taking in another deep breath of him, rubbing my nose lightly against the springy hairs of his groin. When I realized his question was serious I thought he was at first asking about Nathan, then I realized he was continuing with his interrogation about my father.

"Among other things," I said, and I let go of him, leaning back down to recline against the mattress.

He sat first on the edge of the bed beside me, then stretched himself down so that his face rested opposite mine. He leaned into me, ran his tongue along the side of my neck, the wetness on the skin evaporating quickly into the air. "When was the last time you spoke with him?" he asked, and I knew, then, as I lifted my hand up and ran my fingers through his hair like a wide comb, that this conversation would not be over till I had supplied him with some satisfactory answers.

"Is it so important?" I asked.

"I want to know everything about you," he answered. He smiled when he said this, and the hand which I had weaved through his hair I now rested against the warm flatness of his cheek.

"He wasn't a good man," I said, leaning into him, kissing the clavicle of his neck, hoping our cuddling could draw an end to the conversation.

"But you said he was very religious," he said. I felt with my lips the sound of his voice reverberate from the vocal chords somewhere inside his neck.

I drew my mouth up toward his ear and whispered, gently, with an exasperated sigh, "That doesn't keep him from being a bigot." In my peripheral vision I noticed him blink and I could sense the thoughts moving behind his eyes. He seemed to dismiss one further question, then silently regard another, then shifted his body so that he rolled over and could look at my face.

"But you forgive him?" he asked.

"*Forgive him?*" I answered with a hard, irritable laugh. "I don't think so."

"But you'll never have any peace of mind if you don't," he said. Suddenly, he was sitting up, or, rather, sitting on top of me looking down at me, his legs straddling my waist, his hands pinning my wrists against the bed. "My mother still tells me that she can't tell anyone that I'm gay—can't tell anyone about why Stephen died so young, either. I can try to change them but I can't blame them because that's how they were raised."

I shook my head back and forth, seriously so, not wanting to continue this line of dialogue. I pushed my weight against his hands in order to get up, to end this, but Tony pinned me harder to the bed. And he smiled as he did so, knowing he had a stronger advantage on me.

"What was it?" he asked, gently, not forcefully nor demoniacally at all, though still playfully pinning me, leaning his face down toward mine till I could lean up and kiss him if I wanted. "What was so bad you can't forgive him?"

When my mother died I became my father's caretaker; even though I was only twelve years old at the time, death had rearranged our relationship as simply as others would do later in my life. I became in charge of the house; after school I did the laundry, made the beds, dusted and vacuumed, mowed the yard, ran errands on my bike. I learned to cook simple things for my father—hamburgers, scrambled eggs, pancakes, fried chicken—but soon he took to eating out whenever possible, whenever an invitation was extended from one of the ladies he knew from the church, coming home in the evenings after work and a social visit to sit alone at the kitchen table with a bottle of whiskey. My father, in turn, became a teacher for me after my mother's death: "Too sweet," he would remark to me about the way I had made his coffee in the morning or "Don't wash the colors on the hot cycle," he explained after I had ruined his white T-shirts and underwear when I had washed it with a new green towel I had bought the day before. Alcohol soon begun to change my father as irreparably as my mother's death had, and during the lessons I would receive in woodworking in the garage or the basement work room at the church, his body would reek with the pungent odor of someone who drank too much and too early in the day. But there, with his tools spread out around him and the walls behind us full of shelves of glass bottles of screws and nails and brackets and tacking, my father would explain to me how to hold a plane, show me how to work a vise, demonstrate for me how to draw a right angle, illustrate for me why he thought a hand-cranked drill produced a cleaner hole.

As the years passed, however, the drinking got the better part of my father and he resented the way he could no longer exert his control over me, the way I so easily grew away from him, the way, too, when I had finally graduated high school, I looked at college as my way of escaping the control he continued to exert so influentially over me. It was Christmas Day, 1977, that I told my father I was gay and it changed our lives as quickly as death once had. I was at home for Christmas break from the college I was attending in Atlanta, and my father and I had come back to the house from church services and dinner with the pastor and his family. I was flushed with my first love, that year, that Christmas; I moved through the house and church and neighbors' homes with the giddy steps of a teenager, looking at my reflection in capricious disbelief as I passed mirrors and turned over polished silverware within my hands, content, however, to keep the reason for such elation a secret from all those around me who would only offer their disapproval, convinced that my desires were, in fact, transgressions from my faith. That was the year I had fallen in love with Will, my professor, and I had just accepted his offer to move in with him into the house he owned about a mile from campus. My plan, that evening, was to tell my father only that I would be moving off-campus and that my living expenses would be greatly reduced by moving in with Will, describing him simply as a man who owned a house and who was a literature professor at my college.

My father had walked into the house ahead of me that Christmas evening, flipping on lamps as he moved from room to room of the old Victorian house where he still lived. The house smelled, then, of the pine branches my father had placed on the fireplace mantle that Christmas season, the only holiday trappings he would allow himself to indulge in, but the house smelled, too, that night, I remember, like the musty relic of a reclusive maiden aunt, the dark rooms made even gloomier from the deep stained wood furniture my father had built throughout the years. My father had allowed himself a glass of sherry after dinner at the pastor's house, just for social reasons, but as he moved into his own kitchen that evening he pulled the whiskey bottle down from the cabinet over the sink and poured himself a large glass to which he added a small amount of ice. My idea was to tell him I was moving before the liquor enveloped him, or, rather, before the beast he could become could be resurrected by the alcohol.

"Dad," I said coming up from behind him. "I'm going to be living off campus next semester." I knew from experience to be direct with my father, not to try to pull any tricks on him, that he preferred a quick and honest discussion and decision over the needless chit-chat or wandering through possibilities that a conversation between us could often ramble through.

I was only about an arm's length from my father then and I could smell the sweetness of the whiskey moving through the warm air of the kitchen as I stood with my hands on my hips. He was a compact, wiry, older, and weathered version of the pretty boy image I was myself trying to project at school that year. My father turned and looked at me, his eyes squinting as he took in my image, cringing, really, at the way I had dressed myself that day, my hair long and shaggy looking, as was the style that year, a pair of green baggy army fatigue pants, and a navy blue shirt with a wide, pointed collar, unbuttoned to reveal a gold chain around my neck that Will had given to me before I left for Christmas. As I stood before my father I flipped the hair out of my eyes with a wave of my hand, a gesture I realize in retrospect which may have been a too feminine of one, and added to him, "It'll save a lot of money."

My father narrowed his eyes again at me, as if he could see inside me, his upper lip curling slightly as though disgusted. "Where you going?" he asked, his voice already slurring from the rush the alcohol had provided him.

"A house about a mile away from school."

"Who else lives in this house?" he asked. "Any women there?" The idea of cohabitation was a cardinal sin to my father, and he was determined to keep me from falling into the hell he believed existed in such a big city like Atlanta. The year before we had fought about my attending a college outside the county limits; my father had wanted me to attend a Bible College not far from where we lived. Our compromise had found me working a part-time job to pay for the extra tuition for the better school in Atlanta.

"No, just a guy," I answered. "A professor." I had no plans even at that moment to tell my father the real truth about my moving off-campus, but he must have sensed something covert in the tone of my voice, the smug invincibility of a boy who had just fallen in love.

"How much is it going to cost?" he asked.

"Not much," I answered too quickly.

"Not much?" he asked suspiciously in return.

"Just food," I answered. "Just what I eat."

"I don't think it's a good idea," he answered.

"Why not?"

"How old is this guy?"

"He's a professor," I answered determinedly. "In his fifties."

"You should stay in the dorm with guys your own age," he answered. "You shouldn't give that up."

"I'm not asking for your permission," I said, trying to assert myself as an independent adult.

"But you're asking me to pay for your food," my father replied coyly. He filled his glass with more whiskey.

"I can get Will to help me out if you don't," I said.

"Will?" my father looked at me suspiciously. "Who's Will?"

"My lover," I answered, without realizing the impact those two words would have in this house in this small town in north Georgia.

My father, all too aware of what he had heard his son say, threw the back of his free hand across my face. "Satan will not destroy this house," he said, and he tossed his glass into the sink. He took both hands and grabbed the fabric of the shirt at my chest, lifting me close to his face so that the alcohol, now sour from his anger, rose up into my eyes and made them burn. I struggled to get free from him, using my hands to push him off of me, and as I did so his back hit the counter of the sink. The impact, the force of the push his son had given him, enraged my father and this was when his fist hit my jaw hard, snapping it shut.

That was all it took. I fell to the floor and my head felt like it had exploded, but my father did not back away from me then. I felt a thud against my stomach, the white shock registering on my face, then another thud against my back, when I realized my father was kicking me with his boots. "No son of mine will be a faggot," I heard him spit at me, then I heard myself yell, moan, really, from the repeated impact of his boot against my body, yet my body suddenly immobile, as if it had fallen into concrete. I could taste the blood in my mouth, could feel welts rising from the bruises on my body, when I grabbed his leg with my arms and knocked him off balance, hearing him thud against the floor as he fell. "Sinner," I heard him spit somewhere far off behind me, and the sound of his voice floated up into the air like a hiss of steam. I quickly picked myself up off the floor, heard him yell at me, "Don't even think about coming back to this house. Ever. Again."

Who would want to return to this? I remember thinking as I grabbed the doorknob with my hand, felt myself wondering if I had to push or pull it to open it, then sensed the cool air when I was outside, scared about moving too fast, suddenly enveloped in a blinding darkness.

I ran to the church that night; it was the only place I knew that was safe to go. My father would never pursue me, I felt certain of that, and if he were to find me in the church, he wouldn't, under any circumstances, lift his hand to hurt me there. I knew his belief in God was that strong even if his own was so unforgiving. In all those years I was away from home I never desired to become so successful, so rich, so powerful that my father would wish he'd never let me go. I never wanted revenge on my father. All I wanted was to love and be loved by him. He was my family. And so that night I sat in the pews of the church I had helped my father build, heard the creaks of the rafters of the roof I had helped my father repair, and I lifted up my hope to a God I did not comprehend that he would see me not as a sinner, but merely as someone misunderstood, following the direction of his own heart.

I broke into the pastor's office that night with a pocket knife I always carried, a gift from my father when I was seven years old, and called Will at his sister's house in Florida from the pastor's phone.

"Robbie?" he asked, when he recognized my voice and its wavering insecurity. "What's wrong?"

"My father hates me," I said, my heart jumping into my mouth. "I can't stay here." That was the Christmas that I swore I would never return to Galena, that I would never forgive my father for not understanding his son was different from himself, the same Christmas I began searching for another place to call my home.

"I need to get out of here," I said to Will, wanting only to be where he was at that moment. "I have to move on."

What must a father teach his son? How to love and take responsibility for himself and others? How to take pride in his work? What it means to be a man? And what does a son learn from his father? How to love or hate, how to feel insecure or weak, how to be successful or terrified of failure? What does a father learn from his son? How to be warm and nurturing or fearful of intimacy? How to be generous, narcissistic or authoritarian? Whether he is capable of discipline, morality or reliability?

Kenny demanded a lot of me that year; even though Denise's concentration sharpened a little bit more every day and a new enthusiasm had surfaced from her experimentation with Tony's camera, she continued to fade in and out as a thought of Linda or Amy would overcome her and send her into unsolicited paralysis. I found it both easier and safer to be accountable for Kenny, changing his diapers, tying his shoes, feeding him, bathing him—all those parental things that one has to do with a six-month-old baby—until Denise had somehow incorporated this new grief into her life. In fact, I became accountable in every way, now, for Denise and her child. I had arranged with the bank, with money set aside from both Vince and Jeff's estates, to keep Linda's health food store and café open at least through the end of the year, running it as an off-site manager to see if it could continue to provide us with a steady income.

Tony had discontinued his questions about my father and my past once I had told him the story of my leaving Galena, but his question of whether I had forgiven my father had perplexingly lodged in my mind. Hadn't Vince asked the same thing of Jeff about Jeff's father? I recalled. Didn't Denise continually have to make amends with her mother? I realized. I contemplated this new predicament over and over again, whether or not I should be the compassionate one and forgive my father. Every time I lifted Kenny in my arms, to burp him, to carry him to another room, to wash his face, I realized how hard it must be to raise a child and let him go. Had I been too demanding as a son to expect a renunciation from a parent? Should I have found a way to have kept my father in my life, even though he had denied my own existence, my own life, my own beliefs?

And then one morning I was rushing around the kitchen, Denise was upstairs showering, Tony had gone to the grocery store, and Kenny was crying in the high chair where I had left him, when the thought rushed into my mind once again: *I should try to settle things with my father, after all, how could I explain these things some day to Kenny when I hadn't tried to make amends myself.* I was trying to find a pacifier or a toy to give Kenny to settle him down, when the irritation of his moody shrieking washed into me and I wanted to just scream at him to shut up. I knew that I was feeling harassed at that moment, and I was rattled and couldn't think clearly—I had not slept well the night before, a persistent cough had kept Kenny needing attention throughout the night. In the kitchen, I gave Kenny a damp washrag to chew on, lifted him up out of the chair and rocked him in my arms till he quieted down, then laid him in the crib I had built for him before he was born and we had placed off a nook in the dining room. It was then that I went directly to the phone on the kitchen wall, lifted the receiver up, and dialed a number I had memorized years before. It rang three times and a woman's voice answered; my heart pumped wildly in my chest. "Is Robert Taylor there?" I asked. I could hear the forcefulness in my voice and I cleared my throat to calm myself down.

"Yes, just a moment," she said. Her voice sounded nasal and congested, as if the call had caught her off guard while she was crying.

"Hello?" I heard another voice ask a few seconds later—a different voice—a man's voice.

"Hi Dad," I said. "It's Robbie." I had spoken those words quickly, more matter-of-fact than with animosity. But there was a blank pause as the information swept across the continent to my father. I wondered in those few seconds as I waited for some sort of response whether or not he would hang up on me. If he did, I could console myself with the knowledge that I had at least made an attempt to break the silence between us. He didn't hang up on me, however, but he didn't acknowledge me either. I stayed on the line listening to the dead space of air thump awkwardly by, feeling my displeasure rise into a spot at the back of my throat, ready to call him a son-of-a-bitch or an asshole should he even begin to lash out at me. Instead, something then flattened out within me, stretched out, rather, like a piece of chewing gum pulled at both ends. Because of my exasperation over his lack of response or whether it was from a deep breath of air I took or the rush of blood that went suddenly through my arteries, I relaxed the grip on the phone, and a peaceful, unperturbed attitude rinsed over me like a warm shower. And what happened next was I continued to speak. "I'm living in California now," I said. "I had some rough times, but things are good for me now. I wanted you to know that."

I knew he must be as full of questions as I was for him; it had been almost fifteen years since I had left home.

"Are you sick?" he asked me after some more time had passed. The voice was the same as it was decades ago. Thick, authoritative, paternal, distant.

"No sir," I answered.

"Then my prayers worked more for you than for me," he laughed. "I'm not so good myself these days," he said, and it was here I heard the age in his voice, a thinness and frailty cracking in his pitch, and I felt, in that moment, the sorrow once again of a child learning of the vincibility of their parent, an emotion I thought, when I placed the call, I would certainly not have to recall. "I had a stroke last year," he added. "Doctor found cancer last month. Shelly does most things now."

"I'm sorry to hear that," I said, surprised to hear the compassion in my voice and that it had come so naturally and wonderfully out of my mouth in a tone as if it implied that I had forgiven him for all the hatred and misery he had inflicted on me all those years ago.

"Shelly didn't put you up to this, did she?"

"No sir."

"I don't need you coming out here, creating any trouble," he said. The stern, religious father had come back across the line—detached, immovable, direct, unforgiving.

I was about to respond that he needn't worry about that, that I hadn't any plans to travel across country to be insulted and abused by him again, that I had my own home here, in another part of the world—my own life, now, my own responsibilities to tend to, ready to unleash, in a snap of my voice, all the loathing and enmity I had bottled up for years. But Kenny cried out at that moment, and I looked around the corner and saw that he had gotten his leg tangled in the bars of the crib. "I should go now, sir," I said politely, and as I reached out to hang up the phone I felt certain I heard him say, "So long, son," as I placed the receiver against the wall. *Son*, I remember thinking as I went into the next room, untangled Kenny, and lifted him up in my arms. Had I imagined him saying that to me? Had he responded with that naturally, or out of out of deliberation? Had he forgotten how he had beat me? How he hated what I was? Or had he changed even in the slightest, almost imperceptible manner over all these years? Had he once again become my father? Or had he never forgotten that he was my father?

Tony was surprised when I told him later that afternoon that I had briefly spoken to my father, and he asked for details and a replay of the conversation, and I did the best I could to recreate my awkward feelings. Tony felt triumphant that I had made the call, not so much because I had or had not broken down the barriers with my father but because I had listened to the advice he had given me—that I had given him, Tony, an important and credible space in my life.

And then a letter from my stepmother arrived the following week, a few days before Thanksgiving that year, stating that my father had died later during the day we had spoken to one another, and, I felt, then, so distant and heartless; his death felt meaningless, really, compared to the more devastating and closer losses I had already experienced so far. My stepmother's note was brief, saying that I was on my father's mind that day before I had called—he had even mentioned it to her—and that he had died not long after our phone conversation—perhaps, I think, around the time I had told Tony of my conversation with my father. She mentioned that my father had probably undermined to me the seriousness of his condition that day—he had just returned from a two-week long stay at the hospital. Inside the envelope with her note was a clipping of my father's obituary. The newspaper reported that my father, Robert B. Taylor, Sr., had died of a heart attack at the age of sixty-one, and was "a respected figure of the community and a deacon of the First Church of Galena, survived by his second wife, Shelly, and step-daughter, Rebecca, both of Galena." No mention was made of his gay son, Robert Taylor, Jr., who lived in California. How my stepmother tracked me to California is still a mystery to me—my father had always considered me to be dead and forgotten—and she didn't explain it in her note and I never instigated any further contact with her. She may have gotten my address from Elaine Crowder after my father's death—Elaine had surreptitiously written me for years to keep me abreast of my father and my hometown. But I'd like to think it may have had something to do with the fact that my father had always expected me to atone for my sins, atone to him, however, instead of to the benevolent God he professed to worship himself, that he had one day expected me to call even if our actual conversation had not been as he would have wanted it to be. And if I hadn't called that day I think, perhaps, that he may have called me. What he would have said to me I can only imagine, of course, but what I would like to imagine—have imagined, really—is that he might have once again called me his son.

What is a home? Is it something found or something made? Is it a state of mind or a stationary place? Is it a house where one lives or how the heart loves? Is it created by shared blood and genes or from the people chosen to surround you?

When I lost Nathan I thought I had lost my home, for what I had lost, I know now, was my willingness to love. When I left my father, I thought that I was home-less, when, in fact, I found the stronger sense of the place where my life belonged.

A sense of home was well on my mind that year, that Christmas of 1992; that was the Christmas the dead haunted both Denise and myself—the image of los-ing Vince, Jeff, Linda and Amy in such rapid progression fresh within our minds. Even my father's death had begun to deeply reverberate for me against so much other sorrow. If I had not had so much experience with death so far, so many cur-rent obligations to move me through the day, I think, perhaps, that I, too, would have floundered like Denise. But now, it seemed to me, one more loss could sum-mon up a thousand visions of others. A floating memory of Nathan, for instance, could now invoke a string of thoughts within my mind from Alex to Jeff. One evening near dusk while walking out of A Different Light on Santa Monica and carrying Kenny in the knapsack around my chest, I thought I spotted Jeff walk-ing up toward Larrabee, or, rather, spotted Jeff's body as it used to be, pale white skin and weighted with bulky muscles about the arms and shoulders. The light was fading, twilight deepening the sky into a thick blue sheet, and I was on my way to meet Tony at the Abbey, when the guy who reminded me of Jeff passed me on the sidewalk and I felt myself inevitably let out a long, audible sigh.

It wasn't Jeff, of course, I knew that—Jeff had been dead for almost a year by then and he had never worn the kind of tank top and jacket this guy was wearing since he had moved away from New York; Jeff's later L.A. years had been characterized with a more conservative modesty about his body even though his body, the muscular bulk of it, never seemed to fail him even as he progressed through illnesses. And it wasn't just that this guy's body had made me sentimentally sigh as he passed me by. The problem was that when he came forward toward me on the sidewalk and I saw his face, something around the eyes reminded me of Nathan and all at once his presence—this guy's— annoyed me because he reminded me of both Nathan and Jeff and I wanted him only to disappear so I could get on with my own life.

I didn't mention this to Tony when I saw him later; why let him know of my inner hauntings when I was aware that he was plagued by his own now and then? This was also not a new occurrence to me—seeing the dead in other people—I had been seeing the dead for more than a decade; death seemed to intrude on my life every moment of every day. I remember the first time I thought I saw Alex at a bar in the Village, not long after he had died, and I tried to make conversation with the guy, hoping to make some sort of verbal connection to Alex's memory as well—but to no avail—the guy possessed a whiney personality that I would never have tolerated if it had really belonged to Alex, and the guy had naturally assumed that because I was so much younger than he was that I was a hustler looking to score that evening.

The problem was that by that year in California I felt haunted at every step, sorrow so permeated my own composure—even with the pleasure Tony always provided me—that I often found myself walking with downcast eyes, driving like an automaton or a zombie, hoping to avoid being so hexed by memories, or focusing my attention so relentlessly on what needed to be done for Kenny or what I wanted to do with Tony. I wanted to tell Denise outright that the dead never leave you, but I know it was something she would discover herself over time, worried, as well, that such knowledge that I possessed could somehow set her back. Denise had continued to get better—she had started helping out around the house, able to do the laundry and wash the dishes, able to sustain a conversation for more than three minutes, able on days when she had been able to sleep the night before for a few hours to make her way to the grocery store and back, as if to prove to herself the route could be done without impediment, without, really, any misfortune befalling her. I knew she was emerging out of her shell; she read voraciously now, able to make it through one of Jeff's spiritual tomes in less than a day, able to place herself up on the treadmill, which we had moved upstairs, and run for almost an hour.

That was the Christmas we—Denise, Tony, and I—decided not to exchange presents. "No presents," we said to one another, echoing a sentiment I had long ago exchanged with Nathan when he was alive and we were in love; instead of gifts, we wanted so desperately to bring some joy and adventure back into our lives. "We should do something gay," Denise said, as she often had when we had both lived in New York City—and so we decided to buy tickets to Disneyland; what else did we have left except our faith in Mickey Mouse, Goofy, and Cinderella?

The day arrived cool and cloudy that Christmas, much cooler than I expected from the Pacific coast climate; Tony had slept over the night before and was already out of bed, his T-shirt bobbing about his waist as he cooked a breakfast of blueberry pancakes for all of us—he had already gotten Kenny out of his crib and into a green jump suit as well by the time I had wandered into the kitchen that morning.

And so the four of us—Denise, Kenny, Tony, and myself, packed ourselves into the Jeep and headed off to Anaheim, our backpacks stuffed with bottles of juice and diapers and lotion and baby wipes and caps and sweaters and a washrag for Kenny to chew on to relieve the pressure of his teething. The drive, long and hypnotic that day because of the slow, steady traffic, had placed me in a contemplative mood—Denise held Kenny in the back seat humming a tune from *The Little Mermaid* quietly under her breath, Tony rode quietly beside me as I drove, his hand outstretched and placed against my thigh, lifting it up only to point to a sign I should note or to watch out for a car or a bus swerving into our lane.

The park was emptier than I expected that morning; families still gathered in their homes around their Christmas trees opening presents or off to relatives for large holiday meals. But the emptiness of the park was, nonetheless, enchanting, bequeathing a VIP-quality to the way we could move about so easily without any wait for the rides. As the day progressed, the crowds grew larger, but the air retained its sunny lightness. It was, on days like that one— those crisp East Coast autumnlike days—that I found I missed Nathan most, missed the pacifying control he exerted over me, missed the way he would have made everything feel childishly spontaneous, for example, by buying everyone Mickey Mouse hats or pointing out his favorite Pirate of the Caribbean, talking back to the robotic Tiki birds or asking Pluto what he was wearing under his suit. Such thoughts that day made me miss Amy, too, the way she would have tugged against my arm, the quizzical and urgent look she would have given me as she eagerly pointed to Dumbo or Minnie Mouse, or the way she would have steered all of us into a store to buy candy when she wanted something sweet to eat, or pointed to a souvenir stand when an object caught her attention.

Most of all, that day, that Christmas, I was worried about Denise. She seemed too melancholy and self-focused as we walked along the black-top concrete paths, waiting in lines to buy sodas and french fries, waiting in more lines in order to see the Country Bear Jamboree or ride Space Mountain. I did my best to keep her entertained or absorbed in something, asking her to look for Kenny's apple juice in the knapsack, or suggesting she take a picture with the camera she carried across her shoulder. But it was Tony who acted as our navigator and guide that day—Tony, the more controlled and rational of any of us that year—our pillar of strength—our barometer of sanity. I found no fault, of course, in that; at times I especially relished the idea of someone other than myself taking charge of things, someone with a clear, demonstrative purpose, someone in whom I could trust not to get us lost or irritated. I found in Tony an admirable strength I often noticed missing in myself. And I found that if I faltered in my own direction that day, Tony came through with a plan for everything—directing us through the Swiss Family Treehouse and all the attractions we wanted to see in Adventureland, for instance, before we even attempted to explore Tomorrowland.

But it was impossible for any of us to escape our ghosts that Christmas Day. Watching the parade down Main Street I noticed Jeff's body once again in the hunch of a man's shoulders, noticed the blue beardlike stubble of Vince's face on a guy who carried a little girl on his shoulders that had hair the same color as Amy's. Denise noticed them too and we both looked away from them, then at one another but refusing to remark on the incidents. But it was a woman who rode on one of the floats who reminded us both of Linda who disturbed us most.

"I see her everywhere, you know," Denise said and placed her palm on my hand, as we both watched the woman pass, waving her hand back and forth as if she were Miss America. She was dressed in an outfit that was a cross between a Santa Claus suit and a cheerleader's outfit, a red skirt trimmed in white fur, her blond hair pulled back into two pigtails and held into place with a red felt cap. There was something about her slender, All-American look, however, that Linda had possessed as well.

I nodded at Denise, watching the woman wave and pass us by, feeling at that moment as if I were a hundred years old and had survived a war, and for a moment I thought about running up to the float and saying something to her, something to make her stop and join our little surrogate family for a few minutes, telling her that we were trying to heal one another, move on, get on with our lives, but that someone was always slipping off the horizon for one of us and now, today, she looked so much like Linda it made us all want to cry. The feeling passed, though, and the parade moved on in front of us, but Denise walked away and went to sit alone on a bench nearby.

Denise disappeared from us several times that day—I knew it was natural, grief does that to you—snatches up your mind with unnerving visions of the past, unable to accept its finality. I worried about how I could help Denise move through her sorrow, the way she had helped me after Nathan's death, inviting me to live with her and Linda at a time when I was struggling to find a reason myself to stay alive. What could I offer her to refocus her life, when it was clear to me that Kenny was, at that moment, not enough to keep her going? Once, while she was taking a picture of the three of us—Tony, Kenny, and myself—in front of Cinderella's castle, I noticed her lift her head to the side of the viewfinder and frown, as if she didn't understand what was in front of her or why it was so important to remember it with a photograph. Watching her that day it was clear that she was making little pacts with herself to keep herself directed, that if she moved into this line, for instance, and waited with us, she could move on to another line, and then maybe on to another ride— yet underlying it all, I knew, she felt a suspicion that perhaps she had been somehow responsible for all this death in our lives. That made me wonder, too, if I had brought this onto her, that perhaps I had a jinx on me or some kind of curse, guaranteed to bring death and unhappiness wherever I moved. It was then that I first wondered if I should suggest we move again, perhaps make a dramatic change by leaving California, possibly returning to New York. Could Denise find a new direction back in Manhattan? Would that sort of change help her accept her sorrow as it finally had me accept mine?

While we were waiting in line for Mr. Toad's ride, Denise disappeared to wash her hands and refill a bottle with water. Kenny had fallen asleep in the harness and his breath rose up into my nostrils in moist, sweet bursts, and I pinned my chin against my neck and looked down at him, lightly cupping my hand against the back of his head. Denise had remarked before the accident that Kenny was looking more and more like me—the dark hair, the shape of the eyes, the hint of a cleft at his chin. I thought, however, that overall he resembled Denise more and more—the long, petite shape of his face, the joints of his tiny fingers, the way his hair would kink up into cottonlike waves from the humidity. That day, that Christmas, holding Kenny in my arms waiting for Denise to return, I had a revelation of sorts at that moment, that here, with this child, was where my life was supposed to be, that I had progressed through a sequence of paths, passages, obstacles, and obstructions and arrived, finally, at the proper location destiny had somehow planned for me. That day was the day I realized our lives—mine, Denise, and Kenny's—were to be inextricably linked forever, like threads which bind together the mismatched patches of a quilt, and I decided, then, that I had no intention of letting them escape me now that I had realized it to be so. The deaths of those close to me had created a path of responsibility for others; Amy, and even Nathan in his own way before her, had awakened my own dormant parental instinct. Now, it felt important for me to be someone's teacher or mentor, someone and something I had never had in my own life. I wanted to pass along the things I knew and didn't know. I wanted, passionately, to now be this boy's father—the good father, the kind of father my father never was for me.

Looking around that Christmas Day at the other families waiting in line that afternoon, I knew Kenny and I didn't look different from the other fathers and sons who were there that day at the park. But how would I, years later, explain to this boy the journey which had brought us together, the points that lead us from there to here, the stories that bonded us together as a family? Who could ever believe that out of all this horror, this nightmare of AIDS and death, that an aging, thirtysomething gay man, perhaps now too fatigued and bitter could find such an absurd, blissful tranquillity smelling the sleeping breaths of a child? Here was a child for me, a reason to keep going. And how, too, could I explain this to Denise? How could I firmly assert my parental rights without Denise worrying that I would want to take Kenny away from her?

And how do I factor Tony into this picture, as successfully as he had factored himself into our little family? Did I love him? Did he love me? Had we reached those points? I knew I was falling in love with him, felt the same thing was happening to him, as well. But if Denise and Kenny and I were to move elsewhere, would Tony come along if I asked? Or would he want to stay in California and let me go? Let us go?

Suddenly I found myself imagining having to make a decision between Kenny or Tony, when it was clear to me that I needed and wanted both in my life, and I felt myself sweating, my back aching suddenly from the weight of Kenny's harness about my shoulders. Tony must have sensed me faltering—Tony—sexy, self-controlled Tony, for he reached and lifted Kenny out of the harness and held him in his arms and began to chatter in such a nonsense baby language that I had no alternative but to forget my troubles for a moment and smile. How could I keep him, too? I wondered.

But there was something about the way his arm cradled Kenny to his body that continued to bother me as I watched the two of them together; bother is not the right word, really, confused me, I suppose, for there was something very familiar to the shape of it—the shape of his arm and his hand—something that made it something more than just the hand that belonged to Tony. There was something about the way his dark hair twisted around his wrist, the way the wrist, itself, thinned down from the muscles of his forearm, something about the way the flesh padded the palm of his hand that made me think of another hand. And then it came to me that it was Vince's hand, the hand which I could still so vividly recall from that afternoon fourteen years before outside that Village clinic, the one that Vince had offered out for a handshake to a lost boy from Atlanta in the bright summer sunlight, the strong-steady looking hand which could help that boy navigate a vicious, self-driven city— the one that did, in fact, help him—had helped him find a place to live, had helped him with a job, helped him find a group of friends that had become his family.

And then I began to feel euphoric, as if I had been placed centerstage on a carousel and all the world's virtues were spinning around me. I began to feel physical sensations distorting themselves—the sidewalk raising me up as if I were standing on a pedestal, the crowd revolving around me as if I were the gravity to their orbits, the buildings leaning into me as if I were about to whisper a secret to them. Everything seemed heightened—the music from the loudspeakers hidden in the branches of trees, the smell of popcorn and sun-light against black concrete, the color of the sweatshirt Tony wore, the weight of Kenny's harness at my shoulders. Not knowing whether to shout or laugh I looked up at the sky for guidance—a flat, pale blue plane of glass which suddenly came alive with molecules shifting and forming and bouncing against each other like a giant computer screen. And then a flash of light, like a sheet of lightning cracking against the sky, snapped me into a dizziness—a magical, untroubled exuberance, really.

"Are you okay?" Tony asked.

I nodded, regaining my focus, stamping my feet against the ground to steady my balance. It was then that I spontaneously took the silver band I had been wearing on my finger, removed it and nudged it onto one of Tony's fingers. "Merry Christmas," I said.

He shifted Kenny in his arms, his eyes and mouth all wide and huge and big and open. "But you said you didn't want to exchange gifts."

"It's all I have," I said, as if my action had been more premeditated. "So it's not just a gift." And that was when we both saw Denise returning, moving through the crowd toward us, carrying a bright pink pendant she had bought at a souvenir stand, waving it above her head like a torch. She was suddenly smiling, as if she had momentarily found herself again, and I wanted to shout out to her, "*We're here, together, we've made it this far*," but all I did was reach for her hand as she came up toward me, letting her know, in the all too subtle way in which we had become accustomed, that someone was beside her, with her right now—that she was, indeed, not moving through life alone—that somehow things will change again for us, but for now she had a family beside her to help her out.

The stars were vividly bright when I parked the car in the driveway that evening, but a thin cloud interrupted their patterns, like chalk smeared against a blackboard. I only lingered a moment outside, carrying the bags from the back of the Jeep into the garage. The phone was ringing as we entered the house, and when Denise answered it in the kitchen, I heard her say, in such an extraordinarily calm manner, "Hello, Mother, I was about the call you to wish you a Merry Christmas."

Tony had gone into the living room and turned on the television, but I had followed Denise into the kitchen and had taken Kenny out of her arms to give him some juice before taking him upstairs to bed. Denise, in short, dryly comical phrases, described our Christmas at Disneyland to her mother—the way Kenny had laughed through Peter Pan's ride, the pictures we took with the Seven Dwarfs with Tony's very old camera, our holiday meal of hot dogs and ice cream. As I glanced over at her from time to time she caught my stare and smiled back at me, rolling her eyes in mock exasperation as her mother expressed what I imagined to be only alarm and displeasure at our outing and her choice of holiday partners—two gay men and a child conceived in a test tube. I had never seen Denise react so coolly to a conversation with her mother and for a while she was silent, listening to what I knew from experience was her mother's litany of seasonal aches and pains, drawing on the back of a flyer that rested on the kitchen counter as she leaned into the receiver of the phone. By then, Kenny and I were seated on the floor, and I looked up at her again when I heard her say, "But Mother, you know you're always welcome to come out here if you want." I was shocked by the statement; Denise dreaded phone conversations with her mother, not to mention a visit. But Denise dismissed my alarm with a wave of her hand and another smile. I knew, then, their conversation was coming to an end, as it had every year, with Denise's mother saying, oh, so nonchalantly, "Darlin', why don't you just come home and live."

As Denise hung up the phone, with a restrained and somewhat polite return of the receiver to its cradle, so unlike her usual exasperated slam after she finished a conversation with her mother, I wondered, then, if Denise had completely lost it, or if she had somehow been able to unshackle herself from the grip her mother had possessed on her for years like some malicious, bad-tempered dybbuk.

"She'll never understand, will she?" Denise said to me. "When will she ever learn that I *am* home?"

I stood and lifted Kenny off the floor, sitting him in the bend of my arm. It was then that Denise took Kenny from me and I heard an unmistakable clarity within the tone of her voice. "Doesn't she know my friends know more about me than she will ever allow herself to know? Doesn't she understand what you mean to me? Doesn't she know that I want you in my life?" She looked, then, more beautiful and certain than I had ever seen her to be, her face containing a smooth, motherly smile.

It was then that I noticed on the counter what Denise had been drawing, a sketch of me holding Kenny, our smiles so similar that there was no doubt that we could be related. It was the first sketch Denise had done since Jeff had died, and I felt, in that moment, as if I had witnessed a miracle, as if I had stumbled, drenched and disheartened from a thunderstorm, onto the pot of gold where the rainbow ends.

That was the moment that Kenny looked back at me and I caught his eyes, and all at once I realized again that the God I had criticized, mistrusted and abandoned for bringing me such misery and loss had indeed somehow ironically blessed me as well.

And then Denise was suddenly upon us, looking down at Kenny's face and allowing him to grasp hold of one of her fingers. She started humming again, something familiar I couldn't quite identify, a lilting melody of du-tu-du du-tu-du-tu-du. I finally recognized it as a song from *Camelot*, just as Denise broke out into a smile and tapped her finger against Kenny's nose. "What do the simple folk do?" she sang.

Kenny reacted with a gurgle and Denise pulled her finger away. "Listen, Robbie," she said, lifting her eyes up to search out mine. "Something's been worrying me."

I felt, then, my happiness leave me, and a streak of tension raced up my spine and flared across my back.

"I can tell you and Tony are starting to get more serious," she said. She tossed her hair back with a flick of her neck, a habit she had always done when she was nervous. "You're not thinking of moving out or anything like that, are you?"

I searched behind her eyes, trying to find the logic of her question, sensing her own worry now. "I mean, I know I'm being selfish," she continued. "But I like having you around. And so does Kenny—I can tell." And then she shifted the weight of her foot, holding the child closer to her but relaxing the grip of her arms. "He's going to need a father."

I nodded. "I'm not leaving here until you're ready for it, Denise," I answered. "Don't worry about that. I wouldn't do that to you."

"Well, that's sort of the problem," she replied. "I don't really want you to leave."

I felt, once again, a weight of pressure against the back of my neck, as if I were suddenly being forced into a decision before the time was ready for it to be made.

"I thought that when you're ready, you might want to ask Tony to move in," she said. "Here."

I nodded, a warm flush returning to my cheeks as the tension left my body, feeling, as the blood moved through my organs and muscles, pleasant tingles at the turn of my hands and at the end of my nose. I felt, then, as if I possessed my own glow.

"I don't want to lose you," she said.

"You won't, Denise," I answered. "I'm not lost anymore."

And that was the Christmas of 1992, the Christmas my new family began.

ACKNOWLEDGMENTS

I am very indebted to two friends and fellow writers, Anne H. Wood and Brian Keesling, whose constant reading, invaluable comments and encouragement of these chapters and characters helped shape the course of this work. I am also grateful and appreciative for the time and attention my editor at Overlook, Hermann Lademann, invested in this manuscript. Some portions of this novel were previously published as works of short fiction and I would like to thank those editors for their acceptance, advice and edits, particularly David Waggoner, Alex Cigale, Beth Stroud, Kevin Koffler, Jim Berg, Susan Raffo, Glenn Crawford, Jeffrey Williams, Richard Labonte, Kim Smith, Charlotte Stratton, Aldo Alvarez, Maureen Brady, Brian Bouldrey, Douglas Sadownick, Matt Danford, and Lawrence Schimel.

I am also extremely grateful to The Arch and Bruce Brown Foundation for the fiction grant they awarded *Where The Rainbow Ends*.

I am also grateful for a close network of friends who have provided me and this project an ongoing emotional and sometimes financial support, particularly John Maresca, Deborah Collins, Martin Gould, Jon Marans, Jonathan Miller, Larry Dumont, Joel Byrd and Andrew Beierle. I would also like to thank Howard Goldberg for his perseverance and companionship, and especially for providing transportation and accommodations while researching and writing the Los Angeles portion of this book.

Beyond personal experience, several sources were consulted or used in the preparation and writing of this novel, particularly a wide range of periodicals, newspapers and books on AIDS and its affect on the gay and lesbian communities. I must also mention the significance of the *Book of Job* in the formulation of this work; Job's test of faith and continual questioning provided a well-needed inspiration. I would also like to thank the University of Southern California Department of Medicine and the Sperm Bank for the information they provided directly to me, as well as J.A. Verdino for her "AI Diary" in the anthology *All The Ways Home*, which I used as an important touchstone and template for the events of the surrogate process. I would also like to thank the legal department of *The New York Times* for allowing me access to resources and materials during the writing of this manuscript.

I would also like to thank Jim Marks, Elizabeth Weinstein, Rhett Wickham, Boneau/Bryan-Brown, Kermit Cole, Stephen Cooper, Bernard Schleifer and Kevin McAnarney for their assistance and advice. I am also indebted to Ed Iwanicki for his support of my earlier fiction on AIDS, as well as Jed Mattes' comments on the early drafts of this novel. I must also thank Jan Saudek for providing an inspirational image which I used during many hours of writing these stories, and Sarah Saudek for her assistance in granting the final use of it to accompany this novel.

Finally, I would like to remember those members of my family of friends whom I have lost to AIDS, most notably Kevin Patterson and David B. Feinberg; their lives and struggles and encouragement and friendship were responsible for my desire to write about how the epidemic has changed us all.

—JAMESON CURRIER
November 1998

ABOUT THE AUTHOR

JAMESON CURRIER is the author of *Dancing on the Moon: Short Stories About AIDS* (Viking) and wrote the documentary film *Living Proof: HIV and the Pursuit of Happiness*. His short fiction has appeared in the anthologies *Men on Men 5, Best American Gay Fiction, Our Mothers, Our Selves, Man of My Dreams, Mammoth Book of Gay Erotica,* and *Best Gay Erotica*. His writing on AIDS and the gay community has appeared in *The Washington Post, The Los Angeles Times, The Dallas Morning News,* and *Lambda Book Report*. A member of the National Book Critics Circle, Currier was awarded the Arch and Bruce Brown Foundation grant for fiction for this work, which was cited for its historical breadth and depiction of the gay and lesbian community during the AIDS crisis.